ALL THE
DEAD
WERE
STRANGERS

By Ethan Black

The Broken Hearts Club
Irresistible

ALL THE DEAD WERE STRANGERS

ETHAN BLACK

BALLANTINE BOOKS • NEW YORK

A Ballantine Book
The Ballantine Publishing Group

www.ballantinebooks.com

LIBRARY OF CONGRESS CATALOGING-IN-PUBLICATION DATA
Black, Ethan.
All the dead were strangers / Ethan Black.—1st ed.
p.   cm.
1. New York (N.Y.)—Fiction.   I. Title.
PS3552.L324 A79 2001
813'.54—dc21   00052921
ISBN 0-345-43900-7

Manufactured in the United States of America

First Edition: September 2001

10 9 8 7 6 5 4 3 2

For Uncle Dave & Uncle Mannie
AKA: Mr. Martini & Mr. Manhattan
with love & respect

ACKNOWLEDGMENTS

A very special thanks to Ted Combre, Ted Conover, Phil Gerard, Jim Grady, Esther Newberg, and Wendy Roth.

ALL THE
DEAD
WERE
STRANGERS

ONE

"Admit it. You're disappointed," says the dark-haired man across the table. "Things didn't turn out the way you planned."

An old friend. A boyhood pal. A best buddy Voort hasn't seen in nine years, drunk enough to talk too much, sober enough to keep secrets. Meechum Keefe smiles at some private thought, some unshared bit of bitter knowledge. He reaches for his third Johnny Walker Red as eagerly as a cardiac patient picking up a nitroglycerin tablet. He downs the liquid as carefully as a diabetic administering his insulin shot.

"You said you needed help," Voort prompts. "You were afraid to even say the name of this bar, on the phone."

They occupy a rear table in the White Horse Tavern, on Hudson Street, in Greenwich Village, a few short blocks from the Hudson River. The hundred-and-twenty-year-old bar is all dark wood and whirling ceiling fans. The burgers are fat and the beers are dark, cold, foamy. The men, both about thirty, draw glances from admiring women at adjacent tables. Both, to females, are prime-of-life, head-turning males.

But the women might be surprised to hear the dark-haired man mutter, "It's going to sound crazy, Voort. The nuttiest story you ever heard."

"I've heard a lot."

The dark man is shorter but makes up for it with bundled energy, physical power compressed into his wide shoulders and corded neck, and shining in the half-drunken intensity of his Irish-black eyes. His hair is on the long side of acceptably corporate, slicked down on top but rebelling with a slight curl at the tail, over the collar of his fisherman's knit sweater. His hands are smooth, like an office worker's, but powerful, gripping his glass. His ring finger is bare of intimate entanglement. He hovers over his drink, protecting turf.

"People start out believing in things, but then they see the truth," he says.

The blond is leaner but equally fit, more kayaker than weight lifter. His hair is shorter and brushed to the side, his attentive eyes the vivid blue of the sky in New Mexico. He wears a pressed white shirt without a tie, and an Italian jacket of black corduroy. His jeans are stone washed. He's still on his first beer.

"In the end," Meechum says, "people find out their career was dirty. Their boss screwed them. Their girl cheated on them. Their kid shot drugs. Pick an area. The subways are collapsing. The stock market is falling. The good times are over, and getting worse fast."

Over the sounds of the televised Monday night Jets–Buffalo Bills game, the place is packed with a hodgepodge of neighborhood types—brokers still in their rumpled business suits after a hard day on Wall Street; writers who need to get out of their apartments each night, after pounding on

a keyboard all day, alone; tourists who peruse the guide-
books that recommended this historic tavern, reading about
the night George Washington spent here, during his retreat
up the West Side of Manhattan, when it was forest.

"How about a steak to go with that scotch?" Voort says.

"I'm not hungry," says the deep, familiar voice that had
surprised Voort over the phone this afternoon with "The
prodigal best friend, old buddy, is home after nine long
years."

Meechum signals the waitress for a refill by lifting his
empty glass.

He says, with a half-drunken flourish, "The seven deadly
sins all start with disappointment. Greed? *'I don't have
enough.'* Lust? *'My woman got fat, boring, older.'* You know
what I'm talking about. I called One Police Plaza and some
secretary said you quit for awhile and just came back. Something disappointed *you*, didn't it?"

"I took a leave, got out of town awhile."

"Ha! For two months? All you ever wanted to do, all
your whole family ever did, for three hundred years, was police work. Voorts don't disappear for two months. What
went wrong?"

"We're talking about you," Voort says, thinking that the
job hasn't been as satisfying, *nothing* has been satisfying
since his return.

"We're talking about blame. How you get disappointed
and blame someone for it. And then you dwell on it and it
becomes all you think about. And finally you set out to destroy the thing you blame."

"Is someone trying to do that to you?"

"They did already."

"So you're the one who wants revenge on them."

"You're good, Voort, but I told you, I'll get to it when I'm ready."

"I have all night."

Meechum's eyes slide over Voort's right shoulder, across the crowded restaurant, to the front door and back.

In the oak-framed mirror above his friend's head, Voort tries to guess what Meechum sees. Is it a specific person? Or is he worried that a specific person will appear?

"Ah, you were always able to zero in on the fundamental questions, Voort. Or am I too drunk to make sense anymore? Sometimes it turns out, in the end, that a person has everything, even the little pieces, upside down in his head. The devil turns out to be an accountant. Mephistopheles needs glasses, and he's pigeon-toed to boot."

To Voort, Meechum's unexplained fear is not overdramatic. He's seen too much justifiable terror on the job. Usually it's been in women—victims stalked by boyfriends, husbands, fathers, strangers. Women tracked to their apartments, offices, bedrooms, or shops. He's seen the sick mail they receive. He's listened to the perverted messages on their answering machines. Time after time he's answered radio calls, out of the sex crimes unit, to find a body—someone who was once afraid, who perhaps no one took seriously—bloodied and, if lucky under these perverted circumstances, at least half alive.

It had not occurred to him when he became a policeman that he would become an expert on fear. He'd started out with a more romantic vision of the Blue Life. But nine years after graduating from the police academy, Voort understands fear the way a physicist understands atoms. He smells its variations with the skill of a French chef appraising the freshness of a fish. He has come to understand, since

6

he took a leave, that there had been a time when he could have chosen a different area of life professionally—Nature perhaps, or commerce, or the arts.

My father told me to quit if things were getting to me. I just need a little equilibrium now, and I'll be fine again.

And now he sees the thousand ways New Yorkers have incorporated fear into their daily lives, weaving it into the fabric of his city. There's the quiet fear in the subway as passengers clutch bags to their laps, their wary eyes attuned to strangers. There's the nervous fear of pedestrians hurrying home, keeping to the center of dark streets at night, and away from parked cars, dark doorways, alleys. Fear makes women hide their engagement rings, their proudest possessions, in public places. It stalks workers in a suddenly failing economy. They work longer hours. They pore over financial pages, seeking magic in a stock market that may be coming apart. Their fights about money at home elevate over the cost of a new hat, a nine-dollar ticket to the cineplex, or a sixty-watt lightbulb left burning in an empty flat.

Now Voort says, "Let's change the subject if you need time to get to things. Tell me. How's the army? I figured after all these years, you'd be a general by now."

"I quit."

"But it's all you ever wanted to do."

"That's why we're pals. We think the same way. We get disillusioned together. I left Washington two years ago and moved back to New York. Sorry I didn't call you before. I guess I had to keep to myself while I figured things out. Now I work in a . . . you'll laugh . . . corporate head-hunting firm."

Meechum laughs at Voort's stunned expression, and glances, again, toward the front door. "Hey, remember the old army commercial, before they started firing people instead of hiring them? Learn skills for the real world? Well, I took those computer talents and now I use 'em to do psychological profiling. It's the biggest thing in hiring. You sit around with some six-hundred-thousand-dollar-a-year exec, and a ten-page questionnaire, and ask questions like, 'Which would you rather do? Go fishing alone, or watch a Yankee game with friends?' You ask five hundred questions and feed 'em into our trusty analyst computer, and it gauges the guy's suitability to take responsibility to fire workers at General Motors, International Harvester, Calgary Wheat. It's astounding, the way those computers can predict the way someone will act."

"Sounds boring," Voort says.

"Boring," Meechum says, draining the glass, "is my goal in life now."

"The day you got into West Point was the proudest I ever saw you."

"And the stupidest. But now it's time to tell you why I'm here."

Meechum twists around to extract from his wallet a folded napkin, which, Voort sees, has writing on it, in Magic Marker. From his perspective the writing is backwards and has soaked through the paper, so Voort can't read what it says.

"I need a favor," Meechum says. His hand is trembling.

"I'll do it," Voort tells him.

"Don't you want to hear it first?"

"No. I want you to know that I'll do it, whatever it is, first."

A slow smile relaxes the tense expression on Voort's old buddy's face. "You know, Voort, after all these years, I still think of you as the only person, outside family, who I can trust. You and family. That's about it. Even at fifteen, with your parents dead, you were the head of your family. You had that house, and your uncles came to you for advice, not the other way around, and . . ."

His eyes freeze, focused, over Voort's shoulder, on the front door.

Voort is up instantly, even before he sees who is there. He swings around and strides toward the entrance, Meechum's "No!" dying into the general din behind the laughter and Monday night football and the Tony Bennett revival hit, "San Francisco," blaring over a jukebox, forcing people to shout to be heard.

Through the crowd, Voort catches sight of a man in a brown flight jacket pushing out of the restaurant, in a hurry.

He cannot see the face, but from the back the man has the normal quickened gait of a native New Yorker, or of someone from anywhere else, in a rush. Voort remembers seeing no such jacket in the big carved mirror over Meechum's head, although he could have missed it, or it could have been lying in one of the booths, or beneath another coat, on a peg.

Voort follows the man onto Hudson Street, a wide, northbound avenue which retains much of New York's older flavor. The buildings, three- or four-story brownstones, are smaller than structures uptown. The shops are more distinctive than sizable: a wine specialty store, shuttered and grated; a Moroccan restaurant with only ten tables inside; a tailor who's been there for twenty-five years. There are no chain stores, no A&Ps or Barnes & Nobles or McDonald's.

He's ducking into the entranceway of that closed liquor store, pulling out a cell phone.

Back when the avenue was forest, not tar, three hundred and fifty years back, Voorts patrolled a few miles from this spot in the Dutch colony of New Amsterdam, as night watchmen, and later, under the British, as Colonial constables, and finally, as American citizens in the growing city, Voorts passed here proudly as mounted police, beat cops with nightsticks, mobile guys in squad cars, sergeants, lieutenants, plainclothes detectives.

He's talking urgently into the phone. He's gesturing at the tavern.

Autumn in New York is the season of nature's disappointment. The maple trees on the block are bare, their dead leaves in the gutter. The wind whipping east, off the Hudson, reeks of brine, oil slicks, furtively dumped garbage. In the dark sky, vaguely threatening cumulus clouds scud through a night haze of toxic metropolitan pollutants.

Voort's shout makes passersby spin around.

"Curt!"

He rushes toward the man in the flight jacket, a sloppy grin on his face, as if he's drunk, although he has only had the one beer. The man snaps his phone shut as Voort calls out, much too loud, "I *thought* that was you, Curt!"

Voort halts as he reaches the man.

"Whoops," he says, grinning. "I thought you were my old college buddy. Fifty lashes for me."

He is looking into a narrow, balding face registering equal measures of surprise and urban wariness. After all, Voort blocks the man's path from the entrance of the closed shop back to the street. He catalogs, rapidly, automatically, *White man, late forties, flannel collar under the jacket. His tan makes the pale blotches on his neck stand out, as if he's had lesions removed.*

Check the shoes. If you're following someone, it's better to wear rubber soles.

The man tries to inch around Voort and back to the freedom of the open sidewalk. His voice lacks any identifiable accent. "I must have one of those faces. Everyone thinks I'm their cousin Max."

He reaches the sidewalk and turns, already walking off and *He's wearing Reeboks,* and Voort, tagging along like a pesky drunk, says, "You could be Curt's brother. You could be his goddamn twin."

"I said, no problem." Meaning, politely, get lost.

"I didn't see you eating in there, and if you like burgers, that's the primo place around here. The fried onions are the greatest."

"I was supposed to meet someone," the man says, "but she didn't show."

"Stood up?"

"Yeah." The man is looking more put out, which is, under the circumstances, entirely and reassuringly normal. "Stood up."

"Well, if it's any help, just before you came in, there was this woman by the bar," Voort says. "I *thought* she was looking for someone. Man, she was gorgeous. Blond hair down to her ass. White fur coat. I thought she was an actress or something. You're a lucky guy if she was yours."

This time the man slows and his brown eyes fix on Voort's face, and linger there a fraction of a second too long. The posture remains impatient, but that barest flicker of greater interest decides the issue for Voort.

"I never had that much luck with women," the man says. "Excuse me."

He steps to the curb, scans the street for a cab, turns back, and registers Voort's scrutiny.

A cab pulls over and Voort waits until the man leaves.

When he gets back to the restaurant, his table is empty. *Shit.*

Then Voort sees Meechum returning from the men's room.

"You shouldn't have gone after him, Voort."

"Who is he?"

Meechum sighs. "I never saw him before, and that's the truth. The point is, you shouldn't be going after anyone. Next time it *could* be someone I know."

"We're getting out of here," Voort says, raising his hand, signaling the waitress that they are through.

"And you're going home, old buddy. Forget I called."

"Too late."

Meechum shakes his head, pulls money from his wallet. "You know what my problem is? I overdramatize things. I've been listening to myself and I sound like some nervous girl. Tell you what," he says heartily, "I'll call you in a couple of days. We'll hit the old spots. Does Arturo's still have the best pizza?"

Voort grips Meechum's wrist, stops the hand putting bills on the table.

"We're going to Collier's," he says, "where you'll finish telling me what you started."

"Hey, Herr Hitler, don't get so riled. I thought you could do me a favor and no one would know. I reconsidered."

Voort doesn't move. "Collier's," he repeats.

Meechum grins. "I'm impressed, Voort. I disappear for years. I show up drunk. I babble like an idiot and instead of laughing, you take me seriously. By the way, do you know the derivation of the word *idiot*? It's ancient Greek. It means 'he who has no interest in politics.' "

"Meechum, the guy was on a cell phone. If it was

me, following you, and you met someone, I'd call for backup. That way we could watch both targets when they split up."

"Targets," Meechum grins, trying to make a joke of it. "I like that. Targets."

Outside the White Horse Tavern's plate-glass window, Voort sees a cab pull to the curb, and two men get out.

"If I leave here without you," Voort continues, "I'll call your family, the army, find your head-hunting firm. Poke around. My social life's slow these days. I need something to do."

"Since when is *your* social life bad? Is that what went wrong two months ago?"

One of the men outside wears a gray wool overcoat and carries a black briefcase. The other, who looks ten years younger, early twenties maybe, wears a peacoat, and a black wool cap. Both men survey the restaurant from the sidewalk.

"I knew you were an asshole," Meechum sighs, surrendering. "But I forgot how much."

"That's better. Let's go."

Through the plate glass, Voort watches the two men approach the door of the tavern.

"You didn't finish your drink," the waitress tells Meechum, coming up as he lays money on the table. Is she trying to keep him here? Her expression is more flirtatious than critical. "Was something wrong with it?"

"I always order too much. I have big eyes," Meechum says.

"Maybe you need something to eat," she says, standing closer to Meechum. "If you like spicy, the stuffed haddock'll send you to outer space."

She's giving Meechum a come-on smile as the two

men outside walk into the tavern. They head toward the long, wooden bar.

Voort tells the waitress, "We're in a hurry here."

Her irritated look says, The whole city is in a hurry. What makes your hurry more important than mine?

She is quite pretty, long-legged and tall, and she has the kind of confidence that beauty imparts while it lasts. The crimson neckline of her sweater highlights the soft white arc of neck. She probably works here to make money to study dancing, or modeling, considering her superb posture. She's probably pouring herself into some dream she had as a little girl. Maybe she'll be disappointed when she doesn't achieve it. Maybe, like Meechum, she'll be disappointed if she does.

"Keep the change," Voort says.

The man in the wool coat has turned around at the bar now, so he can see the big room, and he rests one elbow behind him as, with his other hand, he lifts a tall drink. He watches Voort and Meechum pass. From the corner of his eye, Voort sees the man say something to his companion.

Outside, Voort passes up the closest cab, which has lingered after dropping the men off. He ignores another which rounds the corner of Christopher Street as he and Meechum exit the restaurant. He flags the third cab, noting with interest that Meechum seems to know exactly what he's doing, and even checks to see that other cabs don't follow as they drive off.

"Hi, this is Artie West," says this month's current and irritating recorded celebrity taxi safety message. In the disappointed society, authorities do not trust citizens to read, and believe they must entertain them to convince them to pay attention to safety. The ex-star of the TV series "Cyber Man" says, "Fasten your cyber seat belt. Have a good cyber night. Enjoy cyber New York."

Meechum has turned in the seat, and monitors traffic as they make a right on Fourteenth, and cross the Village to Union Square, where Voort's grandfather, in the 1920s, helped break up AFL-CIO labor rallies, before cops joined unions themselves, and went out on strike like the men they used to arrest.

Voort waits to see if his old friend will stop the cab before they reach their destination. He wants to know just how skilled Meechum is in basic evasion.

"Drop us by the subway," Meechum says, and the driver pulls over by the green globe marking the Lexington Avenue IRT.

"Well, it's back to Queens for me, Fred," he tells Voort loudly as he pays the bill. If someone asks the driver later where he dropped these particular passengers, he will tell them about the subway station, and perhaps, if he remembers, the remark about Queens, and the phony name, Fred.

Just what did you do in the army, Meech?

They wait for the cab to round the corner, then follow Fourteenth to University Place, and turn south, until they reach Collier's, an NYU hangout, a beery, boisterous, smoky, old-style New York drinkery, with tin ceilings, a mezzanine filled with ESPN watchers, and a long bar made of a single gigantic cedar tree which the original owner had cut down on an Alabama plantation, which he occupied as a Union Army sergeant in the final year of the Civil War.

"Okay, what's going on," Voort says when they take a table upstairs. "And no bullshit this time."

But Meechum is already unfolding the napkin again,

pushing it across the small, wooden tabletop, which is gouged with decades of student names. BD loves LL. SALLY & SAM. Meechum reverses the napkin so Voort sees a list of five names, addresses, and social security numbers, written in black Magic Marker.

1. Charles Farber . . . 1320 Lincoln Pl. Evanston, Ill.
2. Alan Clark . . . Box 1255 . . . Galena Gulch, Montana
3. Frank Greene . . . Rural Rte. 23, Lancaster Falls, Mass.
4. Lester M. Levy . . . 888 Tortoise Lane, Seattle, Wash.
5. Dr. Jill Towne . . . 615 Fifth Ave., New York

Meechum reaches into the side pocket of his peacoat and extracts a pack of unfiltered Camels. His fingertips are stained from nicotine.

"I know I'm being a pain in the ass," he says with a semblance, finally, of earnestness, "but what may be happening is so fantastic I barely believe it myself. I'm not sure I'm right. I don't want to hurt anyone. I need to learn *if* I'm right. You've already put up with more than I would have hoped for. But if you can stand it a little longer, can we do this my way?"

Despite the tense evening so far, Voort bursts out laughing. *Can we do this my way?* He sees his old friend, at age fifteen, toe-to-toe with their high school football coach, on the sidelines, during a play-off game for the Manhattan borough championship. The coach, an ex-marine, towers over Meechum as the stubborn wide end shakes his helmet and argues, "Can we run the play my way?" He sees Meechum at the wheel of his big brother's Jeep, during their first road trip, both of them eighteen, high school grads, crossing the red desert of Utah, bound for Los Angeles in July, to see the place, meet girls, looks for film stars in the street, stand and gape at the Pacific.

Meechum is saying, "Can we take the Zion National Park route? My way?"

Meechum's single-mindedness had been the high school joke. He'd get some notion into his head and push and push and never give up. It was how he'd gotten their congressman to nominate him for West Point. He wrote the man letters incessantly, and even visited his office. You couldn't stop him.

And the truth was, Voort remembers, Meechum was usually right. After that football game, when Meechum's fake square-out running pattern had produced the winning touchdown, the jubilant team had, in the locker room, burst into the old Sinatra hit "My Way" when Meechum walked out of the showers.

Guys singing like Sinatra, or snapping their fingers like Sammy Davis, testosterone rampant, as they stood on benches, bellowing, proud, out of pitch. It was one of Voort's favorite high school memories.

Meechum had stood still during the whole rendition, accepting homage, and then remarked, grinning, when they were through, "Not bad, but sing it my way and you'll make the 'Tonight Show.' "

Voort understands limits when he runs into them. Argument with Meechum, beyond a certain point, has always been useless.

"And what is your way?"

"Check these names out. You can do it. You have contacts in police departments all over the country, whether you're on leave or not. Make some phone calls, off the record. Ask about them."

"Ask *what?*"

"Don't worry about that part. Make up something. Say their names came up in an investigation and see what happens. If I'm right, if there's something to learn, you'll find it. If you come up with nothing, nothing was there. If you can't do it, just say so."

"Why don't you make the calls yourself?"

"Ha! A cop calls a cop, he gets cooperation. A civilian calls a cop, he gets investigated."

"Meaning there's something for them to investigate."

Meechum grins. "See? You sound like a cop."

"Can't you give me a better idea what I'm looking for?"

"It will be obvious if I'm right. And if I am, I'll explain everything." Meechum picks a cigarette out of the half-crumpled pack of unfiltered Camels and lights it, rolling his eyes to indicate that, technically, he understands smoking here is an illegal act. "And you'll be sorry I did."

Voort tries to get more information but finally gives up. There is simply no way he is going to send an old friend away, especially when he remembers the flash of interest in the face of the man in the flight jacket. He says, surrendering, "When do you need it?"

"Two days? How about Wednesday night. Is that enough time?"

"Where can I find you?"

"Like the old saying goes, we'll call you."

Meechum stubs out his barely smoked Camel and the harsher lines around his mouth soften.

"I'm hoping it's nothing. Next time we'll have dinner on me, and talk about you, and whatever the hell happened to make you leave the police, even for eight weeks. I should have called you earlier," Meechum says, rising, reaching for his jacket. "You were always a guy I could count on. I'm glad that hasn't changed."

Voort walks through the chilly streets of Greenwich Village, and at his town house on Thirteenth Street sees lights blazing from most of the windows and silhouettes of people moving behind the curtains. The sound of Wynton Marsalis's trumpet jazz wafts from the three-story home.

When he lets himself inside, the place is filled with Voorts—cousins, uncles, nieces, and nephews. He smells the warm aromas of baked hams and turkeys, October foods, country foods, that will be laid out in the gigantic Dutch kitchen. The upstate families have been coming down each night with pies, roast chickens, squash salads, bags of freshly picked apples. He hears the happy screams of children chasing each other up and down the stairs, or through the bedrooms, study, library, pantry.

"And normally you live here all alone," says cousin Marla, taking his jacket. She provided the drinks tonight, from the SoHo liquor store she owns with her husband. "You ought to get married and have kids."

"Let's lay off Camilla for one day. How's Matt feeling tonight?"

"They gave him chemo today. He's been sick all afternoon but he's up there, listening to the usual war stories. Conrad, it was great of you to let him stay here, instead of the hospital."

"You said it yourself. There's enough room for a hundred people here."

"And you were a prince to take off two months and help with his farm."

"Matt was one of my two best friends when I was a kid," Voort tells his cousin, thinking, *and Meechum was the other. What a night.*

Voort threads his way past the relatives, making his way upstairs, greeting people, shaking hands, kissing cheeks. The tugboat Voorts are here and the Queens cops and also the Bronx detective families. The different branches switch off, so Matt has company every night. Voort swoops up one of his little nephews on the top of the second-floor landing. The five-year-old screams in delight.

"Uncle Conrad?"

"What's that, Buddy?"

"I saw a picture in a magazine of a party, and Camilla was in it!"

"That's terrific, Buddy."

"And then Mommy told Daddy Camilla *betrayed* you. What's '*betrayed*' mean?"

"Tricked."

"She tricked you?"

"It's complicated."

"Who's the man in that painting, with the funny hair on his face?" asks the boy, losing interest in the first part of the conversation, and indicating one of the Voort portraits running the length of the hall.

"Those are called sideburns," Voort says. "A lot of men used to wear them. And Ulysses Voort once owned this house. He was a captain of detectives, and he arrested a lot of bad men who were rioting to stay out of the army during the Civil War."

The boy, released, runs off after one of his sisters. Voort makes his way toward a third-floor bedroom. He hears hearty male laughter coming from the room, and smells, even before he enters it, the stink of shit and the faint aroma of puke.

Matt's propped up in the electric bed, against pillows, his big frame wasted, the tangle of auburn hair gone, so his skull makes him look like an Auschwitz survivor. Tubes of clear solution run into his arms, from suspended bottles. Viler looking green liquid pours out of his body through another tube, extending from his side, emptying into a plastic container under the bed.

It's impossible to believe that this man is Voort's age, thirty-one, impossible to believe that three months ago he looked nothing like this, and that a small pain in his abdomen spread into his back, and sides, and when the doctors opened him up, they found a cancer invading his body as fast as a mechanized army taking over a poor country.

"Anyway," one of the vice cop Voorts is saying, finishing a story, leaning against a windowsill, "I arrest the porno actress, but the whole time I'm putting the cuffs on, she's grinning. Finally she figures out it's a real arrest, and says, 'Wait a minute, you're putting these cuffs on me because you're a *cop*?'"

The half-dozen men in the room break up in laughter, and Matt's is loudest. The emaciated man pounds his bedcovers. Tears of mirth run down his face, and drip onto his baby blue blanket.

"Hey, Conrad, I ought to start paying you rent," Matt says.

"Nah, I save big money when you're here. I won't have to buy food for years with all the groceries everyone brings every night."

"I'm serious. It's been weeks. A couple of the other guys said I could stay with them."

Voort snaps his fingers. "I never thought of that. Pack a bag, and take these liars with their bullshit stories out of here, too."

"Thanks," Matt says quietly.

"I'm going out to Long Island," Voort tells his relatives. "I have to see Mickie. Use any of the bedrooms, even mine tonight."

"A new case?" Matt asks eagerly. "Who needs TV. I'm staying at New York's longest-running cop show."

"That's next week's entertainment," Voort says. To the others, he says, "Who's turn is next?"

"Me," says the youngest man in the room, one of the rookie patrolman cousins from Queens. "Okay," he starts off, "this really happened, last Tuesday, in Flushing . . ."

Voort walks out.

My two best friends when I was a kid.

His heart is breaking.

Things are not supposed to happen like this.

Downstairs, in the garage, he gets into the red Jaguar. He steers the Jag to Third Avenue and turns north, toward the Midtown Tunnel. He calls Mickie on the car phone, hears ringing, out on the North Shore.

"What are you doing?" Voort asks when his partner and current best friend answers.

"Watching TV, that Arizona doctor Robertson killing one of his patients," Mickie says. "Assisted suicide, my ass. He videotaped it! Can you believe it? He likes it. You know what an expert is? A guy who uses facts to support his preoccupations. I just hope when they legalize suicide it's not cops that have to supervise it, if you know what I mean."

Through bad static, Voort explains he's on his way out

to the island. Mickie says, "Good, but there's something you'll want to . . ."

The static gets so bad they have to hang up. Whatever it is, it'll wait, Voort thinks.

He floors the Jag when he gets to the Long Island Expressway. When he hits the Nassau County line, at Great Neck, he holds up Meechum's list, in the dashboard light. The names mean nothing to him. They are a mystery collection of letters. They lack history, faces, problems, passions. They are not yet linked by age, or ethnicity, or sex, or even geography.

Five names, addresses, social security numbers.

He tries to suggest to himself that maybe he imagined the flicker of interest in Leather Jacket's face, outside the White Horse.

I didn't imagine it.

Boys first learn about peer society in schoolrooms and playgrounds. They form bonds with the friends who will mature with them into adults. In playing fields all over the city, they share allies, foes, aspiration, disappointment. They learn to defend themselves. They cooperate on teams. They become representative, as Meechum will always be to Voort, of early standards for measuring friendship—and for that they will remain alive in memory as long as boys live. For that, they will always give one another the extra break.

Voort takes the Roslyn exit off the expressway, heading toward Mickie's oceanfront home. He is in the suburbs now. A storm of brightly colored leaves falls in the headlights.

He envisions Meechum in the back of a cab, being driven through the impersonal metropolis. He sees large buildings going by, and imagines his old pal sunk in fear or gloom, going home perhaps, or going someplace to hide.

He does not see, at that same moment, where a real cab drops Meechum, at a small, nondescript five-story hotel, in Inwood, north of Harlem. "The King Hotel" reads blue neon script above a tattered awning. The establishment is not exactly fit for a king.

Meechum gives the driver thirty dollars, tells him to keep the change, and walks up a half-dozen cracked concrete steps into the modest but spankingly clean lobby. The linoleum smells of lemon polish. The potted palms are freshly watered. Reproduction lithographs of jockeys at Belmont Park racetrack; Angel Cordero, Julie Crone— the riders responsible for the hotel owner's gambling disappointments—hang by the freshly painted black, cage-style elevator that carries Meechum, all alone, to the third floor.

At Room 305, where a DO NOT DISTURB sign hangs on the knob, he runs his hand along the doorjamb; he relaxes when he locates, in the exact spot where he inserted them, three strands of his black hair, between door and jamb.

He inserts the electronic keycard, a modern surprise in these older surroundings, and pushes open the door. He'd left the light on. On the carrot-colored shag carpet he checks the undisturbed expanse of white talcum powder which, backing from the room earlier, he had sprinkled on the floor.

Meechum shoves the door forward, so it swings violently forward and strikes the wall. No one there.

When he enters, he stops and sniffs for any hint of

scent, aftershave, perfume, leather, that was not there before. Detecting nothing, he locks the door behind him.

One more night hidden, but at least safe.

It isn't until he enters the bathroom, and reaches for the lightswitch, that someone blindsides him from the left. An expert blow catches the side of his throat, and even as his hands come up protectively, and he's thinking *I can't breathe*, he knows he's leaving his belly open and the second blow comes fast, doubling him.

The ceiling is whirling. The floor rushes at his face.

He wants to fight but whoever is behind him wields enormous strength. He is helpless as a baby. His larynx seems crushed, and now the man is on top of him, and he feels another pain, sharp and sudden and *it's a needle* going in, by his collarbone, at the base of his neck.

When he wakes he's in the same room, and, senses sharpening, he sees that he's in bed. He reaches to pull the covers off.

I can't move my arms. They tied me.

The TV is on, loud. Very bad sign.

I can't breathe out of my mouth. There's something over my mouth!

"Meechum," a deep, older voice says, through the darkness in his head, and the pain.

There is a pounding between his eyes, and red bursts, dots, ebb and flow behind them. His throat is on fire, and when he tries to turn over, he can't move his legs either.

The voice says, "We lost you. But we found you. Like 'Amazing Grace.' Ever hear it with bagpipes? It makes you weep."

He opens his eyes. The light fuels his pain, spikes it

higher as the voice, and vague mass of dirty brown lines above coalesce into a cotton sweater, as the voice says, plainly, matter-of-factly, "I'm going to loosen the tape on your mouth. Keep quiet or I'll kill you."

Close-up, the speaker is a study in contradiction. He is large, about fifty, with wide shoulders, giving a sense of physical power offset by the bulging stomach, as if he was once in superb shape but allowed himself to go to seed a bit. The left arm hangs at a slightly odd angle. The clothing is pressed, neat but not flamboyant. The wool trousers are the color of milk chocolate, selected well, off the rack. The V-necked cotton sweater is light beige, the crew-necked pull-over beneath that is white. He might be a corporate lawyer, lounging at home, on Sunday. But the whole subdued surface and soft voice are offset by the driving intensity in eyes of the palest blue, magnified by dark silver-rimmed glasses. The hair is steel-colored, cut short and receding from the large forehead. The face is round and Slavic, starting to go fleshy. The mass of creases at the corners of the mouth has a weather-beaten quality, as does the leathery skin, as if this man once spent an unhealthy amount of time in the sun. The entire effect is of a man put together over half a century in layers, each intense, reinforcing the other, until the final complex product was achieved.

Meechum realizes, *My clothes are hanging on a chair. I'm naked.*

And now he sees a second man, the one he spotted leaving the White Horse earlier, and the man is standing on a chair, holding the room's smoke alarm, which he has unscrewed from the ceiling. He appears to be replacing the battery. In his jeans and flannel shirt, he might be a building custodian who strolled into a kidnapping scene and began going about his business. He replaces the alarm.

The speaker says, "Hairs in the door? Really, Meechum. Charley broke in. I stayed outside and put the hairs back. You wrote something on a napkin, in the restaurant where you had lunch. You showed the napkin to the man in the White Horse. What did you write on the napkin?"

Charley wipes dust off his hands and approaches the bed, but stops as he breaks out coughing, a deep ugly sound coming from far inside.

Meechum says, "Napkin?"

The speaker sighs and reaches for a Windsor chair from the room's pine table, and swings it around so he can sit and drape his powerful forearms over the back. A talent at patience is indicated.

"Charley?" he says.

Leather Jacket moves fast, despite the coughing, whips down and replaces the tape over Meechum's mouth. He rears back and drives a finger, a mere index finger, into a spot on Meechum's neck. Meechum shoots up in bed, back arching. The pain blinds him.

"What did you write? Remember, no screaming."

Charley loosens the tape a little, allowing air in.

"Oh, God," Meechum gasps.

"God," the speaker remarks, "is a study in failed expectation." His expression remains bland, but the flatness of the voice shows suppressed passion.

Meechum thinks, *I must protect Voort.*

"Tonight's guests," blares the MC on the television, "are Jennifer Lopez! Steve Young! And that terrific actor, Tom Hanks!"

"Meechum, what did you write?"

The second man leans forward again, replaces the tape and shoves his finger into a new spot. Meechum screams through the fabric, feels saliva dripping down his throat. He can't breathe. Charley yanks him up in bed, enabling a trickle of air to reach his lungs through his nose.

"Meechum, in real life, unlike movies, people tell," the man with the twisted arm says as, eyes bulging, Meechum watches Charley undo the buttons on his flannel shirt, an act which, in its inexplicability, is more terrifying than anything that has so far happened in this room.

The MC says, "Please welcome the star of the new Disney hit, *The Mouse That Snored*."

"We're going to leave that tape where it is. I ask a question. You nod if you want to answer. Then Charley takes off the tape."

A few minutes later, Meechum forces out, through a world of agony, "Names. I . . . wrote . . . down names."

"What names?"

Meechum answers truthfully. "And the addresses," he gets out.

The speaker closes his eyes, calms himself, opens them. "Only those names?"

"Yes."

"No others?"

"No."

"You're sure."

"Yes."

"Charley, I'm not positive he's sure."

Meechum convinces them, at length, that he is sure.

"And who did you give this list *to*?"

"A . . . policeman."

The speaker sits absolutely still, his breathing remaining steady, his gaze never leaving Meechum's face. A small bright light flares and dies in his irises. His tone never rises, never changes. He is perfectly in control. He says, "A New York City policeman. Just a run-of-the-mill municipal policeman. That's what you're telling me?"

"A detective."

"And *why* did you tell this detective you were giving him the list, if that's *all* you told him?"

"I asked him to . . . I wanted him . . . to check . . . the names . . . to check the names."

The speaker runs a hand over his short gray hair.

"You're asking me to believe that you just gave him names and didn't explain it," he says, as much reasoning to himself as repeating information. "You're saying," he begins, but his frown is suddenly replaced by a look of understanding.

"You're saying you weren't sure you had anything to tell him yet, so you were protecting people until your suspicions were confirmed. You didn't want to divulge more unless you were sure it was real."

"Ye-es."

The speaker stands, and frowns. "Or am I fooling myself," he says, "because that's what I want to hear?"

"Charley?" he says. "I'm not sure I believe him yet."

Several minutes later, when Charley has finished another round, the speaker says, "But how is the detective supposed to check the names out, if that's all he knows?"

"Make . . . calls. To friends in those cities."

"But why would the detective agree to this and even listen to you in the first place? He's got other things to do. Why pay attention to your request? A stranger walks off the street and tells a detective to 'check out some names,' isn't that what you said, and the detective, who I imagine has a million cases in backlog, legitimate cases, just snaps to attention and says, Yes sir, right away, sir, I have nothing to do and I'll just run off and do whatever nutty thing you want. . . . Is that what you're trying to tell me? *What aren't you telling me?*"

The tape goes back on Meechum's mouth. Through the foul taste of adhesive, he screams.

"I . . . used to know him," Meechum says when Charley loosens the tape again.

"As in, he's an old friend."

"Yes."

"And the name of this good old friend?"

Meechum shuts his eyes. He doesn't want to watch this time, doesn't want to see Charley, but he feels the hands at his mouth. He tries to bite, to whip his head away. He feels himself arching in agony, feels his spine cresting so far toward the ceiling that he sees it, in his mind, snapping in two.

Donotdonotdonotnotnot say Voort's name.

"Pretty strong," he hears Charley say with grudging admiration. "I didn't think he had anything left."

"Let's hear it for a great actor, who made sacrifices for his work. He put on thirty pounds for this part," the TV host says, and through Meechum's pain comes the tinny thunder of network audience approval.

After awhile Meechum passes out, and the phone starts ringing, which startles the man in the beige sweater. He does not like that someone is calling.

"Are you sure no one saw you come in?" he asks Charley, who now has his pants off, too.

"It's probably someone complaining about the loud TV."

"Probably," the speaker repeats, with some sarcasm. "Are you offering odds backing up this hypothesis?"

"You're the one who said to hurry." Charley breaks into coughs again. He has to wipe away phlegm from the corner of his mouth.

The speaker reconsiders, and subsides. It is the first time he has looked contrite tonight, and the change, in such a big man, a controlled and powerful-looking man, is profound. "You're right and I apologize. I took out my anger on you."

"Don't worry about it," Charley says.

"I mean it," the speaker says with real emotion. "After all you've done, and what you're about to do, I have no right to give you a hard time."

"I said forget it," Charley says.

"Thank you. Put on the pajamas and finish up. Take the pill. Give yourself ten minutes for it to take effect."

"My family?" Charley says.

"Already done," the man with the twisted arm says.

Charley pulls, from a plastic shopping bag, brand-new, cellophane-wrapped green satin pajamas. He slides the trousers over his bare legs.

"Hey! Smooth," he says. "I always laughed at people who wore, y'know, pajamas."

He folds his shirt neatly on a chair. He lays his trousers over that. There is a ritualistic quality to his movements, as if he were a husband, married for years, about to climb under the sheets, onto his side of a double mattress, and pull out a *People* magazine, or channel clicker, or just, tired after a hard day, reach over and turn off the bedside lamp.

The man with the twisted elbow puts on a hooded coat

of fawn-colored wool, button-up style. At the door, he turns and watches the lean man don his brand-new satin pajama top, then climb under the covers with Meechum.

"Charley, I'm sorry it came to this."

He turns his attention to the inert form in the bed.

"Meechum, I'm disappointed in you" is all he says.

Two

Meechum Lawrence Keefe, age nine, stands uncertainly in the doorway of Voort's third-floor bedroom, shifting his weight from foot to foot. It is the afternoon following the funeral of Voort's parents, and, in his first experience with mourning, and in honor of death as something touching people close to you, Meechum wears a brand-new three-piece dark wool suit, a pressed white Van Heusen shirt, and a black clip-on tie as somber as an undertaker's. Conrad Voort lies on his single bed, staring at the ceiling, barely aware that the other boy is there.

"I'm sorry about your parents," Meechum says.

"I keep thinking," Voort says in a flat and terrible voice that chills the other boy, "that they'll walk in here any second. Or that I'll wake up, and they'll be downstairs."

They hear the sounds of adults downstairs, doing whatever things older people do when one of them dies. Outside the town house it is a July day, and the city has managed to continue functioning despite the absence of Voort's parents. He got the news at a softball game, in Central Park. He was just standing in the outfield when an uncle walked out to tell him that the private plane carrying his parents to a fund-raiser for, ironically, families of deceased police, crashed near Albany.

Now dozens of Voorts have descended on the town house, from across the Metropolitan area. Periodically, they come upstairs to try to make the boy feel better, in between their own bouts with tears.

"Want to go to the park?" Meechum says, not knowing what to say, worried he'll do the wrong thing, wanting to help.

"No."

Meechum takes one step into the room. "Want to, uh, take a walk?"

"No."

"Want to play checkers?"

"No."

Voort turns away but senses the other boy coming closer. He hears the scrape of his desk chair and supposes Meechum has simply sat down. Traffic sounds waft up through the open screened window, from Thirteenth Street; from delivery trucks, cabs or street messengers, going about their daily business. It seems impossible that the world is still going on.

The pain feeds off Voort's stomach. His last visitor, an aunt, advised him to "try to sleep" a few minutes ago. Now Voort is seeing that the adults downstairs—his policemen uncles and cousins, the commissioner, and even the mayor, who had seemed until yesterday to have so much power— are flawed by human vulnerability. They provide only limited protection against danger. They offer no shield at all against pain.

At least Meechum is the same skinny boy he was yesterday. Meechum lacked the status to sink in Voort's estimation, being an equal, so has not disappointed him by sinking lower, for whatever it is worth.

But the discussion is different. Normally, when the other boy comes to the house, or Voort goes to Meechum's, sooner or later they pull out photo albums.

"My family was in the army since the Civil War," Meechum boasts, showing off old Mathew Brady black-and-whites of a colonel ancestor, Robert L. Meechum, astride a stallion at Vicksburg, where he was killed by Confederate fire.

"Yeah, well *my* family has been cops for longer than that."

"The army's more dangerous."

"Ha! Army guys don't have to fight for years at a time, maybe even the whole time they're in the army. But police are on the street every day."

Boys. Arguing.

And now, in the bedroom, Voort closes his eyes, exhausted, just for a minute, he thinks, but when he opens them it is the middle of the night, and the moon outside is full and yellow, shining through the window to illuminate, in a rectangular pool of light on the Turkish rug, Meechum, still in his jacket, on the floor, sleeping near Voort, like the pet dog, with a cotton blanket pulled up to his hips.

Meechum's parents, it turns out, coming to bring him home, discovered the boys sleeping. They covered both of them and left them in each other's care.

Twenty-one years later the memory still moves Voort; the sight of Meechum, in his crumpled jacket, unable to help and unwilling to leave. The image remains Voort's archetypical image of boyhood friendship, a silent offering of companionship even against the vastly greater force of death.

God, let Meechum be safe. Let Meechum have content-
ment. Help me help him, whatever the problem is. And make
Matt better. Give him life.

Voort slows the Jaguar before the spiked iron gate marking Mickie's property. Voort and Mickie are the two richest
cops in New York. Through the bars, bright headlights approach along the winding white gravel driveway curling
luxuriously past dwarf evergreens and weeping willows. The
foliage half obscures the sprawling ranch-style home three
hundred yards beyond, on the boulder-reinforced shore of
Long Island Sound.

The gates slide open before Voort can call Mickie on
the intercom. A white Chevy Lumina pulls out and stops.
When the driver's door opens and Voort sees who gets
out, his heart speeds up, and a sour taste surges into his
mouth.

"How many speed records did you break tonight?" the
blond woman asks.

Camilla has never, when he dated her, when she left
him, even when he declined to take her back, failed to
physically move him. Dressed casually tonight, she's model
thin, model tall, with long hair spread along the shoulders
of her chamois zip-up jacket, highlighting the Prussian
blue of her cashmere scarf. The boots are flat, yet she always
seems raised up, as if on tiptoe, or high heels.

"I don't speed, Camilla. Everyone else drives slow."

"That's because police give *them* tickets and let you
pass."

Voort makes out, in the dimmer recesses of the Lumina,
a form in the passenger seat, probably a man, as she has
never had trouble attracting them. But when Camilla shifts
stance and blocks the glare, he sees with some surprise that

it is a teenager, a smaller version of Camilla. A girl with a ponytail, maybe thirteen, in an oversized boy's high school letter jacket, staring at him as she leans forward over the dashboard, eager to watch what is about to unfold.

"That's Tanya, Voort. My 'Little Sister.' She came over from Moscow a couple of years ago and lives in Brighton Beach, with her father. Tanya, come out and meet the famous Mr. Conrad Voort."

"Pleased to meet you," Voort says.

"You saved her life," the girl says breathlessly, out of the car now, speaking in a thick accent, but with an excellent command of English. The child's whole attitude, the heightened attention she's paying, the way she seems to be straining forward on the balls of her tennis shoes, the wide-eyed look of blue eyes, all point toward some enormous importance she's giving this exchange. Voort's run-in with Camilla is not just idle conversation to her. It's some key to the mysteriously frustrating adult world.

"How's the wound?" Voort flashes to Camilla, in the foyer of her apartment building in Tribeca, two months ago, lying in her front vestibule, a red stain spreading along her blouse and jeans. Another body, a woman's body, lies beside her. Voort hears, in his mind, the quick approaching wail of sirens.

"It only hurts when I'm awake," she says, suggesting, as usual, some obscure double meaning. "Antibiotics may be unfashionable, Voort, but pump me full of them any old time."

Once these two couldn't keep their hands off each other. But after what happened months ago, even normal civility is a strain.

"You're handsomer than in the newspaper picture,"

Tanya pipes up, smiling at him in a way that, two or three years from now, will drive teenage boys mad.

Voort can't help glancing down, at the section of Camilla's jacket covering what he knows from once delightful experience to be her flat, hard belly.

I would have been a father.

But all he says is, "I didn't know you and Mickie stayed friends."

"Are you kidding? He never liked me. It's Syl I got close to," referring to Mickie's wife. "We talk all the time. Tanya and I came out for dinner."

Tanya says, "We rode on Mickie's boat, but he had work to do and couldn't come."

"Yes, he was working on his pool game," Camilla adds. "That man would kill for you."

"He's loyal," Voort says, and even through the half light from the floodlights atop the granite pillars, Camilla seems to blush.

She lied to me.

Their breath, in the silence, frosts, rises, and disappears as if it never existed.

"Well, Tanya's got school tomorrow," Camilla says, and turns back to the car.

But the teenager, instead of following, says to her, "Is that all you're going to tell him?"

"We have to go," Camilla repeats, slightly more firmly, woman to girl, warning: Shut up, this is not your business, these are adult things.

"But you can't just drive away," Tanya insists. "He's standing right here."

"Actually, I have to go, too," Voort says.

"Russians," Camilla tells him, "are very aggressive people."

"I'm *not* aggressive," Tanya says, and plants her hands on her hips, turning back, before their eyes, from budding woman into stubborn child.

Standoff. The girl doesn't move, and the Lumina blocks Voort's way into the estate. Tanya shoves her hands in her pockets, as if the two adults, not her, are responsible for the unpleasant scene. "If Camilla won't say anything, I will." And then, restraint gone, she bursts out, "You're crazy if you don't go back with her. She's beautiful and smart and whenever I'm with her every man wants to take her out . . . even on the street, they stop her and talk to her and just because of that baby is no reason to kick her out."

Camilla says, "Stop it."

"Why? The whole city read about it in the *Daily News*. She had an abortion and didn't tell you. But adults always say, in church, that you have to forgive, and then they don't do it. You go to church all the time, the paper said, but you won't give her another chance."

"Forgiveness is one thing. Getting back together is another."

"No! It's the same thing! She cries about you."

"Oh, this is ridiculous," Camilla says. "I don't cry. Stop this right now."

"What about that time he was on TV, after that woman who stabbed you died, and you turned away so I wouldn't see the tears. I bet you'd have his baby now if you got pregnant."

"Are you grooming her at the network to be a talk-show host?" Voort says, embarrassed for all of them. "She goes right for the jugular."

"She's doesn't need grooming. She's a natural," Camilla says through gritted teeth.

Tanya raises herself on her toes, as if she has to make herself taller to be understood, as if greater height will convey extra authority. "Adults always tell you what to do, and then do the opposite when it comes to them. Adults say, if you have a problem, talk about it. And then *they* have a problem, and they shut up."

"Which one of you is the little sister," Voort says, "and which is the big? Tanya, you mean well. I appreciate it. But this is between Camilla and me."

"How can it be between you if you're just going to drive away," Tanya says, "and not even talk to each other."

"Because sometimes that's what's left to do," Voort says.

Moments later, Voort steers the Jaguar onto the grounds, watching the rear lights of the Lumina recede in his rear-view mirror through the electronically closing gates. He tries to ignore the pounding in his chest. The tight throb of stretched nerves starts up along the base of his neck. He'd fallen in love with Camilla eight months ago, in a way he had never before experienced. He'd always had girlfriends, when he was growing up, when he was in college, when he was starting out in the police, but he had never had one he dreamed about at night, never had one he prayed for each day when he went to church. God, he would say, at St. Patrick's, let me make her as happy as she makes me.

For three months they'd been inseparable, but then she'd started going off by herself, into therapy, as it turned out, and then she'd broken it off, telling him she needed "time to think." She'd gotten too close too fast. She needed to make sure things were really over with an ex-boyfriend.

"It's not you. It's me," she'd said.

Later he'd found out that he'd gotten her pregnant, and she'd aborted the child without telling him. To Voort, a

Catholic, a family man without his own family yet, a man linked to his ancestors in a palpable day-to-day way, the notion of aborting a baby, *his* baby, was intolerable.

I would have raised the child myself, if things hadn't worked out between us. I would have paid for the hospital, for help, for child care, for anything. And she knew that all along.

Love, who needs it, he thinks as he pulls up to the house. It's just another four-letter word. Some cultures don't even have the word. Love is nothing more, in the end, he decides, than chemicals gone askew, masquerading as affection or knowledge. A medieval notion, conceived of by professional soldiers who amused themselves by wooing women when they weren't hacking each other apart. The truth, Voort knows now, is that even after falling in "love," whatever that means, any successful future relationship between people is a happy accident. In the end, he sees "love" is one more addiction, and like addiction, it hurts with entrapment, or withdrawal.

At least I'm over her now.

Voort leaves the Jag on a gravel overlook between the main house and a smaller detached building of gray shingle with white trim. "Meet me in the pool house," Mickie had said. Stepping up the flagstone walkway, through floodlights, Voort sees, beyond the dock and cabin cruiser, the flat, dark water of Long Island Sound and, in the distance, the twinkling red-and-green aviation warning lights atop the arched spans of the Throggs Neck and Whitestone Bridges. There's a smoky smell, meaning Mickie is burning logs in there, and the water issues a cleaner and more natural smell than it does downtown, near the White Horse Tavern. There's the sound of surf lapping and, from an open window in the main house, a professional-quality piano rendition of a Chopin nocturne. Mickie's wife, Syl, a surgeon, likes to practice at night, before she goes to sleep.

"Come on in. The market's plunging, in Tokyo."

Voort's partner, standing in his doorway, wears a V-necked cashmere sweater picked up in Scotland last year, at St. Andrews, on his yearly golfing vacation. The pleated Italian trousers are a darker shade of gray and tailored perfectly; the cuffs brush the tops of his Bruno Magli loafers, which match, in black, the crew-necked pressed-cotton shirt. Mickie generally looks like a Hollywood film producer, but provoked, in seconds, can turn back into the beribboned marine. At the moment he holds a crystal tumbler half filled with a clear drink.

"Polish Vodka. I never dreamed potatoes could produce something this good. Want some?"

"Not for me."

"That's what I always loved about the Valkyrie. She brings joy to your life. Syl got friendly with her after you split up. They commiserate together. Boohoo. Aren't men assholes. What's up?"

The pool house, so called because of its centerpiece, a pool table of Indonesian mahogany, has floor-to-ceiling windows, tinted lightly, which provide a view of Long Island sound that would turn a landscape painter green with envy. The couch and sitting chairs are black Venetian leather. The inch-deep pile is gray. On the second shelf of a wall unit, a TV the size of a small movie screen is on, the sound muted and, at the moment, the picture is split between the Humphrey Bogart classic *The Maltese Falcon* on the right side, and rolling lists showing the carnage on the Japanese stock exchange, in white numbers and letters, on the left.

"By the way, what did the Valkyrie have to say?"

"Mickie," Voort warns.

"Don't shoot, Mr. Wayne. Syl said ask."

"I thought you didn't even like Camilla."

"Can you believe what's going on in Asia?" Mickie says, changing the subject, glancing in disgust at the plunging numbers on the left side of the screen. "Total fucking meltdown. They're floating the yen again. I got out just in time. Collectibles, Voort. When things get tight, head for the art galleries, but my ESP," he says, grinning, "tells me you're not here about investments."

Voort explains about the meeting with Meechum, and together, at a large antique rolltop desk set off from the pool table, the two detectives study Meechum's list of names. There's a Dell computer on the desk, turned off, and a modem and black phone connected to three lines. "New York's cop investment genius uses his pool house as a home office," the *Wall Street Journal* said, of Mickie.

"But my true love," Mickie told the reporter, with theatrical modesty, "is watching the Mets at Shea, not making money."

Now Mickie shakes his head. "I never heard of any of these people. What about the doctor in New York. What kind of doctor is she?"

"We'll find out."

"And, Con Man, you trust him, right? I mean, it's a pretty wacky story, and anyone can change in nine years."

"He was as good a friend as you when I was a kid."

"Then we give him the benefit of the doubt."

"Which means," Voort says, glancing at his watch, "we wake people up. Who do we know in Evanston, or Chicago? They're next to each other."

"Santos Brioche," Mickie says, naming a former New York detective who relocated to the Windy City after marrying a commodities broker there.

"And Jack Rosen moved to Seattle," Voort says, going down Meechum's list, picturing a wiry, explosive Jewish lieutenant, one of the most decorated detectives at One Police Plaza, who headed west at the age of sixty. "I wanna die near my daughter," he'd said, "and in a place that has more than two trees per square mile."

"Lancaster Falls, Massachusetts? That's in the western part of the state, right?"

"I can't think of anyone."

"No one in western Massachusetts?"

"I got a speeding ticket there once, but I don't remember the name of the pissass who gave it to me even after seeing my badge."

"Maybe Hazel can help," says Voort, referring to one of the computer girls back at headquarters, the cyberspace geniuses able to access electronic data banks across the country, and dig up, legally or off-the-record, suspects' credit ratings, motor vehicle cards, tax lien information, real estate records, military discharge records, and court records of any suits in which they are involved.

Voort says, "How about Galena Gulch, Montana? Where the hell is ... Wait a minute! Montana's Abel what's-his-name!"

"Drake. Who gave the speech in Vegas. He said any time we need anything, call. Or was he from Wyoming? I mix them up."

"Next time you have time off, you ought to travel farther than the Poconos," Voort says.

Mickie lifts the phone and grins. "Midnight here's only

ten P.M. there. Yahoo. Cowboy bedtime. He was from Helena. I remember now."

Voort pictures the stocky, bespectacled ex-army Ranger, in square-toed boots, cowboy hat, and sheepskin vest, who'd lectured the national detectives convention last spring on "Terrorism in the Twenty-first Century." He'd scared the hell out of even the veterans with his depictions of anthrax bombs going off in rush-hour San Francisco, plutonium balls smuggled into Minnesota from Canada. Basement labs stocked with deadly mustard gas.

"It's not a question of whether these things will happen, but when," the Montana detective had drawled, using a rubber-tipped wooden pointer to indicate, on an easel, black-and-white photo blowups of bacteria or viruses, provided by U.S. Army Intelligence. Bubonic plague. Ebola.

"Not to mention a host of diseases someone's probably coming down with, as I speak, in the jungle in Zaire," Drake had said.

Voort accesses the number they need from his electronic address book and minutes later, clear as the water lapping outside, Voort hears a phone ringing two thirds of the way across the country. A sleepy voice drawls, "Hello?"

The voice cheers up when Voort identifies himself.

"My wife found a photo of your home in *House Beautiful*, at the beauty parlor," Abel says. "I didn't realize you were a celebrity." His whistle, over the line, is long and admiring, like that of a seventeen-year-old boy watching a Victoria's Secret model, or a fifty-year-old man reading about the bank accounts of the Aga Khan.

Abel says, "Did the Continental Congress really give your family the land and house forever, in Manhattan, tax free? Did your admiral ancestor really beat the British navy off New Jersey during the Revolutionary War?"

Voort invites the man to stay at his town house whenever he is in New York, a courtesy he happily extends to policemen from around the country whom he likes.

Matt will be better by then. Matt will be home.

Then he says he and Mickie are working on a case where "a name came up, from your neck of the woods."

"What case?"

"The guy lives somewhere called Galena Gulch. Ever hear of it?"

"Sure. It's close, maybe thirty-five miles south of here, right off the interstate, near the Deer Lodge National Forest. I hunt there, and I'm friends with the state police captain whose guys patrol near there. But the park itself's under the forest service. Let me get a piece of paper. What's the name?"

When Voort reads "Alan Clark" off Meechum's napkin, he hears, in Abel's pause, a deepening of the Montana cop's breathing.

Then Abel says, "Well, unless there's two fellas by that name there, I know who you mean. But he's not around for questioning. Mr. Clark's dead."

"How?" Voort asks as Mickie's brow shoots up. He's listening on the phone extension.

"In an accident. Last winter. He lived up in the mountains, in an old mining claim in the forest. That's the only way you can occupy federal land up there, if you own rights to a claim. The streams used to be rich in gold, and you can still pan for nuggets here and there, but nothing major. Anyway, if you have a claim, you can put up a house, generator, whatever you want. I remember what happened because it was one of our guys who found him. An Indian fella, a lieutenant who worked one of the nearby claims as a hobby. He went up on horseback, after a snowstorm. It's thirty below zero up there all winter. You can't even reach the top with four-wheel drive half the year. Seems Mr. Clark was ice fishing on a lake they shared access to, and he went through the ice."

"Ice fishing," Mickie repeats.

"Come out and stay with us and try it. You saw a hole through the ice. You get comfy in the chair. You drop the line in, and haul out the bass. Try that in the Hudson and you'd probably pull in some great big tires. Haw haw."

"Goodrich or Bridgestone?" Mickie says. "Goodrich is tasty with butter."

Voort says, "If it's thirty below zero there, why was the ice so weak he fell through?"

"Who knows? A freak thaw. A warm spring popping out underwater, where it wasn't before."

"But you're sure it was an accident?"

"Do you have a reason to think it wasn't?"

"Just asking."

"Well, if I remember, and I can check, there were no footsteps in the snow, the deputy said, and no signs of a fight, just a jagged hole and the top of the chair half frozen, sticking out of the ice that had re-formed. No signs of trauma, bullet holes. A person can live for only two, three minutes after you fall in before you freeze, so the body was preserved fresh as a box of Birds Eye baby-sized peas."

Voort runs the other names on Meechum's list past the Montana detective, asks if the man has heard of them.

"Nope. But I'm a little surprised, Conrad. I didn't think

you had a problem with Alan Clark's kind of people in liberal New York."

"Excuse me?"

"Right-wingers. I thought you were all dyed-in-the-wool Democrats in Gomorrah. Welfare-lovers. Is that what you're looking into? Militias?"

Mickie turns the sound down on the TV.

"I think you better tell us more," Voort says, his heartbeat speeding up.

"And then you'll fill me in, right? I'm wondering if there's a connection out here."

"Go."

"I wasn't sorry to hear what happened to him," Abel says, and Voort, trying to judge the quality of the man's opinions, remembers him at the dice table in Vegas. Abel had played prudently but enthusiastically. He had known how much to bet, and also when to stop. "It's always worse when they have a high IQ," Drake says. "Smarts make 'em evil, not misguided. He could have gone to Harvard, from what I understand, but he lived like a hermit and read the bad books, the ones you can't get in bookstores, and he was hooked to the Internet in the worst kind of way. Anyone could call up the hate he put out over cyberspace. The state cops thought he was linked to the bombing of the federal building in Oklahoma City, but they could never prove it, and neither could the FBI. Alan Clark was a rising star in the movement, if you can call an asshole a star, and that bunch of fascists a movement. He was bringing in converts, fast."

"Any possibility that some kind of falling out in the movement caused his, uh, accident?"

"The state police checked into the possibility. Those

guys pop each other regularly and say it's politics, but it's just some shithead shooting the man who slept with his wife. Alan Clark died in a God-sent accident, if you ask me. God sent."

"Any chance you can fax us the reports?"

"I'll call Lieutenant Bottomly at state. But Voort, your turn. Is there something I should be worried about here? I'm itching, fellas. Scratch my back."

"Nothing yet, but if I hear something, I'll call."

A sigh. "You better. Meanwhile, Maggie's holding up that *House Beautiful* and it says the guest bedroom on your third floor has about half a million dollars' worth of Dutch Renaissance paintings in it. And the statuette in the bathroom was plundered off a British ship in the Revolutionary War. Nice statue."

"It was legal booty," Voort says. "Same as seizing a car from a drunk."

"You serious about that invitation to the Big Apple?"

"Any time," Voort says, hoping that Matt is better by the time the westerners take advantage of the offer.

He hears Abel telling his wife, "Looks like you'll get that trip to Broadway in the spring."

After they hang up, Mickie stands at the window, staring out at Long Island Sound.

"You said Meechum was in the army."

"So was his father, and grandfather, all of them, back to the Civil War."

"You said he got disillusioned about something and quit. You think there could be a connection?"

"I don't think Hitler falling through the ice counts."

Mickie nods. "Anyway, he quit two years ago, and Alan Clark died a year after that."

"We have no idea if the accident is the thing Meechum's worried about. Maybe it was the Internet connection, or the militia. Maybe it has nothing to do with the fact that Clark died."

"One name checked. One man dead."

More worried for Meechum now, Voort reaches for the phone. "What's the area code for Chicago?"

On TV, the news has come on, and firemen are fighting a blaze, above the words, on screen, "King Hotel."

Flames reach, in sheets, into the night, roaring from windows on the third-floor level.

Mickie groans, looking at the picture. "Fire. God. That's got to be one of the worst ways on earth to die."

THREE

At one A.M., frustrated and exhausted, Voort and Mickie are dozing in the pool house. The TV is off and in the fireplace the embers are smoking. A light rain has started up outside, and slants through the shore floodlights beyond the tinted windows, to smear the vista out there: the water, which is beginning to roil against the rocks; the distant bridges, with their cable spans supporting all that weight; the sky itself, where airplanes, tiny and vulnerable against the firmament, claw for height, toward cruising altitude, their nervous passengers trying to distract themselves from the turbulence with *Time* or *Newsweek* magazines.

Voort, dreaming, moves his mouth, but no words come out. He is in bed, with Camilla. She lays beneath him, smiling up at him, inviting, gorgeous, naked. He reaches down to put himself inside her. In the dream, he cannot get hard.

Detective Santos Brioche, in Chicago, was "at a bachelor party," his wife had said an hour ago on the phone. Jack Rosen in Seattle was "on duty, at a scene." Dr. Jill Towne in New York, accessed by phone directory, was, according to her answering service, "on vacation, until tomorrow."

"Can we reach her tonight? This is a police call," Voort had said.

"Would you like to talk to the doctor covering for her?"

"I'm not calling for a medical reason."

"Well, I can't page Dr. Towne. It's a rule when she's overseas. But if you leave a number, she'll be here in the morning. I'll leave word that it's urgent. It's the best I can do."

Mickie said, when Voort hung up, "At least she's alive. If she's the right Jill Towne."

"She is. Her answering machine gave her office number."

Now the black phone screams, and Voort, shooting awake, grabbing it, hears the thick Brooklyn accent of former New York detective Jack Rosen. "Well, well, a message from Mr. Getty and Mr. Rockefeller. What are you doing up at this hour? I thought the butler would be answering for you."

"How's Seattle?"

"If you like rain and coffee shops, it's heaven," says Rosen, and Voort hears voices, other cops, he imagines, in the background. "People say hello to you on the street. And that's average people, not nuts. I'm in the middle of something, but you said call when I got the message. What's up?"

"Can you check a name for us, in Seattle?"

"Now?"

"He might be in some danger. I have his address and social security number."

"Let's punch it in and see if anything comes up. By the way, Voort, my son's going to be going to New York this summer and . . ."

"Sure, Jack. He can stay at the house."

"Thanks." Voort hears the sound of computer keys clicking. Rosen says, "There's a rail line running between

Seattle and Minneapolis. The mopes jump onto the train in Minneapolis, do their shit here, and ride back east on the line. They drive us crazy. Ah. Levy. He's here all right. Lester Levy. Dead."

"Dead how?" Mickie says, on the extension.

"Heart attack," Jack says. "Three months ago. We sent a car to the scene, a downtown address, probably an office. But we don't have details in our system for this kind of call. Try Emergency Services. Want me to switch you over? I know a supervisor over there, on night duty. We play in a regular eleven A.M. poker game, on Thursdays. His neighbor thinks we're out-of-work bums. Last week she asked him if he ever intends to get a job."

Outside, the rain intensifies, battering the windows, and the fire pops, and a few minutes later another voice comes on the line, this one thickly southern accented.

"No one in Seattle was *born* in Seattle," Rosen's friend Robert Collins says cheerily. "Athens, Georgia. That's where I grew up."

Collins accesses the EMS computer records, takes less than a minute to call up "Lester Levy," and reads, off his screen, "Forty-five years old. Overweight. He had the heart attack in an elevator, on his way to work at Annselmo Foods. He was dead by the time they got him to the hospital."

"Did he have a history of heart problems?"

"It doesn't say."

"Was anyone else in the elevator?"

"I don't know."

"Was there an autopsy?"

"Not by the medical examiner, but the family could have ordered one of their own."

"How about a phone number for next of kin?"

"That I have," Robert Collins says, gives Voort the wife's name, Sandra, and her phone number, "or at least that's what the number was five months ago. Are you after this guy for something?"

"I'll quote you: 'I don't know.' "

Voort hangs up, punches in the number Collins gave him, and is rewarded with ringing, which means, at least, that it is still in use.

"Hello?"

It's the wife, but, Voort reminds himself, a phone is a deceptive instrument for investigation. On a phone, you cannot see the face of the person to whom you are speaking. You cannot see if they look away when you ask a question, or blush, or if their little finger begins tapping nervously. You cannot tell if they dress with care, or if they are stylish, or garish, or timid in choice of clothes. You cannot stand in their living room, and see the proof that they are cheap, or extravagant. The phone is like the radio. You must guess the surroundings based on the voice.

And now, having no idea if the pleasant female voice on the other end represents a personality, or masks it, Voort introduces himself, apologizes for calling at such a late hour, and apologizes for calling to ask questions about a subject which will be painful to discuss, the death of her husband, five months ago.

"I don't understand," Sandra Levy says, sounding more puzzled than put out. "You're a New York City detective?"

"Yes."

"In Seattle?"

"No, I'm phoning from New York. Your husband's name came up during an investigation of someone else, just in a peripheral way. I didn't know he'd passed away. Please accept my sorrow."

A sniffle. But is it real, Voort the professional has to think, or is it a trick?

"At least you didn't say 'condolences.' I hate when people say that word," she says. "It's so formal, so cold."

"Do you mind if I ask a couple of questions? It could really help us with something we're looking into, back in New York."

"Lester never went to New York. He never went anywhere. And then we were going to move to Paris, but he died."

"I'm sorry. I haven't explained myself properly. We're not really interested in Lester, but in another person he might have known. Lester's name was in his Rolodex. We're phoning everyone in the Rolodex. This is the thirtieth call I've made today."

"What's the man's name?" The woman is slightly less defensive now, and even a bit curious.

"Alan Clark," Voort says, naming the dead man in Montana.

A pause. She's probably thinking, although, Voort knows, she could be recoiling in shock. She could be doing anything.

"I don't believe I ever heard that name, Detective Voort."

"How about Charles Farber or Jill Towne. Either of them?"

"Lester didn't talk much about business," Sandra says. "We had a rule at home. I didn't talk about my students. I'm a kindergarten teacher. He didn't talk about the food business."

"Well, it's possible Lester knew these people from some other area besides business. Political action, maybe. Mr. Clark's fairly active. Was Lester?"

"Ha! Lester wouldn't have been able to tell you the name of our congressman. He hasn't voted in twenty years. He never read the newspaper, except the science pages. He liked to eat, drink, and play golf, in that order, but only if he could drive the electric cart on the course, and take a cooler filled with sandwiches along. He never took care of himself. I told him," she says, voice faltering, "to do a little exercise once in a while."

But she has said it lovingly, not in criticism. Voort flashes to his father telling him, when he was a boy, "When you love someone, you'll find that they'll have two kinds of qualities. Good ones and amusing ones. If you manage to maintain that attitude with the person you marry, you'll have a happy life, as I have with your mom."

Voort lies to keep her on the line and bring her attention back to him, regretting that he has to fool her, but needing the information, "My brother died of a heart attack, last year."

"Oh, God. Then you know what it's like."

"One minute they're walking around. The next," Voort says, and trails off.

Sandra lapses into a pained, rote delivery, which, if she is telling the truth, she has probably given dozens of times before. "Lester was joking around during breakfast that morning, talking about a party we were supposed to go to that night. Then the car pool picked him up. Jay and Ed, those are his . . . *were* his friends, said he was fine during the ride to the office. Then they get into the elevator, and . . . Lester doubled over."

She is crying now, softly. Voort gives her time.

But he also needs to know who else was in the elevator, so he says, "Did anyone try first aid?"

"None of them knew it. It was just the three of them there. For years Ed had been trying to get the other two to take first-aid courses. He'd always say, 'One day one of us is going to get the big one, and the other two'll stand around.' He told me later he tried to do mouth-to-mouth resuscitation, and bang on Lester's chest. But he didn't know what he was doing. The bruises showed that he hit Lester in the wrong place. I'm taking the first-aid course now." A sniffle. "Too late."

Voort says, "My brother'd been under a lot of stress at work. He was a total workaholic."

"Not Lester. He never worked hard. He went in late. He came home early. My gosh, you have a very nice phone manner. You really have me talking, and we've never even met. I'm chewing your ear off."

"No, I called you," Voort says, trying to figure out how to work the Internet into the conversation, since Alan Clark apparently used it to spread hate.

"Look, I'm really sorry to ask you these questions, but I just have one more."

"I don't mind. If it'll help someone else, I'd feel better. And it's not like anything would change if we hung up." A pause. "Lester and I never had children. We figured we'd have a long time together, travel, buy things. We figured a baby would tie us down. But now I look at babies in the neighborhood. They look like their parents. A baby might have looked like Lester. I'm sorry we didn't do it. Do you have children?" she asks, trying to broaden the connection between them herself now.

"I don't have children," Voort says, flashing to Camilla.

"Now I see what a blessing they are. They're like the past, your own past, the way they look, and how you teach them things. And they're also your future. You should have children if you can, Mr. Voort."

Voort changes the subject. "Mrs. Levy, Alan Clark, the man we're looking at in New York, was starting some kind of Internet business, hooking companies up in different parts of the country. Did Lester do a lot of his work on the computer, on the Internet, at home?"

"He hated the Internet. He always said, What's the big deal about it? Lester wanted to get real mail, not computer mail. He liked to go to the library, not read things off a screen. He said he stared at screens enough all day at work, and on TV at night. Also, he wasn't on the business end at Annselmo. He did research. They sell food."

Mickie says, after Voort hangs up, "Well, that was helpful. They're not connected by right-wing politics or the Internet so far."

"Two out of three dead from accidents," Voort says.

They stare at the phone, willing one of the other cops, in the other cities, to call back.

By two A.M., they've fallen asleep again, on the couch, and sitting in the chair.

Voort tosses, and throws the blanket off.

Camilla, in his dream, rubs her swollen belly.

His lips, in sleep, form words.

Save the baby, is what he says.

FOUR

*T*he man with the twisted left elbow is still awake.

It is three A.M., and he is with a woman now, and another, younger man. All three sit attentively in a conference room, where a slide projector is on. The man with the twisted elbow is still dressed as he was earlier in the evening, in the nondescript sweater and trousers. He has not yet gone home.

The woman is about forty, with a cute button nose, a lined face devoid of makeup, a deep tan, and sandy blond hair in a shoulder-blade-length braid. She is dressed in a snug, thick Irish sweater of white wool, and tight black jeans. Her short legs beneath the table are crossed at the ankles. She wears white Reeboks.

The woman is crying.

"Poor Charley," she says.

The other man, about thirty-five, sits opposite the man with the twisted elbow and diagonally across the rectangular table from the woman. He's small, with broad shoulders and a cupidlike face, with bow-shaped lips and thick brows. His eyes are bloodshot. His unbuttoned sport jacket is European, of thick gray corduroy, with a stylishly wide lapel. His

Ralph Lauren white cotton shirt is open at the collar. He sprays mint Binaca into his mouth, and rubs the space between his eyes as if he's suffering a headache. He has been drinking, and smells of it.

"Hey, I was in a bar. You beeped me and I came fast," he tells the older man, who nods that the other man did the right thing.

On the wall, projected, are blowup photographs of a beautiful woman, a lean redhead, always stylishly dressed, against a backdrop of various city locations. The shots are taken from a distance, the subject rarely looking toward the lens, and even when she is, she does not seem to know she is being photographed.

"Dr. Jill Towne," says the woman in the white sweater, holding the projector control in her right hand.

"She's gorgeous," says the man with the open collar.

The photos, like police mug shots, offer views of the subject from different angles. In the top shot, she stands on the balcony of a penthouse apartment, at the railing, a highball glass in hand, as she gazes idly out at the city. The shot has clearly been snapped from above, from a higher building. In the next photo, showing her right profile, Dr. Towne strides out of Lincoln Center, in a black evening gown, on the arm of a handsome black-haired man in a tuxedo. Both are laughing, and it is summer, judging from the crowd's lightweight attire. The man leans toward the woman. Perhaps he means to kiss her.

The next shot is at the airport. Dr. Towne the traveler stands at the TWA counter, viewed from behind, and over the shoulder of the ticket salesman facing her is her destination, Rome, listed on the departure board, with a flight time, nine P.M.

The final two shots show her, respectively, in a one-piece, coral-colored bathing suit, lounging in a folding chair by a rooftop swimming pool, reading a book with an indeterminable title, and, in the last picture, she is frozen, jogging in a park, amid a crowd of runners. She wears lime green shorts and a loose shirt that says "AIDS 30K Run."

"Good work. You could have been a photojournalist," the man with the twisted elbow tells the woman.

"I am, but for a select audience." She smiles. "You."

"Meechum told the detective her name," the man tells the other two, and there is a double intake of breath, an expectation of trouble, and the younger man curses.

"Then he'll be looking, too," the younger man says.

"Since Charley's gone," the man with the twisted elbow says, "I'll do her."

Sighing, pressing his index finger into a pressure point in his neck, trying to stop a headache, the younger man says, "You couldn't learn the name of the cop?"

"He'll show up sooner or later. Why do I feel it will be sooner?"

The woman frowns, says nothing, but looks into the man's eyes inquiringly. She is asking without saying aloud what the three of them will do when the cop shows up.

"Look, it's him or," the man says, glancing at the photos and waving his hand as if to include more photos, lots of people, "all of them."

"You're right. I guess."

There's a click and with the last slide gone, the room is slightly brighter with light from the projector. The conference table is made of polished walnut, and seats ten, although only three are present. The matching chairs are high-backed, with cracked burgundy leather cushions. The carpet is thin and plain, a watery green. The inset wall unit, also of walnut, includes a television which is on, soundless at the moment, and broadcasting a New York One all-news station report of a fire consuming a hotel in Inwood. The screen shows ambulances arriving at the fire. It shows a crowd straining against yellow ropes, craning to get a better view. It shows the full moon half obscured by brown smoke.

There are no decorative paintings or posters on the white walls, but the thick curtains are drawn, and the smell in the room is of furniture polish. There's also a slight burnt electrical odor emanating from the projector, probably from dust being incinerated when it touches the bulb.

The man with the twisted elbow turns to the younger man. "Your turn."

More professional now, less drunk-sounding, the younger man takes over for the woman at the projector. A set of blueprints appears on screen.

"Her building. She owns the penthouse," he says.

The next shot shows blueprints of a one-bedroom apartment.

"She's remodeling. But you have to file plans with the city, so it was easy enough to get them. Ready for this? If you have more than one bathroom in your apartment, and you remodel, you have to provide for wheelchair access. It's the damn law."

"In your own apartment?" the woman asks, astounded.

"Goddamn government is everywhere," the younger man replies.

"Never mind the government," says the man with the twisted elbow.

"Right. Here's the lobby. There's always a doorman, and they change every eight hours. The Hispanic one, the midnight one, is Maurice. The black guy is Felix. The white day guy is Ambrose. He's the crankiest, the hardest to get by . . . but ready for some good news?"

"I'd appreciate it."

"It's a rich building, so *four* apartments are being remodeled now, big-time, walls ripped out, floors ripped out, which means a couple-dozen workmen going in and out every day, minimum. There's a side entrance for tradesmen, and if you go in that way you use a separate elevator. I have the contractors' names. Delivery people also have to use the trade elevator, and if you go in as a delivery guy, do it before seven P.M., because after that you're not allowed in. The owners have to come down to the lobby and pay at the door. No access for the little people."

"Snobs," says the blond woman.

"Final blueprint in this set," says the younger man more enthusiastically, liking his work, "is the roof layout of the building next to hers. Only one balcony—her neighbor's—separates hers from this building. There's a two-foot gap between buildings, but there's a rolled-barbed-wire fence between them, on the other roof. Still, if you get through it, it's easy to reach her apartment. Her neighbor's a bachelor, out almost every night, has a girlfriend on Riverside Drive and usually sleeps there. No cameras on the roofs but both buildings have them in the main elevators and the basement. I have the blueprints of the electrical system, gas system, and there's a drop ceiling in the apartment beneath hers, which shares the elevator, if you want to go that way. But they have a primo alarm system down there, triple backup. Also, you need a key to the elevator. You can't just go up to any floor. You need a special key. Now her office. Ah! New slide! This is the back entrance, on ground level. . . ."

Ten minutes later, the meeting is over, and the blonde

leaves, and at a suitable interval, the younger man heads out, too. The projector is still on. The man with the twisted elbow is alone, in the glow, and the photos of Jill Towne are back on the screen. Jill at the Guggenheim Museum, with the dark-haired man again, arm in arm, strolling up the ramp to the second floor. Jill at a dais at Mt. Sinai Hospital, beneath a banner reading, "Year of the Doctor."

"Meechum, you fucked things up," the man says out loud.

He shuts off the projector. Without the electrical humming, the room is completely quiet, but the TV gives some light.

He hears, in his head, a voice, from a long time ago, and it is saying, *I shoot the dogs. That is what I do. I kill the dogs.*

No time for memory now.

From an interior safe in the wall unit, he pulls out a gun. He also retrieves an ankle holster.

He's thinking, I wish I knew the name of that goddamn cop.

FIVE

At nine the next morning, an hour after Dr. Jill Towne's office opens, Voort leaves the Jaguar outside her ground-floor Fifth Avenue office, at Sixty-seventh Street, in a No Parking zone opposite Central Park. The oaks and maples are luminous in their autumn magnificence. The leaves blaze with trapped sugar. On the avenue, nannies wheel tiny heirs and heiresses in new carriages, through swirling pools of bright light.

After a night of no answers, and a trapped hour on the Long Island "Expressway," the most misnamed road in the nation, Voort turns the POLICE BUSINESS sign out on the visor, locks The Club onto the walnut steering wheel, and straightens his jacket, which Mickie's live-in maid pressed for him that morning. He pushes the buzzer of 1A, an appropriate apartment designation for an overachiever, which a Fifth Avenue doctor is likely to be.

Buzzed in, he finds himself in a waiting room that strikes him immediately as out of the ordinary. It's not the size, as it is appropriately small, given Manhattan's premium for space. Nor is it the receptionist, who sits behind thick glass, with a fist-sized hole for the passage of medical forms or inquiry. But the seats are filled with mostly young adults, in their twenties or thirties. He does not see a single elderly patient, and at this hour, on a weekday, a higher percentage of older people should be here.

He identifies himself to the middle-aged Hispanic receptionist, whose black reading glasses match the color of the braid hanging over her shoulder to her lap.

"You're the detective who left the message last night. We tried to reach you at your office."

"I was stuck in traffic."

"Well, Doctor is busy now," the receptionist says, as if she is the one who is occupied. "Doctor has just returned from vacation." She flicks her eyes toward the patients. "She's booked up until eight tonight. Can I help?"

Voort says he is on "official business" and needs only a few minutes in regard to an "important case."

"One of Doctor's cases?" The receptionist's protective nature goes with her one-track mind.

"No, one of my cases."

Reluctantly the receptionist tells him that perhaps, in a while, "Doctor" might squeeze out a few minutes for him. Meanwhile he's relegated to the waiting area, which is decorated with artwork that would make a Christie's auctioneer go green. Voort estimates that the two-foot-high wooden statuette in an alcove, above a mahogany coffee table, is Roman, and pre-Constantine era. The Christ, carved before the empire collapsed, seems more content than later versions would be, after the Huns swept Italy and brought bubonic plague. The mounted arrowheads, behind glass, are not North American. From the carving on the wood tips, they predate guns if they are from Europe, and predate Europeans if they are from the South Seas. The stone face is

Zimbabwean. The fertility goddess, with its exaggerated girth, came from a ruin in the Mideast. The alarm system, he guesses, must be Metropolitan Museum of Art quality. Just insuring the artwork here has to be equivalent to three months' police salary. And if this is what Dr. Towne puts in a waiting room, then her home, Voort imagines, must be a little Louvre.

"What kind of doctor is Dr. Towne, anyway?" he asks a prematurely gray haired priest, sitting beside him, and grimacing, pressing a hand to his stomach.

"Don't you know? You're visiting her."

"It's a social call."

"She's the top tropical disease specialist in the city," the priest says proudly, as if he himself earned the accolade. So far, everyone associated with Dr. Towne is taking credit for her. The priest adds, "The Archdiocese always sends us here when we get back from a tropical assignment." He squeezes his eyes shut in pain. "I just got back from Bolivia. I always get amoebas and worms when I go. It's the water. I get into a village and someone offers me vegetables. What am I supposed to say? That I can't eat what they touch?"

Voort gathers, from conversation around him, that the other patients include Third World diplomats, a wealthy Indonesian businessman, a plant researcher back from the jungles of Brazil.

"She saved my brother's life," the priest says with some emotion. "He picked up a bug in Turkistan, but none of the other doctors could find it. He was losing weight, sweating at night. He was," the priest says, shuddering, "dying. But Dr. Towne finds the bugs no one else can. And there are all kinds of bacteria in the tropics, ugly little microscopic mutants. Believe me, you don't want to know."

As the man rushes off to the bathroom, Voort notes that the reading material here also differs from the *Smithsonian* or *Time* magazines he usually sees in waiting rooms. He looks over *Tropical Disease Digest*, and, in twin volumes, in red leather, above the couch, *Leishmaniasis Among the Somali Nomads* by Dr. Jill Towne.

"Doctor will see you now, Mr. Voort. Last room on the right."

Beyond a series of small examination rooms, in which he glimpses patients in blue hospital gowns awaiting treatment, he finds Dr. Towne in her office, a larger room with floor-to-ceiling windows looking out on a well-maintained shrub and sculpture garden, protected by a redwood fence.

"May I see some ID?" asks the doctor from behind her French desk.

There are women, Voort knows, whose allure seems perfect for a particular season, and autumn, he tells himself, must have been created for Dr. Jill Towne. She is beautiful. Voort feels the feminine force of her in his weak knees. Mickie had once said to him, "There are three levels of attraction, buddy. Level one is the dick, always ready to go, in the nightclub or at the beach. Level two is when you feel the sex appeal in your throat, and your breath catches. But level three is the danger zone, when muscles fail you, and thought goes out the window. When guys throw careers away. Hollywood is all about level three."

The office is hot, or is it his imagination? Jill Towne is lean, and petite, with a sinuous and vibrant pliancy to even her slightest movements. Her hair is the red of the brighter leaves on Fifth Avenue, and, cut in a jaw-length flip, it frames her narrow face, high cheekbones, and accentuates the shine of green eyes, and the soft white of flawless skin.

Beneath her open medical jacket she wears a single strand of black pearls, a blouse of plain white cotton, and an unremarkable dark skirt, calf length, which proves another of Mickie's sayings, "The babe makes the clothes, not the other way around."

But she has an odd edge to her voice, bordering on suspicion. "Your message said this was urgent."

Voort tells her that her name came up in an investigation. The ploy has worked fine so far.

"Is that so?" she says, staring at him with challenge in those green eyes, eyes which, he now notes, are rimmed with amber. "What investigation?"

"For the moment, if you don't mind, I was wondering if I can ask a couple of questions."

"I do mind," she says, and repeats, "What kind of investigation?"

"The Seattle police asked us for assistance on a case."

"Really!" Now she looks amused. "To think, with all your work in New York, you have time to help police all the way out in Seattle."

This response is all wrong, and she is getting more aggressive. Voort continues, "Their suspect is a researcher in a Seattle food company, and there's a New York connection. Business fraud."

"Not sex crimes?" She leans back in her leather swivel chair, direct antagonism in her eyes now. "I thought, after my call to One Police Plaza this morning, that you worked in the sex crimes unit."

"Not exclusively," Voort says, nailed.

"What do you want to know?"

"Your name was in the man's phone book and we wondered if he's a patient of yours. Lester Levy is his name."

Without breaking eye contact, Dr. Towne lifts her phone and says, addressing her receptionist, "Do we have a patient from Seattle, named Lester Levy?"

She waits a moment.

"No."

"Alan Clark?"

"No."

"Frank Greene," he asks, remembering the name from Meechum's napkin, the man from Lancaster Falls, Massachusetts, whom he and Mickie have, so far, been unable to find.

"Sorry," she says, not looking sorry in the least. "Are we finished now?"

"Meechum Keefe," Voort says.

She drops the phone in its cradle. She leans back in her chair. He cannot tell whether this is because she knows Meechum, or has decided to stop playing the game.

"Let's cut this out. I never heard of him," she says. "And I'm getting tired of you people harassing me."

"The police have been harassing you?" Voort says.

She makes a disgusted sound in her throat. "Police. FBI. Justice Department. Whatever you call yourself this week. I lose track of all the badges and laminated cards. I warned the men who came to my apartment in September, and the woman after that. I've spoken to a civil liberties lawyer who says I may have a case."

"Wait a minute," Voort says, holding up his hands, so they frame, inadvertently, her lovely, infuriated face. It is the kind of face he sees on magazine covers, not in person. "I really don't know what you're talking about."

"Oh? You wandered in here by accident?"

"I didn't say that."

"Right, you made up a story about Seattle instead. This

is the last talk I'm having with you people, *the last one*. Tell whoever sent you that next time I'll get a court order to keep you off my property. And tell him *I'm not going to stop what I'm doing!*"

She stands, her face now almost as bright as her hair.

"I have patients waiting." She starts walking out. "People who are really sick, and need help, and who tell the truth about it."

"You're right. I lied," Voort says.

She halts, at the door, her chest rising and falling with rage.

"I'm not working on any official case. There's no food researcher in Seattle who had your name in his phone book. There's no phone book."

Head cocked, arms folded, she is offering him, stonily, the opportunity for a few seconds of explanation. Above her head, now that he faces the door, he sees a gallery of silver-framed color pictures of Dr. Towne, in a whole series of Third World settings. He sees her sitting on a yak, in snowy mountains, and in a jungle, in an Afghanistani village, and in an African famine relief camp, judging from the Red Cross insignia on a truck beside her. In that last photo she wears a khaki tropical shirt, epauletted, sweat stained at the armpits, and open at the neck, where a stethoscope hangs.

Her patients in the photos seem barely alive, only skeletally human. The wall is a macabre dedication to misery, or witness to it. He can almost smell the flies, and excrement, and hear the wail of hungry infants.

A thank-you certificate from Doctors Without Borders hangs beside the shots.

"I don't know what to tell you," he begins, "because I'm not actually sure what I'm looking into. But your name *was* on a list. A friend gave it to me. He led me to believe that the people on this list—the names I asked you about—were in trouble somehow. But he wouldn't tell me why."

She looks like any second she'll simply leave the room.

"I was hoping you would tell me why," he says. "I trust my friend. I said I'd look into the story, but I have no idea who the names are, or why the FBI talked to you. My partner and I have been checking out people on the list, and if that doesn't make sense to you, it's the best I can do. It's the truth."

"What do you mean, 'checking out'?"

"Asking around. We found out about two of the men so far, in other cities."

"What kind of garbage is this?"

"Look," Voort says, hoping his sincerity shows, "I shouldn't have made up the lie before . . . it's a habit with cops . . . giving less information than we get . . . but you're the only one so far who . . . I don't want to alarm you, but the other two people died, in accidents."

"Accidents," she repeats slowly.

"That's what the police told us," Voort says, "in those cities."

"Get out of here," she says. "Don't you dare threaten me. And don't you dare come here again."

Mickie says, when Voort returns to One Police Plaza, "Doctors Without Borders. That's the group that sends help to any country, isn't it? Cuba, Libya. Like the Red Cross. They'll go anywhere, whether or not they're legally allowed."

Voort thinks about it. "Funny, Meechum was babbling about politics. He said the Greek word *idiot*, from ancient Athens, meant someone who had no interest in politics."

"Greeks had politics, Americans have money. And anyway, we're lowly sex crimes detectives. But the lady sounds tough."

"Tough? She could break the balls off a Rodin statue."

"And she's not going to 'stop what she's doing,' isn't that what she said?" Mickie muses. "*What* do you think she's doing? And what links her to a right-wing nut in Montana? And a food company guy who never even read the newspaper in Seattle, couldn't care less about causes, and played golf?"

Outside and below their private office, unique to the sex crimes unit, steam rises from tugs pushing garbage barges on the glassy East River, and mixes with exhaust off an unbroken line of cars stalled, like a permanent fixture, along the upper level of the Brooklyn Bridge. The office is expensive, thanks to their private contributions. The cedar and Mexican pine furniture was selected by Mickie's interior decorator. The sitting chairs are a rich brown leather. The foldout couch shows a geometric southwestern motif. The walls are soothing terra-cotta color. The carpeting is so thick you could lose an old-style silver dollar in it. Mickie likes to rotate art objects on the walls, and this month has hung a couple of Jean-Luc Godard antique French film noir posters, lithograph sketches of Jean-Paul Belmondo, the Parisian star, smoking cigarettes and looking tough.

Mickie draws a cup of Jamaican Blue Mountain coffee from a silver urn by the mini fridge. A china plate half filled with scones and whipped cream sits on his desk, by a pile of police files—cases they should be working on, and which, at the moment, they ignore.

"Santos left a message from Chicago. He said to call."

Voort accepts coffee, and allows the caffeine to fuel his

frustration. He punches in the Chicago number, and is gratified to hear, almost immediately, an answering voice say, "Detective Brioche. Four twelve."

For the third time since last night he goes into the briefest possible explanation of why he's calling, framing his request as a favor, not an official inquiry. But a favor, to police, is the highest level of inquiry, and Santos tells him that in Chicago and its suburbs, a new cross-referenced, federally funded computer crime program has just been put in place, and may help.

"They're loading every file in Illinois into the program, going back year by year. You give me a social security number, I can tell you if the person is associated, in any way, with a recorded crime. Perp. Vic. Witness. Whatever."

Every city has a different means of accessing criminals. In L.A., cops have personal computers, right in squad cars. In New York, when anyone is arrested, they're assigned a number which is recorded in Albany, and using that number, a cop can call up anything ever recorded on that perp after that, even if the perp beat a particular rap.

"But what we really need in this country," Mickie the Conservative says, as they wait to see what Santos comes up with, "is police access to everyone. Not just perps. Everyone should be fingerprinted. Those damn civil libertarians don't understand it's for their own good."

"Here we go," says Santos Brioche, seven hundred miles away. "I got him. He was arrested, all right."

"Great."

"In nineteen sixty-eight."

"Oh."

"Destruction of property. Resisting arrest. Looks like he was one of those old SDS radicals, at Northwestern University, during the Vietnam War. He was arrested at the Democratic National Convention. He did community service. Rich kid, I guess."

"That's all? Nineteen sixty-eight?"

"Yep. Until two years ago, when the guy passed away, by accident."

Voort sits up on the edge of the desk.

"Let's see," Santos says, and pauses, reading, and adds, "He fell down the stairs at home and broke his neck. But I don't have any details. There was no crime."

"Who might have details?"

"If you want, I can call Evanston, where he died. I have a couple of buddies in the department up there. We go to Wrigley Field together. Maybe I can trace the responding officer, and he'll remember something, if he's still around. Want me to try?"

They say yes, try. And as they wait they attend to paperwork on a backlog of cases.

Victims fill the city, their names typed neatly, more neatly than they died, on municipal forms. A twelve-year-old boy has been found in Riverside Park, by the tennis courts on Ninety-seventh Street, raped and strangled. His parents reported him missing two nights ago. A secretary walking home from work, on Strivers Row, the richest street in Harlem, lined with private homes, was pulled into a gypsy cab, according to a witness, and her body found in an overlook beside the East River, a few hours after that, at two A.M. last night.

Mickie says, as they work, and make calls, "What do you think the odds are that three out of five people in a group, taken at random, died by accident?"

"We still can't find the guy in Lancaster Falls, Massachusetts."

"When are you supposed to talk to Meechum?"

"Tomorrow. He said he'd call us and explain everything then."

No call comes from Santos, in Chicago, and the detectives spend the next hour on their overloaded caseload.

Mickie, working, says, "That doctor was pretty hot-looking, I gather."

"Mickie, I just got out of a relationship. I'm not getting into anything just now."

"Besides, she kicked you out of her office."

Voort bursts out laughing. "Always a plus."

Leaving the office, they spend the day talking to grieving parents, and friends of the two victims. To coworkers. To neighbors. In the Harlem case, they find the witness, who was reading Kissinger's *White House Years* in a downstairs study when he heard a commotion through an open window, and saw the gypsy cabdriver pull the girl into the cab.

By six, back at the office, they've put out an all-points bulletin on the cabbie, who left his fingerprints all over the woman's shoes and leather attaché case, and who has a record for assault. The parents of the dead boy are offering a reward for information. Voort is going over the police press release when Santos Brioche's detective friend calls, finally, from Evanston. Hank Kerkorian is the officer's name.

"You want to know about Charles Farber? I handled that case, and I remember that day because his daughter, the kid who caused the accident, was hysterical," says Kerkorian in the hoarse, thick voice of a chain smoker. "It was pretty cut and dry. The mother and daughter went into the Loop, to the Art Institute. Dad mows the lawn. It's a hot day. He goes inside, upstairs, and trips over a stuffed moose the kid left on the landing. She was screaming like crazy

76

when I got there that she never left the toy out. A doctor had to sedate her. But the moose was on the bottom of the stairs, right beside the body. Poor guy hit a marble shelf in the foyer when he fell, and broke his neck."

"Who found the body?" Voort asks, taking notes.

"Neighbors noticed his mower had been running, on idle, for an hour. The screen door was open, so they went inside. He was on the floor, about ten feet in from the door."

"Was there an autopsy?"

"Actually, yes. The kid was so hysterical that the wife was hoping, I think, that he had a heart attack, so the girl wouldn't blame herself. But the neck was broken. The bruises were in the right places. Nobody saw anyone go into the house, and nobody saw anyone go out. Why are you so interested? There's no chance it wasn't an accident."

"It's probably not connected to what we're working on, but do you mind if I run some names by you, see if any of them came up relating to that accident?"

Hank Kerkorian, unsurprisingly, has never heard of the people on Meechum's list.

"I always felt bad for that girl," he adds, and Voort hears the quick whispery scratch of a match lighting. "I think about her. I have a kid that age now, and she has the same problem, always leaving shit all over the driveway. My wife tells her, someday you'll cause an accident. But kids don't think. They don't have experience. By the time they get experience it's too late. Anything else you need?"

"Do you remember what kind of work he did?"

"The family owns a chain of furniture stores all over the Midwest. I was in the Evanston branch with she-who-must-be-obeyed this weekend, buying a new couch, not that I can figure out what's wrong with the old one. Mrs. Farber runs the business now. I asked about the girl and got the feeling she's still a basket case. You have kids?"

"No," Voort says, and changes the subject. "One of the people we're trying to connect him to was a militia member, in Montana. You don't happen to remember seeing anything in the house, or hearing something that linked him with that, do you? Air tickets. Pamphlets. I know the guy was arrested thirty years ago for being on the other side of things, but maybe he changed."

"What I remember seeing, in the den, was a big blowup picture of him, being arrested back in sixty-eight, dragged into a squad car. There were other photos, too. Farber waving a red flag during the Democratic convention. I got the feeling it was the high point of his life. The way he hung those photos in your face is the way a war veteran brings out the souvenir helmets. But I wouldn't call Farber a militia type. He was more the yuppie type."

"Thanks," Voort says, and hangs up.

"Well, there's just nothing like the telephone to convey the up close sights and sounds of a situation," Mickie says, leaning back in his sixteen-hundred-dollar Norwegian leather swivel chair, and pulling the cork on a bottle of chilled Andalusian apple cider. "Let's sum up. We have one fifty-one-year-old furniture store executive dreaming of the good old SDS college days. One forty-six-year-old, out-of-shape, golf-loving West Coast food researcher, who never votes, travels, or uses computers. And one thirty-seven-year-old fascist Internet nut hermit in the mountains of the West. Oh, and let's not forget our doctor sexpot who threw you out of her office, and her self-important secrets. Other than the fact that three of them died from accidents, what's the possible connection here?"

"I don't know. But someone better tell the doctor," Voort says, standing up, and reaching for his coat, "that she might have accident number four."

Before he leaves they try to reach the police in Lancaster Falls, Massachusetts, again, and get through to an operator who tells them that a freak ice storm is ravaging the western part of the state. During massive power failures, all available officers are manning intersections where traffic lights are out, escorting ambulances to hospitals, and making sure elderly residents have food, and, if they live in electrically heated houses, somewhere warm to stay.

Voort tries directory assistance to see if a "Frank Greene" is listed.

"We have no one by that name in Lancaster Falls," the operator tells him. Voort hopes that means the man is still alive, but moved away.

He takes the number-six train from Chambers Street to Sixty-eighth, and walks east, through crowds of commuters going home, past Park Avenue, and Madison Avenue, toward Fifth. He remembers Dr. Towne's receptionist, this morning, saying Jill Towne was "booked with patients until eight this evening."

It is now 7:50. Voort picks up his pace, and as he rounds the corner of Fifth and Sixty-eighth, sees Dr. Towne herself locking up her office down the block. It's a cold night, for October, and the doctor is wearing a power-walk outfit. Lycra leggings down to her pink-lined Reeboks. Heavier red zip-up warm-up jacket, down to leather warm-up gloves. And white earmuffs over her Walkman earplugs.

Turning to cross Fifth Avenue, toward the park, she catches sight of him, and stops dead.

"I'm calling my lawyer when I get home," she says.

"Do whatever you want," he says, "but we checked out a third name now, Charles Farber in Illinois, and he died, from an accident again, two years ago. If you know something about this, tell me. You're on that list."

"Very dramatic," she says, and, at a power-walk pace, not believing him one bit, starts across Fifth Avenue, weaving around stalled, honking buses and taxicabs.

"You're going through the park?" Voort says. "It's dark out."

"And you're coming along to protect me, it seems."

"Didn't you hear what I said?"

She fiddles with the Walkman, obviously turning the volume up. Her arms pump. She's the good little type-A exerciser. She heads, with Voort keeping up beside her, at a good pace, under a lamppost and into the park.

"As long as you're filing a complaint anyway," Voort says, loud enough so she'll hear over whatever music is blasting under the earmuffs, "I can use the walk."

She ignores him. He is invisible. He has disappeared from the earth to her. She strides ahead like an Olympic walker. At this hour, the roads that are blocked to vehicular traffic are half filled with runners, bikers, joggers, roller skaters.

"Charles Farber fell down the stairs in his house," Voort says, when they cross the fountain area. "He broke his neck."

No answer. Her arms pump back and forth.

He says, a few minutes after that, approaching the new volleyball courts, "Lester Levy, in Seattle, had a heart attack in an elevator. His best friends were with him. Definitely an accident, the doctor said. You would have agreed, I'm sure."

"Leave me alone."

She has stopped now, on the fringe of the softball fields and carousel complex near the West Side. Her furious breaths burst from her, in dissipating puffs.

"Leaving you alone would be," says Voort, "my pleasure."

"Then what do you want?"

"For you to humor me and pretend I don't know why the FBI visited you, and tell me why they did."

"You know why. You . . ." she snaps, and breaks off, and starts walking again, but at a slightly less manic pace, as if she realizes he will not go away, and that speed will not shake him. She even fiddles with the Walkman again, and Voort thinks, since she turned it up earlier, she could only now be dialing it down.

"Fine," she says. "You know anyway, so what difference does it make if I tell you? It's my work. They're bothering me about my work."

"On tropical diseases?"

She bursts out laughing. "You're good," she says. "You really look confused. Yes, I suppose, in a way, you could say, on tropical diseases."

"What about tropical diseases?"

"Oh, give me a break. Not the diseases," she says. "The patients. *You know that.*"

"You mean those other people on Meechum's list *were* your patients?"

She is one of those women who, looking at a man with disgust, can wither him on the spot. "I don't have time for this. I have to meet a friend."

She strides away, tall, lean, disappearing. He has used up his chance with her.

His heart is pounding.

But he follows, at a distance, thinking, helplessly, that at this hour, it would be easy to suffer an accident in the park. A car could hit her. Or, when she leaves the park, a brick could fall on her. The city is a brewing pot for potential accidents, mini disasters waiting to happen. Elevators fall into shafts. Live exposed wires brush against workers. Scaffolding collapses. Commuters, from the pressure of the crowd behind them, flail as they fall before oncoming subways.

Always, these things are accidents.

She looks vulnerable, he thinks, and she is so beautiful.

I wonder who she's meeting. I wonder if she has a boyfriend.

Oh no. Not again, he thinks.

What was it that Mickie said about attraction level three?

SIX

*T*his is going to be bloody," Mickie says. "Watch the left side of the screen."

It's three P.M., next day, but Meechum has not called. Voort has been trying to concentrate on work—on the files and reports on his desk—despite a sick premonition in his stomach. Now the office shades are drawn. The only light comes from the big-screen Sony television set into the wall unit, broadcasting a black-and-white video from the VCR.

"Santos FedExed this," Mickie says. "The three guys in dungarees, hiding behind the Chevy, are Chicago cops."

On-screen, in grainy black and white, like an old war movie, the approaching mob links arms in a skirmish line. Their chants grow louder as they taunt more than a hundred waiting riot police.

"Nineteen sixty-eight," Mickie says. "Welcome to the Democratic National Convention."

The marchers are mostly young, in their late teens or twenties, bedraggled in a stylish way for that time, presenting a cultivated image of reverse prosperity: ripped jeans, tie-dyed T-shirts, leather fringed vests, sandals, and beads. The men's hair falls down their backs, or is puffed into

Afros, even on white guys. The headbands are Beijing red, or have sayings written on them, like "End the War."

"Fuck the Pigs," reads a bedsheet waving above the crowd.

Mickie snorts. "We're pigs until your sister gets raped." He's disgusted at any form of public disorder.

The phone rings and Voort answers hopefully, but it isn't Meechum. The *Daily News* reporter on the other end asks about the arrest this morning of the gypsy cabdriver for yesterday's murder of the woman in Harlem.

"We're not releasing information until her family's been notified. They're away," Voort says, as, on the TV, a brick sails from the crowd to smash against the riot shield of a Chicago cop. "Call PR if you want information."

"Voort, all they ever do is bullshit up there. At least tell me if this was a race crime?"

"It was a sex crime."

Hanging up, he sees that whoever is holding the jerking camera, retreating before the mob, has slipped behind the protective police, so now the protestors are viewed over two rows of helmets and the tips of bobbing batons.

"Why are you showing me this?" Voort says.

"Santos wanted us to see Chuck Farber. He's the guy waving the Coke bottle, on the left."

Mickie hits the pause button when the phone rings again, and the police, who have started charging, stop.

"Conrad? Nice job in Harlem," says New York's chief of detectives Hugh Addonizio without identifying himself. "Clean."

On-screen, the cop faces look as twisted, as hating as the marchers' faces.

"Hugh, the guy left fingerprints, drove home, went to sleep, and even opened the door when we knocked."

"Savor the easy ones," says Hugh, who has recently announced his upcoming retirement. Flyers all over One Police Plaza are announcing the big going-away party in Queens. "Anyway, twenty minutes. The press room. You make the announcement. The woman's family's been notified of the arrest and the photographers love your pretty blond hair."

On-screen, Chuck Farber, turning to flee as the action resumes, has a scraggly beard, rectangular wire-rimmed glasses, and a bandanna that only partially controls the long hair cascading down the shoulders of his military surplus jungle shirt, unbuttoned to show a Grateful Dead T-shirt beneath. The bandanna, rather than giving him a formidable appearance, takes five years off him, so he looks thirteen.

"What a bum," says Mickie.

Voort shakes his head, his mind elsewhere. "Those days must have been weird. While Chuck Farber was marching, Meechum's dad was in Vietnam."

Fighting is breaking out on-screen.

"We used to look at the photos he sent, me and Meechum. We'd dress up, play war games. He had enough military surplus in that house to equip an army. I had to wear a lampshade, which looked like a Vietcong hat, and hippie sandals. I was the Commie. I always lost."

"What happened to his dad?"

"He died stepping on a land mine. And Meechum's brother Al, a marine, got blown up in the headquarters barracks in Beirut, in that terrorist attack. That funeral was awful."

"Christ."

The phone rings.

"Meechum's the last male alive in that family," Voort says, reaching for the receiver again.

This time it's Hazel, the computer department's resident investigative genius, who had been eight when American troops liberated her from a German prison camp in World War Two. Her family had not been Jewish, but the Nazis believed otherwise. She still speaks with the accent.

"None of those names you gave me were in the military. None were ever arrested here. And the doctor, Jill Towne, never even got a parking violation."

"Which means, in this city," Voort says, "she probably doesn't own a car."

"Ouch," Mickie says, watching TV. "our side is killing 'em!"

On-screen, the skirmish lines have merged. The plain-clothesmen Mickie pointed out before have surrounded Chuck Farber, in the grass. Batons rise and fall as the boy curls into a ball, covering his head.

Of course, early in their careers, Voort and Mickie studied "riot control" with other rookies. They dressed in heavy protective vests and knee pads. They learned how to wield electric batons. They formed, with other police, coordinated skirmish lines, and stepped in unison toward plain-clothes police who were that day playing the part of "rioters." The "rioters" screamed at Voort and Mickie, "Child killer!" They used terms in foreign languages that sounded even worse.

Some cops got so carried away with acting that they started fighting. Mickie and one of the "protestors," a rookie named McMillan, ended up punching each other, on the ground.

"What would *you* do if some asshole hit you with a brick," Mickie asks now, as Voort watches Chuck Farber being cuffed by plainclothesmen and dragged from the rear, by his wrists, toward a police van. Blood streams from his forehead. Reaching the van, he kicks out and sends one of the cops reeling, clutching his stomach.

"Turn it off," Voort says.

Mickie clicks off the video. In its place, a CNN anchorman announces that the stock market has plunged another three hundred points.

Mickie says, "Uh-oh. More carnage."

He shuts off the set altogether. The quiet is broken by the soft machine-gun-like *chuk-chuk* of a helicopter outside, probably, Voort thinks, a traffic copter or airport commuter flight, heading to or from JFK from the new landing pad by the East River. He feels sick over the video, and Mickie, for all his bluster, looks slightly embarrassed, as if he agrees. They have dedicated themselves to protecting average citizens, and if average citizens fight cops, that attacks the core of what it means to join the force.

Voort says, "Clark was a right-winger. Farber was on the other side, a long thirty years ago. Plus he stayed in Chicago. He inherited a business. The movie doesn't help."

"He could have nursed a grudge against the government. Could you forget people who beat the shit out of you with batons?"

"A couple of scared cops beat the shit out of him, not the government."

As Voort straightens his tie for the press briefing, Mickie says, "Maybe there's a reason you didn't hear from Meechum yet. He's out of town. He's stuck in a plane. Didn't you say he tried to drop the whole thing in the tavern? You wouldn't let him then, so he dropped it after you left."

Voort smooths down his jacket. "Yeah, he dropped it. Beep me if you hear from him. If nothing happens in an hour," he says, the sour feeling worsening, "check out every murder that's happened in the city since Monday night."

"I'll call the hospitals, too."

"Every death by accident," Voort says, hating that he has to say the words. "Fire Department. Emergency Services."

"Where you going after the briefing?" Mickie asks as Voort takes his raincoat off a peg on the door.

"Into the past."

Voort heads down the hall, into the briefing room, where the reporters erupt into shouted questions. The TV camera floodlights are on. Yes, he answers, the cabbie confessed. Yes, he knew the victim. No, the police did not hit him during the arrest, or afterward.

"Then how come his head was bandaged?" the *Post* reporter shouts from the back.

"Because the woman he killed fought back."

Twenty minutes later Voort's riding to street level in a "Staff Only" elevator. At five P.M., municipal quitting time, it's dark outside with oncoming winter. Workers stream into the rain all over the City Hall area. They are corporation counsel lawyers, secretaries, school administrators, jurors exiting the federal and state court houses. An army pouring down subway entrances, fanning out to Brooklyn, Queens, the Bronx. Taking an hour to make a journey that would have cost Voort's Dutch ancestors a week, camping out.

Voort ducks into St. Andrews Church, beside the State Supreme Court building, where Mass is halfway finished. He kneels in a back pew, recognizing some of the regulars who beseech the Lord daily for strength to cope with whatever the city throws at them.

"God, thanks for order," he says, "and safety. Thank you for family and friendship. If something happened to Meechum, make it so he didn't suffer. And please, help Matt get well."

Voort puts a couple of hundreds into the poor box. Outside, the rain falls in driving sheets, smelling oily, of the river. He shares an umbrella with a lawyer he knows, who was in church, and they run across the plaza to the Chambers Street Municipal Building subway station.

He rides the Lexington line north, to Bleecker Street, where he buys a five-minute umbrella—meaning they work for about five minutes before breaking—from one of the Nigerian salesmen who blossom on street corners as soon as rainstorms begin. They are linked, celestially, to weather patterns. If snow falls, they materialize, instantly, selling earmuffs and gloves. If the sun comes out, they stand in the same places, selling knockoff Rolexes.

Holding the tiny umbrella, Voort walks briskly west, past the NYU housing towers, the jazz clubs near Mercer, and the coffeehouses filled with tourists planning their nights in Village restaurants, theaters, and vintage movie houses on Houston and West Houston Streets. At Murray's Cheese he buys a pound of Greek goat cheese, smoked Gouda, a loaf of long fresh sourdough bread, a half pound of spicy Sicilian cracked olives, a plastic container of hot green peppers stuffed with prosciutto and mozzarella, and a pound of Genoa salami, sliced thin.

He carries the food around the corner onto Morton Street, a narrow cobblestone lane lined by 150-year-old three-story brick town houses.

Maybe Meechum's mom will know where he is.

The third house on the left has only one buzzer, as it has

not been carved into apartments yet. The lights are on, up on the third floor.

"Conrad!" Lynn Keefe, Meechum's mom, says over the intercom, her delight clear, when he identifies himself. "I'll be right down. It's been years!"

Waiting for her, he remembers how the buzzer used to look so high when he was a boy that he had to stand on tiptoe to reach it. And now, as the door opens, Lynn Keefe seems shorter, too.

"At least that four-inch umbrella protects the top of your head. Come out of the rain."

She's put on weight, achieved the fireplug look that can overtake smaller women when they hit menopause. Her skin is still smoothly white, but lined near the mouth, and sagging into folds at the Adam's apple. The gray knit sweater is as plain as the ankle-length wool dress. The hair, her one vanity, is still youthful and free-flowing to the small of her back. It's almost blue-black glossiness tells Voort it has been dyed. The penny-colored eyes peering out through thick lenses are bright with welcome, but her hands tremble slightly as she draws him into the front hallway. The palsy started up with the death of her husband, and comes on whenever she feels strong emotions.

"Is that what I hope it is?" she says, eyeing the wet paper bag sagging in Voort's outstretched hand.

"They were out of Calamatas, so I got Sicilians."

"And I have wine and Brooklyn lager. Or haven't you graduated from Dr. Brown's Cel-Rey soda yet?"

The house was bought by Meechum's great-great-grandfather, a Union Army general and textile mill owner, after he was sent home after the Civil War. It had been paid off a century ago, and after Meechum's dad, Major Keefe, died, veterans from across the metropolitan area who had served under him in Vietnam—carpenters and electricians and roofers and masons—began showing up periodically to do repairs. They would refuse payment, and accept one of Lynn's apricot crumb pies in exchange.

The house looks the same to Voort as it did on the afternoons, hundreds of them, that he came here directly from school. The original gas lamps in the foyer are wired for electricity and softwhite bulbs. The wallpaper has a Colonial-era pattern—men at a tavern, smoking long Dutch pipes, or drinking tankards of ale. The hallways are narrow, the floor made of thick oak planks. The living room, off the foyer, has exposed brick walls and a working fireplace, crackling with flame at the moment. Fresh tulips sit in crystal vases on the stone mantle, below a timeline of photos of Keefe soldiers, going back to the battle of Shiloh, in the Civil War.

In the earliest shot, great-great-grandfather Keefe stands beside General Ulysses Grant, in front of a tent, hat in right hand, left hand on his breast, in a Napoleonic pose, a saber hanging from his hip.

By World War One, in sepia, Voort sees Keefe dough-boys on the deck of a troop ship docking at Cherbourg. There are more shots of the same marines going over the top of a trench at Blanc Mont Ridge, and one of a pilot, a Keefe army flier, standing proudly beside the Curtiss Jenny biplane in which he is shortly to lose his life, trying to blow up a German dirigible, over France.

The Vietnam shots are a riot of color, thick green forest, rust-red rice paddy water. But the faces beneath the helmets are Keefe faces, lean, bony, wise-guy faces.

More modern shots show Keefes in Saudi Arabia,

Panama, and finally West Point, on Meechum's graduation day.

"You know why we live in Manhattan?" Meechum's dad once told Voort. "To explain the real world to all these flaming liberals, not that they listen. It's the enemy you can't see that always screws you up."

Voort takes a seat on the couch where he and Meechum used to watch rerun science fiction movies on Sunday afternoons, laughing at the plastic cities—"London" or "Tokyo"—being destroyed by mechanical monsters. The Giant Behemoth. The Crawling Eye.

"I always wondered," he says, as Lynn comes into the room with the food arranged on an antique silver tray, and a fresh bottle of Oregon pinot noir, "when Meechum used to beat me in checkers, I'd turn around, and you'd be standing there. Were you giving him signals?"

"He would have killed me! Meechum was always a whiz with games and computers. Truth be told, he's a powerful man but more of an armchair warrior. I'm glad he never got into the field. As far as I'm concerned, a computer expert son is just fine."

It would have been too much to hope for that Meechum would be here. Voort doesn't want to alarm her by probing too hard or quickly. He leans back, as if on a social visit. He sips the pinot noir. It is now past six, and Mickie will be phoning the Fire Department, the Emergency Services Department.

Voort simply asks how she is spending her time these days.

"Believe it or not, I went back to school, didn't Meechum tell you? I'm a lawyer now, for the Housing Department. I usually look for you when I'm at the Chambers

Street stop in the morning. I figured I'd run into you one day. No luck so far."

"You should come up and visit," Voort says, and gives her his card, extension, and room number at One Police Plaza.

"And at night," she says, looking content, "I rarely get out of the neighborhood. Mondays is usually New York Cares. I tutor first graders in reading. Tuesday's my book club. I have a membership at the Film Forum. They have a James Cagney retrospective this month. And Meechum usually stops by at least once a week."

"Which night? I'll join him some time."

"It depends on his schedule. They shipped him up here two years ago and they work him like a dog."

"No free time, huh?" he says, wondering, *Who shipped him here?*

"I figured, it's the army, peacetime, and he programs computers in personnel. Some kind of new personality profiling. I keep asking him, What's so important that needs sixteen-hour days?"

Voort feels his heart speeding up but he keeps his face politely interested. He sips the wine.

She says, "Meechum says it's some kind of new army software project. Don't you ever speak to him?"

Voort makes himself look embarrassed. "He left me a message a few months ago, but my machine ate his number. He's not in the book."

She recites an area code 212 number, and Voort jots it down.

But Meechum had said he worked for a corporate head-hunting firm, doing personality profiling.

Did Meechum lie to me about quitting the army, or to Lynn

about working for the army? Was he simply embarrassed to tell her that he quit?

It is possible, Voort knows, that even in New York, Meechum could still work for the army. Contrary to popular belief, the military has a regular presence in the city. The army's got Fort Hamilton in Brooklyn, and the North Atlantic Division runs an office down at 90 Church. The Defense Department has a criminal investigation unit, which Voort worked with on a sex crimes case a few years back: the murder of a receptionist at the Army Corps of Engineers office, at Federal Plaza. The Defense Contract Audit Agency is downtown on Varick, as is the Defense Investigative Service and Supply Agency.

The Air Force Special Investigative Unit works out of 26 Federal Plaza, monitoring the honesty of military contractors around the Northeast, checking progress on military contracts.

Billions of dollars are spent on those contracts.

Meechum told me he didn't want to get anyone in trouble. Does that mean he's protecting people he works with?

"I should have made a better effort to get together with Meechum," Voort says. "Two-one-two area code, huh? So he's living in Manhattan."

"Murray Hill," she says, naming a neighborhood within walking distance of the U.N., on the East Side. "I'd be happy to see you two hanging out again. But he says he's happy, he has a big apartment and a terrific new girlfriend who I wouldn't mind meeting some day. Maybe I'm selfish, but I'd love a couple of rug rats running around. This is a big house for just one old lady."

Voort laughs, the worry twisting his stomach now.

All he says is, "You're not an old lady."

"Anyway, tell me about you," she says, eyeing his bare left ring finger. "What about that television producer that was in the news with you a few months back? Your girlfriend."

"That's ended," Voort says. "It was no big deal. I work. I see family. I kayak. Life's good."

She scrutinizes him, and smiles with the instincts of a mom, who, no matter Voort's age, will always relate to him on some level as her son's nine-year-old friend.

"I remember when you were eight," she says, munching a wedge of Gouda on a soda cracker. "You came here one day, and had that same expression on your face that you do now. That I-don't-want-to-talk-about-it look. Meechum told me, in the kitchen, that some boys had been bothering you on Eighteenth Street. A gang, remember?"

"I thought old people are supposed to lose their memory."

"Only short-term memory," Lynn winks. "Meechum said the boys had read about your family wealth, in the paper. They ganged up on you. They got you on the ground and took turns beating on you. Meechum said you wouldn't talk about it, but later you went up into that neighborhood, waited outside the boys' homes, one by one, and beat the daylights out of them."

"What's the point?"

"That just because you don't talk about something doesn't mean it's not alive inside you."

"I didn't say it wasn't alive. I said it was over."

Voort excuses himself, goes to the bathroom, and uses his cell phone to call Hazel at One Police Plaza. "Can you check out one more name," he asks, then spells Meechum, and gives the birth date, which he still remembers, and the

West Point graduation year, which was written in Magic Marker on the photo hanging in the living room.

"Hazel, find out if he's still in the army."

"Got a social security number?"

"Use what you already have," he says, reluctant to press Lynn further, and alarm her. "If you can't come up with anything, I'll get you more."

He's remembering the morning of Meechum's brother Al's funeral, at Arlington Cemetery. He has never been to a funeral outside his own family that broke his heart so much. He recalls that it was warm, autumn, and that Lynn never spoke, or cried, or even accepted an arm for support during the eulogy, but simply stood with chilling dry-eyed rigidity, staring down as clods of earth began falling on her son's casket.

The volleys of rifle fire, the marine twenty-one-gun salute, had not interrupted her composure.

Standing beside Meechum, wishing he could help, Voort could make out the Eternal Flame at the grave of President Kennedy, a few hundred yards off, and the changing of the guard at the monument commemorating slain union and confederate soldiers. All around Al's grave were the larger, individualistic monuments marking the resting places of fellow officers, occupying high ground even in death, while below, rows of plain white headstones honored enlisted men, an army of dead at attention, in crisp lines, rolling away toward the Potomac, and the capital beyond, in earth that had once been part of the Virginia plantation of Robert E. Lee.

The cemetery had been filled with black limousines that day, coming and going, in a parade commemorating over two hundred U.S. Marines who had died, along with Al, in a terrorist bombing in Beirut.

Now, back in Lynn's living room, he gives the visit a few more minutes, keeping the conversation away from Meechum. He sits while she shows him a photo album and manages to get her to give him an extra, recent shot of his friend "for my collection."

"Next time let's all three of us get together," Lynn says at the door, when he's leaving. "Give him a call. Tell him to bring his girlfriend. I'll make those hot sausages you love."

Voort smiles broadly.

"It'll be good to see him," he says.

"Conrad, you have to stop him!"

The rain has let up and Voort, reaching home at 9:30, finds that most of Matt's visitors have left. Only Voorts who will sleep over tonight remain in the house. The teenagers watch TV or play video games in the rec room. Retired Voorts, from the Queens branch, ex-detectives and sergeants and their wives, clean up in the main dining room, carrying china plates smeared with pizza residue into the kitchen, or plastic garbage bags out front. Marla Voort, Matt's sister, has come out of the kitchen, apron on, spatula coated with chocolate icing in her hand. She looks distressed.

I'll go down to the army offices at the World Trade Center, tomorrow, and check if Meechum still works there.

But of course, if he is still looking into Meechum's whereabouts tomorrow, his friend will almost certainly be dead.

"Matt wants to go kayaking, for Christ sake," she says. "Tonight. He's never been in a kayak in his life."

"I'll talk to him," Voort says.

Did Meechum lie to Lynn, or to me?

"You're the only one he listens to," Marla says. "Yesterday he wanted sushi. He never used to eat sushi. The day before it was the Mets game on TV. He always hated baseball. He's scaring me."

"Marla, be happy he's full of life."

"Let him be that way after the chemo's finished. Now he needs strength."

Voort kisses her on the cheek, and stops, on the way upstairs, to play with his six-year-old niece, Marla's daughter. He swings the girl high overhead, and sweeps her in circles while the child screeches in delight.

"The plane is landing. All passengers to the kitchen for chocolate cake," Voort says, putting her down.

I hope Jill Towne doesn't have an "accident" tonight.

Voort finds Matt in the converted sick room, alone in the big stuffed corner chair, reading Mark Hertsgaard's *Earth Odyssey*. Matt's bald head is polished, white. The angles of his skull reflect light. He's shrunk, from both disease and treatment, but has optimistically refused to buy smaller clothes, so his plaid flannel shirt looks oversized on him, as do his formerly skintight Levi jeans. There's a moss-colored, zip-up jacket with a fawn-colored collar, lying on the arm of his chair, accessible for instant exit.

Matt says, "I never used to read enough. This writer, Hertsgaard, went around the world to look at environmental problems. What a trip!"

"You want to go kayaking?" Voort says. "Now?"

"Everyone tells me to look forward to doing things I used to do, when the chemo is over. I want to take it further and do *new* things, and I want to do them now. It's a question of whether you let bad news get you down or not."

"Marla's worried."

"Marla," Matt says, reaching for his jacket, "thinks the doctor is God, and God told me to stay in bed."

"The river's cold this time of year. If we tip over you'll get wet."

Matt grins. He finished his weekly treatment three days ago, and usually, around now, he starts to feel a small lift. Then, just before his next visit to the hospital, his mood falls.

"When you were trying to get me to try kayaking before I got sick, you said we'd wear wetsuits. And you promised you'd work it so we didn't tip. Or did you get spastic, and now you can't row?"

"It's 'paddle,' not 'row.' And if you start feeling sick, you better tell me."

"Conrad, I'm not a masochist. I want to have fun, not drown."

Ten minutes later, in the Jaguar, they are driving through the heart of Greenwich Village, past crowds, cafes, jazz clubs.

"My God," Matt says, "I never figured just a restaurant could look so special. Marla's got me cooped up. Next time I'm out of chemo, phone one of your girlfriends and let's all eat out."

Voort flashes in his mind to Jill Towne, imagines her in a restaurant with him, across a small round table. There is a candle on the table. There is a bottle of white wine in a bucket at the side.

Jill, in the vision, goes off to the ladies' room.

A minute later, in the vision, he hears a scream.

They take Seventh Avenue south to West Houston Street and turn right toward the West Side Highway, and boathouse.

"Who are you dating these days, anyway, Conrad? Give the patient vicarious thrills."

"You want thrills, rent a porno movie."

Voort leaves the Jaguar in a temporary parking area formed by construction dividers, beside the Hudson River promenade. The full moon floods the velvety black river with light. The boathouse, on pier 26, lies a few blocks north of the World Financial Center, and across the West Side Highway from the Traveler's Insurance Building. A few late-night joggers and RollerBladers pass, wired to their earphones, their private cocoons. Voort unlocks the boathouse gate, noting that Matt, in his weakened state, has to lean against the building to stay up.

"Are you sure you want to do this?"

Close up, the river looks a bit rough.

"Conrad, you know what I've learned about disappointment? That it's easy to give in to it. That the world *wants* you to give in to it. I see all these old-looking people shuffling around New York and then it turns out they're only sixty. They started acting afraid of things when they were our age, and look how they ended up. Now get the damn kayak out."

Voort remembers, as he slides a two-seater fiberglass model from its wooden berth, that it was Camilla who introduced him to this sport. He sees her in his mind, in her little mad river racer, on the Hudson. Sees the sun flashing on the wet spots on her shoulders. He instructs Matt on how to put on his wetsuit, as she instructed him, and he selects a lifejacket and spray skirt for his cousin.

Voort turns the kayak upside down and kneels and wedges his head and shoulders into the opening. Standing, he balances the kayak on his shoulders, the way Camilla showed him, and walks it out of the boathouse, across the wooden pier, to a ladder leading down to a floating dock.

"Remember when we were kids?" Matt says. "You brought your buddy Meechum to the farm, and we went out on the sloop. That kid was some sailor. You ever see him anymore?"

"The other night," Voort says.

Matt laughs. "He kept wanting to sail the thing himself. He kept saying, Can we try this my way? Can we sail this my way? He cracked me up."

Voort says. "You sit in front. When you paddle, don't lean to either side. I'll steer from the back."

They push out into the river. It is turbulent, rolling, but Matt's a natural athlete, even in his sick condition. Their arms and shoulders move in slow synchronization. Voort feels tension lifting as they glide choppily from the floating dock, into the protected area flanked by piers which block the swifter current marking the river farther out.

"This is great!" Matt says, as Voort carefully monitors his cousin's tone for pain, stress, weakness.

They stay close to the rock-lined shore. Technically, Voort knows, he should display lights on the kayak at this hour. If a coast guard outboard spots them, they'll be ordered back.

"The city seems unreal when you're in this thing," Matt says. "The hospital is a billion miles away."

Spray hits them in the face.

There's a briny smell. The river is at its loveliest at night, when you can't see the floating condoms, ginger ale cans, plastic Silvercup wrappers, and snouts of creatures that you would rather avoid. Voort hears water slapping the rocks. There's the hum of traffic from the West Side Highway, engines where once were horses, and there's the drone of a tug somewhere, and the deeper throb of a big ship or barge. A *chuk-chuk* comes from a helicopter coming into the landing pad to the north, near the docked museum aircraft carrier *Intrepid*. All these sounds form layers in a familiar and comfortable blanket, a steady presence for those who have chosen to insert their lives into the humming urban mass of New York.

They do not speak. It is a masculine moment. They do not need words to enhance the closeness they feel. Voort watches his cousin's back as they move in a slow arc, bouncing beneath the stars, within sight of the glittering offices. He is enormously proud of Matt. For a man in Matt's condition, this excursion requires the equivalent energy an Olympic athlete might spend in a race.

Voort thinks, first Matt gets sick. Now Meechum is gone. Maybe loss is one reason why people form their own families, drawing themselves in together like pioneers circling wagons, for protection.

Why people have children.

Steering, he goes back again to the winter night last January when he went after Camilla here, in a blizzard, in in a small kayak. A night when the Bainbridge case culminated, and both he and Camilla almost died.

He is surprised that at the moment, at least, his sharp anger at her has diluted itself into a dull acidic regret.

Matt turns to him, and even in the moonlight, Voort sees that the little color that had brightened his cousin's face is gone.

"I think we better paddle in now," Matt says quietly.

Voort gets him back fast, puts him in the Jaguar, turns the heat on, and runs back to carry the bulky kayak to its berth.

I should check on Jill Towne. But how?

On the way home, Matt's breathing goes jagged, becomes labored, yet he forces out, "Let's go skiing this winter. Downhill. I've only done cross-country up until now."

"Great idea," Voort says, accelerating smoothly, trying to avoid potholes, trying to take corners easy, trying to apply the brakes with the lightest touch.

"If I'm still on chemo, we could try Massachusetts, one of those Berkshire places the kids like, Jiminy Peak or Butternut. But if I'm in remission, let's go to Utah. I want to speed down those steep black diamonds and go so fast I can't think."

"I'll get brochures," Voort says.

"You better . . . ugh . . . stop the car."

Voort is helpless watching the man's last meal flow into the gutter. He can only put his hand on Matt's back, provide a small human contact, as relief.

When Matt's finished, and they're driving again, he says, still fighting to maintain enthusiasm, "In one of those books you brought me, I read that all life comes from corruption. Everything has to die before new life can be born."

"You're not going to die."

"What I mean is, I'm going to kill this damn cancer, not the other way around. Then I'll be a new person."

"And what new thing should we try then?" Voort asks as they reach Thirteenth Street.

"Nothing active tonight. But when we get home,

maybe there'll be a science fiction movie on. I never liked them before, but I'm starting to understand the advantages of seeing the monster coming, if you know what I mean. Of understanding what you're dealing with."

Trying to grin, Matt looks like death.

"If you see it, you can kill it," agrees Conrad Voort.

SEVEN

You shoot the dogs? *You shoot the dogs?*"
The man with the twisted elbow is dreaming,
clutching his bedsheets, the knuckles of his hands white
from effort. The lightest sheen of sweat breaks out along the
ridge of his brow, above rapidly twitching lids.

He whispers a name, "Lupe."

He begins to thrash, slowly, ponderously, legs pushing
off covers, hands shoving away blankets. Sweat spreads on
his forehead, and froth bubbles and dribbles down the un-
shaven left side of his face.

"Where's the little dog?"

In his dream he cannot find it. There's too much smoke,
and explosions, dull reverberating thuds, and a girder is
swinging in flying dust, in the wreckage of a kitchen, and
there is a Coca-Cola bottle on a table, with blood dripping
down the side. The man with the twisted elbow reaches to
pick up a plastic dog collar that lies on the floor.

"Here dog! Hey! Dog!"

He jerks to full consciousness a full second before his
alarm goes off.

I'm in my office, on my pullout sofa.

His breathing seems louder to him than the tinny clanging of the "Lifelong" clock buzzing on the end table. He shuts the alarm. He needs a minute to slow his breathing. It is still dark beyond the third-story window's open curtains, and Manhattan glows with a faint, early-morning deceptive peacefulness. Ten million people, slumbering out there, are about to have their collective consciences jerked rudely awake.

He makes it to the bathroom, and retches, but nothing comes out except his own bile.

Everything is ready for Jill Towne. Now it's time for Frank Greene, the last one on Meechum's list.

He wills the dream away, brushes his teeth, runs the shower so hot that it raises his body temperature, that the skin of his belly and back erupts in red blotches. Back in the office, he pads over soft carpet to a closet behind his big desk, and pulls from a top shelf long thermal underwear, faded stained blue jeans, a red-and-black-plaid flannel shirt, and rubber-soled waterproofed hiking boots. The hunting jacket, Day-Glo orange vest, and fur-lined matching peaked cap are folded into a large sliding drawer. The rifle case is in the hidden compartment in the rear of the closet. It's a fine leather snap-up home for, according to the ad in *Internet Gun*, "the finest armament available to the modern hunter today."

Before he dresses, he slides on a flexible elbow brace, wincing from the pain of it. But it straightens his arm.

Once Frank Greene is gone, there will be no way for the detective to find us.

A musician of accidents, he will play the rifle today the way a saxophonist coaxes notes from metal. He will use his knowledge of speed, trajectory, and impact to send an inch-and-a-half-long steel projectile to change the world.

Downstairs, down a long narrow hall, he slips into a kitchen, a box of a room, as office kitchens usually are, an alcove, really, cramped but functional with linoleum flooring, a Formica-topped counter, and a row of triple-shelved steel cabinets painted white. He switches on the Braun coffeemaker. Humming a single repetitive note, more a mantra of focus than a song, he removes from the small, overworked refrigerator half a carton of eggs, from which he removes two Grade A larges, and heats them sunnyside up in a Teflon frying pan.

He is the only one in the office so early.

He heats two pieces of wheat bread in the toaster, burns them dark. He does not pause over the rich smell of brewing Colombian coffee, or the sizzling eggs turning brown, or the charcoal aroma of intentionally burned toast. Food is fuel.

Fuel is logic.

A voice in his head from years ago, a friendly and respected voice, says, "Don't forget what Sun-tzu said, pal. 'Go forth where they will not expect it. Attack where they are unprepared.' "

He cleans the last of the dishes, and makes his way past the ground-floor supply rooms and empty receptionist's desk, to the street. He retreives a green Chevy Lumina from a twenty-four-hour garage—one he does not normally use—six blocks away, tips the attendant a dollar, inspects the chassis for damage, and places the rifle case, shaped like a saxophone case, in the trunk.

"I play the trumpet, myself," the attendant says. "Do a gig in Astoria on Friday nights."

The man heads out into Manhattan, through gray, misty predawn light. There is a sense of expectation, of energy building, about to erupt with the day. Steam wafts from manhole covers. Traffic lights direct empty space, as if practicing for the cars that will appear an hour from now. Here and there light illuminates a window in the glass-and-stone towers he passes. Listening to all-news radio, learning about a labor riot in Detroit, he heads north on the FDR Drive to the Willis Avenue Bridge, crosses the steel grate roadway into the Bronx and accelerates onto the Major Deegan Expressway, the Cross County Parkway, and the Hutchinson River Parkway, north into Connecticut, staying within the speed limit, not wishing to be noticed by police.

By nine he has crossed into western Massachusetts and reached the historic town of Great Barrington, where, passing white churches and chain restaurants, a construction tug-of-war between traditional and new, he locates the main shopping center. A red Ford pickup with a dented passenger door sits in the third row of parking spaces across from the Price Chopper supermarket, in the second slot from the left, where the cupid-faced man had told him he would find it. The magnetic key box is under the left rear wheel well. Minutes later he is driving east on Route 23 out of town, through the autumn Berkshire hills.

The voice in his head says, "Hey man, Sun-tzu said, 'The highest realization of warfare is to attack the enemy's plans.' "

At a sign saying REVERE STATE PARK, he makes a sharp left up a steep forested incline, through pine forest. Within the first half mile he sees at least half a dozen other pickups, belonging to other "deer hunters," who have taken the day off from work, to shoot guns, stock their winter freezers, drink rum, and stumble around in the woods wearing Day-Glo orange vests and hats.

Monitoring his odometer, he drives 2.6 miles up the narrowing road, until he sees, exactly as the cupid-faced man said he would, a gap between two evergreen trees, and a boulder on which a wiseass vandal has spraypainted "Wendy & Scott" on gray rock.

A hunter, one of a thousand in Massachusetts today, he carries the rifle and scope, at a brisk walk, up the forested mountain, following well-placed blue trail markers.

He passes no other hunters, but sees landmarks the cupid-faced man told him about; the oak with "Gay Love" carved in it, the pond smothered by dying lily pads, the two-hundred-year-old rockpile remains of some settler's log cabin chimney.

When he leaves the trail, brambles cut his face. *Good sign*, he thinks, because the thorns will keep most hunters away from here today, and judging from the undisturbed state of things so far in this area, he is alone.

At length, unmistakable from the cupid-faced man's description, he sees a rock wall, some dead pioneer's property boundary, and a pile of granite boulders from which has sprung a fat, hardy oak, its twin limbs leaning right and left in a gigantic V, for the victory of survival. The right-hand branch is so low he can drape himself over it. The view beyond thirty yards of wood is of another dirt road, empty at the moment, rising up a hill to a crest where it disappears.

Moving unhurriedly, deliberately, the man checks his watch, arranges himself comfortably over the bough of the oak, cradles rifle on elbows, and trains his scope on the top of the rise. The elbow brace makes his arm throb, but he wills away the pain.

"Frank Greene hits the top of that hill on his mountain bike,

doing exercize, every morning between ten o'clock and ten-twenty, rain or shine," the cupid-faced man had said.

It is 9:49 now.

"The bike's a red Trek model. His helmet's blue. He always rides alone, and usually wears a Walkman."

He hears a shot from somewhere in the woods, but today, gunfire sounds as natural as a car backfiring in this part of the state.

9:55.

9:59.

At exactly ten, he sees a flicker of movement at the top of the rise, readies, and in the scope watches an immense stag leap across the road into the trees on the other side.

He has no interest in deer hunting.

At 10:18 the wind comes up, and its sighing makes him strain to hear any approaching vehicle, or mountain bike that might be laboring toward the rise in the road.

At 10:41 he mutters, "Shit."

At 10:52, as he is giving up, starting to push himself off the tree, he makes out the labored sound of someone grunting up the road, on the other side of the rise.

The scope comes up.

A lady jogger staggers into view.

Massachusetts law prohibits gunfire within a hundred yards of any road. Choosing to believe that the law protects them, each October, dozens of walkers, runners, and hikers venture onto forested roads during hunting season. They amble along as confidently as Chinese Boxer rebels charging guns to which they've been told they are immune.

Every year some get shot by accident.

But this morning, at least, that does not seem like it will be the case for Frank Greene.

At eleven, the furious shooter leaves his perch and returns to the shopping center. He finds a pay phone, always more secure than a cell phone, and calls New York.

"You better check the stables," the cupid-faced man suggests.

Keyed with frustration, driving back on Route 23, toward the hamlet of Lancaster Falls, the shooter feels a hole open inside him, feels the dream that is always just beneath the surface. He smells the dust and hears the screaming of dying dogs.

Lancaster Falls turns out to be such a speck of a town he almost misses it, a cluster of rural buildings in a dip in the road. There's a post office/general store, white steepled church, redbrick volunteer fire department, and an out-of-place, arty-looking furniture-maker shop, serving higher income summer visitors to the Berkshires, who come for the symphony at Tanglewood, the dance performances at Jacobs Pillow, the Shakespeare on the Mount Theater, and not to murder Frank Greene.

The bulletin board outside the general store advertises an ashram where visitors can chant mantras, a shiatsu masseuse who will travel to your home, a "light therapist" whose products, her card promises, will "soothe pain, relax the soul."

But unrelaxed, the man with the throbbing elbow searches through the tacked-up business cards, and finds one advertising "W&R Stables." A quarter horse is outlined on the card, carrying a western-style rider. The rural address is listed underneath.

Back in the car, he passes more dairy farms and clap-board homes, telling himself, hopefully, that the reason Frank Greene did not show this morning is that he has the flu, or a broken leg, or was forced to work today.

At the big W&R STABLES sign, nailed to a tree by a white split-rail fence, he turns right, drives another quarter mile past a mare and foal in a paddock, until, across a field of grass and daisies, he sees a red house and barn come into view.

He backs up, pulls off the road, parks beneath trees, and walks back, carrying binoculars. He takes up position in a copse of oaks, this time to observe the ranch.

He sees a black man with white hair coming out of the barn, carrying a pitchfork.

A black woman, also white-haired, is at a kitchen window in the house, wiping dishes with a rag.

He waits. The breakfast he ate has long ago been burned up, and his stomach is growling, but he ignores it. After an hour, a Plymouth van passes, heading for the ranch, where it discharges a half-dozen adolescent girls at the barn. The black man leads an equal number of saddled horses to the girls, and all of them, man and girls, trot off across the pasture, into the state forest beyond.

An hour later, they return.

At six, the black man goes into the main house, and at seven he comes out, dressed in dark brown slacks and a moss-colored zip-up jacket. He disappears around the side of the house and the man with the bad elbow hears an engine start up, and then a white Volkswagen Passat wagon churns toward him, up the dirt road. After it passes, he runs for his own car, and follows.

The black drives east, onto Route 8, and into the town

of Lee, where he parks outside a carriage house restaurant called Morgan House.

By the time the man with the damaged elbow gets inside, the rancher is already at a small rear bar, with a scotch or rye in front of him, nibbling pretzels from a bowl, watching "Who Wants to Be a Millionaire" and muttering answers to the questions to himself. Beside him is an open stool, which the assassin occupies.

And of course, at length, they begin chatting about the quiz show's questions. They fall into the easy bar conversation strangers are prone to have. The man with the twisted elbow pretends that this is the first time he is learning that the black man's name is Norman, that he owns the stable, that he moved here from Brooklyn, "for a change," four years ago.

The rancher hears the lies that the assassin lives in Boston, is a wine company representative, has taken two days off to go deer hunting, but has been disappointed in even seeing a deer.

"The worst part," he says, signaling for another Sam Adams for himself, and another Wild Turkey for the other man, "is, my old buddy, who told me how good the hunting is around here, isn't in the phone book. I haven't talked to him in two years and I think maybe he moved away."

"Who is he? It's a little place."

"His name is Frank Greene," says the man with the twisted elbow, and the black man breaks out laughing, because, he says, it is a small world, and Frank Greene, believe it or not, worked at his stable, only leaving yesterday morning.

"You're kidding," says the man with the twisted elbow,

also breaking into laughter, hoping that his monumental rage, his killer fury, does not show. "He worked for *you?*"

I missed him because of Meechum.

"I gather he had some problem in New York and moved back. Too bad. He was good with horses. To Murphy's damn law," the black man says, lifting his glass.

"Good with horses, huh? I never knew Frank had that talent."

I missed him because Meechum slowed everything up.

The black man orders more drinks, and says that, in a way, Frank Greene was better suited for dealing with animals than people. Frank had an affinity for four-legged life, he says, adding that Frank could talk to the horses, and brush them, for hours.

"But when it came to people, he was shy. I hired him because I felt sorry for him. He saved his money. He read books. He stayed in his room."

"Do you know where Frank moved to?"

"Queens, I think he said, or the Bronx. One of those places. He bought an old van, with cash he saved, and loaded it with fertilizer. He said he'd sell it to plant stores in Manhattan. He said he bought it cheap up here, and could get a bundle of cash down there."

The man with the hurting elbow raises his glass, as if toasting the business acumen of the vanished Frank Greene. "Here's to making a fortune any way you can."

"Amen," nods the black man, as, on "Who Wants to Be a Millionaire," tonight's winner beams over the $125,000 he has just won, to massive applause.

"I didn't understand at first," the black man says. "I said, Frank, you crazy? What the hell are you going to do with a thousand pounds of fertilizer in a city that tars over streets. I said, *fertilizer?*"

The man with the bad elbow shakes his head and grins, but his stomach is burning.

Fertilizer usage in New York is not the usual kind of question that gets asked in "Who Wants to Be a Millionaire," but he knows the answer, unfortunately.

You build a truck bomb with it, is what he thinks.

EIGHT

Lieutenant Colonel Renata C. Wilkes wears, on her green U.S. Army jacket, the elongated red-and-white "A" patch of the First Army, whose command encompasses the northeast United States. The gold twin-towered castle insignia denotes the Corps of Engineers, and the trio of silver badges, service in Iraq, Bosnia, and Haiti under President Clinton.

"Meechum who?" she says.

Voort faces her, over her desk, in her corner office at the World Trade Center, sixty-two stories above the underground parking garage where, in 1993, terrorists detonated a truck bomb, hoping that the 1,350-foot tower would collapse. Colonel Wilkes's office is decorated with potted palms, children's finger painting, and color photos showing her directing pontoon bridge construction, in a snowstorm, outside of Sarajevo. Double-pane windows look south over New York Harbor, toward Governors Island, where the corps is dismantling barracks which at one time housed two thousand troops.

"Soon we'll have only a handful of personnel left in New York," she says. "Fort Totten is gone, in Queens. Fort

116

Hamilton's closing in Brooklyn. Schuyler's cut people. Now we spend half our time dismantling facilities, not building them.

"I know most of the people in this office, and I'm sure I never met any Meechum Keefe," the small, dark-skinned black woman says. "But let's check."

Voort's remembering how he first met the lieutenant colonel, during an investigation into the murder of a New York State auditor who worked on the same floor. The woman's body had been found in a nearby landfill park, a strip of chemically enhanced green running behind Stuyvesant High School and along the Hudson River promenade, to the World Financial Center. The park is fenced off at night, for safety reasons, but one July morning a custodian had unlocked the gate to find the half-naked body of a woman who had been raped before she was strangled, medical examiners said.

Police arrested a civilian engineer in the corps, who had dated her, been dumped in public, at a restaurant, and shouted "I'll kill you" in front of two dozen customers. But Voort and Mickie cleared the man, and arrested a Belfast businessman as he headed to JFK Airport and his flight home. The chase, on the A train, had made the evening news.

"I owe you," Colonel Wilkes had told Voort, only then revealing that she also dated the engineer. They were married six months later.

Now Voort's cell phone goes off as he and the colonel wait to see if her staff has any records on Meechum Keefe.

"Go ahead. Answer it. I have drawings to look at," she says.

"Bad news, Con Man," Mickie says, when Voort picks

up. "I'm in Clinton," he adds, naming the neighborhood formerly known as Hell's Kitchen. "Twenty-fifth near eleventh. The clerk from the King Hotel lives here, the guy who was on duty when it caught fire Monday night. He's ID'd Meechum's sketch as one of the two John Does that burned in the fire. I'm sorry."

Voort feels blackness edging against the periphery of his vision. His throat has become scratchy, and the pulse has picked up on the side of his head.

"Is he sure?"

"There were sixteen accidental deaths since Monday: heart attacks, stroke, a car crash, a kitchen fire in Staten Island, a guy falling off a ladder in Bayside. Fourteen were ID'd by the time I started. Both the John Does were at the hotel, so that's the first place I checked."

"Burned to death," Voort whispers. The room feels warmer now, and spins slightly, and he remembers seeing, on TV, orange flames shooting from a third-floor window of the hotel.

A wave of rage is rising in him.

He has, over the years, seen victims of fires, close-up, with their features burned off, their skin charred as cooked chickens, their torsos swelled with gas, their whole aspect robbed of human identity.

Mickie says, "The Fire Department's citing the hotel for failing to keep a functioning smoke alarm in that room. There were no batteries in the thing, but the clerk swears he installed a Duracell the day before, when they tested the alarms. And Meechum was asleep when it happened," Mickie adds, but of course they both know that Mickie has no idea as to Meechum's level of consciousness when the fire broke out. He is simply trying to make Voort feel better.

Voort cannot speak for a few moments. Then he says, "You said another guy died, too," and Colonel Wilkes's head swings up sharply, away from her blueprints, at the word *died*. Voort tries to push grief away for later, to make himself concentrate on work. "What about the smoke alarm in the other guy's room? Did it work?"

"That's the other part," Mickie says, faltering slightly, from more bad news, or embarrassment. "Meechum and the other guy were in the same room. They were in bed together."

"What do you mean, 'bed'?" But Voort knows exactly what Mickie means.

"The other guy, the John Doe, wore flammable pajamas. They're banned from stores in this country. They're Indonesian. Someone smoked and the fabric went up like gasoline."

Voort's headache spreads down his spine, clenching the muscles of his back.

"Meechum wasn't gay," Voort says.

A pause. "Con Man, what do you want me to say? You didn't see him for nine years. Things happen, people change. Those two weren't playing Scrabble."

"No," Voort says stubbornly. "But if we include Meechum on the list, that makes four out of six people dead from accidents. Over sixty percent, Mickie. Give me the address and try to keep him there. Wait for me. I'm almost finished here."

Voort hangs up to see Renata Wilkes staring at him, and simultaneously another officer enters the room; a rotund, lethargic-looking lieutenant named Frank Mitchell, to whom Voort had been introduced earlier, and who works with computerized records on the same floor.

"Colonel, there's no Meechum Keefe here," he tells Renata Wilkes. "No one by that name ever worked here, at least going back to 1983, when our records start."

"How about elsewhere in New York?" Voort says.

The lieutenant answers but keeps his eyes on his commander. "I'd have to pull his jacket to see if he's in the metropolitan area."

He looks like he'd prefer to get back to whatever he'd been working on before Voort arrived. But Colonel Wilkes tells the man, firmly but softly, "Do it, Frank."

"Sure thing, Colonel."

"Now, please. How long will it take?"

The lieutenant shrugs. "At most, twenty minutes. All I have to do is tap into the mainframe in D.C. Mr. Voort, do you have your man's social security number? It would be helpful."

He's finally looking at Voort.

Voort considers calling Meechum's mom at work, considering the urgency of things, but she won't have the number there, and she'd know something was very wrong right away. No. He'll visit her in person to break the news, before doing a search of Meechum's apartment. But at the thought that he'll be making a death call, the sour sensation in his stomach turns to nausea.

He says, "I know what year he graduated West Point. Will that help?"

"Probably. We did a project up there. They're usually pretty cooperative. Maybe I can access his number from their files. Why should I say I want to know?"

The colonel tells him, "Say I'm trying to get a message to him."

"Yes, ma'am." The lieutenant swings on his heels and strides out.

"You knew the man who burned, I have a feeling," Colonel Wilkes says.

"We grew up together."

"How about a cup of coffee? Washington keeps cutting our personnel but increasing our food quality. It doesn't attract recruits, but at least it's real coffee, not the mud like before."

The quality of the silence has changed now, become pained, and Voort, looking down from the window, sees smoke or steam rising from factories across the river. It makes him think of cremation, and to distract himself, he says, "What does the army do in New York, now that the Cold War's done?"

"At this office, I told you, construction. Or rather, destruction. Other offices audit defense contractors. There are still a few of those out on Long Island. And the intelligence branch tries to monitor all the bad guys going in and out of the U.N."

"That sounds a little right wing to me."

"No, it's a fact," she says, putting Sweet'n Low in a steaming ceramic mug and passing it to Voort. "Foreigners, diplomats, at least the ones from poorer countries, want to work at the U.N. for two reasons. Either they want to live in a place where they can drink the water, or they want to spy on the place where one day they may try to poison it."

"What are you talking about?"

"Iraq. North Korea. Libya. Countries we have no diplomatic relations with can still slip people into the country by sending them to the U.N. Baghdad wants to place a spy here? Just give him a diplomatic passport. Send him to the U.N. as a 'commercial attaché.' Once he's here, he can try to lose himself in the country. He can drive out to the defense contractor factories on Long Island, or hire a private plane in Islip and snap photos of the entrances, truckloading docks, parts waiting to be shipped out. He can meet a disgruntled engineer in the McDonald's on Sixth Avenue. He can hop a red-eye to Silicon Valley, or disappear into the subways to meet whoever is selling him information this week, in a thousand cubbyholes in the city. And it doesn't have to be a Baghdad agent either. It could be an agent from Tokyo, Beijing, Moscow, Tel Aviv."

"There must be restrictions on their travel."

"On paper, Voort, sure. But who can follow around five hundred people every minute, in New York? You never know which diplomat is real, and which is phony. Hell, the army, FBI, Justice, we're probably all here. That's why regular people can't find a goddamn apartment to rent in the city," she grins. "They're all rented by spooks."

"You sound like a spook yourself."

"I sound like someone whose ex-husband was one. It's the perfect job for a man, Voort. Don't want to talk to your wife? Just get a job where you're ordered to shut up, or to lie. Ah, our lieutenant is back. What do you have, Frank?"

The man says, "West Point was completely cooperative." Lieutenant Mitchell holds up a printout. "They gave me his social security number. Your man left the army two years ago."

The date is in sync with Meechum's tale the other night.

"He got an honorable discharge," the lieutenant says.

"Does it say why?"

"No, but everything looks normal. Fort Drum, Fort Bragg," the lieutenant says, listing Meechum's postings. "He worked with computers, looks like. Updating systems at the different forts."

"But he left before his time was up."

"Yep."

"Why does a man get an honorable discharge?"

"Plenty of reasons. Medical, oftentimes. He hurt his back playing basketball. Or stress. My brother-in-law got an honorable discharge because he didn't get along with people, and they all agreed they'd be happier if he was out."

"Can I take a copy of this?" Voort asks.

"Sorry," the colonel says. "Privacy laws. I need an official request to hand over a soldier's file." But she lays the printout on her desk, facing Voort.

"Lieutenant, I want to have a word with you outside," she says.

The instant they close the door, Voort takes out his notebook, and scribbles down all the information on the printout. But nothing there strikes him as odd.

When the colonel comes back in, she says, "Oh no, did I leave that printout on the desk? What was I thinking?"

"Can you call anyone you know and get details on the honorable discharge?"

"Let's see. His last posting was Fort Bragg, North Carolina. I have some friends there. I'll see what I can do and call you later today."

Bradley Licht, now the unemployed night clerk at the King Hotel, turns out also to be a Columbia second-year law student working his way through school. He's a medium-sized, baby-faced, balding blond with a pear-shaped body. He's dressed in a denim workshirt and jeans. His two-bedroom apartment, on Twenty-fifth Street, was willed to him, under the city's medieval rent control laws, by his deceased mother. Since the mother originally occupied the nineteen-hundred-square-foot apartment in 1943, and claimed in her will that Bradley never moved away from it, his rent remains a paltry $150 a month, and the enraged landlord cannot dislodge him.

"A big help since I'm not on scholarship," Bradley says.

Voort and Mickie sit with him in a third-floor living room with a picture window looking out onto a narrow street spotted with auto repair shops whose robber prices underscore the advisability of never breaking down in Manhattan. Voort's visited this street often enough on official business. At night it is lined with hookers, who give blowjobs in cars or shoot heroin behind parked tow trucks. During daytime, the more desperate hookers are still out there, working around the clock to support their habits, pimps, or AIDS-infected kids.

"That's definitely the man who rented the room," Bradley says, when Voort shows him Meechum's photo, which Lynn had given him.

"Describe the other man."

The description, especially the part about the discolored patches on the neck, matches that of the man Voort now knows had been following Meechum at the White Horse Tavern.

"Do you remember his name?"

"He never gave one. He just came in asking for the first guy. He had a box of candy for him. I thought they were lovers, and he was trying to make up after a fight."

"Do you remember anything either of them said?"

"The hotel was busy that night. There was a church reunion up the block and people were coming in from out of town. They had a million questions. Is it safe to go out? That kind of thing."

"Do you remember *anything* Meechum said?"

"He looked quiet. No, not quiet. Worried, you know, frowning."

"Did the men ever come in or leave together?"

"I never saw them together. I remember telling the second man that I couldn't let him up without permission. But people sneak lovers in all the time, to save on the double rate."

"How about anything you heard about them from a maid, or another guest. And we'll want to contact the maid."

"Now that you ask, a German guy in the room next to theirs phoned down to complain that their TV was on too loud. I called up, to ask them to turn it down, but nobody answered. We were too busy to send a bellboy. Then the fire started."

"Did the neighbor hear anything else?"

"If he did, he didn't say." Bradley lets out air. "Those poor guys," he says. "You'd think, in the twenty-first century, gay guys could just do what they want without embarrassment. But we still get 'em coming in, hiding who they are from friends or families. I have a friend who's gay and his parents still don't know it. It kills him."

Voort just listens, hoping that Bradley, rambling a bit, might remember something, or, relaxing, reveal something he thinks is unimportant, but which will be a solid clue. The room is large and quite sunny from floor-to-ceiling windows, despite the protective wire embedded in the panes. Law books, piled on the floor, between potted plants, also double as legs for a lumpy couch, a 1950s wingbacked monstrosity probably inherited with the apartment. There's a black-and-white Zenith TV, lots of board games like Scrabble and Monopoly on a bookshelf, and an antique poster reproduction of the film *The Wasp Woman*, in which a wasp with a beautiful woman's face clasps a tiny, screaming man with its legs.

"Look at that guy. He reminds me of half the cases we investigate in the unit," Mickie says when Bradley goes to the bathroom.

"Did anyone else visit Meechum while he was at the hotel?" Voort prompts when Bradley returns.

"Not that I remember."

"How about any calls he made?"

"Calls go out automatically, not through a switchboard. And all the records burned when the fire spread downstairs. And I don't remember the German guest's name."

"What are you going to do for a job now?" asks Voort, who is actually concerned, but also remembering, as always, to ask a source about himself, to open the conversation up, to give the person an opportunity to remember something important, or failing that, to create a link so that later, if the source remembers a relevant fact, he'll pick up the phone, and call.

"Columbia has a pretty good job placement service. I have a couple of interviews this afternoon. The Hilton needs a night clerk."

"Want us to drop you anywhere?" Voort says. "We're heading downtown."

"I appreciate it, but no thanks. I have studying to do before the interview. I . . . I checked the batteries in that smoke alarm myself," Bradley insists, frowning, shaking his head. "The fire investigator looked at me like he didn't believe me, but I swear, I know how important alarms are. When I was a kid this apartment caught fire, and the alarm woke us, saved me and my mom. I'm telling you, that alarm worked the day before. Maybe the heat made the batteries explode, or maybe when the plastic melted, they just dropped out."

"That's probably it," Voort says, seeing that Bradley, like any good person, questions whether he may have been responsible in even some small, negligent way, for the deaths.

"That smoke alarm should have woken them," Bradley says. "They had time to leave."

Voort thinks, *Meechum's problem wasn't lack of warning, Meechum's problem was he couldn't get out.*

As Voort heads downtown, dreading his upcoming meeting with Lynn Keefe, Lieutenant Colonel Renata C. Wilkes, back in the World Trade Center, checks her harbor-dredging schedule and munches on one of her homemade chicken enchiladas for lunch when the intercom buzzes.

"Colonel Grey on line one," the receptionist says, naming the colonel's old friend from basic training, now in charge of Military Transport at Fort Bragg, Meechum's last posting, according to his file.

"Hey there, Sugar Ray," she says, using the man's nickname. The diminutive Colonel Grey resembles the famed boxer so much that, when he wears civilian clothes, strangers ask him for autographs.

"Renata, I asked around about that officer," Grey says in his west Arkansas drawl.

"Why was he discharged?"

"On the record or off?"

"On."

"Back problem."

"Off."

"Sex problem. He had an affair with a married officer. A male married officer."

Colonel Wilkes puts down the enchilada. She'd overheard enough of Voort's phone conversation this morning to understand that Voort's old friend was gay. But she's puzzled. "How come there's nothing in the record about it? Why not a dishonorable discharge?"

"Because a general here knew Meechum's father, served with him in Vietnam, and didn't want to embarrass the family. The other officer resigned. Nobody wanted a stink. Old White Boys network, Renata. Meechum promised to get counseling, so instead of lockup, they eased everybody out. I could use those kind of connections. I can't even get a damn traffic ticket fixed."

"Can I tell the police here what you told me?"

"That boy had a real love-hate relationship with the army, I gather. Trying to live up to his brother and father. But also feeling trapped in his body, that kind of shrink shit. If you want to tell that detective friend of yours, do it off the record. We've gotten enough bad press about who's pumping who. Journalists don't want to write about how the army needs new weapons, or money, or why we're losing recruits each year. They'd rather concentrate on sex. Who trains these people, the National Enquirer?"

"Voort can keep a secret."

"Why the interest in Meechum anyway? Did his pecker get him in trouble again?" asks the drawling voice over the line.

"His pecker days are over," Colonel Wilkes replies.

By three o'clock, having received Colonel Wilkes's call, and after finding nothing useful at Meechum's apartment,

Voort is watching New York City Chief of Detectives Hugh Addonizio pace in his thirteenth-floor office at One Police Plaza. Addonizio's rottweiler Ernie, named after Ernie Harwell, the old Brooklyn Dodger broadcaster, sleeps in a corner beneath Addonizio's framed front page of the *New York Mirror*, his last unpacked wall decoration, proclaiming, sadly, "Dodgers Go to L.A."

"Nobody stays put anymore," Addonizio says. "Those guys leaving was the greatest disappointment of my life."

In his pause, which implies, "until now, with my retirement happening next week," Voort says, "I said, can I go to Chicago?"

"I want to get this right," Addonizio says. He's a blocky, sixty-one-year-old with the muscles of a weight lifter, the white thick hair of an Italian fashion magnate, the pallor of a cancer victim, and the cunning of a Ugandan dictator. "The Fire Department says Meechum died in an accident. The army confirms the gay story. There's no connection between the accidental deaths, and the doctor on Fifth Avenue is perfectly all right, doing exercise, walking around."

"The FBI may be investigating her," Voort says.

"Meaning what? We haven't the slightest idea. And *you*," Addonizio says, "after taking weeks off, are neglecting your legitimate cases, throwing yourself into one that isn't even official."

"You can make it official."

"Because *you*, without proof, decided Meechum was murdered."

"He gives me a list of people who died accidentally. That night, *he* dies accidentally, too."

"You decided he's not homosexual, notwithstanding the army report on him."

"Whether he was homosexual or not is not the point."

"And now you want to take more time off, fly around the country, and figure out what happened to all these other people. Like we don't have enough to do around here."

"Meechum was murdered here. Jill Towne is still here. All the deaths are connected, and the starting point is here. I'll go on my own money."

"But on the department's time."

"I have vacation time coming separate from the leave."

"Fuck vacation time," snaps Addonizio. "I'm not going to take away your vacation time. If it's worth you going out there, it's worth doing it on department time."

"Look," Voort says, "I spent the last two hours on the phone with every corporate head-hunting firm in the Yellow Pages in New York. None of them ever heard of Meechum. We'll try Westchester and Nassau, but he said he worked on the East Side."

"Maybe he was with one of those ultra-private firms, that don't advertise in the lowly middle-class Yellow Pages. That pluck their clients from the rarified stratosphere, from which their HAHvid," Addonizio says in a mocking imitation of a Boston Brahmin accent, "MBAs never come down."

"I contacted them, too. I called people on Wall Street and got the private numbers."

"Is Mickie ignoring his caseload, too, or should I fire just you?"

"The cops in Lancaster Falls called thirty minutes ago to tell us that the living, breathing guy we asked about doesn't even live there as far as they know. My father used to say that when you've got a lot of facts that don't make sense, there's usually one big one underneath them that does, and ties them all together."

"Your father also used to say never try to bluff Lieutenant Fahey in seven-card stud, but he did it all the time. No offense, but you didn't know the human side of the guy."

"I spent two hours this morning with Meechum's mom. She's in the hospital, sedated."

"Two hours for a notification. Two more hours on the phone. Let's throw in travel time. How many cases are in your basket? Did it occur to you that your personal involvement in this whole thing is clouding your vision?"

"It's improving it."

"But you admit your involvement causes you to ignore other, legitimate cases."

"Every case I work on causes me to ignore other ones."

Addonizio growls, "Well, I'd say we're into a sizable degree of distraction today. Not to mention," Addonizio adds, heating up, "that despite a lack of any evidence to the contrary, despite the fact that this buddy of yours showed up out of the blue after nine years, and you haven't the slightest idea how he spent those years, instead of accepting that he swung both ways, which makes sense to me, seeing that he was in bed with another guy when he died, you would rather rely on your flawed loyalty, and conclude that the other guy wasn't his lover—no, *that* doesn't make sense to you. What makes sense to you is that the other guy climbed into bed with him, *not* to have sex with him, but to intentionally put on flammable pajamas, knowing he was about to kill them both, and he just reached over and clicked his Bic on the Sealy Posturepedic grill. Does one and one equal twelve here, or what? And by the way, with all due respect to your friend, he just lies there through all of this, humming dum-de-dum. Do you know how nuts you sound?"

"You summed it up accurately," Voort says. "Except for

your deciding that four dead people out of six means 'no evidence,' means just coincidence, and except for your ignoring that the same guy who was following Meechum in the bar turned out to be the guy who died with him in that room."

"His lover followed him to see who he met in the bar. Jealousy, Voort, is a big motivator."

"Let me tell you something. Whoever that guy was, he was *not* Meechum's lover. So if we assume, for the sake of argument, humor me a minute here ... if we assume Meechum's *not* gay, and that the guy *was* following him, which seems pretty damn reasonable to me since the clerk identified him, then the TV was on loud in that hotel room for a reason, which was that they were hurting Meechum *before* the fire. Maybe they were asking questions. They knew he met me in the bar. Maybe they were trying to get my name or find out what he told me. Because he damn well knew something about *something* going on. Also, if he's not gay, we're dealing with a group that's so committed to whatever they're doing that one of them was willing to die to hide their existence. What else are they hiding? *What else are they planning?* What did Meechum want me to help prove?"

"It's nice to know you haven't lost perspective," Addonizio remarks sourly, shaking his leonine head. "You are a sex crimes detective, probably the best I've ever known. You are *not* a conspiracy theorist, or a goddamn secret agent. Do you know who you sound like? You sound like my brother's son Gus, who lives in a basement in Washington and tacks articles about John F. Kennedy all over his walls. You work the streets, Voort. Why don't you stay there?"

"Does that require an answer?"

"I'd like to get an answer to *something* around here," Addonizio says, and stands up, goes to the window, and runs his fingers through his thick hair. "My problem is, you're right ninety percent of the time."

Addonizio blows out air and turns back. "Go to Seattle. Go to Chicago. Go wherever the hell you want and call every once in a while and tell someone here you haven't had an accident yourself. If someone's screwing with us, nail 'em," he says. "If someone's after that doctor, stop him."

"Thanks."

"Have Mickie and Hazel run the names on Meechum's list past the FBI, Justice Department, whoever else that doctor mentioned. Work on her more. Also, I'm not kidding, watch yourself. Cops have accidents, too. I can't believe I'm even listening to you. And charge the trip to us."

"I'll pay for it," Voort says. "It's not going to be cheap. And the department needs money more than I do."

"Voort?"

"What?"

"Everyone needs money more than you do."

NINE

Thousands of Americans die of accidents each year. They drown while swimming. They run into the street, between parked cars, into the paths of oncoming vehicles. Cleaning their basements after floods, they stand barefoot in water, unthinkingly plug a lamp into a socket, and the current surges into their heart through frayed wire. They overdose on drugs. They are allergic to bees. They get struck by fluke bursts of lightning, or by panes of glass falling from tall buildings. They die when a bus brake fails on a steep hill. They perish when they bite into a hero sandwich, and a piece of roast beef lodges in their throat.

Voort, sitting in coach class, feels the airplane lift violently, so that the overhead luggage rack opens across the aisle. A Samsonite attaché case topples out, narrowly missing a Japanese businessman trying to concentrate on his *Wall Street Journal*.

"We've hit a little turbulence," the pilot announces. "But we should be on the ground at O'Hare in twenty minutes."

Voort leans back and puts accidents from his mind as the jumbo Delta Airlines L-1011 breaks from the clouds, and the flat, dreary autumn patchwork of shrinking fields and expanding suburbs spreads below, unremarkable as safety. Rain pummels the Plexiglas window. Lake Michigan comes up as the plane banks. Voort sees, in the distance, Oz-like, the rearing glass tower of the Sears building above the Chicago skyline, modern wonder-of-the-world of the Midwest.

"Business or pleasure in the Windy City?" says a voice to his right. The woman has been immersed in the paperback best-seller *Terrorist* since they took off from La Guardia two hours ago. Her overly controlled voice means she is a fearful flier trying to distract herself.

"Business," he says, pegging her for a New Yorker. New Yorkers, he's decided, rarely start conversations on airplanes until late in flights. Passengers from other cities have no trouble slipping into sociability with strangers, but New Yorkers equate strangers with discomfort. Talk to a stranger too quickly on a flight, and they will think you're a nut, or turn out to be one.

"I'm visiting my sister," she says. "But every time I get in a plane, I fly through a storm."

Her knuckles are white on the seat divider. She's about forty, with a plain, squarish face, reading glasses suspended from a black elastic cord, and a nervous, vulnerable smile.

The jet lifts, plunges, settles. "They test these planes against all kinds of dangerous conditions," he says, to calm her, unable to keep from thinking, given the events of the last week, *but not against bombs in the cargo hold. Not against phony mechanics fiddling with the controls.*

He learns, as the woman talks, that as a birthday present, she has given herself this trip to Chicago. Her sister has three children, and works as a nurse in the Loop. Her husband, a vice president at IBM in Westchester, is being wooed by a high-end Manhattan head-hunting firm for a job in Chicago.

"What's the name of the firm?" he says, more interested now, hoping this coincidence may be helpful.

But it turns out the firm is one he already checked, one where Meechum did not work.

"What are some other high-end head-hunting firms?" he asks.

"Oh, I don't pay attention to that. Having four kids is my full-time job."

The wheels touch down, and the passengers break into applause, for life, safety, mechanical achievement. For the fact that a four-hundred-thousand-pound steel machine has conveyed them, without disappointment, through the sky.

Voort's brought only a small leather bag, in the overhead rack, so he retrieves his coat and jacket and heads for the taxi stand. His air ticket lists three more cities he must visit over the next few days, and he is hurried. But the instant he exits the terminal, he gets a relieving sense of space opening up.

"I'm going to Skokie," the woman says, back again, catching up to him, carrying a smaller suitcase than he would have imagined. Skokie is the northern suburb adjacent to Evanston, where he's headed, a fact he had not mentioned to her. She smiles up at him, his big pal now that they have chatted for fifteen minutes.

"If you're headed in that direction, let's share a cab," she says, looking into his eyes.

How did Chuck Farber's "accident" happen, Voort wonders. Did some friendly stranger ask to come into the house for a glass of water? Did Lester Levy's "heart attack" begin when some inconspicuous man, carrying a sharply tipped umbrella, maneuvered close in the lobby of the building where he worked?

I am getting paranoid, he thinks.

"Actually, I'm going in the other direction," he lies, at the taxi stand. "I'm in no rush. Take this cab. I'll get the next one."

Did Meechum gave them my name?

The woman says thanks, hands her little pink traveling case to the driver, climbs in, and waves good-bye. She does not glance at the license plate of Voort's cab, rolling up to him, next in line.

But Voort notes *her* license as she pulls off.

"If you're ever following someone at an airport," he re-members a senior detective advising him once, "and you think he suspects it, take the cab *in front of him*, have the driver pull over to the side, y'know, before you're out of the airport, and wait for your guy to pass."

There's the sound of a crash, and horns honking. Thirty yards back, along the curving terminal access road, Voort sees a harmless fender bender has occurred between a Range Rover and an Avis passenger van.

He does not see the woman's cab again, and traffic is light at nine A.M., on the John F. Kennedy Expressway, as he heads toward the lake. Voort called ahead last night, and Mrs. Lila Farber, as the widow still prefers to be known, said she'd wait for him at home.

"I'm the boss so I go into work whenever I want, but I don't understand why you want to talk to me," she'd said. "What does Chuck's accident have to do with something in New York?"

"Do you mind if I explain when I get there?"

In Evanston, the cab proceeds north up Sheridan Road, a four-lane, oak-lined avenue that intersects the campus of Northwestern University. Classes are changing, judging from the volume of students strolling or cycling through pools of brightly colored leaves swirling in a stiff wind coming off Lake Michigan.

Following directions, the driver turns left on Lincoln Street, at the northern edge of the campus, and proceeds two blocks west, into an area of private Tudor-style homes, wealthy-looking, reminding Voort of Riverdale or Westchester, back home. The grounds are well kept. The oaks are big enough to have been around when Woodrow Wilson was president. The sidewalks are as bare of pedestrians as Beverly Hills. The vehicles in driveways are newer, and the whole neighborhood, when he climbs from the taxi, resounds with the high-pitched buzzing of lawn machinery, as handfuls of Central American refugees, working out of old trucks, blow leaves off lawns or suck them into gigantic bags with gasoline-driven lawn vacuums. The decibel level exceeds that of Times Square.

Mrs. Farber answers the door so quickly he assumes she watched him from a window as he came up the walk. She's a trim blonde, clearly a good twenty years younger than her husband would have been when he died. She wears her hair mid-length, in a shoulder-length flip that was stylish in Manhattan two years ago. The tailored red jacket has three brass buttons fastening the front, showing white blouse beneath, and snugly revealing a good figure. The calf-length black skirt matches the pumps and bow tie. She has the sororitylike, girlish, put-together, eager-to-please air of a real estate agent, but he reminds himself that she has run a twelve-store furniture company since her husband died.

And that interpersonal signals vary in different cities. Outside New York, people feel less obligated to show their toughness right off the bat.

"I kept Tabitha home from school, like you asked," she says, after checking Voort's ID, and matching the department photo to his New York license.

"These pictures look like mug shots," he jokes.

"You must have gotten up before dawn to get here by nine. I have coffee and bagels, the water kind, not the egg kind. My sister-in-law always tells me, pizza and bagels are never the same out of New York. She's a food snob."

"A bagel," says Voort, who is hungry, and smells the coffee, "sounds great."

"Should I bring Tabitha downstairs?"

"Let's talk first."

In the kitchen, she takes cellophane wrapping off a china platter of bagel halves, on a cedar table in a breakfast nook. There's a plastic tub of cream cheese, sliced Nova lox, and a small plate of cornichon pickles. "I didn't sleep last night, trying to figure out what you want. Tell me, Mr. Voort, why are you here?"

"I'm hoping you might be able to help me with something."

Pouring himself coffee, trying to keep the mood as relaxed as possible under the circumstances, he launches into the story, leaving out his friendship with Meechum, but telling her about the list, and the death of the man who had provided it.

"That's one crazy story," she says.

"I know. But when that fire happened, we decided to visit the places where the other people died, to check things out."

"I don't know what to tell you."

"Your husband's name was on the list. But so far we haven't the slightest idea what the list means."

"Can you repeat the other names?"

Voort does.

"I never heard of them," she says, shaking her head, looking like she means it, but her breathing, Voort notices, has deepened, with her color. "You're asking me to believe that Chuck didn't die by accident."

"It's possible. I'm sorry to open this all up again. But this is why I didn't want to tell you on the phone."

"But everybody here said, after he fell . . . the medical examiner . . . the police . . . the way he hit his head . . ." She is silent for a few moments. Then she says, "Murdered?"

"He tripped on a toy, officially, I understand," Voort says.

"My daughter always claimed she put that toy away that morning. And she's never been the same since. She stopped seeing friends. Her grades dropped. I took her to a therapist. He told me she feels guilty. She's punishing herself. She thinks everybody blames her."

"Do they?"

"You should have heard the remarks, nasty, ugly things, from kids at school. Now you're telling me she may have been right."

Mrs. Farber's mouth has drawn into a hard line, has changed into the mouth of an old lady, shrunken with accumulated experience. She is unsure what to think. Voort's words are too much to absorb all at once. *Murder* is a word most people relate to from television. It doesn't happen to them, or to people they know. Her cup is trembling and when she puts it on her saucer, it makes a clattering noise and liquid sloshes out. Voort appreciates the ugliness of the choice she is facing. Did her daughter accidentally cause the death of her husband? Or did a stranger murder the man?

"But nothing in the house was missing," she says, making the jump, in memory, to the day Chuck Farber died. "We weren't robbed. The neighbors didn't see anyone go into the house. Tabitha!" she calls, and a couple of minutes later, they hear a slow stirring up there, and muted footfalls coming down the carpeted stairs.

Lila Farber says, "Her grandparents, Chuck's parents, blame her. They try not to, but they don't act the same way with her anymore. I guess no one does."

"Maybe they need time," he says, uttering the platitude, but he knows, as he hears himself, and flashes to Camilla saying "I aborted that baby," that time has nothing to do with it. There are disappointments that cannot be cured by time, that cut off a piece of human heart.

And now the girl is standing in the doorway, fidgeting in her own home, a place where she should be comfortable. A child's face should never have to show such misery, Voort thinks. The mouth is downturned, the brown hair frumped up, ignored, the denim shirt bunched out of the jeans. The kid is unconcerned with how she looks. The brown eyes dart between Voort and a bare spot on the wall, as if Tabitha Farber associates any human contact with unpleasantness. She reminds Voort of dogs he has seen in the New York pound, mutts wary of contact, sulking in a cage, needing food and water from the very strangers they fear.

"This is Detective Voort, who I told you about," the mother says. The child moves stiffly to the table, and starts eating, not even looking at him. There is a compulsive quality to the movements, which do not reflect hunger, at least a caloric kind. She stuffs half a bagel into her mouth. She reaches for the pickles, but her mouth is still full.

Voort explains that he is working on a "mystery." She can help him. He is sorry she has been kept home from school today. She reaches for a plate on which Mrs. Farber has arranged, in a cute circle, small frosted black-and-white cookies. Tabitha knows quite well this is going to be one more interrogation. To her, he is one more adult ready to accuse her of murder in his own direct or indirect way.

"Aren't you going to say anything?" Mrs. Farber says. "Mr. Voort came all the way from New York to talk to you."

"Who cares."

"Tabitha!"

"I left Choosie on the stairs," she mutters. "Can I go now?"

"Choosie's her stuffed moose," Mrs. Farber tells Voort.

"Actually," Voort says, "I think maybe you put the moose away, in the closet, like you said."

"I don't care what you think."

"Stop it," Mrs. Farber snaps.

Voort ignores the mother. "Why *should* you care?" he tells the girl, who is now eating cookies. "You never saw me before. I could say anything to get you to talk. Nobody else believes you. Why should I?"

"Mom, can I go upstairs?"

"No."

"I have a stomachache."

"I bet you do," Voort says. "Have more cookies."

"I will if I want to."

"Hey, am I stopping you? Eat the whole plate."

"You want to know if I was angry at my father? If I had a

fight with my father the night before he died? That's what everybody keeps asking. I had a fight with him. Okay? I killed him."

"If you say so."

"I do say so! I do!"

"Oh, God," Mrs. Farber says, burying her head in her hands.

"Well, that's that, then," Voort says, to the top of the girl's head, now pointed at the parquet floor, where a small circle of crumbs is growing. "You think I'm just one more stranger here to bother you. You're thinking, I bet . . ."

"You don't know what I'm thinking."

"You're thinking I don't care about you. And you're right. I never met you. Why should I care? Hell, you don't even say hello when I come to your house."

The kid looks up, her mouth full. "I didn't ask you to come here."

Voort nods. "But I'll tell you who I do care about," he says. "It's this lady in New York. She's the same age your father was, when he died. She has people she loves, like your father did. She won't talk to me, just like you. She's sort of a jerk, actually," and he is gratified to see the girl's mouth twitch, as if she suppressed a giggle.

Voort continues, "She's a doctor, and someone is trying to hurt her. *Just like someone hurt your dad.*"

"I hurt him. I said so."

"Maybe someone will push *her* down the stairs, the way they pushed him. And maybe some innocent girl will get blamed for it in New York. And maybe no one will believe *her* either."

The hand reaches for the plate of cookies. It takes a cookie. But it doesn't put the cookie in the mouth.

"Yep," Voort says, leaning toward the kid, concentrating on her. "We both know *someone* left that stuffed animal on the stairs, because it was there. So if you didn't leave it, who did?"

The girl looks up sharply. She is a child, and for two years has concentrated all her will on defending herself, on denying accusations, on blocking the fact that the stuffed animal was lying on the top of the stairs in the first place. It has never even reached the point where she has been required to even try to imagine a stranger sneaking into her house and moving her toys around.

"I said," Voort says, "if you didn't leave that stuffed animal on the stairs, someone else did. Unless you're telling me your father played with stuffed animals. That, after you left the house, he went into your closet and took out Choosie and dropped it himself. Is that what you're saying?"

"Yes, if you'll go away now," the kid says, but she sounds slightly less aggressive.

"Good," Voort says, rising, "we know what happened. Your father put the toy on the stairs, and then tripped over it. I'm glad to hear you confirm it. Because if someone *else* hurt your father, then he's still out there, he got away with it, nobody even put him in jail, and now he's going to hurt someone else."

"Mommy, I have a headache."

Voort, shaking his head, says, "Of course, if you're not telling the truth this time, and the lady gets hurt, this time you *will* be responsible. Because this time you can stop it. You can help save her. You can be a hero."

"Leave me alone." But the girl's shoulders seem to be caving in.

Voort says, more softly, watching her posture, and face,

and throwing all his will into the truth, "Why else do you think I'd come all the way out here. It isn't my job to find out what happened to your father. It's my job to help the lady. She treats kids who get sick. She helps kids like you. If you tell me you left the toy on the stairs, I'll walk out of here right now and go back to the airport and you'll never see me again. But if you lie, and the person who hurt your father hurts the lady, I'll be back to tell you what happened, and show you pictures of it."

The girl starts to cry.

She looks up. "Why would someone hurt my father?" she asks.

Mrs. Farber slides her chair close, and puts her arms around the girl. Her eyes are streaming, too.

"Look at me," Voort says, putting the truth into his face. "All you have to do is tell me what you remember. It's not a test. There's no wrong answer. It's impossible to say the wrong thing. Anything you say is a big help."

She says nothing.

Then she says, doubtfully, "I don't know what I remember anymore."

"That makes sense, especially since no one believed you before. We can stay here all morning and talk about it. We can play games, memory games, to help you remember. I can come back this afternoon if you like, or tomorrow, if you want to think about it."

"Tomorrow?"

"Do you want me to do that?"

And the girl, looking up, says, "But if we wait until to-morrow, what if that lady gets hurt?"

Half an hour later, after she's calmer, after he's told the child the story, the details, made her feel a part of it, let her see his own confusion, he says to her, willing to break it off at any second, if she resists, "I know you hate doing this. But close your eyes and imagine when your father was alive."

"I miss him."

"Remember, I don't care what anyone else told you to think. I don't care if the whole world told you that you left Choosie on the stairs. Think back. Picture that morning. Do you see Choosie?"

A nod.

"Where is Choosie? I want to know what *you* remember."

"What I *really* remember?"

"Sometimes the adults can be wrong and the kid can be right."

"I don't have to close my eyes. I know what happened."

Voort's heart is pounding.

The girl says, "In my closet, the dolls are on the top shelf. The stuffed animals are on the next shelf. And the games are under that. I always put Choosie in the closet."

The buzzing of the lawn equipment outside grows enormous, fills the room.

Tabitha bursts out, in a fury, "I never left Choosie on the stairs in my life!"

Half an hour later Mrs. Farber comes down from upstairs, where she's put the sobbing girl to bed.

"I don't know what to think," she says. "It's back to her original story, but with your extra information . . . I just don't know what to say."

Voort is standing at the front window, looking out at a vision of normalcy, safety, achievement, prosperity. An

Evanston City squad car cruises past, down Church Street, stirring up leaves from the gutter. He inhales a vestigial aroma of last night's wood fire. Maybe Mrs. Farber sat around reading a book, or watching a television show, while the girl did math homework upstairs.

"There are all kinds of specialists in the world," he says. "A safecracker makes breaking into a bank look easy. A forger does it with a counterfeit bill."

"Is that what you call it if someone made my husband's death look like an accident? A 'specialist'?"

"I'm just saying they exist."

She stares into space. "While I was upstairs I called New York. I talked to someone named Mickie. I understand you're quite a respected detective out there."

"Do you mind if I ask a few more questions?"

"I didn't mind before, why should I now?"

"If you imagine that it wasn't an accident, how could someone have gotten into your house that day?"

"The door was open."

"So your husband was mowing the lawn, he goes inside, someone follows, is that it? I don't see a lot of people on that street right now. Is it usually that empty?"

"Not in the summer."

"The killer," Voort says, "and stop me if this is too upsetting, breaks your husband's neck and throws him down the stairs. Maybe he hits his head, going down, on the shelf. The killer then goes into your daughter's room, and puts the toy on the top of the landing, so everyone thinks it was an accident."

"But why go to the trouble? And why Chuck?"

"That's what I want to know."

"You started this."

"Well, was there anyone who hated him, who fought with him? Did he owe money or have money problems in business?"

"No. And I run the business now. I know it was sound back then."

"Forgive me, but was your marriage happy?"

"He wasn't sleeping around, if that's what you mean."

"Excuse me, but how about you? I have to ask."

"You're pretty damn polite with all those 'excuse mes' and 'forgive mes.'" She closes her eyes. She says, in a voice indicating that she is controlling her temper, "I wasn't sleeping around then. I haven't even slept with anyone since he died."

"Was he active politically?" Voort says.

She looks surprised. "Politics?"

"It's just one thread. One of the other people was active in that area. I know your husband was arrested a long time ago in a demonstration."

"Thirty *years* ago. And no, he wasn't active politically, if you're talking about the Democrats and Republicans. And his fund-raising was humanitarian, not political."

Voort lets the curtain fall back. The pace of his heartbeat has just picked up. The living room has all the earmarks, from the casual look of the place, of a room used for day-to-day family activity, not just guests. The couch is deep, of Haitian cotton, in pastel blue. The sitting chairs are matching, faded and soft. The Tibetan carpet is deeper blue, and thick, with pillows on it large enough to allow people to lie on them as they watch the television in the cherrywood wall unit. Paintings show winter scenes: a New England village in a snowfall. A boy rushing down a hill on a sled.

"What kind of fund-raising?" Voort says.

"For overseas kids," she says. "He raised hundreds of thousands for the SAP program. He was great at it."

"SAP?"

"Serbian Aid Project. The money went for food and blankets, for children displaced by the fighting. My husband's mom was Serbian. There's a huge Serbian community in Chicago, and let me tell you, they have a bad reputation over there, undeserved. They're the nicest people in the world. We went there for a visit. Nobody helps the Serbs except other Serbs."

"I guess you have to be born there to really understand," Voort says, who is remembering scenes he's seen on television of Muslim women machine-gunned by Serb soldiers, and lying dead in the snow.

"People even try to stop the aid program. One time a woman came here, right to this house, from the government, to ask him to cut out the fund-raising. A bureaucrat. A big fat woman. She made up some story about SAP being a terrorist front. She told Chuck only a little bit of the money went for food. The rest went for explosives, and guns, she said."

"But your husband didn't believe that."

"He said, Who are you? CIA? The CIA isn't supposed to operate in this country, and the lady said, I remember this, she said, 'I'm not "operating." I'm just talking.'"

"Your husband didn't stop it, I take it."

"My husband," Mrs. Farber says, "hasn't trusted the U.S. government since the cops broke his legs at the Chicago convention. And the woman had no proof. Chuck asked her, Where's the proof? And she says, get this, 'Trust me.' Any time the government doesn't like someone, they call them terrorists. Have you ever heard of a Serbian terrorist? Was it the Serbs who bombed Saba and Shattila? Was it the Serbs who blew up that Pan Am flight?"

"Nope."

"Our government has an agenda, believe me. Have you ever heard of a single Serb hijacking a plane?"

Voort is amazed at the transformation in a woman who, until a few moments ago, had struck him as peaceful, friendly.

"You want to know who the real terrorists are?" she says. "The Israelis, the way they treat Palestinians. They *bomb* them. *That's* terrorism. They *bombed* a refugee camp. And us, our very own government, we give guns to people and then ten years later we fight them. Gadhafi was our friend, then an enemy. Afghanistan was a friend, then an enemy. Serbs don't have time to be terrorists. They're just trying to hold on to their own land, and feed kids."

"How much money did your husband raise for them?"

"Plenty," she says, in an exaggerated way that gives him a feeling that the SAP is actually a small, unimportant operation. "Although since he died, the project fell apart. He was special at raising money. He had a talent for it, a passion. What nationality are you?" she asks, peering at him in a different way now, which he finds unpleasant. She seems ready to change her opinion of him based on his answer.

"Dutch, but my family's been living here for three hundred years."

"Ah, Dutch," she nods, as if some preconception has been confirmed, as if he is an immigrant who just stepped off the boat from Rotterdam. "Everybody loves the Dutch," she says. "What's your secret?"

"Nonaggression."

"Meaning the Serbs defend themselves, and that counts as aggression?"

Voort holds up his hands. "I didn't say that."

"Are you suggesting the CIA killed my husband to stop his money-raising activities?"

"That sounds as ridiculous to me," he says, "as I hope it does to you."

She thinks about it. Her breathing returns to normal. Her flush fades. "I guess," she says, and subsides back into the friendly hostess role, the antagonism gone from the surface, deep down inside again, out of view.

He takes the next two hours searching through Chuck Farber's old papers, and finds nothing. Then he gets the phone numbers of some friends, and people in the SAP organization. He gives Lila Farber the address of the hotel where he's staying, and asks her to call if she thinks of something.

"You want some oatmeal raisin cookies to take with you when you go?" she says. "I made them last night."

"That would be nice," Voort says. Now they're back to being polite.

"What do I say now? Thanks for coming? It's been interesting? I'd hate to have your job," Lila Farber says.

The Serbian Aid Project, Voort discovers, an hour later, in the western Chicago suburb of Cicero, turns out to be two guys in a basement, surrounded by posters of hungry children, who are apparently having trouble even paying the rent. And Chuck Farber's old friends and coworkers, who he meets over the next day and a half, add nothing of seeming value to what Voort knows about the man.

By Tuesday afternoon Voort's in a cab, heading back to O'Hare, for a flight to Seattle, when his cell phone rings.

"I think someone just tried to kill me," says the frightened voice of Dr. Jill Towne.

TEN

I would have been dead by morning, and the medical examiner would have called it an accident."

At midnight, Voort, Mickie, and Jill Towne sit amid the disarray of construction in her Fifth Avenue penthouse apartment, thirty floors above her ground-floor office. The fingerprint crew has left. The living room is cluttered with furniture that has been moved from her den and bedroom while workers redo walls, paint, build closets, varnish floors, rip out plumbing.

Plastic sheeting blocks off rooms in the apartment where work has been progressing.

"I'm allergic to the dust," she says. "I've been sleeping and eating in the living room while they finish the job, which should happen one of these years."

"What happened tonight?" Voort says.

She seems smaller than she did in her office, but perhaps that comes from vulnerability. She is curled on an easy chair, with a wool afghan over her knees and ankles, so that socked feet stick out. She's wearing matching denim jeans and long-sleeved shirt, open at the collar to show a white turtleneck. Track lighting strategically located in the room highlights the auburn in her hair, and Voort can see, from the couch, where he sits with Mickie, directly across a glass coffee table from her, that her green eyes are rimmed with amber, and that iridescent bits of light float in the black pupils, like tiny stars. She is a constellation of attractions.

"Tuesday's are always the same," she says, holding a mug of spiced cider in both hands, and taking small, comforting sips every once in a while. "New York's so busy that you have to give yourself at least one night of quiet a week, actually schedule it, or it never happens. Tuesday's that night for me. I quit at five. I do my exercise walk through the park. I come back and change and do laps on the twenty-ninth floor, in the pool. I order takeout at Taste of Bombay, light a fire," she says, indicating the glassed-in fireplace, off at the moment. "I open a bottle of Merlot, and a novel, and I read until it's time to go to sleep. I even take the phone off the hook."

"Every single week," Voort says.

She nods. "By nine o'clock, I'm in this chair."

The room, like her office downstairs, showcases a tasteful collection of expensive artifacts collected from travels overseas. The rugs are western Turkish, woven kilims, dyed with dull vegetable colors: dun, moss, mustard. The fertility goddess is red clay, with painted lips, and it occupies a locked, glass display case, lit as if in a museum. Built-in mahogany shelves fill the east wall and contain, in their alcoves, medical books, photo books, novels by women authors, Voort has noticed, and an occasional musical instrument: a small stringed Turkish lyre, a wooden drum from Kenya, a hand-carved ivory mouth flute from Madagascar.

"I can't believe this is happening," she says.

The sliding glass door is open to a wraparound corner

patio, which is larger than the interior space, and fronts both Fifth Avenue and Sixty-seventh Street. From below, above the distant swoosh of cabs cruising Fifth Avenue, Voort hears a rougher sound, a roar which it takes him a moment to identify. It's a big animal, in the Central Park zoo; a bear or lion confined in an exhibit, doomed to perpetually voicing its confused rage, its bestial disappointment.

"Tonight started out the same. I turned on the fire. Reading, I started to feel sick after awhile," she says. "I was having trouble focusing. I noticed a dull throb in my chest."

"You were thirsty, too, you said," says Mickie, who heard it all before Voort arrived, whom Voort dispatched here the second he hung up with Jill Towne, when she called Chicago, hours ago.

"If I weren't a doctor, I would have thought it was the flu. My assistant has it, in the office."

"What told you it wasn't the flu?"

She laughs wryly. "You. You freaked me out the other day, even though I didn't show it. I've been jumpy since you showed up, thinking about those 'accidents' of yours. So I think, when I started feeling bad, that in another corner of my mind I was matching symptoms to other kinds of ailments. Wooziness. Blurred vision. Chest pain. Like the flu, all right, but it's also like," she says, sipping hot cider, "carbon monoxide poisoning."

"So she checks the gas fireplace," Mickie says, "which is on."

"I thought carbon monoxide came from cars," Voort says.

"It's an exhaust by-product," Jill Towne says, more comfortable with an academic explanation than an admission that someone just tried to kill her. "It can also come from a gas stove, or even an automatic clothes dryer. The exhaust gets blocked from escaping fully. The CO gas leaks out. You can't smell it even normally, and in here," she adds weakly, indicating, with a small feminine swish of her right hand, the construction on the other side of the hanging plastic sheet, "the place smells of paint anyway. There was no chance I would have detected it."

"How did you know, then?"

"I checked the monitor," she says, this time nodding up at a small, white, squarish plastic apparatus on the ceiling, shaped similarly to the adjacent smoke alarm. "And the battery was loose."

"You connected it," Mickie says.

"By that time I was seeing double. It went off."

"The Duracell killer," Mickie says, "strikes again."

"Where do you get your sense of humor?" Dr. Towne says.

"What's the matter with *mine*? What's the problem with yours?"

"Could the battery have gotten loose by itself?" Voort asks.

"Of course."

"So it could have been a real accident."

"Absolutely," she says.

Voort wants to scream with frustration. He is accustomed to dealing professionally with overt acts of violence. Shootings or stabbings which, horrible as they are, are at least usually clear in terms of what they mean. He can tell how they happened, and, generally, why. The brutality of these acts is an unmistakable public display of intent, an acknowledgment of the conflict lines between detective and criminal. The crude violence is a laying out of rules, in a way, a dare, an admission, and it usually gives him the sense, even if it is occasionally misleading, that he is ultimately smarter than a killer, and will identify him or her in the end.

But this quiet malevolence is something new, in scope, in sophistication, and in a subtlety he has not until now encountered in the sex crimes unit of the New York City police.

So now the three of them go over the apartment, finding nothing stolen, or even out of place. The medicines in the bathroom vanity are exactly where she left them. The cups and dishes in the kitchen cabinet have not been moved, even an inch. The books are slightly dusty, from the day's construction, and this means no one has touched them. Since the elevator opens directly into the apartment, and requires a key to open, he knows that whoever dismantled the CO alarm either arrived with the work crew or entered from the patio.

"But we're thirty stories up," she says.

"Could someone climb over from the next penthouse?"

"I know my neighbor. He's the nicest guy in the world."

"I'm not talking about him. I'm talking about using his patio."

"I guess so. But his patio is sealed from the building next door to him by a big roll of barbed wire. He's in England this week. No one's in his apartment, but I have a key to the divider separating our patios."

She stretches, as if tired, a completely natural movement, arms out, back arched, toes out, but to Voort, it is as if he has been struck by a blast of raw sensuality. He has often heard the expression, uttered by women of men, that they "undressed a woman with their eyes." But Voort has always known that the term is untrue. It implies that a man works backwards, sees the woman, makes the conscious decision to envision her naked, and proceeds, in order, in his mind, to strip her of clothes.

The truth is that, under circumstances like these, to a man, the woman he is admiring might as well *be* naked. Her clothing seems irrelevant to him, a stage prop. He sees the bare body and responds accordingly, as Voort, who feels an itching in his groin, does now.

"Let's see if the wire's been cut," he says, a thickness in his throat, and, leading the other two, goes outside where she unlocks the redwood divider separating the penthouse patios of Dr. Towne and her neighbor. The lights are off in the neighbor's apartment. The sliding door is locked. A security light is on, on the adjacent roof, and in its glare, reflections moving in the window, they thread the maze of white patio furniture and reach the barbed wire on the other side.

"It's not cut," Mickie says.

They also find no fingerprints on Jill's sliding glass door. No footprints tracking construction dust anywhere. A twenty-four-hour locksmith arrives to change her locks, and Voort keeps the old one. He will bring it to the police lab, to see if scratch marks inside the cylinder will show it was picked.

By the time the locksmith leaves it is one in the morning, and Jill Towne asks if they are hungry.

"No thanks."

"Then why is your stomach growling?" she asks. "I have roast beef and kaiser rolls, hot mustard, pickles, and cole slaw from the deli downstairs. The creamy kind, not the vinegar kind. I'm starving."

She seems fully recovered, and sways into the kitchen. There must be automatic controls for the stereo in there because it comes on abruptly, emitting a soft saxophone melody, a jazz tune Voort recognizes, a Ryebeck song called "Blue Love." Voort has to admire her toughness. She returns, humming along with the music as she lays out an assortment of cold-cut deli meats, sliced kaiser rolls, a liter of Coke, and a couple of frosty unopened Sam Adams beers.

"You recover fast," Mickie says.

She says, spreading mustard on rye bread, "Thanks, but I'm terrified. I'm just hiding it." And to Voort, "What's the next step?"

"I think you know that," he says, reaching for an opener. "I asked you a question in the park two days ago, and you still haven't answered."

"You mean, about my patients."

"About why all those government types have been visiting you, and asking you to stop doing something."

She takes a bite of sandwich, and nods. "They want me to stop treating one of my patients," she says, surprising Voort. "That's what they want."

"Who?" Mickie says. "And why?"

"You ever hear of a man named Abu Bin Hussein?"

Mickie straightens in his seat. "The Saudi heir who funds terrorists? The one hiding out in Afghanistan? I saw an ABC Special on him. *He's* your patient?"

"I'm a doctor," Jill Towne says. "Not a politician. Do you know what Doctors Without Borders means? It means just that. Like the Red Cross. He's sick."

"He's the one the FBI blames for blowing up the U.S. embassy in Dakar."

She has colored, deeply. "They haven't proved it."

"But you treat him anyway."

"I'm not going to justify myself to you," says Dr. Jill Towne.

In the silence Voort gets up and opens the glass sliding door and walks out to the long, wide, wraparound patio. His heels click on the stone. There's a grill here, and redwood outdoor furniture. He sees small, hardy potted trees. Leaning over the brick wall, he looks down at the glow of cruising headlights on Fifth Avenue, and yellowish orbs, lampposts, dotting walkways meandering through the dark expanse of Central Park.

Again comes the deep animal complaint from the zoo, of rage or confinement. A wild creature has been caged by humans down there, and its disappointment mounts to a breaking point.

Voort is remembering the day the embassy was bombed, in Africa. He remembers seeing rescue workers on TV carrying bodies from the rubble. The scene shifts, and now he is remembering a different bombing, this time of the marine barracks in Beirut, where Meechum's big brother Al died.

Voort remembers sitting in Meechum's den, with his friend, just like they did almost every late afternoon, watching "Star Trek," or "Combat" reruns, except this time they were hearing the tinny wail of real ambulances from the set, and watching real marines, not actors, with tears streaming down their faces, as they carried stretchers on which lay their bleeding comrades.

On the TV, the marine barracks had resembled, in an odd, enlarged way, a cutout of a little girl's dollhouse. The front facade had fallen off, from the explosion, and inside, the rooms were exposed, some of them preserved perfectly, death dioramas, complete with beds, dressers, posters of sexy actresses in swimsuits.

Stray beams had swung like pendulums amid dust clouds, and he and Meechum had heard, over the shocked announcer, who was talking about "low-impact explosives" and "shock waves," the cries of bystanders, and sharper, more terrible moans of pain coming from beneath wreckage.

"Maybe Al was out when the bomb went off," he'd told Meechum, as phones had started ringing all over the house; in the front hall, and kitchen and bedrooms, a cacophony of extensions, of electric warnings, like church bells signaling alarm in a town. Both Meechum and his mom had been afraid to answer, but of course they had, and throughout the next few hours, while Al's fate hung in the balance, more calls had come from Washington. They were from Al's friends, officers he'd served with, the mayor, a congressman from Schenectady. A captain from the marine PR office kept phoning to say, comforting them with news but torturing them with uncertainty, "No word yet."

But finally the captain had told Lynn, "Your son died instantly. The ceiling collapsed on him while he slept."

Now Voort blows out air and steps back into the living room. Jill is still on the couch, but is not eating. Mickie has retreated to a corner, and pretends interest in the artifacts he's examining, from her shelves.

"A lot of people find it hard to understand what I do," she says.

"You get paid for it?" Mickie says.

"Prime Minister Begin, of Israel," she says, "at one time was called a terrorist. So was Nelson Mandela, and then he became President of South Africa. So was Thomas Jefferson."

"Give me a break," Mickie snaps.

"I'm only saying," Jill Towne says, having reconsidered her earlier touchiness, "that he founded a movement. That he led resistence. Sometimes these things all depend on your point of view."

"Lady, you have one fucked up point of view," says Mickie, the ex-marine.

Voort switches the subject back to business. "I wonder if we've found our link."

She swings toward him, her green eyes bright with interest. "What is it?"

"Meechum warned me it could sound crazy. But you, Alan Clark in Montana, and Chuck Farber are all connected to terrorists. Or at least the government says you are."

"Serbs," Jill Towne disagrees, "haven't pulled off any terrorist act here that I know of."

"But a Chicago cop told Mrs. Farber they might be planning one," Mickie says. "The government knows more about these things than us. At least I hope they do."

"Are you suggesting that some government 'hit squad' is going around, arranging the accidents?" Dr. Towne says, making a face that shows how absurd she considers the thought.

Mickie shrugs. "You ask me, knocking off terrorists is not such a bad idea."

"I'm not a terrorist," says Jill Towne stiffly, standing up.

"Keep telling yourself that, then go fix up the guy who is."

"Stop it," Voort says. "We know about three attacks so far. All have a political element, but none involve the same cause. In fact, the victims are pretty far apart on the spectrum. Geographically, too, although they're all in the

United States. What I don't understand is, if someone wants to stop Abu Bin Hussein, why not go after *him*? Why you? And why not track down the alleged Serb terrorists overseas? Why a fund-raiser in Chicago?"

"Because they can't get to them overseas," Jill suggests.

"Because we're not dealing with government people," Mickie says, addressing Voort, ignoring Jill. "Our boys," he says, meaning the perpetrators, "have highly specific information about their victims. They're sophisticated on one level. But at the same time they're operating under limitations. Our government has plenty of people overseas to carry out operations, so it's not going to turn out to be government. And anyway," he adds, "the government doesn't go around arranging 'accidents.' That thinking is bad TV. Hell, the army kidnapped General Noriega in Panama, and brought him back for trial. They could have killed him. The FBI spent weeks talking cultists out of their compound in Idaho. They didn't go in shooting. And they didn't arrange for the boiler to blow up by 'accident.' They put them in jail."

"So we're looking for a small group, you think," says Dr. Towne. "But who?"

"It's a guess," Voort says. "So far we only have skeletal information on three of the five people on Meechum's list. We don't know if the list is a complete rundown of victims, or the tip of some other plan. And we might not even know that after we check the last two names."

Mickie tells Voort, referring to the doctor as if she is not there, "She follows the same schedule every Tuesday. Were they watching her? Did they know she would turn on the gas tonight, or did they fix up the fireplace days ago, and bingo, tonight's the night she stayed home?"

Voort, turning, catches his reflection in the dark sliding

glass window, and becomes aware suddenly of other apartments, higher up, taller buildings across the park, or diagonally across Sixty-seventh Street. Thousands of New Yorkers own expensive telescopes, and turn them not toward the moon, but at neighbors' windows. Others stroll into electronic surveillance shops, street-level stores where they can buy electric listening devices, or directional microphones as powerful as those employed by the FBI.

Voort is now very aware that at least a dozen balconies and watertowers look down on Jill Towne's rooftop fishbowl.

Mickie is saying, "I don't mind flying," meaning, Voort knows, that his partner has no desire to baby-sit for Jill.

Voort says, "I think we should cover these windows up."

"Shit," Mickie says.

"Why?" Jill asks, and then puts her hand to her mouth. "Oh, my God," she says. "Are you kidding?"

"I'll change my air tickets over to you," Voort tells Mickie minutes later, when the curtains have been drawn.

"And Hugh?" Mickie asks, meaning, Do we tell Addonizio what's going on yet?

"Not until we have more. Dr. Towne, I'm curious. Do you have some trip planned soon, to treat your special patient?"

She looks surprised. "How did you know?"

Voort nods. "I think whoever is after you may know we have Meechum's list. But it hasn't stopped them. They still came after you. That tells me they're on a timetable, and willing to take risks. Also, if you don't mind my asking, how did you end up with this patient? There are a million other doctors in the world. Iraqi doctors, friendly to his cause. Why you?"

"I took care of him when he was a teenager, in Saudi

Arabia. He trusts me. And he has a special medical problem that's hard to treat."

"What is it?" Mickie asks.

"I'd rather not say."

"As in, doctor-murderer privilege?"

"As in, I tell you and then you tell someone else, and they use it against him. His medicines dry up. Labs bar me from entering, or visas disappear, or someone is waiting for him at the treatment location. I'm sorry. It's against my principles."

Mickie snorts. "Your principles."

Jill Towne colors, then reaches for the plate, and, quite deliberately, picks up her sandwich and begins to eat. But now that they are coming up with a plan of action she does not seem furious, or frightened anymore, or even defensive. She seems, to all appearances, quietly secure.

Voort cannot afford to judge her at this point. He is seeing, in his mind's eye, his first detective teacher, his very own father. In his head he is at the dinner table, and his father, between mouthfuls of beef Stroganoff, is saying to nine-year-old Voort, "You're a kid now, so the law looks like it's always right. The bad guys steal, or murder, or hit old ladies. The good cops catch them. But if you become a cop, sometimes you'll see that the good guys are worse than the bad, but the bad guys will be protected by the law. Do you know what you will do when that happens?"

"I don't, Dad."

His father, looking down at him with love, and sympathy for the choices he will one day face, says, "You'll enforce the law, pal. You'll hate it. But I hope you do it. The law is smarter than you in the end. It is older and wiser and you serve it, not the other way around. But one of the hardest parts of being a cop is when the law will seem wrong."

"But what if it *is* wrong?"

"If it's that wrong, Connie, quit. But be honorable either way."

He can't quit now. Meechum is dead and Jill Towne may be the link he needs, and he tried quitting for a while anyway and it doesn't work. Plus, despite her disclosure and his disgust over it, he cannot help the powerful chemical draw that he feels for her. He is a breeder. He was put on earth to multiply. He has not experienced sex with a woman in months, and is filled with rampaging chemicals. A part of him is every man who ever threw away a career for a woman, charged in front of traffic for a woman, followed a woman the way a moth mindlessly flies toward a fire on a summer night.

He knows, without having seen them, that her legs will be strong, and lean, and that when she runs, the cords will stand out on the sides of her thighs, and on the back of her calves, as they flex. He knows, from the way her shirt hangs loosely, that her belly will be flat, from her exercise walks, and her swimming. Her breasts will be small. Her rib cage will be slightly visible when her clothes are off. Her ass, from the way it moved when she went into the kitchen, will be firm, and round. Despite himself, Voort experiences an itching in his groin.

He smells her, even over the other odors in the room, the construction, paint and dust, and the general urban grittiness washing in, even thirty stories up, through the vents of her air conditioners. She has a fresh-laundered scent. She smells clean. Undiluted.

"What now?" she says, staring back at Voort, and it occurs to him that she is also feeling a physical draw.

"Mickie will check out the other names on Meechum's list, and he'll fly to North Carolina, where Meechum was last posted. I should be able to arrange a police guard for you."

"You mean a patrolman?"

"For this kind of thing, if it's done, usually the department assigns a detective."

"What about you?"

Mickie, across the room, makes a sound in the back of his throat, a guttural reproach, a warning.

"Well, I have things I need to do. I have to talk to people in New York," he says. "I can't be sitting around in your office all day."

"I'll come with you. I want to know what's going on, too."

"You're going to close your practice?"

She's silent. She can't close her practice. Her patients need her, her frown says.

"Anyway," Voort says, "interviews go easier when I'm alone. But I can keep you informed. The department has good people to stay with you. Besides, I'll work closely with you because you're our best link to figuring this thing out."

"Then share something now. Who will you be talking to?"

"I'd like to start with," Voort says with a professional calm that masks his concern, "the FBI agents who interviewed you. I want to try to access their files. Maybe Chuck Farber's in there, or Lester Levy."

"You think the FBI is involved?"

Mickie snorts. "Let's not forget the White House," he quips from across the room.

"No, I don't think they're involved," Voort says, "because of what we were talking about earlier. But I'm hoping they may give us a way to find out who is. Maybe there's a rivalry between terrorist groups. Or what if they're forming coalitions? Alliances? I just hope they're all in someone's files somewhere."

Mickie goes to the phone, calls Delta Airlines, and checks if there's a flight he can catch in the morning to Seattle. Voort tells Jill Towne, "I also want to visit West Point, and try to trace whatever Meechum did in the army before he quit. Mickie'll work from the present back to the past. I'll start in the past and try to work it up to the present. Meechum lied about where he worked, so I'm thinking it's important. I need to find out where he worked."

"What about the press? Why not tell them what's going on?" Jill suggests. "Let them publicize it."

"My favorite people," Mickie says.

"We don't *know* what's going on," Voort says. "There's no proof of anything, not a single piece of proof of any kind. Now, do you want me to stay here tonight? Or would you rather sleep somewhere else?"

He wants to sleep here, he tells himself, because, rattled tonight, she may remember something useful. She is vulnerable, and in that state, people often talk too much.

"You don't have to stay," she says, looking him full in the face in a way that suggests she does not want to be alone. He notices her lips, the enticing fullness of them, as she says, "I'm pretty tired."

But of course, when he insists on staying, she looks grateful.

Mickie throws on his coat. "I'm outta here, Con Man. I'll call you from Seattle."

Then he has left, and Voort is alone with her in the

apartment. With the back rooms closed off, and the curtains shut, the place suddenly seems cramped and intimate. It's like the first time a date brings you to her apartment, Voort thinks, and you see her bed, except in this case the real bed is covered with plastic sheeting, in the bedroom. Tonight's makeshift bed will be the foldout couch.

"Thank you for staying," Jill Towne says, as he helps her get the couch ready, as their hands touch spreading the fitted sheet to the mattress, as they fluff up pillows together. They stand on opposite sides of the bed, patting down a quilt.

"I'll take the floor," he says.

"You'll take the bed," she says, the utterance of even the word seeming to have meaning. "I've slept in the back of cargo planes, and huts in Zaire, and sitting in a wooden chair once even, in a Ugandan police station. The air mattress is as good as a Sealy Posturepedic."

"Good. I love air mattresses," says Voort, taking it from her, starting to blow it up.

She disappears into the bathroom, and he hears the noises of her nightly preparations. He hears a bathroom vanity close. He hears water running. He hears the frothy noise of teeth being brushed, just the way he used to hear it when Camilla used to stay over, and ready herself for his bed.

When she comes out she's wearing lemon-colored silk pajamas, buttoned up front, and her toenails are painted red, and there's a new smell, Crest or Colgate, a minty smell, the hygienic smell of a woman who takes good care of herself.

When the light hits the pajamas a certain way, he sees

the outline of one slim, tapering thigh. Then she turns back to him, and the silhouette is gone.

"Thanks," she says, turning the light out.

"I'm doing my job," says Voort, lying on her air mattress, under her quilt, in her apartment. He can't believe that he already has a hard-on.

She says, stiffly, "I'm doing my job, too."

ELEVEN

*H*e shouldn't be kissing her. He tells himself to stop. He tells himself not to get involved with her while the case is active. But he can't reason, he's helpless before the chemistry. He was sleeping when she woke him with the lightest touch on his shoulder, and the embarrassed words, "I have to admit that I'm scared."

Now it's still night and the room is black, even the city lights blocked by drawn curtains. It's dark as a bad mistake, and when he pulls away from her, trying to stop, he feels her gaze on his body without seeing it.

Then her arms pull him down again. Her legs clasp his hips. Her silk pajama top is unbuttoned, so her breasts bunch against his chest with the cool fabric.

Drunk with the perfume and sex smell, he enters her.

"Oh, Voort."

He turns her over and takes her from behind. Her heat rises into him. He relishes the power of her muscles, pulling him in, clenching him inside her.

But an alarm is ringing.

Voort opens his eyes.

He is alone, lying on her air mattress, on the carpet of

her living room, and the quilt on top of him is wet from his own sweat only. Not from hers.

Amused, Dr. Towne stands over him, looking down. The lights are on and the curtains closed, but he sees the bright fringe of daylight shining between the lengths of fabric.

"You talked in your sleep," she says.

"What did I say?"

She winks. "I couldn't make words out, but you seemed to be having fun."

Voort's penis is so hard he is unable to get out from under the quilt, lest he reveal himself. He is still breathing deeply, with excitement but not satiation. Sweat slides down his spine. His groin is moist, his throat parched. The sense that they have just made love is not dissipating. He knows it never happened, but the dream was so overpowering he feels as if he has kissed those lips, run his hands over her breasts, shoulders, white sloping neck.

"Go ahead, lie there," she says. "You like eggs?"

"Scrambled, if you don't mind."

She turns away, in the buttoned-up, lemon-colored silk pajamas, and she pads into the kitchen, on bare feet. He hears a refrigerator close, and the sharp metallic clang of a pot hitting an iron burner. His hard-on begins to fade.

"There's an extra toothbrush in the vanity, still in the pack," she calls out. "Use the green towel. If you want to shave, there's a man's razor on the top shelf, with a new blade."

Voort feels a flash of jealousy. A man's razor for whom?

Twenty minutes later he's downing a hearty breakfast of scrambled eggs with melted cheddar and green peppers mixed in, wheat toast with butter, crispy bacon strips, pulpy orange juice, and hot sweet coffee rivaling the taste of Mickie's expensive brands.

"All things in moderation, including moderation," she jokes, picking at her own, smaller, girlish portion. "I like to watch a man eat."

The intimate comment goes with the sensation, which he cannot shake, that they *did* make love, and that he is already on familiar terms with the contours and private places of her body. It is an awkward feeling, because it gives him a natural urge to lean close when he speaks to her, as he would with a real lover. It makes him want to touch her neck, a familiarity that a lover would welcome. It gives him a false and dangerous sense, under present circumstances, that he knows her better than he really does.

The only positive aspect of the situation is that he is at least aware of it, and he can keep himself under control.

"More coffee, sir?" She's definitely flirting.

"Thanks."

"I didn't open the curtains, even though it's morning. That was the right thing to do, wasn't it?"

"Do the same at your office. With those big windows there, someone could be able to watch you talking on the phone. And speaking of the phone," Voort says, writing down a number on his business card, "call these guys and have them sweep the line. It's just a precaution, but until they do, and even afterward, actually, don't talk about your plans, where you're going, anything like that."

"That sounds a bit extreme, don't you think?"

"We don't know who we're dealing with, and what kind of access they might have to you. Try to make sure you aren't alone when you go out. Skip the power walk after work, until your escort arrives. Same thing with the swimming. It's safer to assume, all the time, that someone is watching."

"That's horrible."

"It's just for a while," he says, but the truth is, he has no idea how long this state of affairs may last. He uses his cell phone and calls One Police Plaza, and arranges for an officer to be dispatched to Dr. Towne's office to "watch her today."

"But we'll have to discuss whether or not she deserves full-time protection," says the lieutenant Voort talks to.

Voort tells her, when he hangs up, "I'll ask you not to be alone with any new patients."

"That's pushing it," she says angrily.

"Keep a nurse there, or an aide. Also, you're a tropical disease specialist. Do you work with hazardous viruses or bacteria in the office ever, or in a lab?"

"My patients come back from Zaire, Sudan, all over the African Rift Valley, Mr. Voort." Now he's back to being called "mister." "Some of the diseases they pick up stew inside the human body for days, even weeks, before they break out. It's less than twenty-four hours' travel time from Nairobi to Kennedy Airport; an infected person might not know till they're home on Fifty-fourth Street that something is wrong."

"Meaning yes."

"I have to draw blood, and take samples. I have to look at slides under microscopes. How am I supposed to treat people if I don't know what they have?"

Voort frowns. "We're dealing with someone who arranges accidents, and you're telling me you work with infectious diseases. I don't suppose you'd consider stopping working until we solve this thing?"

"Let me put it this way: If I stop, and one of my patients *is* carrying something, untreated, they can die in two days, not to mention spreading it."

"That fast?"

She chews toast, her appetite unaffected by talking about deadly viruses. "The first time I went into the Amazon, it was to treat an Indian tribe that was being wiped out by the plain old flu that would put you in bed for ten days at worst. The Indians caught it from a *New York Times* reporter who went down there to 'help' them. He sneezed into his hand, and shook hands with the chief when he got out of the plane. Three hours later the chief was coughing and running a fever. Within two days they were *all* running fevers. Reverse the process, and you'll understand how vulnerable you are to a virus, especially a level three or four, that comes from there."

"Be careful in the lab then, will you?"

More softly, she says, "Thanks. And I wasn't mad at you."

There's something about the way she looks into his eyes that makes his knees weak, even when he's sitting down.

By eight, they're in the elevator, heading downstairs, when it halts suddenly, with a jolt, between the twenty-eighth and twenty-seventh floors. Voort hears banging in the shaft. He punches the "Help" button. There is no response.

"It's probably nothing," he says, doubting it, cocking his head, listening for other noises, creaks, sawing sounds, in the shaft outside.

The elevator lurches down a couple of inches.

"Sometimes it does this," she says, and he sees she's white, but trying to control her fear. "But it was supposed to be fixed last month, or at least that's what the flyer from the co-op board said."

They hear a grinding noise, a mechanical straining, and the metallic violent clang of something heavy striking the top of the elevator.

"Sounds like it fell from a few stories up," Voort says, trying to envision a wrench or hammer that had accidentally been dropped upon them. He eyes the little square emergency exit door on the ceiling, and considers pulling out his .38. His hand drops down around the gun.

But the elevator starts moving again, abruptly, then smoothly.

When they reach her office, they are met by a uniformed officer who says he has been assigned to stay with Dr. Towne today.

Voort calls headquarters and confirms the man's identity. He resists the ridiculous urge to kiss her good-bye, fights off the carnal sense of familiarity that still has not entirely gone away. He heads home, changes into fresh clothes, and takes the Jaguar downtown, parking it in a Commercial zone, near Federal Plaza, with its POLICE BUSINESS sign displayed on the visor, and The Club locked across the steering wheel.

The New York field office of the FBI is located in the number-one tower of the World Trade Center. Voort takes the elevator to the well-marked suite on the forty-ninth floor.

Dr. Towne has given him the business card of the agent who visited her last month, and who asked her to give up Abu Bin Hussein as a patient.

Waiting for "Agent Jack Bogdonavich," in the open reception area, with its view of the bigger main room beyond,

Voort is thinking that federal offices all look the same to him, whether they house auditors, engineers, or agents dealing with terrorists. The gigantic rectangular room, brightly lit from translucent panels overhead, is broken into partitioned-off areas, each with a desk, an agent, and a corkboard pinned with information—sometimes a photo of a baby back home in Westchester. Sometimes a photo of the Pan Am jet destroyed over Lockerbie. Phones are ringing. The conference rooms and offices for senior agents will be at the far end of the room, by the windows. The agents, both men and women, are dressed more plainly, conservatively, and expensively than their New York detective counterparts, reflecting a difference in federal versus municipal pay scales, as well as respective organizational attitudes toward public image.

"I'm Jack Bogdonavich," says an athletic-looking dark-haired man, in a gray suit and striped shirt, coming up to Voort. He has the cordial air of someone who is busy, but not too rushed to see a visitor. "Mind if I ask for your ID?"

Voort provides it and Bogdonavich says, "You're the one who caught that woman last year, the, uh, 'surgeon.' " Bogdonavich grimaces, the typical male reaction to the Nora Clay case, and then he leads Voort back to a small conference room on the outer rim of the main one. Voort doesn't need privacy to ask questions, but Bogdonavich probably doesn't want him standing around where he can hear FBI conversations.

There's a rectangular table in the room with eight empty seats around it, an easel with dollar figures written on it, and the words AK-47s and assault rifles in Magic Marker on the board. There's an unplugged electric coffeemaker on a side table, and, on a small round plastic platter, a half a dozen sugar doughnuts, and two empty Dunkin' Donuts boxes.

"What do you want to know?" Bogdonavich says, standing below a humming machine suspended from the ceiling, the size and shape of an air conditioner. Voort recognizes it as an air purifier. First the architects design these buildings with windows that can't open, to save electricity. Then half the people inside them, disappointed with the environment, plug in space heaters to mitigate the air-conditioning, air conditioners to cool off the heating systems, and purifiers to clean recirculated air.

Voort explains why he is here, and asks if it might be possible to look at any files or notes concerning Jill Towne. The request could have been made officially, department to department, but he has learned that personal appearances usually achieve better results. The FBI likes to cooperate when it can.

"Someone tried to kill her?" Bogdonavich says, frowning more with puzzlement than surprise.

"It looks that way."

"Well, you involve yourself with Bin Hussein, you never know what can happen. Wait here," he says, disappears, and returns ten minutes later with an older, white-haired man, whom he introduces as a senior agent, and who shakes Voort's hand and says, by way of introduction, "Mike Kaye."

Voort goes over the story again. The agents glance at each other as he speaks, their brows going up when he gets to the "accidents" in Seattle and Chicago. Like Mickie, it is inconceivable to Voort that the FBI is killing people. He would rather risk telling them the whole story than leave something out and regret it later.

When he is finished Agent Kaye says, "That was better than the bullshit my uncle Tony used to throw around, when I was growing up in Indiana. Jack, you and Detective Voort tell war stories for a few minutes. Give me the list of those names and social security numbers. Jack, fill him in with anything he could have learned from *her*."

Voort understands that Agent Kaye will now go into a more secure area in this office, and call Washington, or access files that the Bureau may have on the people on Meechum's list. If he finds anything he will, depending on his status, call Washington for instructions, or decide on his own whether to share the information with Voort.

"I bet you never figured when you signed up for your job that you'd be protecting people like her," Jack Bogdonavich says with disapproval, when the glass door swishes shut.

"What can you tell me about her?"

The agent rises, goes to the side table, and puts a sugar doughnut on a paper napkin. Voort indicates that he is not hungry. "Our guys overseas tell us Hussein caught some kind of tropical parasite. His doctors can't kill it, and it can knock him out for months at a time, lay him right out. Sweats. Fever. He can't do shit when it's active. He certainly can't operate an organization."

"How do you know?"

"We know. We also know she's the expert on this worm, bug, whatever it is. She comes up with a medicine that knocks the thing out for a while. Abu Bin Hussein can work during that time. Then the bug evolves, gets strong, and he needs her to redesign whatever she treats him with. And la-de-da, she does. She thinks if you're nice to him, he'll come around. She quoted Bible verse at me. Love your enemy. That kind of thing."

"But where does she meet him, if he's in hiding?"

"She's a member of Doctors Without Borders, for Christ sakes. She flies to Khartoum, Libya, Havana, a dozen places where she works in refugee camps, where he's welcome, and we can't stop it. She's there for weeks at a time. One day, he just shows up."

"What did she say to you when you tried to talk her out of it?"

"What do you think she said? Her parents were missionaries and she's got the do-good bug. Peacenik bug. Those are the first people who always get killed when fighting breaks out."

"Missionaries?" Voort imagines Dr. Towne as a little girl, standing next to a man wearing black, and holding a Bible. She has pigtails in the vision. She's wearing an ironed white dress, shiny black shoes, and her hands are folded in front of her. She's in a tropical place, under a palm.

"In Zaire," the agent says. "She grew up in a mission, in the middle of nowhere, believe me, if you look on the map. Apparently her parents had a bad experience with the CIA, and now she won't listen to anyone from the government. Us or them."

Voort just waits for the explanation.

Bogdonavich chews his doughnut and says, "Back in the late sixties, there was a Congolese leader, Lumumba was his name. Zaire was called the Congo then. Patrice Lumumba. He was a Communist, and in those days, that meant something. The CIA helped overthrow the guy. Hell, the whole Congo would have turned Red if they didn't do it, and I guess at one point Dr. Towne's father helped them, gave them information about Lumumba's people. He didn't realize what was going to happen. It was a bloodbath. When the fighting started, half his parishioners were slaughtered. He spent a week burying bodies. And Zaire landed up under a dictator anyway. Her father never listened to anything that anyone from the government, any government, told him after that. The CIA tried to use him to get information, but he turned them away. He died blaming himself for those deaths."

"How do you know this," says Voort, thinking, shaking his head, great, now we can throw the whole country of Zaire into this gigantic spreading mess.

"She explained it while she was telling me to fuck off."

They are interrupted by Mike Kaye returning, carrying a couple of manila folders. He seems relieved, which turns out to mean that the FBI had information on only two of the people on Voort's list; Dr. Towne, and Alan Clark in Montana. The relief is apparently over the fact that the FBI's not going to be dragged into an embarrassing incident, or so Mike Kaye believes.

"Clark was the kind of person you *want* to see have a fatal accident," the supervising FBI agent remarks.

Voort scans the files, "Can you imagine any possible connection between the Bin Hussein organization and Alan Clark's people?"

A shrug. "Maybe weapons sales, but it's a reach. Those militia guys, the bad ones, support themselves by robbing banks or selling weapons, and you never know who the buyer is, and when it comes to profit, they don't ask. Check with the Bureau of Alcohol, Tobacco, and Firearms. They might have something on arms sales."

"Isn't there a law you can use to stop her from treating Bin Hussein?" Voort asks.

"No one can prove she treats him, and no one has

proven he's responsible for any bombings. We know it but we can't prove it, and you have to prove it to arrest her as an accessory under the Terrorism Act."

The files don't help him. By eleven, Voort's got an inquiry in with ATF, one more government agency now involved, and he's back in the Jaguar, heading over the George Washington Bridge, to New Jersey, where he turns north, along the Palisades, and heads for West Point.

He is having trouble reconciling his conflicting strong feelings for Jill Towne, with whom he is barely acquainted; his disgust over her commitment to treating one particular patient, and his admiration for the courage and risk involved in her exposure to disease in helping others overseas. His powerful attraction to her is rising, clashing with his professional judgment.

He tells himself, *Is it so different, her being a doctor, and treating anyone who comes to her, and me being a policeman, arresting killers, even though I know they may be released? Because that's the job description. How many times have I caught them red-handed, and instead of shooting them, I put handcuffs on them, knowing a lawyer might get them off?*

He tries to concentrate on the professional questions, and review what he knows about Meechum's death, but the information covers such a broad area, such a wide array of groups by now, and such a range of theories that he remains baffled, and, at bottom, worried for Jill Towne. He calls her office and finds that she is having a normal day so far, and that the patrolman has been helpful around the office, telling stories to nervous children in the waiting room.

Voort experiences a flash of jealousy at the helpful patrolman.

Mickie should have landed in Seattle by now, he thinks.

West Point, which he last visited to see Meechum graduate, occupies a fifteen-thousand-acre campus along the Hudson River, near Storm King Mountain, on the west side of the river, and below the ruins of Fort Putnam, where Voort's ancestors in the Continental Army fought the British marching up from Fort Lee. As Voorts still occupy farms and own businesses along the river valley, he spent many Sundays with his parents, as a boy, visiting riverside towns, parks, and forts.

His predominant memory of West Point, though, comes back as he enters the parade grounds, on foot, beneath the shadow of the institute's towering chapel. He remembers Meechum, on his graduation day, in a sea of cadets on this field. Meechum throwing his hat into the air. Hundreds of white hats swept into the brisk Hudson Valley wind.

Voort has not called ahead, as he is unsure how the academy bureaucracy might react to a police request over the phone. "Sometimes," his dad used to say, "it's better to let sources know you are coming, so they can prepare. Other times a cold call produces results you might otherwise never get."

Voort asks a passing cadet for directions to the office of the commandant of cadets, the man responsible, he remembers Meechum saying, for the military side of cadet life.

When he gets there, Brigadier General Randolph Pratt seems close to retirement age, but still powerful, with a broad chest beneath his olive jacket and a full head of cropped, steel-colored hair above a penetrating gaze from light blue eyes. He introduces himself with a hint of a southwestern accent. He examines Voort's police ID, and listens intently, in his large, comfortable office, while Voort explains that a former cadet has been murdered in New York.

"And you think it's connected to the academy?" asks

the frowning general, in the gravelly voice of a smoker. "But you said he graduated nine years ago?"

"We're trying to reconstruct his life after he left, to get an idea of what he got involved in, later. My partner'll visit Fort Bragg, Meechum's last posting. Other detectives are talking to Meechum's friends and family, tracing," Voort lies, "a lot of threads."

"Very thorough," the brigadier general remarks wryly, the tone asking a question as much as making an observation. He is sitting in a leather swivel chair, behind a desk of massive oak, flanked by a bust, on the right side, of General Dwight Eisenhower, a graduate of West Point, and of General Robert E. Lee, another alumni, on the left. The paperweight is a brass Bradley fighting vehicle. The oriental carpet is thickly woven in reds and blues.

"It was a gift from a Kuwaiti friend of mine, after we helped them out," the general says. "I'm impressed that the New York police," he adds, protective of the academy's reputation, and clearly a man accustomed to having his questions answered, "have so much manpower to concentrate on one case, unless there's something more to it you'd like to share."

"His death may be tied to three other killings. And he was my best friend when I was a kid."

The brigadier general pauses, says he's sorry, and Voort can see that the man is remembering someone he has lost, someone once close to him. He leans over his desk and asks his secretary, over an intercom, to find any files still existing on a former cadet named Meechum Keefe, class of 'ninety-two.

"I wasn't here then," the general says, as they wait. "But a few of our professors were. Perhaps they'll recall something about the cadet."

But first, of course, the general has to check Meechum's files, to make sure there is nothing potentially embarrassing inside to the army or the academy. Apparently there isn't. Apparently, if he was homosexual, it isn't in the files.

"He got good grades. He was some kind of computer genius. He received excellent recommendations, particularly from Colonel John Szeska, one of his instructors who left here some time ago. Let's see what else," he says, scanning information. "Average athlete, which means he was pretty damn good because we've got the best in the country. Graduated twenty-first in his class. No disciplinary problems. A solid cadet."

"What did John Szeska teach?"

"Tactics. But he's gone, like I said."

"Who can I talk to about Meechum who's still here?"

It takes only a few minutes, and a single phone call from the general, to arrange. Of the three instructors who taught Meechum, and remain at the academy, one is in Washington today, researching a book on nuclear strategy, one has the flu, although Voort is welcome to visit him at home, on campus. The third, Colonel Mark Jaxx, is apparently out, right now at Trophy Point, the academy's famous riverside walkway.

"He paints every afternoon. But we reached him on his cell phone. He's waiting for you. Good luck."

Voort leaves the office, and strolls through the campus. In late afternoon, classes are finished for the day. The trees are gold, and the grounds swarm with cadets in gray shorts or sweat clothes, playing football, or soccer, or doing calisthenics. He passes the superintendent's quarters, a center hall brick classic, across an expanse of lawn and garden from the MacArthur Barracks. He comes eventually to Trophy Point, the curving walkway lined with stone benches, and captured cannons, overlooking the river.

A man sits painting, at an easel, twenty feet off.

Colonel Jaxx turns out to be a Vietnam, Iraq, and Cold War veteran, a widower who teaches battle strategy in the mornings and paints, judging from the sample in front of Voort, fairly decent Hudson Valley landscapes in the late afternoons, liking the dusk light. He is powerful-looking yet oddly graceful, on his little stool. His paint smock, dabbed with blotches, is probably the most anarchistic piece of clothing in his wardrobe. It covers his knees like an apron. But the posture is rigid, the haircut crisp, and even the rectangular frames of his silver wire-rimmed glasses give him a geometric aspect at odds with the soft river scene; sailboats tacking against fall mountains, taking form on his canvas.

"I remember Meechum well. I met him before he was actually a student of mine, at the annual service for the marines who died in that bombing in Beirut. I had a nephew who was killed. Meechum's brother Al was killed, too. I liked that cadet. He was serious. He thought about things. My wife and I, she was alive then, had him over a few times for dinner. He was going to be a lifer. I'm surprised he dropped out."

"People change," Voort says.

"Not cadets like him," the colonel says. "Something must have happened if he quit."

"Was Meechum homosexual?"

The man looks surprised. "Is that what happened to him?"

"I'm only asking," Voort says.

Jaxx remarks, "You know who you really ought to talk to about him? John Szeska. Meechum worshiped him. They spent a lot of time together. Szeska was a hero to Meechum."

"Who's John Szeska?" Voort says, pretending he has not heard the name before.

"Big war hero. Vietnam. Iraq. He had a rare combination of talents. Brilliant in the field. Brilliant in the classroom. I think he was posted to the Pentagon after here."

"Is he still there?"

"I couldn't say."

"What did he teach?" Voort says, asking the same question that the brigadier general already answered, but the rule is, always ask the same question to different people, and see if they answer the same way.

The colonel dabs little bits of color on his canvas, turning a sunbeam slightly more orange.

"He taught them how to win," he says. "He was a TA expert, a *real* expert."

"TA?" Voort says.

"Sorry. You use initials so much you forget other people don't know them. TA means threat assessment," the colonel says. "Intelligence gathering and analysis. It's easy to get the information. It's harder to figure out what to do with it. There's a science and an art to it. So many threats out there, but which ones do you take seriously? Which ones will become deadly? Which potential enemies will you have to fight?"

"We could use that skill in the police department," Voort says, his pulse suddenly, at the man's words, speeding up in his head.

"TA," says the colonel, shaking his head, "is the great talent. Guess right and you're prepared when the fighting starts. You save thousands of lives. The Israelis plaster the Egyptian Air Force before they can even get off the ground. The Somalis are monitoring our radio frequencies when the

Rangers make a raid. Guess wrong and you suffer Pearl Harbor, or you have the French building the Maginot Line, before World War Two, sinking all their resources into the wrong strategy."

"What about more modern threats?" Voort asks, the pulse thick in his throat now, connections starting to come together, telling himself it is too soon to jump to conclusions, but knowing, as he hears himself speaking, that he has finally hit an intersection point of every far-flung story he has heard in the last week. "Where are the enemies today, now that the Cold War is done?"

The colonel puts down his brush, and turns, and seems for a moment, despite the paint-smeared frock, to be lecturing a class. "The threats are smaller, but deadlier. It's not Russia anymore we worry about, not a whole army coming at us, but one man with an anthrax bomb in the subway. One pip-squeak country that doesn't even have a paved highway, finally buying a nuclear warhead. One professor who never did a pushup in his life, not carrying an AK-47, but a chemical formula which could wipe out Los Angeles. The threats are less visible, the ramifications more terrible. The wrong person, one single person, can do more damage in this country than ever before."

Voort's throat is dry.

"And that's what Colonel Szeska, Meechum's hero, excelled at, threat assessment," Voort says.

"That's what he taught," Colonel Jaxx replies, reaching for his paintbrush, and going back to dabbing color to his personally created dusk river. "And that's what he did."

"These enemies you've just mentioned . . . the modern ones," Voort says, looking down at the Hudson, where his ancestors sailed ships, and fought the British for freedom, where they joined into Colonial militias for safety, "are not overseas anymore. They're here. Right in this country."

The colonel looks up, a gleam in his eye. "I know, but tell that to the civil libertarians," he says. "You ever read that book, the *Turner Diaries*? It describes, in detail, how to make a fertilizer bomb, and then someone reads it and blows up the federal building in Oklahoma City with one. Free speech? Or something worse? You're right, Mr. Voort. A lot of people in the military think the next fight will be here, not overseas. How do you handle threats that are already here? Where's the line? You tell me. Where's the line in a free society between opening your mouth legally and shutting someone else's forever?"

"I'm a cop and you're a soldier. That's not our question to answer."

The man leans over his palette, considering which color to use next. "You're right," he says in a way that disturbs Voort. "They make the rules. We only enforce them."

Voort leaves the man to his painting, and, walking back toward his car, it seems to him that the wind coming off Storm King Mountain has intensified. The trees are bent sideways. The leaves blow into his face. The water below is churning up angrily, and the regatta of small sailboats race for the protection of their little marinas and harbors on the east side.

At the commandant's office he makes one last request, and it is for a way to contact Meechum's old teacher, Colonel John Szeska. The commandant considers it, then asks his secretary to see if she can find the information.

She's back ten minutes later. "Looks like he retired from the army two years ago," she says, naming the same period when Meechum quit.

Trying to look professional and nothing more, to seem vaguely curious and nothing else, Voort asks if there is any forwarding address, or phone number for the ex-colonel, and they tell him no. He asks for the social security number, and they tell him it is private. He asks for any army ID number, or last posting, or full name, including middle name, or initial, and that they do provide.

"Last posting, as of two years ago, was the Marine War College at Quantico. Then he retired."

"Check the veterans organizations," General Pratt advises. "They have thorough mailing lists. And the Veterans Administration. The VA is alerted automatically whenever someone retires."

Voort thanks him, and he's crossing the parade grounds, heading back toward the Jaguar and the main parking area, when his cell phone rings.

"You're not gonna believe what I found," says Mickie's voice, wavering from a bad connection, but clear enough to make out okay.

"Are you in Seattle?" Voort has noticed a couple of cadets, walking toward him, about twenty feet off now.

"Land of coffee shops and rain."

"I think I know what you found, but not over the cell phone. Call me in ten minutes," Voort says, which means he'll find a pay phone in the interim.

"Ah, time for another cafe latte," Mickie says. "At this rate I won't need a plane to fly east. I'll do it on caffeine."

Voort hangs up and finds a pay phone off the main lot. He waits a few minutes, and when Mickie calls his cell phone he gets Mickie's pay phone number in Seattle and calls his partner back.

"Okay, Con Man, what are you so sure I found?"

"That our engineer out there who didn't care about politics, and never traveled, was into something dangerous, but it was unconnected to the other victims. In fact, it opens up a whole new area, as this thing keeps spreading and doesn't stop."

"You win the champagne, pal. First I talk to his wife. He was an angel, she says. I talk to neighbors. Mr. Happy, that was him, they say. He dressed up like a clown for kids. He brought tuna sandwiches to the Salvation Army kitchen, from Annselmo Foods, where he worked. Then I go to the office, a fucking *food* company, right? And they take one look at the badge, even a New York City badge, and next thing I know, I'm in the president's office. He's terrified. The lawyer's there. They're swearing they had nothing to do with it. They've been waiting for someone to show up. They figured, nothing ever really happened, so they weren't going to volunteer information, but if someone ever showed up, they'd tell the truth."

"Which is?"

"Ready for this? The logo says food company, but they're really a global conglomerate. With a shitload of divisions, and the one *he* worked for had nothing to do with food. *He* worked for a division doing chemical research, for the Department of Defense. He worked on antidotes to chemical attack. And his division was to be sold to a French company, lock, stock, and personnel. Our guy was going to move away, to Paris."

"With the information."

"Right. He wasn't supposed to, he signed a nondisclosure agreement, like all the other engineers in that division, but after he died, and they went through his files, which were already packed up to move, by the way, they found all kinds of stuff he wasn't supposed to have in there. Dia-grams. Formulas. Major secret shit. Meanwhile, the French company backs out of the sale, so everyone here is guessing they knew he was bringing the stuff with him. They must have promised him the world once he got to Paris."

Voort, in the phone booth, watches the same army cadets he saw on the parade ground walking toward him again. They stop just outside the phone booth, as if waiting to use the phone.

"A French company's not so bad," Voort says, feeling the weight of his .38 on his hip, and noting that the cadets seem older than others he has seen. "At least they're friendly. Not like, say, an Iraqi company."

"That's the point, Con Man. The French company does business with all kinds of people U.S. citizens are embar-goed from selling to, people who would be very interested in knowing which chemical weapons the army's developed antidotes to."

One of the cadets says something to the other one, and they both burst into laughter. The second cadet puts one hand against the glass of Voort's booth. It's a casual move, but provocative. It means, get out of that booth.

Voort is reluctant to turn his back on them. He says, "But the people you talked to must have had some idea Lester Levy was crooked. In Chicago, and also with Jill, the FBI or police came by, gave a warning about things."

"Now you're calling her Jill, huh? Not Dr. Towne?"

"You seem to know who I mean anyway."

"No one from any investigating unit ever came by in Lester Levy's case, if they're telling the truth, and frankly, they looked too scared to be lying, but we can check. Levy had his heart attack. The French company pulled out of the deal. Annselmo discovered the stolen material in his boxes, and decided to regard it as a near miss, not a breach. Why confess to the government and jeopardize their relationship? They clamped down on security. They made new rules for other personnel. They decided, if an investigator ever showed up, they'd tell everything they knew immediately, but otherwise, zilch. After all, Levy was dead, and couldn't be questioned, and to their knowledge, the stolen information never changed hands. There was no obstruction of justice, no danger, nothing they could be charged with, unless, under direct questioning later, they lied. They were clean, they said.

"Yeah, I said, two clean assholes. How can you be sure he didn't pass over information, and next time our soldiers are in Iraq, or Iran, or Korea, their chemical antidotes don't work, and they fucking turn blue with their eyes popping out? But all the chickenshits wanted to know is, Did I tell the military about Levy yet? I told them, I'm calling them tomorrow. Which gives you the rest of the afternoon to do it yourself today."

The cadet outside raps sharply on the glass, and points to his wrist, miming the annoyed question, How long are you going to stay on the line?

Mickie says, "Since you knew what I'd find, did you figure out who killed him, by any lucky chance?"

Voort looks at the phone in his hand. A wire, a tappable route for conversation, extends out of this booth and into the Putnam County phone system. A directional microphone, aimed at the glass, could translate the vibrations of a human voice against glass, into words. A lip-reader, watching with binoculars, could have "heard" everything he just said.

"Paranoid," was the word Jill had used earlier.

But if I'm dealing with some kind of intelligence organiza-
tion, they have all those means at their disposal.

"I'll call you tonight," he says. "Leave word where I can
reach you."

"Can't talk?"

"I'm not sure."

"Okay then. Off to Massachusetts," Mickie says. "Piling
up those frequent flier miles. Con Man, do you think
Meechum was involved with whoever killed these people?
You think he was one of them and had a change of heart?"

I don't want to get anyone in trouble, Meechum had said.

Meechum didn't work for any head-hunting firm, Voort
tells himself. *That's why I can't find it. My guess is, some-*
how, he hooked up with these killers. All that talk about
disillusionment. Maybe he didn't realize what his own peo-
ple were doing at first. But he came to suspect it.

Threat assessment? Or threat removal?

But now, on a public phone, all he says is, "Someone
was watching Levy. Now maybe they're watching you."

Just like those cadets are watching me.

But they don't follow him, don't talk to him, don't even
look as he walks off toward the car. Glancing back, he sees
one of them in the phone booth, and the other, back to
Voort, tossing a rubber ball into the air.

On the way back to the city, he spends much more time
than usual studying other cars in the rearview mirror.

I have to find John Szeska. I think that may turn out to
be the starting point.

He hears Meechum's words again, fearful, in a bar, a
week ago.

I don't want to get anyone in trouble.

Feeling sick, Voort asks himself, as he reaches the George Washington Bridge, *Who else are they planning to assassinate?* Because they clearly are not stopping.

Who else do they regard as a threat now?

Mickie? Jill? Me?

Lots of cops have accidents every year.

Every single year.

TWELVE

*T*he future assassin does homework. It is April 1969, and he bends over his bedroom desk, delighting in escape. Homework is easy, and its secrets, deciphered, are logical and clear. When a history book tells John Szeska that Vietnam is in Southeast Asia, it is an immutable fact that never changes, as predictable as the appearance of the sun in the east.

The man in the doorway says, "Hey, Book Boy. What will you do when the darkies pour across Cicero Avenue? Throw your fucking textbook at them?"

The bedroom is small, but neat, with a single bed, and well-read history books and a barred window overlooking an alley where, on warm nights, the boy hears cats fighting, their screams mixing with the shouts of Dad and Grandma in the house. On the walls are a Chicago Cubs banner, a map of Vietnam, pinpointing troop movements, a wrestling team photo, featuring him, the star, and a *Time* magazine cutout of the murdered president John F. Kennedy, who died when the boy was thirteen.

"Hey, Fat Boy, I love your poster of Martin Luther Communist King. Maybe when the Sheenies flood across

Cicero Avenue they'll spare you while they rape your grandmother."

Without even looking up, the boy says, "I'm not fat anymore."

The boy draws down the flexible neck of his Tensor lamp, so a circle of hot light illuminates homework questions. He finds the trick query with which his twelfth-grade teacher has tried to fool his class. He replaces the incorrect country on the map, Laos, with the right one, Thailand. In geography, he thinks, you erase mistakes and they are gone.

"You make me sick," the man says.

The man radiates the kind of disproportionate fury that compact men can produce, in the muscles of his torso, the grime on his jeans and T-shirt, the skin burned raw from labor in the sun, from loading trains in a railyard. He is blond but his legal son is dark. He has brown eyes but the boy's are blue. He has a narrow face while the boy's is rounder. And the boy is the large one. His shoulders, in his ancestors, provided power to dig coal, butcher cattle, carry rocks, skewer soldiers.

"Dad," he says with a lack of emotion equal to the man's fury. "The only one who crosses Cicero Avenue is you, to shoot off your gun on Saturday nights."

"You're an expert on gorilla psychology now! Go live with them if you love them so much."

"Someday you'll pick the wrong person to scare. They'll shoot back."

"What you don't understand," Michael Szeska retorts, stepping into the room, propelled by a bottomless and directionless rage, "is that keep 'em scared, and they'll stay on their side. There are more of them than us."

And the boy says, "Us? Like you and me are the same?"

"The real enemy is here, not somewhere else, asshole."

Asshole. Fat boy. Shithead. The song the boy hears each day when he walks into the house.

But despite the taunts, he is athletic. In the room is a workout bench, and weights he lifts each day, building his biceps, forearms, wrists, neck. There are devices for strengthening hand muscles. A chinning bar is attached to the doorway. He works on his body the way he works on his homework. Both are necessary forms of protection here.

The boy says, finally looking at the man, "Oh, the real enemy is here all right."

"Shut your mouth or I'll shut it for you."

"You're not strong enough to do that anymore."

His guidance counselor had written of him, a week ago, in an evaluation form, "John can be reserved at school. I suspect problems at home, but he never allows personal difficulties to affect his performance."

His wrestling coach had written, "John is a silent leader. The other boys want to follow him. But I have never seen a wrestler erupt with the kind of controlled savagery I see in him. I'm afraid there's a monster in that kid waiting to get out. I hope he figures out a way to harness it."

His girlfriend had told her best friend, "I know he loves me but he never talks about emotions. He tries to pretend he's a dead fish but there's kindness in him. I see it. I'll help him."

But right now the boy eats dinner with his dad and grandma, in their little kitchen, beneath the Byzantine eyes of his grandmother's plastic icons, bloody Jesuses and saints and crusaders killing Muslims in Turkey and Jerusalem and Malta and Spain. There is a whole series of photos of the current pope.

The mother died in a car accident, with her lover, who the boy resembles, when the boy was one year old. The apartment is spotless. The magazines on the couch are *Gun & Ammo*, for Michael Szeska, and *Commentary*, for the grandmother, who taught herself English after coming from Europe, who watches Public Television, who belongs to the League of Women Voters, and who is a political and social aberration in Cicero, Illinois.

The boy sits between father and grandmother, in the middle, where referees generally preside.

"At the railyard today," the father begins, tearing off a hunk of hot fresh bread, "a fight broke out between a nigger and a Pole. The nigger cut the Pole."

"I hate that language," his grandmother says, pouring potato vodka into a jelly glass. She is a lean, tough woman who immigrated to Chicago after her husband was killed in Slovakia, by rival Croats.

"Mama," the father says, as if this is the first time they are having this discussion, as if he is explaining how a bicycle works to a ten-year-old, "the only thing that holds this country together is money. When it dries up, everyone'll be at each other's throats."

"Are you my son? Did you actually come out of me?"

"Pass the peas," John says.

"It'll be a bloodbath," the father says, swigging Welch's grape juice. A doctor has forbidden him to consume alcohol, because of a blood condition, and he craves sweets. Nestlé chocolate bars. Hostess cupcakes. Pineapple fruit pies. "You can't have so many races living together."

"I should have left you overseas," Grandmother retorts. "You'd fit right in."

"Pass the cabbage," says John.

"I cooked it for you, John," his grandmother says lovingly. "I added raisins, the way you like." She runs her leathery palm down the back of his neck, the affection for the grandson as strong as the disdain for the son. "John, we live in a special country, where different people get along," she says with the passion of an immigrant, who has chosen the place where she lives, instead of considering it a birthright. His grandmother regards politics as more than a talk-show subject. She's seen the consequences of bad politics. In Eastern Europe, bad politics kill.

" 'Ask what you can do for your country.' That's what President Kennedy said, and, John, if you love this country, if you fight for it someday, keep it from the hands of those Communist murderers overseas, you'll make me proud. John Kennedy knew that violence isn't always wrong. It depends on what you use it for."

Politics instead of personal matters. Personal matters are too incendiary here.

"I do love it," he says with the most feeling he has shown tonight.

"Do you know what real love is? You feel it even after you've been disappointed. Who's banging at the door?"

John finds, out in the hallway, his father's best friend: Ratko Milovicek, a fourth-generation Ciceran, a thick, jowly man, scarred from bar fights, who also works at the trainyard, and who is almost shaking with excitement as he rushes in, clutching a Browning automatic.

"They shot Martin Luther King in Memphis! A sniper finally got him!"

Michael Szeska bangs both fists on the table, in an unleashing of righteous fury.

"Who did it?"

"The whole South Side is going to riot," predicts the visitor. "Get your gun. We're going to patrol the neighborhood. All the guys are."

"I told you this would happen," says Michael Szeska, shoving his chair back so hard it topples over. "Mama, I'll be out all night. And *you*," he says, flashing a disgusted look at the boy, "if they come, throw your history book at them."

By midnight the sky to the east is lit, and the air is alive with cars filled with men with guns, driving toward the border with Chicago, and on the news, wafting from the open window, John Szeska hears of fires burning in Los Angeles and in New York.

"Promise me you'll never be like my son," his grandmother says.

He sits with her on the porch, rocking, hearing distant popping sounds of gunfire, and sirens, as helicopters fly in the sky to the east, like they do in Communist countries, Grandma says.

"I promise," the boy says.

"I hate to say this, but sometimes I wish he would have an accident, or leave."

"Me, too."

"One man caused this," she says, shaking her head, meaning the rioting, the burning. "John, it's terrible to say this, but I'm glad you had a different father. Promise me, *swear* to me you'll never forget how much damage one twisted man can do."

Voort, like most cops, has come to see his city in terms of the threats it poses. He is overly aware of the broken streetlamp, the man in a hooded sweatshirt, lounging in a shadowed doorway, the teenager peering furtively into the window of parked cars, eyeing a new radio or suitcase left in view, or even a mere dollar's worth of quarters lying on the floor.

In the past, the threats have tended to affect individuals. But after talking to Colonel Jaxx at West Point, they suddenly seem wider. A whole city seems to be holding its breath, awaiting attack.

Colonel Jaxx had said, *The danger isn't war anymore. It's one man with a bomb, with anthrax germs.*

Now it's seven P.M., the stragglers' end of rush hour, and Voort, driving across the Queensboro Bridge, finds himself in possession of the kind of fear that might occupy a policeman in Beirut, or Tel Aviv. He is unusually aware of the vulnerability of the cars massed on the spans, just idling. They seem perched in air, dependent for safety upon a strategically placed girder, a thin strip of tar.

And the evening shoppers on the Queens side, when he reaches it, seem to invite attack. Even the 747 overhead, clawing for air as it leaves JFK, hangs like plastic in the sky. Falling, it would burst into flame, become a plunging meteor instead of a rising star.

I found out where John Szeska lives. He's right here, in Queens, Hazel had told Voort, on the phone, twenty minutes ago.

He steers the Jaguar through the busy revitalized neighborhood filled with old Greeks and new immigrants, nestled by the East River, within view of Manhattan's lit towers, empty but burning power nonetheless. The narrow commercial streets are filled with a mélange of languages and cultures: Jamaican, Indian, Ecuadorian, Afghanistani. It is the new century's version of old immigrant New York—populated by people so recently arrived that they cluster by ethnicity rather than economics. Each morning, Astoria fills the slow-moving, Manhattan-bound F train with Manhattan's cabdrivers, floor scrubbers, news vendors, immigrant medical students. Each night Manhattanites flow the other way, to Astoria's Greek nightclubs, curry restaurants, and galleries showing the work of artists who have fled SoHo's high prices for an easier place to live.

Hazel had said, *I tracked him through his social security number. He's not registered with the Motor Vehicle Bureau but he has a driver's license. He's not listed owning real estate, so he rents, and I can't find him when I cross-reference rent rolls with the big real estate companies, so he's probably in a small unit.*

Voort gets directions from a Sikh attendant at a Mobil Station, and locates Weprin Street off Continental Avenue. He rolls past well-kept shingle or clapboard homes with neat lawns, chain-link fences, and lots of adolescent boys and girls in the street, on bikes. The neighborhood has a safe, homey feel. He can hear, from open windows, bits of foreign music, notes and scales that to Westerners seem more discordant than melodic. Checking addresses, he parks in front of a two-story, white-shingle home, with lights burning behind the downstairs curtains, and the upstairs unit dark.

I have to meet Jill in an hour.

No one answers Szeska's bell at first, another frustration that ratchets his sense of urgency up one more small degree. The attack on Jill Towne last night showed that whoever is killing people on Meechum's list is not stopping. The fact that neither he nor Mickie have been able to locate Frank Greene, the last name on the list, in Massachusetts, makes him worry for the stranger there, too.

No one answers Szeska's bell, and Voort tries the downstairs apartment, where the door is opened by a swarthy man just home from work, judging from his un-knotted tie, rumpled white dress shirt, and off-the-rack jacket.

The man is young, in his late twenties, with a narrow frame, small paunch, and expression which strikes Voort as more curious than wary—one more indication that this neighborhood is, at least, by the standards of the metropo-lis, considered safe.

Voort hears a TV in the background, tuned to a Spanish-language sitcom, judging from the canned laughter. There is a spicy smell that makes his mouth water.

The man tells Voort, after examining the detective shield, "John rents the upstairs unit from us. He was mar-ried to my wife's cousin before she passed away."

"Do you know where I can find him," Voort asks.

"Is he in trouble?"

"No," Voort says, having no idea whether, in the end, John Szeska will be in the worst trouble of his life, and curi-ous why an army genius, a West Point instructor, a teacher of modern military tactics at Quantico lives on the second floor of this shingled walkup in Queens, whether distant family owns it or not.

Voort says, "I just want to talk to him about a case I'm working on. Do you know when he'll be home?"

The man looks apologetic. "He travels. I take in his mail when he's away. I haven't seen him for a week."

"Does he travel for his work?"

"He is very busy."

"Where does he go?" Voort asks, wondering if he will hear Chicago, Montana, Lancaster Falls, Massachusetts.

"He doesn't discuss his business. I think it is very boring to him."

The man's shrug tells Voort that in this house, work matters are no big deal. Jobs provide money so people can enjoy more important things in life: food, family, soccer games, movies.

"Do you know when he'll return?" Voort asks.

"He never stays away more than a week. Can I give him a message?"

Voort hands over his card, keeping the mood light although his frustration is chewing at him. He tells the man that the block looks peaceful, pleasant, and the man nods.

"Before I came from Quito, people told me New York is dangerous. But it is safer here."

Safer, Voort thinks. Right.

Back in the car, driving to meet Jill, he puts on the news, and listens to an announcer worrying over the Mideast situation, and the president's health. The police commissioner is deciding who to appoint as the new chief of detectives when Hugh Addonizio retires next week, the announcer says, and dramatically makes it seem as if, without Addonizio, crime will wash over the city, bury neighborhoods like the one Voort just left, thrust the metropolis back to the dark ages, when people huddled inside at night, afraid to go out.

Pushing down the accelerator, speeding up so he can meet Jill Towne in time to replace her daytime bodyguard, he wonders where John Szeska is traveling?

To Massachusetts, like Mickie?

Or is he the one trying to kill Jill Towne?

There will be a valley to cross, the captain tells the new lieutenant from Cicero, John Szeska. There will be thick jungle, the captain adds as they bend over a green-and-brown topographical map, in the air-conditioned Quonset hut.

"Yes, sir." It is 1972.

"Several patrols in this area have been ambushed. We've had reports of enemy arms hidden in Doc Ho."

The captain rolls up the map, and pulls, from his desk, a manila personnel folder. He's an army lifer, on his third tour of duty in Vietnam, and he's seen plenty of lieutenants come and go, but he tells Szeska that he is doing a terrific job. He is impressed that Szeska has learned Vietnamese, that he's fit in so well in Intelligence, and that, like the captain, he volunteered to come to Vietnam.

"You're a patriot. You've performed well under fire. If they hit you, radio for the gunships we have standing by."

John Szeska, hours later, in a hot rain, leads a dozen specialists, one corporal, and a sergeant named Charley Mann up a foot-wide trail zigzagging up a mountain. The rain soaks him, and pours off his helmet. Something small, wet, and alive seems to be chewing at the sole of his right foot. Yet there is something in the rampant anarchy in the forest that makes him feel at home in the way it pushes away alleged civilization. You don't have to deal with people here, not in a personal way, just with logistics, just strategy, just mathematical odds.

The truth is, he felt free leaving Chicago, his girlfriend, his friends, his father. Now the sweat drips inside his uniform, making his skin slick, and it runs down the inside of his thighs. The heat is deadweight in his lungs. The liquid air is filled with the aroma of rotting timber and sopping soil.

He hears a long, faraway *Caa! Caa!* Probably a crabeater monkey, but it might be a human, pretending to be something else.

That pile of leaves doesn't look right. I haven't seen other piles on the trail, so why is that one there?

He squats, waves the patrol around the leaves. He studies it and, from five feet off, notices that the vegetation seems browner over that spot. Deader.

No trip wires visible.

He finds a piece of bamboo, wipes it clean of grubs, extends it, and brushes the top level of leaves away.

Under the leaves are a crisscrossing arrangement of palm fronds.

"Shit, Lieutenant. It's a pit!"

The floor of the two-foot-wide hole is lined with razor-sharp bamboo sticks with dark brown dried shit smearing the tips.

"Fill it in," he tells the admiring men who might have stepped in the pit.

Two hours later Doc Ho appears abruptly, at a break at the edge of the jungle, and from a half mile off seems to be a peaceful cluster of huts, pigs, and pathetically tiny rice paddies clinging to the terraced side of a mountain. The name sounds like the punch line of a GI joke. Hey, buddy, what doctor do you never want to visit in Vietnam, if you want to get well?

Doc Ho, my man. Doc Ho Ho Ho.

The rain has let up; it is late afternoon, and there's a

dripping sound as huge drops of water continue to fall, even after the storm is over, working their way, in shafts of sunlight, down from the upper canopy, across immense ferns and fan-sized leaves.

From the tree line he studies the objective through binoculars, and across a field being prepared for burning, an expanse of ex-forest now littered with felled mahogany trees. There is no way to reach the village without exposing the patrol. Ahead, chainsawed stumps alternate with rotting logs, whose timber will not even be sold, just burned. The scene is as peaceful as an innocent countryside, or as a prepared trap.

He is thinking that there is no such thing as "normal" here. At best, the country is a shifting illusion, which, at the moment, in the round binocular O, consists of a pig rooting in the ground. A boy is talking to an old man who wears the woven reed conical hat of a peasant.

Well, at home everything was a lie, too. At least here it's obvious.

"You two, follow me. The rest, wait until we signal you to come."

The men nod, ease back, move up behind him.

They trust him.

But before John Szeska even steps from the protection of the trees, the enemy ambush erupts.

By the time Voort walks into the Museum of Modern Art, to meet Jill and take over bodyguard duty, he is realizing that his hopefulness got the better of him earlier, at John Szeska's apartment. The ex–military man, or whatever he is now, is merely one more possible lead, among dozens, to help find Meechum's murderer. Odds are any one strategy will turn out to be a dead end.

By now Mickie's in Lancaster Falls, Voort thinks. Hazel's still running computer checks. Detectives are canvassing Meechum's neighborhood. And other detectives in Evanston and Seattle are double checking the "accidents" that killed the victims there.

Voort pushes through the museum's revolving door into the crowded lobby and sees her striding toward him. He is assailed by a wave of lust so powerful that it robs him, for the moment, of rational thought. There are women whose allure grows each time you see them, as if beauty comes in layers, and each meeting reveals more.

She's dressed in a tight-fitting gown of white silk which outlines the curve of her hips, the taper of her legs. Her left shoulder is bare, her right crossed by the thinnest spaghetti strap. Her red hair is braided and coiled above her head, and her neck encircled by a single strand of white pearls. He has not seen her in high heels before, which make her taller, jut her small breasts forward, and create the impression that she is moving toward him on tiptoe, even though he hears the sharp click of approaching heels above the sound of stringed instruments, and the murmur of the crowd.

"Conrad, what did you find out?"

"Nothing."

She slides her warm, bare arm through his, like a date, like an intimate. "Are you sure you don't mind being stuck here tonight? Sponsors have to be here, but if you hate it, we don't have to stay the whole time."

"No problem."

The atrium beyond the entrance area is packed with

men in tailored jackets or tuxedoes, and women in gowns. Much of the jewelry present is normally stored in strong-boxes, or wall safes, and insured for amounts that, in Astoria, protect entire homes. A Juilliard string quartet plays Mozart on the mezzanine. Two champagne bars do a brisk business on either end of the main atrium, by the escalator.

"The money goes for medicine for Doctors Without Borders, she says, pulling him into circulation. "There's cholera in Sudan and Nigeria, and also Palestine now."

Up until a week ago Voort would have taken this at face value, but now he can't help thinking, *Or does the money somehow go to Abu Bin Hussein?*

His thoughts are broken by the crash of glass breaking behind them, and Jill jumps right as Voort whirls, hand going into jacket, fingers touching the butt of his gun.

"Sorry," a white-jacketed waiter says, bending to pick up the shattered champagne flutes which broke when his tray hit the marble floor. Small pools of champagne bubble, and shards of glass glitter or crunch underfoot.

"I hope I didn't get any on you, sir."

Jill has gone white. Voort feels sweat dripping under his armpits, and sliding down his back. He never got the gun out. He had not seen the accident, not even picked up whatever violent movement caused the tray to fall. He'd been blind, and now his throat is dry, and he is thinking, *If it had been an attack, it would have been successful.*

"It's just a few spilled drinks," he tells the man, reaching to replace her arm in his with an assurance he does not feel. Their hips touch, and a jolt of electricity surges through him.

"I always get nervous hosting fund-raisers," she says, pretending ease as well, and he appreciates the effort. But he'd rather leave. He's remembering that being out in public has not stopped the "accidents." Lester Levy, in Seattle, had his heart attack in public, in an elevator, going to work.

"Actually, it's better if we go," he says.

"A half hour more. I can't just disappear."

The mood between them is changing. They look like a circulating couple, not a detective and ward. Voort is no stranger to this kind of scene. He spends a couple of nights a month at fund-raisers. Last week it was the Hudson River Cleanup Project. Last month it was the Rainforest Alliance. You mail your check. You put on your tux. You chat with the men who make the city's fortunes and the wives who give the money away.

He finds now, moving through the galleries holding the museum's permanent collection—Monet's *Water Lilies*, the Mexican Zapatistas—that he is introducing her to people as often as she introduces others to him.

Meet the city commissioner for housing, Voort tells Jill, as they shake hands with an energetic bald man with a younger, taller wife. The woman's hatchet face swings from Voort to Jill, appraising.

"You two look good together," she says indelicately, assuming some greater relationship.

"Thank you," Jill says, not correcting the mistake.

"Mr. Trump? Mr. Voort," Jill says, as they chat with the pudgy-faced construction magnate, whose name headlines casinos, condos, and notoriously public divorce suits.

"Mr. Voort and I have met," Trump says.

Voort introduces her to the editor of *Rolling Stone*

magazine. She introduces him to the head of Mount Sinai Hospital, and the chancellor of Rockefeller University. Voort shares a joke with the owner of the New York Mets.

"You get around for a detective. Uh-oh," she says as the *Daily News's* gossip columnist pushes up to them, as the stringed quartet plays a spirited medley from "The Goose of Cairo."

"Jill! Where did you pick up Conrad Voort? And more important," she whispers theatrically to the doctor, "how do you keep that derriere so small? I want a derriere like that. I *try* to get a derriere like that. I *run*. I hang off this *horrible* metallic contraption my husband bought me, out of the Spanish Inquisition. Even the Canyon Ranch spa doesn't help. But tell me. Is this a romance with you two?" she says, her job a license for asking obnoxious questions, a public permission to pry.

"I just support the cause," Voort says, nodding toward the DOCTORS WITHOUT BORDERS banner.

"We're friends," Jill says, and Voort feels her hand playfully squeeze his forearm. The pressure does not let up.

"Ah, friends," winks the flamboyant columnist, clutching her trademark mug of Blue Mountain coffee, as Voort's beeper goes off. "Friends," repeats the pixie snooper, her voice a swooping dulcimer. "You mean like Anthony and Cleopatra were friends? Like Romeo and Juliet were friends?"

"More like Babe Ruth and Lou Gehrig," Voort says.

"Darling, you mean they were gay?"

Jill says, "Have to dash," and steers Voort toward the nearest escalator, which carries them up toward the mini-helicopter suspended from the fourth-floor ceiling. But Voort notices a tall, gray-haired man get on the escalator behind them. He's staring at Jill, and his right hand has disappeared beneath his right side pocket.

The man, he realizes, feeling the sweat start up again, has been maneuvering close to them, trailing them, for the last ten minutes. He's been somewhere close behind them, every time Voort checked.

I should have insisted we leave.

"Let me cook you dinner, to thank you for putting up with all this," she says.

The man's hand has not come out of his pocket. On the top of the landing, they are separated from him for a moment by the press of people, and Voort thinks he misjudged things, but then he spots the man again, standing, back to Jill, five feet behind her, looking up, toward the ceiling, at the minicopter suspended by cable wires.

"Let's get out of here," Voort says.

"It won't be fancy. But it'll be good," she says.

But the crowd has suddenly grown thicker. The natural fluctuating movement of guests has placed, for a moment, too many of them in the small top-floor area, and a ripple of bodies pushes against Voort, wedges him away from Jill, like a human undertow. A couple of feet separate them and the gap is growing.

She's pushed back. Voort sees the tall man, behind her, start to turn toward her, as if he has waited for the opportunity, as if he is now finally moving decisively. The area to Voort's left explodes in loud laughter. It drowns out his cry, "Jill!" and she's lost from view, but he knows where she is because he sees the tall man has found an opening in the crowd, and taking advantage of it, drives through. Gray eyes meet Voort's.

I'm not going to be able to stop it.

The tall man's hand goes into his cummerbund, as a woman brays, beside Voort, "I'm over here, Fred! *Fred!*"

Voort bulls into the woman, violently shoving her into a fat man to her right.

But he is moving too slowly. The room has filled with the awful sense of too late.

THIRTEEN

The ambush erupts behind Lieutenant John Szeska, explodes from the forest as he steps into the clearing, toward the village ahead. Bullets clip ferns and trees, and advance in crisscross patterns across the spongy earth, disintegrating their field of fire as thoroughly as lines on graph paper.

Birds are screeching. Foliage explodes in green bits. Four men go down in the first second.

One of them is screaming "Mary!"

Yet despite the speed of the attack, Szeska's mind works logically, experiences entire thought processes in fractions of seconds. He issues orders instinctively.

"Smoke grenades!"

Expressed in words, his decision would be: *They're behind us and on the right. Our only chance is to run toward those fallen trees, and use them as cover. If we stay here, we'll die.*

"This way!"

And now they are running, Sergeant Mann laying down covering fire, and another private has fallen, and Szeska, hearing bullets passing his ears, watches for bursts of enemy fire to erupt from the logs ahead.

If they're waiting for us there, we're dead.

But the firing comes from behind.

That enemy commander should have posted men behind the logs, but he was overconfident. One of his men fired too quickly and gave away the attack.

Szeska makes it to the nearest log, an immense, truncated, termite-gored length of mahogany, against which bullets thwack as they are absorbed into the wet spongy wood.

Only three men left: Szeska, Sergeant Mann, and a private from Chicago. The radio and its operator lie in the open, ten yards back. There is no way to call for air support.

The shooting tapers off. The silence is immense.

That commander made one mistake. Can I cause him to make another?

The attackers, Szeska guesses, in the pause, are preserving ammunition, probably moving around for better angles. He raises himself slightly, still protected by the log. He throws out his voice, trying to make himself sound furious, and in fact finds himself calm. He calls in perfect Vietnamese, Szeska the stage actor, Szeska the gambler: "Comrade, you have made an error!"

The worst that can happen is that nothing changes. But maybe I can cause them to delay.

He yells, as if furious, "You have attacked your Soviet allies! Is this the way you treat friends?"

Preposterous. But the silence remains unbroken. Szeska, committed, continues, forces himself to sound disdainful, outraged.

"We are a Soviet intelligence unit wearing American uniforms! We are returning with maps of the U.S. base at Da Nang! You should have been told to expect us! You are supposed to escort us to the border, not shoot!"

A fucking joke. The biggest whopping lie of the war. But Szeska has heard reports of occasional Soviets moving around with the enemy. Szeska must make his voice into a weapon. Szeska forces all the fury inside him, rage over his men who have died, rage accumulated over a lifetime, into his powerful will.

I need to keep them from attacking till dark.

"I demand to know your unit!"

He hopes that his wounded men on the hill don't wake up, scream in English, give the lie away.

Charley Mann is staring at him, with awe in his narrow, older, West Virginia face. The sergeant understands a smidgeon of Vietnamese. He's a gutsy veteran, four years older, tough and smart, and he crosses his index and middle fingers, for luck.

And this time a voice answers, in Vietnamese, saying, essentially, you are full of shit!

But they have not fired.

They believe he is lying, but are not one hundred percent sure, and in a matter like this, they don't want to make a mistake.

Szeska becomes the European colonialist mocking the inferior Vietnamese, the way he read about in his history books. "Does Ho Chi Minh share *all* of his battle plans with you? Does General Giap telephone you each time he plans an intelligence operation? Make another mistake and you will be sorrier than you can imagine. I demand to speak to your Soviet liaison officer."

It can't possibly work, he thinks. But the voice curses again. There is, of course, no "Soviet liaison officer."

If they're North Vietnamese regulars, and have a radio, they're using it. If they're Vietcong, they may not have one.

The voice calls, "Come out and we will check your story!"

"I demand that you contact my superior, Colonel Alexi Grudonov, at his temporary headquarters in the village of Lu Noc," he says, making up the man's name, identifying a hamlet occupied by the enemy, thirty miles away.

"Let us pick up that radio!"

And Szeska laughs!

He really turns the acting on. He is so good at this that the other two men stare at him, at the well of talent bursting from the young lieutenant who they only met a few days back. Szeska has actually turned red and his features have gone hard, contorted. He looks the part of the incensed overseer. "Do you think Grudonov talks on the radio so the Americans can hear? None of you are getting closer to us. Send a runner."

They curse again, but do not shoot.

Maybe, he thinks, they have sent the runner.

After a few hours, the light starts to fade, and the clouds come back, and soon the tropical darkness is complete.

Szeska shouts, letting them know he is still there, "Don't you have an answer yet?"

Turning to his men, seeing their eyes, their panic grown wide and terrified and close to the surface, he mimes a crawling motion. They slither from the log.

Ten feet safely.

At fifty feet, the enemy commander demands proof that Szeska is behind the log.

One of Szeska's wounded men wakes up behind them and begins to scream in English. "Medic!"

Firing erupts from the tree line, only this time Szeska sees where the enemy is, from the flashes. There are too many of them.

He whispers, "If they come out of the trees, mow 'em down. Otherwise, no shooting."

But the enemy doesn't make that third mistake.

A half hour later the Americans are back in the forest, using a compass, fleeing home, when he calms them, halts them, actually makes them double back and take up positions beside the trail they have used to flee.

"Lieutenant, are you crazy?"

"Those fuckers will come after us. They're too angry and they'll be in a hurry. They'll make mistakes."

Which is exactly what happens. Szeska and his men wipe out the enemy patrol. And later, the report of Szeska's ingenuity, coolness, acting ability, and controlled fury is passed from his captain to a major, who has a rare specialty, and a particular need, and this major requests, in turn, all of Szeska's files.

The major is especially gratified when he reads Szeska's psychological testing results. He sits in a special office, away from any base, and he hums while he reads, and occasionally says out loud a word or phrase that impresses him.

"Great compassion," he says at one point, reading.

A second later, he says, "No remorse."

The major from public relations, Szeska thinks, is big and garrulous, and looks more like a rock-and-roll guitarist than a military man, with a thick unruly beard, and an idle attitude more suitable for an actor in the recent hit show *Hair* than the army.

"Call me Nick, not Major Rourke," the major says.

He doesn't even wear a uniform, but khaki shorts that show his pale, heavy legs against a bright tropical shirt, adorned with red orchids. Nerdish white socks cover his feet beneath the straps of leather sandals. He looks like a tourist visiting Hawaii. Talking loudly, annoyingly, he leads Szeska to a small table at a popular Saigon outdoor cafe.

The street is packed. The Grateful Dead are playing over a loudspeaker outside a nearby bar. If not for the men in uniform walking past, there would be no sense that a war exists.

"I caught this damn fungus on my feet," the major says. "So I have to let air circulate around my toes. That's why I wear sandals, and since I gotta wear sandals, I might as well wear the rest. But it makes the reporters think I'm antiarmy. Those chickenshit liberal assholes. What do you wanna drink?"

Szeska orders a San Miguel beer, but he'd rather leave. It's been a week since the ambush, and he only agreed to the meeting after being ordered to come. In his mind, he keeps going over the patrol, the sounds, the trail, the call of the monkeys.

Could I have done something differently that would have saved lives?

He does not care that the army later found that the Vietcong had been waiting like deer hunters in a blind.

"They knew you were coming. You're a hero," Major Nick Rourke says, sipping a black market Johnny Walker Red, buttering Szeska up and clearly building toward some kind of half-assed public relations request.

"That Russians bullshit story you came up with saved your men, and that, my friend, would be one hell of a piece for," he says, dangling bait, "*Life* magazine."

"No."

"Buddy," insists the major, like some hotshot Ogilvie & Mather adman on Madison Avenue, shaking his head, as if

Szeska is missing a crucial point. "Don't you know what happens to heroes? They go home! They give speeches. *It's a ticket out of here!* Don't you have some girlfriend, family you want to see?"

"Twelve men died."

"Don't you want your name in public?"

"Those reporters don't care who they screw."

The PR man looks, as he cajoles Szeska, surprised, baffled, irritated. Finally he shrugs. "Hell, I tried."

But when Szeska stands to leave, the major growls, in a tougher voice, "Did I say we were through?"

Szeska sits, surprised at how the big man is now eyeing him more intently. The dopey laugh lines have rearranged themselves into military directness. The change is startling, goofball to commander.

Major Rourke says, "See that woman inside, in the blue dress?"

He nods toward a Vietnamese whose back is turned, at the bar, as she talks to a man in a light tropical suit.

"She teaches Vietnamese to a captain in Intelligence, sleeps with him, too. When she learns things from him she comes here and tells that man at the bar."

Szeska feels the color rising in his neck.

"My patrol route?"

"Among other things."

Szeska starts to stand again but the major growls, "Finish your beer."

He leans back, spreads his arms theatrically, becoming the nerd again, and lifts his face toward the sun. "I don't get rays like this in Minnesota! All I get is months of snow."

Okay, I'm supposed to wait for something, Szeska thinks,

and sips the beer, not tasting it, and the major chats about fishing, and Superbowls.

"Who would have thought Namath could beat the Colts," he says.

At length the woman walks by their table, and Voort sees she is pretty, no more than twenty-three, with long black hair, hip bones so sharp they are outlined against the deep blue silk of her slit dress, and white high heels that make her long legs seem even longer.

She steps into the street.

"Watch," the major from PR says, as the woman climbs on a motor scooter.

Suddenly there is a screech of brakes, and a scream, and the woman, flying through the air, resembles a life-sized doll, her arms and legs whirling as if made of stuffed cloth, not human muscle.

"Looks like she had an accident," Major Rourke says, reaching for his wallet as a crowd surrounds the body.

He pays the bill. In the street, the two men are picked up by an army Ford.

"Who are you?" Szeska says.

In the back of the car, he smells the major's Old Spice aftershave, and sees, this close, the pores in the man's face, the remnants of some long ago case of acne.

"One time it was a professor," the major says. "One time a businessman who travels to Hong Kong, and smuggled arms from Beijing. One time it was even a professional flutist. He traveled the country giving concerts. He was very high up in their intelligence system."

"I'm listening."

"You're superb in combat. You speak Vietnamese. You can act, even under pressure. You know the difference between a calculated risk and a foolhardy one. Your profile is right. You're violent, but you have a sense of decency, which is important so things don't go out of control. Finally, you have a grudge. We've found, in this area, revenge motives help."

"Area?"

"Accidents," the major says, "happen to anyone. That woman's bosses will never know if we knew about her, or if she just got hit by a car. It's the person who *told* us about her we need to protect. Protect him, get rid of her. Sun-tzu said, 'Warfare is the way of deception. . . . When committed to employing your forces, feign inactivity.' "

"Who's Sun-tzu?"

"The greatest Chinese military man in history. Learn from the enemy. Do you like history?"

"Yes."

"I'll lend you some books. Sun-tzu. Machiavelli. Clausewitz. Napoleon. Sun-tzu said, 'Subjugating the enemy's army without fighting is the pinnacle of excellence.' "

Rourke stares hard at the boy.

"Decide. Now."

But Szeska just says, "You're telling me you knew, before I went out on patrol, they would be waiting."

"Sending you was the only way to prove it. If we had gunships there, the Cong wouldn't have hit you. We were ready to come the second you radioed us. Do you see an error in logic?"

"I lost twelve guys."

"And saved a few hundred in the end."

Szeska says nothing for a long time. After a while he asks, "Why *Life* magazine?"

"If you wanted publicity, I could have arranged it. But

that's where it would have stopped. A guy who likes reporters is not the guy we want."

"Are you looking for other people, too, with grudges?"

"Like?"

"Sergeant Mann," he says, naming the person who will,
years later, die beside Meechum. "Also, Major, if you don't
mind my asking, do you always wear those clothes?"

"I wasn't lying about the tropical fungus. It really fucks
up your toes!"

Voort, in the Museum of Modern Art, lowers his shoulder
and lunges toward the man who has been following Jill,
who has now reached her, whose white hand is now half an
inch from her bare shoulder.

I can't see if there is anything in that hand.

He has to settle for knocking someone else back, into
the man. Time slows. The woman he has struck, falling
backwards, sets up a human ripple, a domino effect. The
world breaks into pieces. A gown collides against a tuxedo.
A glass breaks. An elbow swings into a stranger's belly. A
bit of the canvas *Echo of a Scream* disappears as the wall of
bodies blocks out Voort's view.

A collective complaint of pain and inconvenience
erupts from the crowd, but the hand has not reached Jill's
shoulder.

Voort bulls through an opening, grabs the wrist and
twists it, and is rewarded with a grunt of pain, but now the
crowd becomes aware of what he is doing, and a man's voice
is ordering "Stop that!" And other people seem to be trying
to get away.

"What's happening!"

"He hit the other guy!"

Voort's got the attacker facedown on the floor, knee-on-back.

And Jill's voice is saying, over his shoulder, horrified, "Dr. Feingold? Is that you?"

Shit.

Jill is pulling at his shoulder. "Stop! Dr. Feingold was my supervisor at Columbia!"

Voort is drenched with sweat. The doctor, Feingold, the noted internist, picks himself up, dazed, not angry yet, a sixty-year-old hero in his profession looking more at the moment like an eight-year-old punished for an infraction he did not commit. Wincing, he rubs his wrist. He doesn't understand what just happened. He is unaccustomed to violence, to things happening this fast. He seems older close-up, and tussled, than he looked through the crowd, when the tan and lean carriage, the tailored clothes, the excellent posture, had made him seem younger. Now Voort sees the pate beneath the thinning hair. The body had felt soft, not muscular. Atrophied with the pampered life.

"I thought that was you," Feingold tells Jill. And to Voort, when Voort tries to explain, the doctor is still more relieved to be unhurt than outraged, "Police? You're police?"

Jill apologizes, soothes, skillfully maneuvers the man to the side of the room. The gapers lose interest. The little conversations around them start up again.

Voort's heart is beating hard. He thinks, I could never be a Secret Service agent. Every time the president goes out, every time a stranger even looks at the president, you have to watch, and tense, and follow the movements of their hands. You have to figure, from a fraction of an expression, whether the person constitutes a threat.

As Jill talks with Dr. Feingold, explaining, Voort realizes that his beeper has started buzzing. He sees that Hazel is
calling.

He ducks into a small hallway five feet off, providing,
on one side, a view of Jill and, on the other, the entrance to
the men's room. He punches in Hazel's number.

"I work while you party," Hazel says, hearing the laughter in the background, festivity returned to normal.

"Yeah, I'm having the time of my life," Voort says, wiping sweat off his face.

"Well, I've been checking more databases on Szeska,
just to see if I could find something. State by state, and I
mean everything: mail-order lists, tax rolls, civil suits."

Knots of people, Voort sees, are discreetly watching him.

Hazel says, "Then I tried retirement records. You were
right. After soldiers are discharged they're moved to Veterans Administration files, automatically enrolled for benefits. Medicines. Commissary access. Retirees have a lifelong
relationship with the VA."

"And?"

"He's not there."

Voort pauses. *Jill is gone.* But then he sees her weaving
toward him, smiling, a drink in each hand. He bats down
the anger that surges because she left.

He says, to Hazel, "What do you mean, he's not there?"

Hazel says, "The army says he retired. He's definitely
alive, we know that. So why isn't he in the records?"

"Just tell me," Voort says impatiently, remembering
Szeska's dark house in Astoria, and the words *he travels all
the time.*

"Hey! I'm a lowly computer genius and my only pleasure is torturing you. I checked Meechum, too, for the hell

of it, with the VA. He was honorably discharged, right? He should be listed with them, too, right?"

"But he's not," Voort says.

"First prize for you."

"Which means they're both still in the army," Voort says. "The discharges are lies. There might have been a mix-up transferring one guy's records, but not two."

"It's called sheep-dipping," Hazel agrees. "Falsifying records. Hell, the Pentagon gets hit by electronic hackers over a thousand times a month, and every once in a while, they succeed. It's not like the old days where the secret was in a paper file in a safe somewhere."

"But records aren't falsified just against hackers," Voort says.

"Right. They close 'em against people like me, too," Hazel says, with her Germanic accent. "Or against one of their own generals who has clearance but he's out of some loop. Sheep-dip. Cover the white sheep with shit. The real record is somewhere under another name, accessible through a code. I always loved the way in movies someone calls up a computer file, and in plain letters it says Top Secret. But if something's really secret, it's secret that it *is* a secret, if you know what I mean."

Voort thinks, all Meechum's secrecy is making more sense now.

Jill slips her arm through his.

"I calmed Feingold down," she says.

I can't leave her alone until a replacement arrives to stay with her. And the inquiry required now, in Washington, would be more effectively made by someone with more clout than a sex-crimes detective.

He waits until she's occupied with someone a few feet

off, and punches in Chief of Detectives Hugh Addonizio's private number. If the army's involved in this, the problem's going to the commissioner and the mayor, Voort thinks, and hears, a moment later, the phone answered by Addonizio's number two, a veteran detective named Lou Barbieri, a burly winner of a half-dozen bravery medals, who used to play seven-card stud with Voort's father, in regular Tuesday-night games at the house.

"Long time no see," Barbieri says, glad to hear Voort's voice, but when Voort asks to reach the chief detective, Barbieri sounds sorry.

"He's at his five-thousandth farewell dinner, with Hizzoner and His ass kisser the commissioner. No calls to go through unless it's an emergency."

"It is."

"I gotta screen it. Emergency as in, did Madison Square Garden blow up? Otherwise I can get you in to see him first thing, tomorrow, at the office, seven-fifteen."

How do I explain?

"Does your pause mean it's not an emergency?" Barbieri asks, sounding satisfied that, in his mind, one more time, he has protected his boss.

"Lou, it sounds nuts, but there may be some kind of . . . assassination group in New York. They've already hit three people in other cities."

"They *may* be here, or they are?" asks Lou, who listens to exaggerated stories all day.

"Probably they are."

"Probably," Lou says, not liking the word, "doesn't sound like an emergency. You gotta give me more. Who are they?"

"It might be the army." But even as Voort says it, consumed with frustration, he thinks, *It doesn't sound right. I just don't believe the army would do this.* He thinks, *Meechum would never be part of it.*

Lou says, "Halloween's not for two weeks."

"Look, I have to talk to him. Someone has to call Washington, to clear it up, to get information."

"Gimme your number. If he wants to talk to you, I'll beep you. Otherwise, come in tomorrow morning. The army? Man, you better know what you're talking about. All the lines are ringing. I gotta go."

Voort thinks, hanging up, *What's the piece here that still doesn't make sense?*

Jill returns, grinning. "I think I avoided Feingold's million-dollar lawsuit," she says. "I told him, from a few feet away he looks like a man who's been threatening me, who you're protecting me against. A big powerful man. Feingold liked the 'powerful' part. He'll be telling this story for weeks. Would you prefer to eat Mexican? Or Chinese?"

"We need to make two stops first."

"Yes, sir! I dragged you here. It's your turn now. By the way, are these stops of your's police work? I always wondered what it was like."

Voort uses the key the superintendent gave him the last time he was here to get back into Meechum's apartment. When he pushes the door open, he and Jill enter a small, drab, one-bedroom flat which, considering Meechum's rich love of history, strikes Voort as almost intentionally devoid of personal mementoes, or even of any special effort to achieve comfort. It's as functional as a motel room. In a way, that's what it had been.

Maybe there'll be a piece of paper, an address, a note that I missed last time.

"Can I help?" she asks.

"Stay on the couch."

She leans back, reclines so her long legs stretch over the cushions, and her arms drape over the ridge, in an open, exhausted posture. Even now she exhudes femininity, fueling his interest.

The sense of Meechum's presence is so strong that Voort expects his friend to walk out of the bedroom, or in through the front door, even though he knows that will never happen.

Voort starts with Meechum's utility bills, like last time, moves to the mail, never to be answered, junk, mostly, and no help. He goes through the kitchen drawers, the IKEA build-it-yourself hutch in the hallway, the bathroom vanity, laundry closet, shoes, shirt pockets, TWA travel kit.

Hazel can check with TWA and find out what flights Meechum may have been listed on, that is, if he flew under his own name.

"I'm getting hungry," she calls, from the other room.

"Soon," he answers from the bedroom, aware that the dynamic has changed between them. Just now, in her voice, he'd heard the familiarity of an equal, not the wariness of a suspect, and definitely not the fury of the woman who had ordered him from her office less than a week ago.

Voort runs his hand under the mattress. Nothing. He checks the edges of the wall-to-wall carpet for loose spots, where something could have been slipped underneath. He finds none. In the closet, just like last time he was here, he carefully goes through Meechum's trousers, raincoat, the inside of his umbrella, the lining of his hiking coat. He turns the leather gloves inside out. He turns the mirror on the wall over, telling himself he must be missing something. A cop has to be a peculiar sort of optimist, his father used to tell him. Despite odds to the contrary, cops have to believe in luck.

What's this?

It's a slip of paper, behind a desk drawer, in the bottom of the cabinet, where he touched it, probing in the dark with his hand.

Pulse quickening, Voort pulls out a dry-cleaning bill from a shop thirty blocks north of here, in Midtown.

People bring laundry to shops near their home or office. And this one isn't near his home.

It is nine P.M., so the laundry will be closed. But tomorrow Voort will bring Meechum's photo there, hoping that someone might recognize it, and provide information about him.

Jill looks impressed when she sees the bill.

"You said there would be two stops. What's the other?"

"My cousin," he says.

Flirting again, she says, "Meeting the family already?"

"You'll meet plenty of Voorts, all right."

When he explains about Matt on the way downtown, she is aghast that he's been spending nights at her apartment while his cousin lies sick in bed, in his home.

"Believe me, he has company. At least two dozen relatives every night."

It's a replay of the museum when they get there. The Voorts at the house regard them as a couple. Jill takes in the paintings and artwork while Voort cops and their husbands or wives size her up.

"Where'd you meet *her?*" Matt asks Voort, when she

excuses herself from the sickroom to go to the ladies' room. "I thought Camilla was beautiful, but *she* looks like a movie star. It makes me feel better just to look at her."

"She's part of a case," Voort says.

"She didn't kill anyone, did she? Tell me she didn't."

"No."

"She likes you. Anyone can see that. Ignore her and *you're* the case. The nut case," Matt says.

Jill fusses over Matt when she returns, checks his temperature, asks about the pain, where it is, how often it comes, how well he sleeps, what he eats. She gets the name of Matt's doctor, and it turns out she knows the man.

"I'll call him tomorrow," she says, to Matt and Marla's satisfaction.

Voort admires her bedside manner, the way she holds Matt's hand, as if she has known the sick man for years, and the way she focuses on him entirely.

Jill, meanwhile, clearly likes the way Voort has opened his home to his family. She's impressed with the history embodied in the portraits of policemen and -women, going back over a quarter of a millennium.

The truth is, Voort would rather stay in the house tonight with his cousin, and normally might ask Jill to take a spare room, but he is reluctant to keep her close to the family because whoever is near her might be in danger, too. So they leave, and in a cab, on the way to her apartment, the talk turns more personal. She tells him about growing up in Zaire as the daughter of missionaries.

"When I got to Harvard, lots of students weren't sure how to treat me. They expected me to be a Bible-thumping fanatic. They didn't think anybody *was* a missionary anymore. I was exotic to them."

All over the city, couples are returning home from evenings together. They unlock doors, and in the privacy of their homes, remove their coats, trousers, dresses. They turn on bedroom lights, or music, or late-night TV. They brush their teeth. They put on pajamas. They pour brandy, or make tea, or if they are older, they take their medicine together, turn down the covers together.

Voort, paying the cabbie, walking into her building, finds himself sharing stories about growing up in New York. When he mentions that both his parents died when he was nine, she squeezes his hand. They are in her elevator now, just the two of them, rising up inside the city.

"I lost mine when I was young, too."

In her apartment, she hands Voort a corkscrew and a bottle of Australian Shiraz. She cooks penne with arugula, pine nuts, and Parmesan cheese. There's a fresh salad of red lettuce, sliced egg, tomatoes, kirbys, kiwi fruit, and apple bits.

Voort answers questions about his father, about the way the man introduced him to the police life when he was a boy.

She tells him about working in the Palestinian refugee camps during summers while at Harvard. Giving vaccinations. Teaching health education. Treating ringworm, tuberculosis, measles, polio.

For dessert, she produces leftover brownies studded with nuts, and makes almond tea, which they drink, sitting on the couch in the living room. The windows are still blocked by curtains, and Jill has halted all renovation work in the apartment, halted all access to strangers, for a while.

"I'll give him up," she says.

"Who?"

"Abu Bin Hussein. I'm scared. I don't want to live like

this. I hated it, in the museum, when I freaked out every time a stranger looked at me. I'm a coward, I guess. I'll call the FBI in the morning, and tell them they won."

"Good."

"You say that because you didn't think I should be his doctor in the first place. But that's not the reason I'm stopping. There's nothing glorious in being frightened. I only hope the right people will get the message, and leave me alone. There are other patients who need me. Do you think they will leave me alone when I stop?"

Her hand, holding her teacup, is trembling.

"Yes," he assures her, but has no idea if that will be the case.

"Then you can go back to your regular life, and stop baby-sitting."

She is looking into his eyes, and the meaning is clear.

It is no dream this time when Voort leans over, unable to stop himself, and she is leaning toward him also. He's wide awake when they kiss.

They do not draw back. They kiss harder. Her tongue slips into his mouth, and he feels it gliding between his teeth. He sucks at it. He is unhooking her gown, and she is unbuttoning his shirt, breathing faster. The bedroom is off-limits, under construction, filled with plastic tarps, and they slide off the couch, onto the thick living room carpet.

"It's been a long time," she says.

He kisses her neck. She is biting his shoulder. The gown glides up, the fabric bunching in his hands, and the smooth feel of cloth in Voort's fingers is replaced by the hot sensation of flesh. He loves kissing her, loves the warm feel of her, loves her hips thrusting against him, and her frenzied hands on his shoulders, chest, his groin, and sliding to his engorged penis.

"I want you in me," she says.

Voort enters her and she reaches up, grasps him fiercely, and he can smell the mixed sweat off them, the juices, and he sees the lamp stand by the couch has slid to the right, and when he turns her over she reaches back, massaging his penis as he jerks against her, wanting to come, wanting to keep from coming, locked in sensation.

"Come inside me," she says. "I want to feel it. I'm safe."

Safe, he thinks, still moving, Voort the animal, and just what is it that constitutes safety anyway?

But then he is lost in the sensation again, and when he comes it is with vast shudders, hearing her moan, feeling himself spurt into her.

At length they roll off each other.

They lay on the carpet, gasping.

Snuggling against him, she says, "I've wanted to do that for days."

"Me, too."

"Let's do it again."

An alarm is ringing, pulling Voort from sleep. It is dark, and at first he thinks it is morning, that the lack of light means her thick curtains are blocking out the sun. But then he sees the red numbers on the clock beside the pullout couch read 2:21 A.M.

"Jill?"

She does not wake up at first. Her naked leg hangs over her side of the pullout. Her right arm remains flung over her eyes.

No wonder she can work in war zones, he thinks admiringly. Nothing wakes her.

Then he realizes it's not the alarm that's ringing, but the phone.

And now, struggling from sleep, she gropes for the receiver, her voice honeyed, drowsy. She's a doctor who's been woken a thousand times by late-night phone calls, and clearly she has trained herself, until she hears the reason for a call, not to grow alarmed. "Dr. Towne," she says, as her free hand brushes his chest, warm and smooth and affectionate, gliding across his pectoral muscles.

Then suddenly she sits up.

"Yes, Detective Voort is here," she says, and hands Voort the phone.

"Voort? It's Lou Barbieri," the thick smoker's voice says, over the receiver. "We called your house and they gave us her number."

"Where are you, Lou?"

"Downstairs."

"Addonizio's here?"

Voort, astounded, envisions the chief of detectives in the marble lobby of Jill's building. He envisions Lou on the doorman's intercom telephone, while Addonizio waits beside him, or more likely, sits outside in the back of his LTD. He envisions the uniformed doorman, having seen Lou's badge, relishing the emergency late-night show.

Normally, New York's chief of detectives summons detectives when he wants to see them. He doesn't drive to their apartments, or their lovers' apartments, and Addonizio has certainly never, to Voort's knowledge, shown up at a detective's door at 2:22 A.M.

Barbieri says, "I'll explain when you get down here," meaning, *The doorman is listening. Hurry.*

"Right."

Minutes later, Voort strides from the elevator into the lobby, where his father's old pal leans against the doorman's station, shooting the breeze about the Giants Wild Card chances in the playoffs.

Barbieri always had the ability to get along with anyone. He's smaller than his booming voice implies, with a copper-colored crew cut, a Brooks Brothers dark blue suit, pressed white cotton shirt, and muted gray-and-blue-striped tie.

He steers Voort by the elbow, through the lobby, which is long enough so he has time to whisper, "He doesn't sleep with retirement coming up. He has no family. He hates that he's leaving. We drive around all night, every night, visiting places where he made arrests."

Voort says, "I called you hours ago. You just got around to telling him?"

"He was drinking with the commissioner till two, and that's when I finally got the chance. Voort, what's he gonna do when he retires, play the stock market like Mickie? He doesn't even want to go back to his apartment. There's nothing in that damn apartment except police awards."

But he stops talking as they leave the building, and the back door of a black Ford at the curb opens. Addonizio gets out, thick, tough, full of liquor but not showing it. A rock, is the way Voort's father used to describe Addonizio. The guy can drink and stay awake and keep going for days. He's a rock.

"Lou just told me about your call," Addonizio says gruffly.

"Don't put this on me," Lou says. The two of them often bicker like an old couple. Detectives affectionately call them Hughie and Louie.

"Yeah, it's my fault, okay? I told him not to bother me

unless it was bodies. You're like a goddamn wife, Lou. Voort? Talk."

They stroll on Fifth Avenue, Lou hanging back, and at this hour, there are only the cabs out, the lonely people, the disappointed ones, the sleepless ones.

Voort recounts the sequence of events leading up to this evening. When he reaches the West Point part, Addonizio says, shaking his leonine head, "That was eight years ago."

When Voort gets to Meechum's army records, and Szeska's, Addonizio says, "You don't *know* the records were falsified."

"That's why someone has to call Washington. So we know."

"What can you prove?"

"If I could prove things, I wouldn't need to ask questions in Washington," Voort says. "All the victims were on one federal list or another. FBI. CIA. Frank Greene's missing. Someone tried to kill Jill Towne two nights ago. Hazel's sure Meechum's still in the army, and if he is, everything relates to that."

"Hazel," Addonizio snorts, "is a conspiracy nut going back to Nazi Germany."

"Which turned out to *be* a conspiracy. All I'm saying is, someone should be calling Washington along with other strategies. You want me to do it? I know Phil Hauser," he says, naming the congressman from his own district, to whom he's given money, who he grew up with, and went to high school with. "But I thought at this point the mayor'd want to make the call. He'd get faster results than I would. Or maybe I should talk to the commissioner direct."

"What kind of results do you have in mind?"

"The truth about whether the army is involved.

Whether Washington is running some sort of . . . I don't know the right word for it, Hugh. Operation or intelligence or assassination group here."

"You know what you sound like?"

"Yeah, all the people who used to say the FBI kept illegal files on people when I was a kid, and it was a big joke until they turned out to be right."

Voort isn't even sure the mayor can help. But he has no experience in Washington, and the mayor, and commissioner, have a little. In his imagination, at least, he hopes the mayor can begin some high-level chain of inquiry. Mayor to New York's senior senator, perhaps, who, Voort knows from the newspapers, heads the Senate Armed Services Committee, and who might be angry as hell to think the army was running some illegal operation in his state. Senator to White House maybe. White House to Defense Department, or FBI, or CIA, or *something*.

However these things go.

Addonizio says, "He hates asking favors. When he asks, he has to pay back."

"He hates being kept in the dark about things more."

"We're not keeping him in the dark if there's no proof of anything."

"Hugh," Voort says, starting to get an idea of why his boss seems so reluctant to proceed. "This could be your last big case, your most famous one. Do you want people to say you hesitated if it turns out to be real?"

Hugh says nothing.

"Or are you more afraid they'll laugh at you if it turns out to be a false alarm?"

"I'm not afraid, Voort."

"All I'm asking you to do is tell the mayor. If he doesn't

want to call Washington, he won't. And if you don't want to tell him, I will. So far I didn't do it out of respect for you."

Addonizio snaps, "Don't tell me my job."

They are alone now, on Fifth Avenue. One detective at the end of his career, and one with years to go on the job. Voort, looking at the older man, for an instant sees the way his face will look ten years from now. The skin around the eyes and at the neck will droop, and turn yellower. The ears will be bigger, the face narrower. The dandyish shirt collars will seem too big for the neck they encircle. The shoulders will jut up, as if the head weighs too much to keep it up straight.

Voort flashes suddenly to a baseball game he'd been taken to by an uncle, when he was a boy. A hot summer day at Shea Stadium, and they'd watched the Mets play the Cincinnati Reds. Johnny Bench, the great Cincinnati catcher, soon to retire, had played third base that day, because his injured knees would not permit him to squat any longer behind the plate. Bench had dropped the first ball hit his way, and then the second. Bench had made so many errors at third, because he was playing past his prime, that when he finally made a play, and threw out a Met, the New York crowd, embarrassed, gave him an ovation.

At that moment Voort, sitting near the third-base line, had seen the legendary player turn to the stands, and had caught a glimpse of the man's humiliation. He had seen fear in Johnny Bench's eyes.

Voort had thought the man was thinking "I fucked up because I didn't quit playing in time."

Voort says, "You know what you told me a long time ago, Hugh, when I was a kid? *You*, and not my father? You said there comes a point in every detective's career where their instincts tell them to look in a place they don't want to go. You said probably, sooner or later, if I get good cases, being connected the way I am in the city, I'd have enough evidence to start poking around some sensitive place, and I'd try to convince myself that I really didn't. But it would just be that I was protecting myself. I'd hesitate, you said. I was twelve. You were working on the Vizzini case," Voort says, naming a police corruption scandal that resulted in Addonizio's putting two of his best friends in jail.

Addonizio has stopped, and looks into Voort's face, and Voort knows that he guessed right.

Voort says, "You said detectives are at war, Hugh. You quoted a French politician. You said, 'All delays are dangerous in war.'"

"What politician?"

"It was your quote. How do I know?"

Addonizio stops, and puts his thick hand on Voort's shoulder, and squeezes hard while he smiles. "You'd make a good infighter, Voort. Maybe you'll be a chief someday. I wouldn't doubt it. Look, if I ask the mayor to call Washington, he'll do it. If he thinks they're screwing around in his city, he'll call out the dogs. He has a temper."

Voort says, "You want me to file a freedom-of-information request with Washington? Maybe in a month or two, if we go through channels, if we even *can* use channels, we can get answers. By then, someone else could be killed. What do you think the mayor's temper will be like when *that* comes out? What do you care, anyway? You'll be gone."

Addonizio sighs, reeking of disappointment. Then he straightens. The old man is gone. The tough chief of detectives is back.

"I'll call him in the morning. Go back to sleep. Me and Lou have some driving to do. It's so late anyway, what's the point of going home?"

Three hours later, when Voort and Jill wake at six, they're at it again, a marathon couple, unable to stay away from each other. And when the alarm goes off, an hour later, she finds her robe, and says, happily, wet with sweat, "I'll make breakfast."

She pauses, regarding him for a moment, thoughtful and slightly playful. She says, with some delicacy, "By the way, my handsome detective, you aren't married or anything, are you?"

"Nothing to worry about."

She shakes her head, her grin widening. "That would have been too much to ask for."

Voort raises himself on his elbows, thinking he must have heard wrong.

Then Jill says, "Because I am."

FOURTEEN

Maniya Oasis, a twenty-mile-wide desert eden, lies on the border between Saudi Arabia and Iraq, north of Al Litiyah and due southeast of the strategic town of Judayyidat Ar'ar. It is cool, shady, and wet, with date palm trees and streams to feed camels, sheep, nomads, or soldiers. On July 18, 1990, Major John Szeska stands with Colonel Nick Rourke, at the northern fringe of shade, beneath the last palm tree, peering north with binoculars.

The temperature is over 120 degrees. The normally still air fills with the sounds of men and machines mobilizing.

The allied land invasion of Saddam Hussein's Iraq, coordinated by President George Bush, is scheduled to begin twenty minutes from now.

"Did you know biblical scholars say the Garden of Eden was out there, in southern Mesopotamia?" remarks the always cool Rourke.

"What do you want me to do," Szeska replies, taking in the burning, dun-colored landscape, rock and sun-blasted rubble, devoid of water, as hostile to him as his human foe.

"How does it feel to be back commanding men in the field again, buddy?"

They are dressed for desert warfare, in lightweight khaki uniforms, with pouches for gas masks, handguns at their sides, packs nearby filled with survival gear, medicines or chemicals especially prepared for the upcoming fight. The tools of war have changed since Vietnam. There are computers now, and smart bombs, and laser-guided missiles. But the strategies still resemble the ones Sun-tzu wrote about in the second century B.C.

"I want you to bring me something back," says Rourke.

"What?"

"Ordnance. Chemical shells," Rourke says. "We can't blow 'em up and we can't leave 'em there. The bombs are in a cave thirty miles north."

At their back are a dozen Bradley fighting vehicles, and soldiers who have been assigned to Szeska's command. They are checking weapons, filling gas tanks, coughing from diesel exhaust, or getting a last few minutes of sleep before the invasion begins.

Rourke kneels on a rare tuft of grass, grinding brown strands into sandy soil. He unrolls a topographical map. Its colored contours are reflected in the aviator lenses of his olive-tinted sunglasses.

"When you cross the border, you'll stay with the main group at first," he says tracing the route through a slightly green strip meandering north, between two jagged lines of beige, connoting mountains, and white, to show no rain ever falls.

"You'll peel off from the main group, into a mountain pass *here*. It'll be narrow and flat. You'll know it because there'll be a shitload of Soviet tanks, at least two dozen, burned-out motherfuckers, smoldering at the entrance, where our planes caught them. Take Interstate Ninety here through the valley fourteen miles north. You should be fine. No opposition, nothing moving under the air cover, and right *here* the valley'll fork right and left. Turn left at the Howard Johnson's, and the ammo dump's in a cave, three hundred yards later. You can't miss it, on the right, between the deli and the pizza place. Oh, yeah, one potential problem."

"Only one?"

"The man who told us about this never got the whole transmission off. He said most of the Iraqis fled the place, but you may get opposition. Take 'em out fast. Sun-tzu said, 'The army values victory, not prolonged warfare. . . . If the enemy opens the door, you must race in.' "

For Szeska, after Vietnam, the next assignment had been Beirut, where he helped Christian Phalangists arrange "accidents" for Syrian officers.

"In the middle of peace negotiations," he told the Phalangists, "you don't want to provoke the other side. But if their general dies in a swimming accident, no one will blame you."

Then, around the time his father died in Cicero, in a bar fight, there was a stint in Athens, with the Greek secret police, designing "accidents" against Bader Meinhoff Germans preparing to bomb a TWA plane.

TERRORISTS BLOWN UP IN THEIR OWN BOMB FACTORY, the headline in the *International Herald Tribune* had read.

He has helped Afghan guerrillas arrange "accidents" for Soviet officers, and trained anti-Communist contras in Nicaragua and worked in War Plans in NATO. He has, in a distinguished and varied career, drawn up tank defense strategies in war games against the Soviets, and coordinated land and naval troops in a computer "battle" against the Chinese over Taiwan.

The army is his home now, and his family. His grand-mother died years ago. There is no one he corresponds with in Chicago. No one he misses. No one he loves.

"How's it feel to be commanding troops again?" Rourke repeats.

"Ask me when I bring back your shells."

At that moment green flares go up all along a line one hundred miles long, and Szeska spins on his heel and moments later he is atop a Bradley fighting vehicle, leading his smaller column of men inside a larger one, all part of a huge, coordinated pincer sweeping north.

They pass smashed Iraqi trucks, and smoldering troop carriers. They pass vultures feasting on charred corpses, the birds too engorged to fly away. They pass fields of grass turned blue by chemicals, as, to the east, black smoke rises from burning oil wells, and from the north comes the thump of ten-year-old artillery. When they look behind, they see roiling walls of dust thrown up from oncoming men and machines.

A Kuwaiti Beduin guide, handpicked by Rourke, rides along with Szeska. "One who does not employ local guides will not secure advantages of terrain," the colonel had quoted from Napoleon.

Two hours later, without seeing any enemy, Szeska peels his group off the main one, threads the field of smashed, Soviet-made armor, only weeks ago the pride of Iraq, and pushes north into the narrow valley that Rourke described.

The sky is a slit of washed-out desert blue between rock. The cliffs tower above them on both sides, making them vulnerable to the kind of mass destruction they witnessed twenty minutes ago. If Rourke is wrong, he thinks, and the Iraqis are up top, we're finished.

Five miles.

Ten.

At fourteen miles, almost to the decimal point, the valley splits right and left, and Szeska slows the Bradleys, waits for his point vehicle to return, and soon he sees dust churning toward him, and his scouts are back, laughing, confident, young bulls already taking credit for victory, already composing letters in their heads to their girlfriends, basking in relief that the Iraqis were not here to fire back.

"Go in slow, and spread out," he instructs through his microphone.

A good precaution, because five minutes later, all hell breaks loose.

The firing erupts from the cliffs, from behind rocks, from the gigantic cave entrance he can see ahead, gouged into the rock. Tiny figures, gutsy or stupid men, run from the cave and crouch, facing them, and then there is a trail of incoming light, and a hissing noise, and the Bradley to his left explodes in a cloud of flame and smoke.

But the firing from up top is small arms, mostly, and the enemy is driven back in a barrage of bullets. Inside his vehicle, Szeska directs operations, skillfully pinning down more attackers on the cliffs with three of his Bradleys, while the others drive directly into the cave.

And now he is *in* the cave, with his men, and from *outside* it may have looked older than Moses, but *inside* he's in a depot as sophisticated-looking as anything he might find in Cheyenne Mountain, Colorado. There are computers and railroad tracks for armaments, fluorescent lighting, bunks, mess rooms, modern toilets, giant TVs.

In one cavern he finds Vietnam-era fieldpieces that

were obviously hauled here, for storage. Pieces that could throw a shell eight or ten miles.

Saddam's plan, never used, had clearly been to keep these old fieldpieces close to the front, and use them when the invasion started. The plan had been to match the antique ordnance to whatever newer ammunition this place contains.

He has no idea why the plan was never instituted. Maybe, because of Allied air cover, the Iraqis had been reluctant to move the pieces outside. Maybe they just got scared and ran.

But it's a good thing they did, he'll see, when he discovers what they would have fired.

Meanwhile, the fighting remains steady outside, the rattle of Iraqi small arms versus the bigger guns of the Bradleys. Szeska, searching, finds, in a lower-level supply "cave," two hundred artillery shells, the heads screwed open to reveal empty compartments. In the same cave are shiny chemical storage tanks, each with a red rubber hose at the side, each marked, in vivid red, with the international warning symbol for biochemical hazard.

"Damn."

Szeska bends down to read the writing on the nearest tank. "Made in USA," it says.

He also finds a pamphlet from a chemical company in Cincinnati.

"Under U.S. Law, these chemicals cannot be exported for military purposes," reads the pamphlet.

Right.

At that moment, as he is hit, Szeska hears a sound like a car backfiring in the cave, except he knows it's not a car, and something hard and hot smashes into his left elbow, spinning him around, and blood is spraying while someone shouts, "Sniper!"

In the end his men kill the shooter, and collect the shells. A medic bandages the smashed elbow, which hurts quite a bit on the way back, as Szeska wafts in and out of consciousness. He is hospitalized after they cross the border.

"Were you surprised to see those labels on the shells?" Rourke asks, visiting the hospital the next day.

"How'd Iraq get our chemicals? Steal them?"

"Well, let's see," Rourke replies, showing, for once, anger. "Some congressman probably passed a special bill allowing certain exports to be legal, benefiting a company in his district. Then some asshole in the Commerce Department stamped the shipment 'Approved.' Then some middleman in Chicago, who never fought a day in his life, earned a big commission. And in the end you've got bone splinters in your elbow, and two dozen of our guys are in heaven. It stinks."

The war is over, but Szeska will be in the hospital for another month, recuperating.

"Here's a book to read while you get better," Rourke says. "*The Letters of Chinese Gordon.* He was a big hero of mine." Rourke holds out a leather volume.

"Chinese who?"

"A British general, in the time of Queen Victoria. They sent him to Khartoum to evacuate it against a Muslim army. But he dug in. He thought he could win. And he *would* have if he'd been sent the reinforcements he asked for. But the politicians talked, and argued, and months later, when the reinforcements got there, they found the city in flames, and Gordon's head on a spike. They missed saving him by a day."

"They screwed him over, like our politicians did to us in Vietnam," Szeska says.

"Right, but because of Gordon, the Brits stayed in Africa another hundred years. They stayed instead of getting out. He saved the empire, at least for a while. Gordon understood eternal truths."

Rourke draws himself up to deliver Gordon's quote.

"I'll put it in my words, not his, since the Brits are too reserved for me. He said," Rourke says in a very bad British accent, "half the time, your own side fucks you in the end."

Years later, on a cold October morning, Voort rounds the corner of Madison and Sixtieth Street, striding downtown from Jill's office, where he'd left her with her daytime bodyguard, heading toward the dry-cleaning shop on Meechum's laundry ticket. He's hoping the clerk will remember Meechum, will have chatted with him, will relate a clue about his job, friends, hobbies.

But Voort's finding it hard to get Jill's words out of his head, and concentrate on work.

My husband lives in Rome, and works for the World Health Organization. He sleeps with other women when he's overseas. I can sleep with other men. But I haven't wanted to, until now.

The day is bright and blue, the city too sophisticated, and with Halloween—the night celebrating illusion—coming, Voort passes cutout goblins taped to a hair salon window, and witches taped to a toy shop door, as gorilla and space monster masks glare out at him like decapitated heads from the shelves. A bakery offers orange cupcakes. Clothing shops, perpetually out of sync with natural seasons, feature mannequins swathed in winter parkas and wool hats. Mannequin moms eye mannequin kids. In their perfect world they are shielded against winter disappointments: busted water pipes, heat that doesn't work, snowdrifts dirtied by car exhaust.

Confetti "snow" blows in the show windows, propelled by electric fans.

It's funny, Voort. After five years of abstinence when he's away, I finally like someone, and you're the one who disapproves. Bit of a role reversal. I thought men will jump into bed with any woman they want?

"There are all kinds of convenient points of view," he had replied.

"Are you hurt?" she'd asked.

"Just surprised."

"Should I have said something earlier? Loyalty is important to you. It's why I like you. But you don't have to be loyal to a man you never met, who doesn't mind what we're doing. Do you want to phone him? You can, you know. You're even sweeter than I thought, and you're naive."

"Naive is a word that people who don't care about things use to describe people who do," Voort had said, wanting to leave, except now he already desires her again. He can't help the way his body responds to her. He can't help recalling her finger tracing lines of seduction, affection, simple human contact along his chest. In his mind, the finger slides down his deltoid muscle. Her leg loops over his hip.

He is hard as a rock.

Voort, I used to think the same thing about marriage until I evolved a realistic point of view. Europeans have a lower divorce rate, and their marriages work. The spouse is in one place. The lover is elsewhere. In America, we want perfection so much we'll wreck anything to get it, so we jump from marriage to marriage, and in the end, perfection doesn't exist. How can you be a detective, live in the real world, and not realize that?

"You're making it out like I'm telling you how to live your life," Voort had said, eating her ham and cheese omelette. "But the question is how I want to live mine. Maybe, because I'm a detective, I want my private life to reflect better things."

Sipping hot sweet coffee, she had lain the cool fingers of her free hand against his. She had said, conversationally, "The detective accepts human fallibility in enemies, but puts inhuman expectations on people he loves."

"No offense, but I'm not in love."

"That's my point. Also, you do seem excited."

"He has no mind," he had said, looking down at himself.

"Or maybe he knows what's best."

As he reaches the right street now, Voort remembers her coming around the table, moving his dish back, massaging his shoulder, kissing the back of his neck, running her hand down the inside of his thigh when he stood up. She'd touched the places where he loved to be touched, almost instinctively. The spot on his lower spine. The bit of tender flesh below his right nipple. His heart had pounded, and despite the fact that he was half dressed, her randiness had gotten him crazy again, and they'd made love again, and it had been the best time of all.

Voort walks faster, frowning, unaccustomed to leaving a lover's bed feeling furtive. He has seen enough open marital "arrangements" to regard them as the first step toward divorce, which is none of his business, or violence, which is. He's seen the wreckage that comes from testing fidelity, has answered calls out of the sex crimes unit and found men and women who'd thought they'd "evolved" past "traditional" arrangements, as Jill might say, bleeding, sobbing, tortured, dead.

I want her right now.

But he must banish Jill from his mind. When he enters the dry-cleaning shop, he must present a calm, unreadable demeanor. He must not show emotion, which gives clues as to how a detective wants a source to respond.

At exactly ten o'clock, from across the street, Voort watches a short, curly-haired, heavyset woman inside London Dry Cleaners pull up a steel grate shielding the front door, and, one hour after she was supposed to, reverse the plastic CLOSED sign on the knob so it reads OPEN. As he pushes inside a bell chimes like a faint blooming of hope.

The woman, beginning one more urban workday, already seems to him an apparition of boredom, having waddled to a steel swivel stool behind the counter, where she scratches New York Five lottery tickets with the edge of a penny, hoping, probably, to win her way free of this job.

A calendar shows Moscow's church domes through snowfall. A gigantic rack of pressed, bagged clothing stretches into the rear of the shop, on an electrified rail, and the whole place is saturated with the crisp tang of cleaning chemicals.

Voort hands the woman Meechum's ticket without a word, as if he is Meechum. She sighs, put out by duty, shuffles on backless terry-cloth slippers to the carousel, and pushes a red button setting the rack into grinding motion. A line of used jackets, trousers, and dresses slides past.

But suddenly the woman stops the rack and peers at the ticket.

She says, accusingly, in an Eastern European accent, "You are not Meechum."

Voort's hope begins to race.

He shows his badge and her suspicion disappears as if it never existed, but it's replaced by a stolid unreadable look in the puffy face. Russian immigrants, he knows from experience, are tough to question. Suspicious from experience, and trained to hide emotion, they seem to Americans either cold or obsequious, depending on whether they view the cop as threat or superior. Their home country lacked middle ground.

"I never talk to Meechum," she says flatly, arms folded, as if daring him to contradict her. "I just recognize name."

Voort explains that Meechum is not in trouble, and the woman nods curtly as if she believes him, but of course she does not. She climbs back onto her stool, and pulls the pile of lottery tickets close again. She picks up the penny. With a steady machinelike pace, she starts rubbing.

Voort sighs inwardly and explains, threat slightly present in his voice, that if he leaves here without being satisfied, her shop may receive visits from city inspectors.

"How's your electrical wiring?" he asks.

"You theeenk I run firetrap?" But her look has changed to sullen wariness.

"The Environmental Department," Voort says, looking toward the rear of the shop, as if he has spotted some infraction, "would be interested in testing your chemicals. The rules call for stiff fines if you use toxic ones."

"Maybe I talk to Meechum one time," she admits, as if this is the first time Voort asked the question. She opens a drawer and takes out a pack of Junior Mints. She pops one in her mouth. She does not offer one to Voort. She simply needs to occupy her hands.

"What did you talk about?" he asks.

"He makes jokes with me," she tells him, bringing up an aspect of Meechum that Voort remembers from high school, but never saw in the tavern the other night. "And he mentioned he works on this block."

"Where?" Voort contains his excitement.

The woman's fingers dip in and out of the candy box with the same pace with which, earlier, they rubbed lottery tickets.

"He did not say, but one time, when it is raining," she says, so Voort knows that she chatted with Meechum more than once, "he tells me his shirts will not get wet because office is on block."

Voort gives her the police stare, the special look of scrutiny designed to unnerve sources, to make them more pliant. It is a look his father taught him in front of a mirror, as both of them laughed, posturing, when he was eight years old.

But the woman's been stared at, back in Russia, by experts. "You want to send inspector? Send. You are all same." Voort supposes she is referring to cops around the world.

An American source, especially an innocent one, he knows, would be throwing questions at him now, like *What did Meechum do?*

But a Russian? Hear no evil. See no evil. Eat mints.

"I told you everything I know. Good-bye."

Minutes later, he is on Meechum's street, the hunter's excitement building in his chest, sharpening his senses. A breeze has come up from the west, and gray clouds scud toward Manhattan, bringing a smell of incoming rain.

I work in a corporate head-hunting firm, Meechum had said.

Voort surveys the brownstones, redbrick postwar apartment houses, shoe store, Turkish restaurant, furniture showroom, printing business on the ground floor of the warehouselike building across the street.

Meechum's office may be close, but thousands of people live and work in the few hundred feet that make up this one block. Hundreds of offices, shops, and apartments fill these buildings. Voort could spend a week trudging from door to door, riding elevators, ringing bells, never leaving the block and never finishing the job. He considers calling for help but has another idea, at least for the short term.

He goes back into the dry-cleaning shop, where the woman, rubbing her lottery tickets again, does not seem surprised to see him. To a Russian, policemen always come back. But she *is* surprised when he asks, "What's the best pizza place around?"

"At ten in morning?"

But Voort knows that the delivery boys in the neighborhood, spreading out along this block each lunch hour, afternoon snack hour, and dinnertime, will have served a healthy percentage of the residents. He remembers an article in the *Times* about the first person in Washington, D.C., outside of the White House to usually know when a late-night crisis is brewing. It's not a reporter but the owner of the local Domino's Pizza, who receives, on crisis nights, orders for vast amounts of pies to be delivered to 1600 Pennsylvania Avenue, fast.

The woman names a restaurant called Antonio's, and Voort, trying the long shot, finds the tiny stand on the corner, where a dark, compact, vigorous man dressed in white mops the linoleum floor, in preparation for the lunch-hour hordes, beneath a sign saying TRY THE BEST. The shop serves walk-in trade. It has a half-dozen tables where customers can stand while they eat slices. The place smells of ammonia, olive oil, oregano, dried cheese.

The owner is much more cooperative than the Russian, but who isn't? He peers at Voort's photo of Meechum.

"I don't know him, but my delivery kids show up at eleven. Come back then, but meanwhile try the breakfast place across the street. They got three, four juvenile delinquents running sandwiches and coffees all over this neighborhood. It's a work program for dropouts. The diner gets a tax break. If it works for them, I'll try it here."

Voort thanks the man, crosses the street to a Greek diner, and this time when he produces the photo, the cashier, a dark-haired woman who has the same features as the waitresses, calls over a delivery boy, who is heading out the door, toward a locked bicycle. The kid holds a paper bag smelling of coffee and doughnuts, which, from the size of it, probably contains breakfast for a half-dozen people. He looks about nineteen.

The cashier asks him, "Mannie, did you ever deliver to this guy?"

The kid stares at the photo with a mixed look. He hustles for tips, so he's eager to please. But he's also reached a stage in life where he understands that bad choices have bad consequences. He looks to the cashier for a clue how to answer.

"I'm not sure."

"Tell me who you *think* he is," Voort says softly. "Don't worry about making a mistake."

"Well, there's a brownstone halfway down the block. They send out for egg sandwiches and coffee every morning. Two guys switch off paying. One tips like shit. The other gives a couple dollars even if they only get coffee, but I haven't seen him for a couple weeks. The picture looks like the good tipper. The secretary said his name last time. What *is* it?" The boy frowns. "It's a weird one."

"Think."

"Ethan? Beechman? Something like that."

"Meechum?"

"Yeah! The secretary said Meechum."

"What kind of work do they do in that office?"

"Who tells me anything? He comes downstairs and pays for food."

Five minutes later Voort watches the boy pedal into traffic from a croissant and bakery shop across from the brownstone, which the kid pointed out. He sips hazelnut coffee and watches to see if anyone goes in or out. If this is where Meechum worked, Voort thinks, if this building is where things started to go wrong for him, then whatever is going on in there may have led to the deaths of at least four people.

He phones One Police Plaza to let one of the other detectives know what he has learned, and he asks for backup.

He says, "Get hold of a reverse telephone directory, and find out who's listed at that address."

No one goes into the brownstone. No one goes out.

I don't want to get anyone in trouble, Meechum had said.

Waiting for backup, and information, growing restless, Voort considers the brownstone as if it is a fortress, as if by simply knocking on the door, he would alert an enemy inside to his presence, and the beginning of an assault. It looks like a thousand other brownstones. The walls are covered with trimmed ivy, and the windows are protected by wrought-iron bars. The roof looks well maintained, and as no air-conditioning units jut from windows, he assumes the owner's installed central air-conditioning.

Voort's phone buzzes as the detective calls back.

"The phone's unlisted to the public, but Verizon's got some company called the Baxter Group inside."

"Check with corporate head-hunting firms. See if anyone's heard of the Baxter Group. Also, where's my backup?"

"You gotta wait. There was a shooting in Greenwich Village, in a health club. Three people down in an aerobics class. No one'll be free for hours."

Voort snaps the phone shut and crosses the street beneath four stories of brownstone windows. He has, over the years, gone on many police raids, and the quickening feeling as the door gets closer is always the same.

I shouldn't go in there alone.

There's only one bell on the stoop when Voort mounts the steps, which means the company owns the whole building. There is no name by the mail slot, and Voort sees gray electrical alarm sensor tape running around the periphery of the windows on the first floor. A bright, well-placed sticker on the glass door, below a picture of a snarling Doberman, reads "Sherlock Security. This Building Is Under Surveillance!"

The camera above the door is trained on him. Inside, someone is probably watching him, watching the man on the stoop just standing there, not ringing the bell.

Here goes, he thinks, once again telling himself that the smarter thing to do is wait for help, for witnesses. *You are part of a team,* his teachers, his father, his captain has always stressed.

But Voort's prudence is overcome by a vision of

Meechum, at the morgue: a charred, dead thing, robbed of animation.

He can't stop the wave of rage that crests inside him.

If you're ever too angry, take a walk, calm down. Don't go into an apartment when you're not fully in control of your emotions, his father had told him.

But he can't stop his finger from punching the bell.

FIFTEEN

W hat do you mean you think Voort went into the brownstone alone? *You haven't sent backup?*"

Detective Mickie Connor, on a pay phone at Hartford-Springfield Airport, listens disbelieving to the excuse he is getting from New York, and snaps at the detective manning the line, "I don't care if a *thousand* people got shot in Greenwich Village. Get him backup right away!"

He slams down the phone.

We shouldn't have split up.

He hefts his Calvin Klein overnight bag, a present from Syl, and pushes through the morning rush-hour crowd—or what constitutes a crowd outside of New York—to the Hertz rent-a-car counter. It's been a long sleepless night. First his Delta Airlines flight was delayed in Seattle because of heavy wind. Then he missed his Salt Lake City connection because of the first delay, and had to take a turbo-prop jet to Cincinnati. In Cincinnati he discovered that his six A.M. flight to Springfield was canceled due to equipment failure.

I wonder if Frank Greene is still alive.

Now, at the rental car counter, he finds that the Chevy

he reserved is gone, since he never showed up to get it, but the Asian attendant surprises him with an upgraded new Avalon, and twenty minutes later, Mickie's on Interstate 91 heading south from Springfield, and then west on Massachusetts Highway 20, the route British settlers used three centuries ago, when it was a dirt track instead of a two-lane blacktop, when Voort's ancestors were patrolling the muddy streets of New York, and Mickie's were half-starved bog-trotting potato eaters in Ireland.

He tries to call Voort on Voort's cell phone. No answer.

He rockets through small Berkshire hamlets which are as picturesque to travel writers as they are boring to him. Mickie hates the country. It's filled with insects, mud, blocked radio reception, pollen. It lacks theater. Its restaurants close early. In the country, he thinks, you can't buy an Armani tie.

"What do people do at night around here anyway," he mutters, "watch bats flying around?"

Speeding past pine forests, and summer camps closed for the season, he tries to pick up a New York City radio station; rock, or hip-hop, even a talk show, but he gets only a local station playing oldies from twenty years ago.

But he knows his irritation masks worry. He's violated rule number one of police work: Don't leave your partner alone.

Voort's judgment is off because of Meechum, and Jill Towne's got him thinking with his dick.

What he does not admit to himself is that he feels alone, too, in a state in which he has never worked before, and where he has no jurisdiction, not to mention that Voort has him spooked with this talk of assassination. To Mickie, the very nature of his job seems to have changed in the last week. Flying over the brown pollution haze blanketing the country, looking down at the mountains, cities, and deserts, he has begun to appreciate the scope of whatever force killed Meechum. It's enormous, and invisible, and for all he knows, it's looking for him, too.

What's it going to turn out you're involved in, Frank? Do you sell secrets to the Chinese? Are you plotting to shoot the president?

"Mickie," he says, out loud, "stick with sex crimes and leave this other stuff to the FBI."

He reaches the hamlet of Lancaster Falls by ten forty-five, but still can't reach Voort on his cell phone, and when he tries One Police Plaza, he learns backup has still not been dispatched.

"It's a bloodbath in the Village," the detective on the phone says. "Some guy's girlfriend was screwing her aerobics instructor. He walked in and started blasting. Voort was supposed to wait."

"*Did* he wait?"

"He's supposed to."

As if the words are an incantation that will protect Voort.

Mickie again tries to reach Voort on his cell phone. No answer.

Frank Greene's town of Lancaster Falls turns out to be a pathetic-looking cluster of clapboard buildings around a rural intersection. There's a dot of a village center, a white steepled church, combined post office/general store, a town hall that looks like an old garage and doubles as a volunteer fire department; Mickie also takes in a VFW lodge fronted by a World War Two–era cannon, its long barrel probably as blocked as the intestinal tracts of the men who go there to drink.

No one is in the volunteer firehouse to give directions, and in the store, the fat, white-aproned postmaster supplies Mickie with a county phone directory while slicing smoked turkey for a woman trying to quiet a screaming baby. The baby seems to have more chocolate on his face than skin.

Mickie mutters, thumbing pages, "Would it be too much to ask you to be in here, Frank?"

But the postmaster turns out to be useful. He tells Mickie, without even asking for ID, that Greene used to rent a P.O. box here, but canceled it a week ago, over the phone.

"He had quite a cold. It didn't even sound like him. Anyway, he worked at the stables off of Route Twenty-three. That man is a letter writer. I swear, all he did was post letters to everyone from the president of the United States to the mayor of New York. Big fat letters."

"About what?"

"Well, sir, I asked him that exact question," the man says, his enormous belly spreading over the lip of his wooden checkout counter, his chubby hand unwrapping a Slim Jim, his voice as slow as a tree sloth in the Amazon. "I said, 'Mr. Greene, what are you complaining about to all these folks?' And he said, ready for this? 'The monsters,' and I said, 'What monsters are you worried about?' and *he* said, he was one angry sonofabitch, Mr. Greene was, 'The two-legged uniformed kind.'"

"The army, you mean?" says Mickie, not appreciating Frank Greene's absence, anger, or point of view.

"He didn't play with a full deck is what I mean. The stables are only a few minutes away. Want directions?"

Mickie tries Voort's cell phone number.

Still no answer.

Back in the Avalon, heading through wooded valleys, past Berkshire country taverns, farms, apple orchards, and new A-frame vacation homes, Mickie thinks, *Why'd you disappear, Frank? Did you die of a heart attack like Lester Levy? Did you hit your head on the edge of your bathtub? Were you crushed in a car accident? Did you drown in a lake?*

A dirt turnoff road takes him bumpily past a pasture, a copse of oaks, a paddock inside of which he sees half a dozen quarter horses, and finally up to a three-story Victorian-style home, with turrets, gables, and a wooden porch with an empty hammock on it. The sight of it reminds Mickie how tired he is. His bones ache.

The air smells of horse manure. He steps in dog shit as he exits the car, and the perpetrator, a mustard-colored mutt, rushes him from the shadows of the porch, braying. A gray-haired black woman steps out of the house, holding a dishrag, shouting, over the barking, "Cleon, shut up!"

She's about fifty, Mickie judges, wearing a long denim dress, her hair in braids, her round face pleasant, her accent surprisingly Brooklyn. She calls out an apology for the animal, seems disappointed that Mickie is not a customer, and then, when he shows his badge, the welcome look turns worried. The dishrag twists in her knobby hands.

"You're here about Frank, right?"

"Is he here?" Mickie says hopefully. It is always better to ask questions than answer them.

His evasiveness confirms her worry. "I told my husband not to hire him," she says. "I told him there was something wrong with him. But Ed said he was a good worker, and he was that, at least."

"Was?" Mickie says. "Where is he now?"

"Who knows. He bought that old Ford van, worked on

it for a month, collected his last paycheck, and he left no forwarding address."

Mickie's relief that the man is all right subsides into a new kind of concern now. "If you don't mind my asking, why were you so sure, when you saw my badge, that I was here for Frank?"

The sun is warm, and there's a smell of burned firewood in the air, and of mulchy autumn woods, and the dog has come compliantly up to the porch, where it lies by the woman's side as if it had never considered Mickie an enemy.

The woman squints at Mickie, sighs, and shades her brow with her hand. She seems torn.

"That was a New York City shield you showed me. You don't have jurisdiction here, do you?"

"No."

"Hmmm. You want some iced tea?"

Mickie tries to gauge the nature of the woman's nervousness. Is she worried over Frank? Her husband? Or herself?

He says, "That would be great, and is that a New York accent I'm hearing?"

"East New York," she says, naming one of the toughest areas in Brooklyn. "Come on in."

Welcome words, but they barely mask the nervousness. Trying to come to a decision, she's keeping him here while she thinks. He forces himself to relax, outwardly at least, keeps himself from pushing her, reminds himself that he has no legal power here. Chatting, she leads him into a wide, sunny kitchen, opens a new refrigerator, and brings out iced raspberry tea. Her husband is in Pittsfield, she says, at the chiropractor's, and won't be home for an hour. They bought the stable four years ago, having decided to leave

Brooklyn, where she was a nurse, and he was a medical supplies salesman.

"We like it here. It's peaceful. The people are nice. And Frank Greene showed up one day," she says, finally getting around to things. "He'd seen the card my husband tacked up in the village, offering minimum wage for a handyman. We needed someone to clean the stables, feed the horses. My husband has a bad back."

"Was Frank from Lancaster Falls?"

Now they're at a small wooden table, in an alcove, overlooking, beyond lacy curtains, a vegetable garden. Mickie sees plum tomatoes on a vine, still coming in, in October. He sees pumpkins. Squash. Pear trees.

"No, it turned out he'd left the city, too," she says, referring, like any New Yorker, to her birthplace as if it is the only city in the world, *the* city.

"I had the impression he'd been in trouble there, but he never talked about it. He was angry, a good worker, but raging inside," she says, touching her chest. "He was always writing letters to people, scribbling away in the middle of the night. Muttering while we watched the news every night. And his clippings."

"Newspaper clippings," Mickie prompts.

The thing that is bothering her, the thing she is reluctant to just say, is slowly coming out. "They were tacked up in his room. I saved them after he left. My husband said throw them out, leave Frank alone. But I always had a feeling that he'd be in trouble. *Is* he in trouble?" the woman asks.

"He might be," Mickie admits, sipping the tea, appreciating the tart flavor, and picking a homemade butter cookie off a plate she pushes toward him.

Don't rush her.

"Would you like to see the clippings?" she asks.

"Definitely."

She sighs, emits a deep breath of trouble, premonition, dread. She leads him through the ground-floor living room, which seems comfortable, filled with big stuffed furniture, colorful woven Appalachian throw rugs, pine cabinets which she says she and her husband stripped and refinished. The windows are open and he hears horses running outside, and smells hay, which makes his nose itch. The curtains are blowing. Photos of children, and grandchildren, he guesses, from the shiny newness of them, decorate the top of every available surface: the upright piano, TV set, tables, shelves.

"Frank slept in here, behind the study."

It's a small room, painted in cheery yellow. The window looks out on the horse paddock. The bookshelves are held up with cinder blocks, and Mickie makes out titles. *How to Improve Yourself. The Turner Diaries. The Failing Presidency. Serpico.* The walls are bare, but there are small discolored patches, as if from Scotch tape that once secured paper to the walls. There's a TV, a single bed, made up, and an antique steamer trunk in the far corner. That's it.

"He hated men in uniform," Mickie prompts, remembering the words of the grocer.

"So you know about him," she says.

"Actually, you could tell me more."

"Look in the trunk."

Mickie crosses the room, feeling her anxiety, and that something of import is about to happen. He lifts the lid and sees, inside, piles of newsclippings scattered on neatly folded quilts and pillows. He picks up the first pile, starts reading *New York Post* headlines.

COPS INDICTED IN BRUTALITY SLAYING.

POLICEMEN BEAT HAITIAN IMMIGRANT.

FEDERAL PROBE OF GRAFT IN BRONX PRECINCT.

The articles are all about men in uniform, all right, but all the men in uniform are cops.

"He hated police," the woman says. "He never talked about why, but if anything bad was on TV, about cops, he'd start ranting. He read all the New York papers. It was the one thing he spent money on, except for his van, and that fertilizer he was going to sell. He said cops are evil, they shoot innocent children. Devils, that was what he called cops. He *hated* cops."

Fertilizer?

The woman's worry is clear now. She fears that her former handyman has attacked a cop.

"Mr. Connor, he was gentle with horses, popular with riders, good to kids, but if the subject of police came up, he got wild."

Mickie thinks, Cops shoot kids? *His* kid?

"Well, he doesn't have any police record," Mickie says, to calm her, as he looks over a *Time* magazine piece headlined THE DECLINING QUALITY OF POLICE.

She seems surprised. "Really? Then he hasn't done anything? But then why are you here?"

Mickie makes a face, chuckles at the irony of it. "To protect him from someone else," Mickie says, although a new kind of alarm, that he had not considered before, has begun sounding in his head. The purpose of his visit has just changed a bit.

"You have no idea where he went?"

- "No. He bought his van. He drilled holes in the back of the cab, between the driver's seat and the rear. I asked him," she says, coming out with the really bad part now, that *really* concerns her, now that he has alleviated some of her fears, "I asked what are you doing that for. He said, ventilation. Ventilation?" she says, going to the bookshelf, removing the volume *The Turner Diaries*, flipping pages. Mickie understands that he and the woman are both imagining the same nightmare now.

Shit, fertilizer, Mickie thinks, remembering the speech on terrorists that he'd heard from Abel Drake, the Montana cop, in Las Vegas last year, remembering how Abel talked about this book, and the way it outlined how to make a truck bomb.

Mickie, angry now, says, "You never called the police."

She has turned a darker shade of brown. "A man comes into your house. He's good to you. It's hard to believe he would really hurt someone. My husband thought Frank was a talker, not a doer, that he was blowing off steam. So Frank bought a book. But it's not illegal to have this book. A lot of people have it. And the book's racist, but Frank didn't hate black people. I don't even know if he *read* the damn book. It's not underlined or anything."

"I understand," Mickie says, controlling his anger, but he does not understand. He never understands why people don't call the police.

"Look, Detective, when we lived in Brooklyn, we had a BMW. My husband saved for *years* for that car, *dreamed* of buying it, and the very first time he drove it he was pulled over, frisked, and humiliated by police, all because they were sure a black man could only have stolen that car."

Mickie feels himself turning red.

"The police were always stopping us, but my husband refused to get rid of that car. We grew to hate the sight of a squad car. We never knew when we left the house if we'd get all the way where we were going without being stopped. You want to know the truth? It's why we left New York in the end. A person can make themselves blind for a lot of reasons. My husband decided Frank was harmless. My husband said, leave him alone. We have no evidence. He said, the poor guy probably had the bejesus kicked out of him by cops one time. He said, after we heard about the dynamite theft at the quarry, hell, *anyone* could have broken in. I *still* don't know it was him."

Mickie sits down, heavily, on the bed.

Oh Christ, he thinks.

The woman is saying, with an undertone of pleading, of trying to protect her husband and herself, "It's not like the movies. There's no music playing when the bad guy shows up. It's not like TV. He smiles. He sings songs. You don't really think someone you know personally might do something bad. It seems far away. Do you know what I mean?"

And Mickie is thinking, *Why didn't I expect this? Everyone on Meechum's list was accused of being a public threat. We've been worrying about helping them instead of about what they might be doing. Why didn't we guess one of the threats might turn out to be real?*

And now Mickie, peering down into the trunk, sees something else that catches his attention amid the old magazines and pieces of cloth and scattered balls of twine.

Drawings.

"Frank made those," she says as he picks them up. They're pencil, on thick artist's paper, loose-leaf paper ripped from a book.

Shit, Mickie thinks, as a cold finger brushes his chest, as he considers the charcoal-colored lines, finely drawn, by a talented person, straight and accurate. They form, in the first picture, the facade of a mid-sized city building, with diagonal parking spaces outside, along a narrow street. In the next drawing, of the same block, he's looking at the facade from another direction.

The last, most complete sketch shows a different structure, from street level, as Frank Greene's carefully drawn lines crisscross the unlined page.

Mickie's looking at a fourteen-story building, with satellite antennas on top, and a concrete ramp leading to the glass front doors. There's a broad plaza outside, with benches, and a couple of trees, small ones, for shade. There's a steel sculpture, modern style, and a little church beside the building. Concrete safety barriers, roughly two feet tall, shield the section of building visible.

"Why did you keep this?" Mickie asks.

"Maybe," she says, slowly, "in the back of my mind, I thought I might need to show it to someone someday." Curious now, she adds, "Do you know these places? You look like you do."

Mickie, despite the coolness in the house, feels sweat running down the hollow of his back. He turns the drawings over. He sees, on the last drawing, a date . . . October 20.

Two days from now.

"Yeah, I know them. The first one's a precinct house in Manhattan. The other one? I work there. It's One Police Plaza," he says.

There are no lawyers in the room, but there are rules of evidence. No judges, yet indictments are handed down. No juries, but there are verdicts.

"This next slide is Conrad Voort," says the blond

woman, the photographer, as she is known here, working the slide projector, eyeing the detective whose handsome visage shows on screen.

"This is his house, on Thirteenth Street. This is him kayaking, on the Hudson. Here's Voort at the Museum of Modern Art, escorting Dr. Towne."

"Dr. Towne is of no interest to us anymore," says the man with the twisted left arm. "She's canceled the activities that brought her to Washington's attention."

"Colonel, *he's* still of interest. This is Voort at West Point, yesterday. He asked questions about you."

They are on the third floor of a brownstone, on the same block where Meechum brought his clothes to be dry cleaned. The building sits across the street from a croissant and coffee shop, down the block from a pizza stand, two hundred feet from where Conrad Voort sips coffee, deciding whether to go in.

"What do we do about him?" says the researcher, the cupid-faced man, the third person in the room.

But Szeska, at the moment, is preoccupied.

He is thinking, *Today would have been her birthday.*

The photographer suggests, "A kayaker could get hit by a powerboat. They're so low in the water."

Szeska hears a woman's voice saying, in his mind, *I shoot the dogs.*

In the room, the blond woman, a captain of Intelligence in the marines, leans toward him, raises her voice to get his attention. "Voort's people are making inquiries at the Pentagon."

And Szeska snaps out of it. "Have they figured anything out?"

"No, but they're getting closer, judging from the questions."

"How good are our sources in the Police Department?"

The woman shrugs. "We're not set up for that. We only get an idea what they're thinking by monitoring the questions they ask."

"Shit," the other man says softly.

"Forget the kayaking," Szeska says slowly. "Forget an accident. He's looking into Meechum's accidents. He must have notes written down somewhere, must have told someone about it. His partner. His superior. If he dies in an accident, that's waving a red flag to the police."

The researcher, who is a naval lieutenant in Intelligence, looks worried. "So we do nothing?"

"Not for a month or two," Szeska says. "Then we'll see."

"You want us to let him run around for a *month?*" the researcher says, horrified.

"*Or,*" Szeska says, thinking, the beginning of an idea forming, "if he dies, it has to look like murder. Not an accident. Obvious, unsophisticated murder. I wonder what other cases he's working on. Or maybe there's someone he arrested once, who just got out of jail."

The researcher brightens. "Yeah! Someone *else* he's investigating went after him!"

Szeska says, "There are no good choices here."

"Those New York cops work on a dozen different cases," the researcher persists. "He's worked on hundreds of cases. There have to be people pissed off at him all over the place."

Szeska says, considering, "And then we hope that whoever inherits Meechum from him doesn't have a personal stake. Because if we've done our jobs right, no one can prove we're linked to any list. Once the personal motive is gone, the thing should lapse. Then we can finish what we started."

"Good," the blonde says.

"It's that or do nothing," Szeska says.

"We can't do nothing," the researcher repeats.

The blonde says, "Although it's too bad. He's just doing his job, like us. What a good-looking guy."

"Find out who else he might be investigating," Szeska says slowly. "Someone he's close to arresting. A lowlife would be good. Sex crimes suspect, druggie, crackhead. A repeater with a record. A street person bombed out of his mind, who can't remember anything. I'll do the rest. A death that calls attention to itself. A big death, not a little one. We *use* that Voort's a cop."

The blonde is nodding.

The researcher says, "No accidents."

Szeska shrugs. "And we're protected in Washington, from inquiries. Right now it's still just him, looking for us. But he reached West Point, eh?"

The others trust him implicitly. They have done their jobs right, and if Szeska says they are safe in Washington, he must be correct.

"I'll find out what else he's working on," the woman says.

Lupe, I miss you.

On her birthday, Szeska can never fully shut the nightmares out. On her birthday, history assails him as a series of ravaging emotions. History is a pain in his heart that never goes away.

He can even smell Quito, the rain that never stops in October, the green of the Andes Plateau the city occupies, the exhaust and bad sewage odors of a Third World capital, the air freshener pumped over the air system of the Conquistador Hotel, where he is eating dinner in the ground-floor restaurant, across from Colonel Rourke, allegedly an embassy commercial attaché, and diplomats or businessmen from France, and Germany, and across from the woman who will become, in a short time, his wife.

In the present, the blond woman says, "Colonel?"

But he is barely listening, not in that fraction of an instant. He is back to Quito, at the end of the President George Bush years, after his stint in Iraq.

I shoot the dogs.

In Szeska's mind, in the hotel restaurant, the Frenchman is mocking America.

"At McDonald's and Burger Keeeng, you *eat* in your *cars*."

It is the kind of offensive conversation he's been subjected to so many times overseas, in all the capitals where he has worked, and listened to the never-ending criticism of America's military power, or businesses, or teenagers, television programs, educational system, lack of universal health care.

The German clothing factory owner says, "You have heavy metal instead of Wagner. Stephen King instead of Shakespeare. Norman Rockwell instead of Picasso."

Colonel Rourke, an actor himself, pours Chilean red wine and laughs and acts like the good old boy, everybody's buddy. But Szeska knows he seethes inwardly. "We saved Europe's ass for the last fifty years," is what Rourke always says in the embassy, when he and Szeska are alone, planning strategy to aid the Ecuadoran national police.

"American television!" laughs the Frenchman. "So many channels! So little substance!"

"Americans have no knowledge of other cultures, yet you want to tell us what to do," the German says.

"You are infants trying to run the world!" the Frenchman agrees.

But suddenly, the woman across from Szeska snaps at the critics. "You are wrong!"

She is not someone Szeska has really noticed until now. She is the niece of their Ecuadoran host—an airline owner—back from the Galapagos Islands, where she works as a scientist. Not a pretty girl, not dressed to flatter, but to conceal, with that big dress and squarish glasses. She's on the large side, her black hair curled naturally, stiff as a permanent, around a squarish face. Her skin is good, although at the moment it has gone purple with anger. Her lips are thin, almost bloodless with political rage.

"You critics of America are the ones who disgust me!"

It is her fire that draws Szeska, shocks and warms him and makes her beautiful. He has slept only with prostitutes for years, has kept the private part of himself aloof, offered loyalty to his country only.

In his memory, at the table, he recognizes his grandmother's passion in another woman. A fire, an incendiary reaction.

A woman who is not even American, yet she is defending America!

In the present, the blond woman is saying, "We haven't been able to find Frank Greene. He's not shown up at the house he used to live in, in Brooklyn."

In the past, Szeska can feel Quito around him. The shantytowns on the hillsides. The immense basilicas and cathedrals, constructed by the Conquistadors. The wealthy diners at the other tables. The fledgling guerrilla group, to the west, in the Amazon, who were planning to kidnap Americans, that he has just helped Ecuadoran soldiers wipe out.

The blond woman is saying, "He bought a 'ninety-two

Ford van, blue, registered in Massachusetts. He hasn't started a bank account in New York, at least under his own name."

But Szeska is hearing Lupe say, "America is the greatest social experiment in history! In America people come from so many places, and flourish peacefully together. Serbs and Croats! Jews and Muslims! Greeks and Turks! Of course they break down their old cultures before they form a new one! Give them time!"

The photographer says, "We've confirmed that Frank Greene bought two hundred pounds of racing fuel in Massachusetts. That gives him the fertilizer, fuel oil, and dynamite. Coupla days, his profile predicts, and he'll use it."

Lupe says, in his mind, "You French sell anything to anybody! You Germans go crazy every forty years and slaughter half of Europe, and mope around, guilty, the rest of the time."

Lupe stares at Szeska, right into his eyes, as if she has some special knowledge about him. It can't be, yet he feels it so strongly he wonders whether one of her relatives, high up in the government, told her something. So many of the upper class in Latin countries are related, that the notion is not wild.

"You are John Szeska," she will say, consuming him with her eyes, when the meal breaks up, and they are in the lobby, waiting for their cars to be brought out front.

Her face is round, her eyes startlingly black, and she has thin brows, a small nose, a forehead that seems lined with intensity. Her hair is blue-black, and she is deeply tanned.

"What is it that you do in the Galapagos?" he asks her, to change the subject.

"Me? I shoot dogs."

And two weeks later, when they have become lovers,

when she has become the first woman that John Szeska has not paid, since high school, to have sex with him, she is *showing* him her job. They sit in a launch, in the Galapagos, landing on an island as she loads a rifle.

The Remington is big for her but she handles it expertly. It is a bright, sunny, equatorial day, and the island is composed of the remaining three sides of an ancient volcano, jutting above the ocean, plunging a full mile to the floor of the Pacific, where he cannot see.

Inside the crater the water is blue, and red-breasted black frigate birds wing over the crest of the rock, as sea lions roar from caves.

"As a naturalist," she says. "I must protect the ecosystem. These birds and seals have no natural defenses against predators, because there *are* no natural predators in these magnificent islands. But every once in a while someone, the owner of a boat maybe, releases a pet dog on an island. The dogs become feral. They kill innocent animals. A single wild dog can wreak terrible havoc. So someone has to kill it before it does."

John Szeska's future wife, in 1991.

"Someone must shoot wild dogs before they do damage."

John Szeska stands on the black sandy beach of a volcanic island, watching Lupe load a rifle, pause, turn to him shrewdly.

"I bet you know how to use one of these," she says.

"I used guns in the army, years ago."

"I bet you shoot dogs also," she says.

"Excuse me?"

He never tells her the truth, not during their whole three-week relationship, but she knows about him, and he never finds out how. She is letting him know without using words that he is a hero to her, and that she understands him. She is inviting him to love her back, without fear.

In his mind, a rifle fires.

He remembers a small black dog, a mutt, an abandoned innocent, limping on three remaining good legs, the fourth a mass of red, and the animal topples over a volcanic escarpment, howling, dropping into the blue sea.

Lupe is crying.

But in the present, a buzzer is ringing, and it captures all Szeska's attention, finally.

The blond woman, the photographer, is standing and holding a phone out to him. She looks as alarmed as the cupid-faced man looks frightened.

"Colonel Szeska," the blonde says, "that detective is downstairs. What do we do?"

SIXTEEN

V oort, age eight, watches his father interrogate a lawyer. He stands in a small viewing room on the second floor of the Upper West Side's Twentieth Precinct. On the other side of a one-way glass wall, a middle-aged man in tortoiseshell glasses, a "witness" in the murder of a lady, on Seventieth Street, tells his tale.

"And then I looked out the living room window, and saw her in the playground across the street, trying to fight the black guy."

All over the city this September day, boys have gone to work with their fathers. They sit in doctors' offices and TV studios, and watch their mechanic dads fix Volkswagens. On the other side of the police glass, William Voort, detective first class, sits across a small wooden table from the lawyer. Both are polite and dressed well; Voort Senior in an extra-large well-fitting Brooks Brothers dark blue jacket, white shirt, and muted red-and-white-striped tie below his button-down collar. Shiny oxblood loafers rest on the floor below the table, beneath the cuffs of his fawn-colored slacks.

His father asks, "You mean the tall guy, not the one who

drove the green car? The one with the gold chain around
his neck?"

"Right, the bald one," the lawyer says.

The lawyer looks washed out from working indoors,
gray-skinned, gray-suited, prematurely gray-haired, with a
fat brown leather briefcase beside the leg of the table. The
man came in on his way to work. Under the table, Voort
watches his thin hands twisting on his lap, above his black
wingtips.

"I can't believe I actually saw him stab her. It looked
unreal. Then the guy just walks out of the playground,
toward the car, and she takes two steps forward like nothing
happened. Then she stops and presses her hand to her
chest," the man says, doing it. "When she fell, I called
nine-one-one. Do you think those guys are the same ones
making the other attacks in the neighborhood?"

"Could be," Voort's father says.

It is a Friday, after school, and the boy, as always, has
the general run of the precinct where his dad is temporarily
stationed. Sometimes he sits with the desk sergeant, like a
war orphan mascot for an army squad, and listens to the
complaints of people who walk in off the street. Sometimes
he eats RingDings with the precinct captain, his uncle, who
is also in his dad's poker group. On quiet days he rides in
squad cars with the Blue Guys, or goes out with detectives,
which is against department rules, but they let him anyway.
Voorts are police royalty. And this boy is the prince.

Now his father says, jotting notes with his big hand, "So
first, sir, the teakettle went off and then you heard the
woman scream from the street, and went to the window."

"That's how I knew it was eleven o'clock. My wife and I
always have peppermint tea just before the beginning of the
nightly news."

"Do you remember what item started the news that night?"

"How could I? I ran to the window."

Voort's father looks embarrassed, as if he had forgotten this fact, when of course the boy knows he didn't. His father was testing the man.

"Oh yeah, right," his father says.

To the boy, the interrogation room, the cracked green walls of the hallway, the Pepsi machine and holding cells and old Smith-Corona detective squad typewriters, the smells of coffee and polished leather, are as familiar and homey as the antique Colonial furniture in his house.

His dad shakes the lawyer's hand, seemingly impressed with the man's civic-mindedness, and says just "a couple more questions." He asks if the lawyer would mind talking to another detective, his partner this month, a Harlem resident named Jesse Ray.

"So, pal," his father says minutes later, putting his arm around the boy, when he brings Voort to the coffee room. "Any observations? Remember, there are no wrong answers. There's only what you think."

"He's dressed nice."

"Which means?"

Voort thinks about it. "That he has money, but I guess it doesn't make him more honest than other people."

"Anything else?"

Voort says slowly, understanding that he is being tested, going back over the scene, "Everything he said made sense, about when he got home, and the man standing under the lamppost. . . ."

"Then what's bothering you?"

"I didn't believe him."

His father's brows go up. "Why?"

"I'm not sure," says the boy, who is at an age when children would rather absorb the knowledge of adults than dispute it. He gets no signals from his father indicating whether he is right or not. "Should I believe him, Dad?"

"Let's figure it out."

His father, handing him a soda, emits the love he feels for the boy, in his patient voice, in his smile. He is every father who ever taught his son to hunt a bear, fix a car, bait a fishing hook, drive a truck. "Why do you think you don't believe him? Take your time."

"His hand was twisting under the table," Voort starts out. "He was nervous."

"After seeing a dead body, most people are."

"He was looking at you the wrong way. He never took his eyes off your face. I think he was scared you wouldn't believe him."

"A lot of people are afraid when they come here. Even innocent people."

"Then I'm wrong?"

Voort's father stirs sugar into his coffee. "I'm not saying that yet. If you were me, what would you do to test your theory?"

"I'd find out if the lawyer knew that lady."

"How?"

"I'd do the things you told me about. Check where he works, and his neighbors, and her apartment, his phone book, her friends."

"Is that all?"

"No! I'd ask his wife about that night, too, and see if they give the same answers. But, Dad, if he's lying, why come here to talk to you at all?"

"Good question. Does that mean you're wrong?"

Voort says nothing.

"Think about it, pal. Everything is logical if you look at it the right way. If someone is guilty, and I'm not saying that man is, but *if* he is, why voluntarily come into the precinct, and put himself on record?"

"Maybe he wants to send you off in the wrong direction."

"But why show himself? Why not call on the phone, anonymously. You know what anonymous means?"

"That you don't want anyone to know who you are. Maybe the man thinks you'll believe him more if he says it in person."

"Or maybe," William Voort suggests, a devil's advocate of police thinking, "the man likes risk. It's exciting to him. Maybe he's a certain kind of person, sure he can convince anyone of anything, who thinks he's smarter than me, so he took a risk. He's afraid if he doesn't come in fast, we might find evidence showing something else happened. You think that might be it?"

But the boy doesn't buy this. "He doesn't think he's smarter than you. He's scared of you."

"Ah! So go back to your original question: What is wrong?"

The boy thinks hard, trying to put everything he has heard into a sensible framework. The soda is sweet and delicious. He reasons out loud, "If he's lying, maybe *he* was with the lady, or . . ."

"Yes?"

"Maybe he saw someone *else* hurt her, not the black man."

"Then why lie about it, pal?"

Voort's head hurts. This is so complicated. "He's protecting the person who did it?"

285

Voort's father nods, but never stops pressing. "But if that's the case, why risk himself? That lawyer, if he's lying, is risking going to jail. Pretend you're him. If you were him, never mind a murder, make it something less important for you, why would *you* protect someone?"

Which is an easy question, now that murder is out of the equation, especially since Voort sits with his father, with the obvious answer lying between them. "Because I love the person," he says, and then it hits him, and he bolts up, experiencing a kind of certainty, a meshing of fact and emotion, a thrill of expectation that he has not before sensed, but which he will enjoy many times, one day, when he joins the force.

"Who does that scared lawyer love?" Voort asks his dad.

William Voort stretches, which means, Voort knows, that it is time for him to join the interrogation. The lesson is over. "Remember, always look at the personality, not only facts. One day, even if you don't become a detective, if you get a feeling about someone, trust it. It doesn't mean it's right. But take it seriously."

And days later, after the lawyer's nineteen-year-old son is arrested for the murder, Voort's father takes Voort out for pizza, in a little ceremony that occasionally accompanies one of the boy's minor investigative accomplishments, suggestions, or better observations.

"Pal, always balance out facts and feelings, because feelings are information processed a different way. So, Detective, how about another slice?"

And now, years later, Voort watches his index finger pull back after pressing the buzzer that will alert anyone inside the brownstone where Meechum worked—where Mee-chum's "corporate profiling firm" is allegedly located—that he is outside. A two-note chime sounds. Voort has commit-ted himself. His throat is dry. He did not wait for backup. He looks up at the camera above the heavy oak door. There is a small, square, translucent window in the door, of thick wired stained glass, and a shadow appears behind it as he hears the click of the lock opening.

"Can I help you?" says the man who opens the door, but partially bars it, and Voort pegs him, from the jacket and tie, and the noncommittal look of professional scrutiny, as security.

I'm looking at a tall man, dark, fit, dressed well enough to be corporate, but if this place were corporate I'd probably be stopped when I reached the receptionist. Why would a head-hunting firm need security at the door?

Voort shows his badge and says he is part of an investi-gation that concerns businesses in this neighborhood. He asks to talk to "whoever the boss is here."

"What's the investigation about?"

Voort thinks, *Corporate security police are usually in awe of real police. This guy wants to keep me out.*

"I'd rather talk to the boss."

"Wait here," the man says, and closes the door. When he returns, he says, "Dr. Szeska says come up."

Szeska!

Voort hides the surge of emotion, the sense, coursing through him, of hitting pay dirt.

The heavy door shuts behind him, cutting out sound from the street, which means even the windows are sound-proofed. A woman receptionist sits ahead, in the foyer, eye-ing him with more curiosity than welcome, from behind a modest wooden desk that seems to have been dumped there as more of an afterthought than a means of making visitors feel welcome. Voort sees a narrow hallway, typical of brownstones, behind her, leading to the rear of the ground floor, and a wider carpeted stairway going up.

The walls are of dark wood, polished, and wainscotted. The carpet is thick and maroon, but also slightly worn. There's no coffee table with magazines, which would be typical of a reception area. There are no potted palms, prints or paintings on the wall. He sees no courtesy telephone for guests. The room is functional, a buffer zone. The room is like an air lock separating the outside world from whatever lies up those stairs.

Is this really where Meechum worked?

"What kind of business is this anyway?" Voort asks the security man as he leads him up the stairs, and the receptionist's white-haired head swivels to follow their progress.

"Corporate head-hunting," the man grunts, only the way he says it makes it sound more like some New Guinea cannibal rite than a hiring process.

Voort's cell phone buzzes, but he ignores it. He does not want to distract himself, does not want to miss any possible clues. He is experiencing the heightened sense of clarity that comes in times of professional stress or import.

The whole building is obviously a single office. The bland decorating scheme is consistent, reflecting a single point of view. He hears phones ringing, a Xerox machine running, voices chatting, arguing, or talking softly.

They reach the third landing, and another narrow hallway, lined with open doors casting rectangles of light on faded carpet. Up here computer keyboards are clicking and a woman's voice is saying, loud, as if on a phone, *"I can't hear you? You say he went into the ambassador's office or residence? Which?"*

Now!

Voort halts, presses a hand to his belly, groans and says, "Excuse me," which makes his security escort turn. "Sorry. You got a rest room?" Voort says. "This won't wait."

The man's face flickers with indecision, as if he is under orders not to let Voort out of his sight. But it would be too obvious to accompany him to the bathroom, so he waves a hand down the hall, and says, reluctantly, "Second door on the right."

Which will give Voort a look inside at least *one* of the rooms. Passing it, halting as if his cramps have momentarily gotten the better of him, he glimpses a man and a woman at work behind gray steel desks, one on the phone, one typing at a computer. He is too far away to make out the snapshots or work schedules tacked to corkboards over the desks, too far to know exactly what the aerial photos beside them are. But it's clear, whatever they are, that this whole place is too functional, too drab to be serving high-end, well-paid job-hunting executives.

In the two seconds Voort has to take in the view, he also sees a third desk in the room is empty, and he hopes the occupant will be in the men's room.

"I said the second door on the right, not the first," the security man growls from behind.

Voort walks into the men's room, to the urinal, gratified to see another man there, who, Voort guesses, unlike the guard and receptionist, won't know he's a detective, and who, if Voort handles this conversation right, won't call upstairs to repeat anything Voort might say.

Voort unzips himself. "I'll be glad to fly home to-night," he says wearily, providing a logical business reason why the man has not seen him before. Voort uses the urinal. He says casually, going to the sink, "I hate this goddamn city."

The man moves to the sink, too.

"Where you from?" he asks.

"Bethesda," Voort says, knowing that the name of the Washington suburb will reassure the man, if this office is government. The principle is, Voort knows, nine out of ten times, mid-level people in offices have no idea what the bosses are doing.

"I used to be stationed at Fort Myer," the guy says.

Voort dries his hands. "Poor Meechum."

The man's head jerks around. "What happened to him? I haven't seen him for a couple weeks. I thought he got fired."

Voort makes himself look surprised, as if *he's* the one who should not have revealed anything. "Forget it," he says. There's nothing like superior knowledge to convince a person you belong somewhere and they don't.

"Dr. Szeska will release the news tomorrow," Voort says. "Do me a favor. Don't say I said anything."

Which means, of course, that the guy will tell everyone he works with, but odds are that Szeska won't hear it until after Voort talks to the man.

And minutes later he is on the top floor, the boss's floor, where the security guard stands back to allow Voort to enter an office. A man behind a desk is rising, smiling, reaching to shake Voort's hand. He's a big man in a chocolate-colored crew-neck sweater, and he has a fleshy round face inside of which oblong pupils glitter like obsidian inside irises of pale blue.

"John Szeska," the man says, gripping Voort's hand powerfully. Something seems wrong with his left arm.

"Conrad Voort."

The room, with its stained walnut wall unit, nondescript maroon carpet, and matching shades would not impress a million-dollar-a-year executive.

"I thought I paid that parking ticket," Szeska jokes, waving Voort onto a couch.

"I'm not with the parking unit," Voort says.

"That's a relief."

"I'm with homicide," Voort says, and watches the pale blue eyes widen appropriately, hold his gaze an instant, and slide to the photo that Voort holds up.

"I'm looking into this man's death."

He does not say the name, does not give more information. He wants to see if Szeska lies, volunteers the truth, or hesitates while he makes up his mind.

"That's Meechum Keefe," Szeska gasps, looking shocked. "Dead? Is that what you said? Oh my God! *Homicide?* Oh Christ!"

The big man closes his eyes, squeezes them shut as if to dispel reality, and when they open again they are as appalled as any eyes Voort has looked into in all his time on the force. "Tell me what happened," Szeska urges shakily, either meaning it, or he's the best off-stage actor Voort's ever seen. Szeska totters to a sideboard, pours water from a glass pitcher and gulps it. He's so off-balance that he doesn't even offer any to Voort.

If he's this good, and he's involved, I'll only have one chance to trick him.

Szeska repeats, in a small, shaky voice, "Dead," as if it is sinking in. And then he provides the opportunity Voort needs, by asking the natural question, "How?"

Voort maneuvers closer to get a direct view of the roundish face. "He and another man," he says softly, starting the way it really happened, the way Szeska, if he knows what happened, will be prepared to hear it, "were shot in Central Park."

And just for an instant, Voort sees the wrong kind of surprise. The barest change of facial musculature, the hint of puzzled relaxation instead of shocked contraction, as if the answer contradicted whatever Szeska had expected. But Szeska should not have expected *any* particular answer. It was not even a twitch. Just a flare of half light in the black pupils, gone as fast as it appeared, but it was there.

Definitely, it was there.

Szeska had been ready to hear the story of the fire.

"Have you made an arrest?" he asks hopefully, pouring water again.

Voort tries to block out his memory of Meechum's funeral. Rage will only get in the way here.

"We have leads," he says.

"Do you have a suspect?"

Voort says, fighting off his loss, "We have that."

Szeska's desk is large but empty. The wall unit is polished walnut, lined with books, including *The Life of Chinese Gordon, The Arms of Krupp, The Second World War, Napoleon*, and *Sun-tzu, The Art of War*.

But there are also oddly situated gaps between books, as if items had just been removed from the shelves. On a hunch Voort strolls closer to the wall unit. Sure enough, the gap areas are more polished than the rest of the exposed shelves.

"It would be helpful," Voort says, pulling out a pad, "if

you could tell me about the last time you saw Meechum Keefe."

"Of course. It was a couple of weeks ago. He was . . . how can I put it . . . distressed. Having difficulty with a lover, I gather from office gossip. He came in to tell me he was quitting. I tried to talk him out of it. He is . . . was . . . good at what he did. But he was adamant. *Two* men were killed, you say? Who found the bodies?"

Acting again.

"A jogger."

"That must have been a shock," Szeska says, shaking his head, every attempted deception, every lie fueling Voort's growing rage.

"It was a big shock," Voort agrees.

The dance with a suspect can last for months, Voort's father used to say.

"Who was the other man?" Szeska asks.

When Voort shows him the sketch of the second man, drawn from the hotel clerk's description, Szeska sinks into his chair and groans. "That looks like Charley Mann. He worked here, too. I think he and Meechum were . . . the rumor here is that they were . . . well . . . gay. And he quit, too."

"What kind of work do you do here?" Voort says. "The Baxter Group?"

Szeska waves his hand as if the topic could not possibly be important to Voort. "We perform locating services for companies. Head-hunting. That sort of thing."

"And Meechum Keefe's part?"

"Will this help you?"

"Everything may help."

"Meechum was a computer whiz. He designed software

to help us match executives to jobs. He was the best I'd ever seen. Profiling is an art as well as a science," Szeska says, speeding up, as if talking about professional matters might make painful personal ones disappear. "People make fun of profiling, but I assure you it is quite sophisticated. The wrong person at the helm of a company can lose billions of dollars. Meechum knew what questions to ask, and more important, how to process the answers."

Szeska sits back down in his swivel chair and says, "Meechum made the questions more objective. He came up with a system for coding respondents, numerically, rating their suitability for a job."

"And that actually works?"

"More than you might imagine."

"I trust human judgment more than computers," Voort says.

Szeska answers dryly, as if protecting the reputation of his company. "Many corporate boards have made that same mistake."

"Maybe you can give me a list of executives Meechum worked with."

At this, Szeska frowns, as if considering it, and he leans back, and sighs, looking genuinely distressed. "I want to help but I can't," he says. "Our files are private. Companies pay a lot for that. What good would the names be?"

"Who knows? A disgruntled client? A disappointed corporate suitor? We haven't made an arrest."

"I thought you had a suspect."

"How do you know the suspect's not a client of yours?"

Szeska looks shocked. "One of *our* clients?" he says, although Voort's fairly certain there are no "clients" at all. He also notices that Szeska apparently does not find it odd that

Voort seems less interested in the second dead man, the alleged "Charley Mann."

"I like to be thorough," Voort says. "If Meechum quit, perhaps he went to work for one of these companies."

"I doubt it. He said he was sick of profiling."

And now even the lies in the room begin to harden into positions. Voort insists, "Either way, I'd appreciate the list."

"Then I have to say no. But if you get a court order, I'll be glad to oblige," Szeska says. "That way the clients will be satisfied. Not happy, but they won't feel we shared information without having to. My God. Meechum and Charley. Meechum and Charley. Both of them. And you say they were shot?"

"And robbed. I would think you'd want to help."

"I *do*, I *really* do, but," Szeska says, helplessly, "even the president of a company is a cog in the greater scheme of things. I imagine even the president of these great United States sometimes feels like just a little cog."

"Can I see Meechum's software?" Voort says, switching subjects.

"You mean the system he designed?" Now Szeska looks as shocked as any CEO hearing that a detective wants to see his corporate secrets. The two actors are going head to head. Both good, both committed, both convinced now, Voort is sure, that their rival is lying.

Szeska says, "My Lord, no. That's classified."

"You can trust me," Voort says.

"I know I can," Szeska says, as a wooden pendulum clock on the wall begins chiming. "Let me think about it. Is there anything else you need?"

"What exactly did Charley Mann do here?"

"Personnel. He was good at it."

"Ever hear of someone named Frank Greene?"

"Who?" Szeska looks perfectly curious.

"Jill Towne?"

Szeska sips water. "Is that Meechum's girlfriend? He said he was having love problems. Maybe I spoke too soon when I suggested he and Charley were gay. And I've been rude. Do you want something to drink?"

"Lester Levy. Ever hear of him?"

"Sorry," Szeska says, more confident now that Voort is clearly fishing. Szeska glances at the clock. "I have a meeting. I hope you'll excuse me. My God, murdered. My God! Look, I'd like to help you, but when it comes to our records, get a court order. Help *me* help *you*. I have to answer to people, too. I want to keep my job."

Voort stands up to leave. Is it really over for the moment? "I'm sure you do," he says.

But he is wondering if he should up the stakes before going. Normally, in an investigation, he has more time. He's looking into a death that has occurred already, so, identifying a prime suspect, he has days to stalk the person, to alternately soothe or worry him, to walk away as if satisfied of the suspect's innocence, and then surprise him at his office, apartment, girlfriend's house, neighborhood Indian restaurant.

But things are different here. Jill's in danger, and so is Frank Greene, if the Massachusetts man is even alive.

The clock ticking on Szeska's wall seems to emphasize the lack of time; *Trust those instincts,* his father used to say. Voort imagines that he actually feels Szeska's ire growing: an emanation, a malevolence hidden on the cooperative surface but pulsating beneath, boiling and alive.

If I just walk out of here he may feel free to make another try

*at Jill or Frank. But if I put more pressure on him, maybe he'll
back off for now.*

Voort makes the decision to protect the potential victims. Voort takes the plunge.

"Colonel Szeska," he says, using the title for the first
time, watching for reaction, "let's be straight here."

A nod. The man settles back in his swivel chair. "That's
fine with me," he says smoothly, making the perfect transi-
tion. You lead and I'll follow, his noncommittal smile conveys. You initiate and I'll react. You thrust, I'll parry. You
reveal, I'll obscure.

Voort even senses that Szeska seems more comfortable
with things in the open. Perhaps he knows how much
Voort's revelations reflect frustration. Knowledge is ammunition, and once you use it, you cannot fire it again.

"This place," Voort says, indicating the room, the building, the "business" with a sweep of his left hand, "isn't really
a head-hunting firm, is it?"

"Nope."

"You're army."

"No again."

Voort shakes his head angrily. "Five people are dead.
Meechum Keefe's murdered and he worked here. So did
Charley Mann. And other people, Jill Towne and Frank
Greene," he says, watching Szeska's bland expression, "are
in danger. You're trying to tell me that what you do has
nothing to do with the government?"

"I said we weren't army."

"Then who?"

Szeska says, "Sorry."

"I can get a court order."

"Feel free."

"And open your records."

"I doubt that very much."

"Someone killed two people who worked here."

And the big brow actually clouds over, as if the man is feeling pain, *real* pain, and Szeska says, "Yes, I hear that, I liked them. Perhaps I can even help," Szeska says. "Would you consider sharing what else you know about their deaths with us? Tell me what happened in the, eh, park?"

"*Me* share with *you*? Who the hell *are* you?"

"I can appreciate your position. I'll tell you what," Szeska says, getting up slowly, having somehow turned the meeting on its head, having managed to accumulate the power in the room over the last few moments. Or did he have it all along? Is he only now hinting at the extent of his connections, his reach.

"Give me a few days and I'll make some phone calls. Two, three days, okay? Then it might then be possible to share more. Is that too much to ask? I think that's very reasonable. We work out an agreement. Bring in the lawyers, hell, those worms are everywhere. You agree to basic secrecy precautions. Believe me, we want whoever hurt Meechum and Charley to be caught."

"You want me to keep *your* secrets?"

Soothingly, Szeska is walking toward him.

"First, I need to know how you found this place," he says.

Goddamn government, Voort thinks. They turn you down. Then they want your help.

Szeska is five feet and closing.

"Colonel, I'll be back," Voort says, and spins, although he feels uncomfortable showing this man his back.

I should have come with backup.

He remembers what he had heard at West Point: Szeska's a war hero. And only now does he think about what that means. Szeska's a soldier. A tough, lifelong veteran who has faced enemies on the battlefield. He's not going to be intimidated by a single sex crimes detective, who is twenty years younger, to boot.

Voort reaches for the door.

It's locked.

Szeska says, two feet away now, closer, that twisted elbow starting to move around, to come up a little, "I hope you'll forgive me, but I'm not sure I can let you leave just now. It won't take long. Do you mind waiting while I check?"

Szeska, twenty minutes earlier, sits behind his desk, watching Voort walking toward him. The detective looks exactly like his picture, impossible to miss with that blond hair and blue eyes.

Is he alone?

Szeska's danger bells are sounding. He is hiding a heart-popping, stomach-churning, head-throbbing rage. His meeting with the detective will require one of the greatest tests of his acting ability. He shakes the man's hand, waves him to the couch.

Kill him now or let him go?

But of course the response to that question depends on the answers to other ones, more immediate ones that Szeska must find out or guess the answers to.

Are there other cops in the street? And even if there aren't, did he tell anyone he was coming?

Who else knows whatever he's found out?

"I hope I paid that parking ticket," Szeska jokes.

"I'm not here for a ticket," the detective replies.

John Szeska sits, chats, answers questions. He is facing one of the toughest choices of his life, and as always, allows instinct to guide him. But if his impulses were slowed into words, they would be:

I have a few days at most to stop Frank Greene. But if I tell the detective, I might as well admit my connection to Meechum's list. If I let him go, I could lose my chance to stop Greene. If I kill him here, what about my own people who saw him come in? Even in a security zone, not all the staff know exactly what we do.

Voort tells Szeska that Meechum and another man were shot in Central Park.

What a fucking good trick!

Szeska has, over the decades, faced combat, bombs, prisons, enemy police. He has evaded guerrillas. He has killed Russians, Cubans, Vietnamese, Chinese.

How can I just run off now and let that bomb go off?

Not to mention Lupe.

Dear Lupe.

Lupe, who I loved, who I made a promise to.

I'll shoot the dogs, darling. I swear.

Voort is saying, "Colonel Szeska, let's be straight with each other."

"By all means."

And Szeska makes his decision. He commits himself. Things seem to slow in the room.

Szeska's hand slides under his desk, and presses a button, locking the door as they talk.

Voort at the door, is trying to get out. He looks nervous.

There are no other cops outside or he would have brought it up. He'd threaten to call them.

Szeska, knowing he has made the right choice, rises, thinking *I must kill this man, now, quietly, so the wrong people in the building don't hear. The photographer and re-searcher and I will move the body tonight. We'll make up an excuse for the police. We'll say he left at seven. We'll think up something that gives us extra time. And even the people here who don't know our real job are trained, and will shut up if queried by police.*

Szeska starts his attack with a soft walk, and reasonable tone, strolling toward the enemy. He is a fifty-year-old mur-der machine putting itself into motion. And he is saying, "I'm not sure I can let you leave just now. It won't take long. Do you mind waiting while I check?"

"Check?"

"With my boss in Washington," Szeska lies. "Hell," he grins, "everybody has a boss, even me. This will take a few minutes. Help yourself to anything at the sideboard. Scotch. Seltzer."

Almost there.

But Voort, at the door, reaches for his shoulder holster.

He pulls the gun out, but he still hasn't said that more cops are outside.

"Yeah, yeah, you're armed," Szeska says reasonably, halting. "Listen to reason. I don't want a problem any more than you. But you've demonstrated sufficient knowledge of what we're doing here for me to temporarily hold you, un-der the National Security Act. If you know Meechum worked here, you must also see that whoever killed him may be a bigger threat than you imagine, the kind of threat my people deal with, not yours. So don't compound your problems by pulling *that* out."

Voort shakes his head. "Holding a person against his will is . . ."

"Kidnapping? Give me a break! *You* hold people against their will all the time! It's the law. The same here!"

The damn gun is still up. The cop's instincts are terrific.

But he won't fire, Szeska decides, and starts coming again, drifting across the room, keeping his eyes on Voort's face, his voice soothing. The cop appears to be in good physical shape. His reflexes will be younger, his muscles stronger, and to Szeska, that means he will have, at best, one really good chance if he times the attack right.

Szeska, coming, shakes his head at the difficulty of things, "Think for a second. If you won't agree to basic security precautions, you're the one on shaky ground. You're a cop in a federal situation. A coupla phone calls . . . my boss talks to your boss . . . everyone is happy. You go home."

Voort says, "What precautions?"

"Usually they involve a legal statement. Lawyer secrecy stuff. Hell, those guys are into everything these days." Szeska grins. "Background check. Sign a few papers. Everyone does it."

"Stay put, please."

Szeska stops.

Voort thinks a moment. "Papers saying I won't tell anyone what I know, right?"

"What else did you think I had in mind? You may have information more dangerous than you imagine. You're the one over the line here, not me. I'm supposed to know things. You might be sitting on something valuable, and you won't share it."

Voort looks as if he is starting to feel unsure.

But then he shakes his head. "Background checks take more than an hour."

"Okay, a bit longer. I exaggerated," Szeska says, inching forward. "What are you going to do with that thing, shoot me?"

Voort lets out air, and lowers the gun. He doesn't put it away, but he's not pointing it anymore.

Szeska says, "I won't tell anyone you pulled that. You're upset. We'll do the conference call."

They are a foot apart. The cop is almost relaxed. He's in good shape and his reflexes will be terrific, so Szeska needs him relaxed.

"We want to find whomever hurt your friend."

A mistake, because Voort steps back. "How do you know he was my friend?"

"He had a background check. Everyone here has a background check. He told me about you, his old buddy Voort the detective. Your family. The history. Meechum loved you."

Szeska, close enough, is turning his body slightly, to place his good, right side closer.

Voort seems to sag from grief, and memory. Szeska knows how debilitating both can be.

He presses the fingers of his right hand together. The weapon is cocked now. It's been years since he had to use it this way, but he has no doubt it will function perfectly.

Then someone starts banging on the door.

Damn!

The banging is something which would only happen in this particular office if there were an emergency.

"Later!" Szeska calls.

But the interruption works in Szeska's favor, because Voort glances away, toward the door, and *do it now*, and the hand begins moving.

But the photographer's voice calls, from the hallway, "There are more police downstairs."

Opening the door, feeling sweat break out along his spine from the close call, Szeska learns, moments later, that the cops downstairs have the same last name as his visitor.

"They're Voorts," the photographer is saying, confused. "All of them are Voorts, same as him."

SEVENTEEN

Manhattan District Attorney Warren Aziz is a somber thirty-seven-year-old who favors off-the-rack dark brown suits, white shirts, wide olive-colored ties, and whose stated hero is consumer advocate Ralph Nader. His conviction record is dazzling, his politics liberal, his low-key approach to conflict legendary, and his career, since he graduated NYU Law, has carried him in a carefully planned upward trajectory that he does not care to slow.

"I won't ask a judge for a search warrant until tomorrow," the third-generation Iranian-American tells Voort, in his fourteenth-floor municipal building office. "Let's give the mayor a chance to get Washington moving first."

Aziz, Voort knows, started his public life by showing his shrewd form early, holding fund-raisers around Manhattan at private apartments, introducing himself to influential people, explaining that he had not targeted the exact office he was seeking yet, but would choose one vacated voluntarily by a Democratic Party incumbent.

"I'm not interested in giving people I respect a hard time," he said then, and still repeats in speeches, interviews, or low-key negotiations marking the high-profile cases he wins, leaving opponents dazed and jailed.

Now he tells Voort, "If you want to learn what Szeska's up to, don't go in shooting or he'll stonewall. Plus, if he's smart, he started moving material out of that building the second you left. He knows you'll want a warrant. The only purpose I can see in getting one is to turn up the heat, but the mayor and Eisenstein," he says, naming the state's senior senator, "are doing that in D.C. Just say 'bomb' to them and they're on the phone. Let's not get carried away because we're eager to do something."

Voort says, "But at his office, Szeska . . ."

"Locked you in? For five minutes?" The D.A., who looks under twenty-five years old, shakes his head. "Thirty minutes, an hour, and *maybe* we could go for unlawful imprisonment. But at this point, are we after cooperation from the guy, or a fight? Didn't you say he may know where Frank Greene is?"

"I said he's probably trying to *kill* Frank Greene. They're *both* a threat."

"Says you." Aziz remains composed. "And I respect you, but without evidence"—he shrugs—"the mayor tries first. It's a mess! If Hizzoner gets no answer by eight tomorrow, you'll get your warrant. You'll be in that brownstone in half an hour, with your sledgehammers if they won't open up. But first we go over Szeska's head."

Mickie snorts. He's been back from Massachusetts for hours, with Frank Greene's drawings, and a state police sketch of the man. He's in no mood for delays.

"The date on those drawings is two days from now," he reminds Aziz.

"That date could be his birthday," the D.A. says.

"Which means he could set off his bomb tonight, while you're watching *Gershwin Lives Again* on Broadway," Mickie says. "Maybe we don't even have two days."

But the prosecutor doesn't take the bait, doesn't raise his voice, or turn red, or vary the inflection in his modulated tones. "I understand how you feel, but you've got no proof he's got dynamite. Buying racing fuel is not illegal. You want a warrant that stands up? Or one that gets thrown out because we arrested him too soon? The FBI says they never heard of him."

"But Meechum's list . . ."

"Exactly! It's only because of that list you're after him. You show me drawings. You say he bought fertilizer. A thousand people buy fertilizer. Unless we're in China here, there's nothing I can do. And *you*," he says to Voort, shaking his head, "want to plaster Greene's face all over TV. I agree with the commissioner. We're not doing that, so he can sue us, like that bomb suspect did to the FBI, in Atlanta."

All three of them form a triangle of human impotence, at the fourteenth-floor window of Aziz's office, his legendary "crime war room," incongruously decorated with family photos and finger paintings made by the D.A.'s twin six-year-olds. The furniture is modest, of stained oak. From the no-frills room, they look down at the scene of possible disaster to come, One Police Plaza, the urban fortress, shielded, at a distance, by concrete barriers on three sides, and by police cruisers guarding street access to the place— and allowing through only vehicles showing ID—on the fourth.

But, Voort thinks, what about the vulnerable pedestrian plaza outside the barriers, the sculpture, the steepled form

of St. Andrews Church? Hundreds of people stream in
and out of those openings between barriers, from all directions all day; from Chambers Street or through the arch
of the municipal building, or up the wide steps that lead to
the back.

Voort and the D.A. are reflected face-to-face in the
double-paned window. Voort urges, "Then publicize the
sketch for another reason. Say we need help in a murder
case. He may have information but we can't find him.
That's the truth!"

Aziz considers it. "I'll recommend it."

The worst part is, they both know, all police buildings
will remain open as usual to tourists, cops, visiting officials
from overseas. The public will have no idea what may be in
store down there.

"We'll assign extra security to headquarters, and to the
precinct house he drew, hell, to all the precincts," the police commissioner had told them an hour ago, at a meeting
where he'd ordered a task force set up, to look for Greene
and investigate Szeska.

"But no massive alert. No panic until we know more.
Everything is pure conjecture at this point. Greene's not
even made a threat."

Now it is three P.M., four frustrating hours since Voort
left the brownstone, after half a dozen of his relatives,
phoned by Mickie at Matt's bedside, rushed over and got
him out.

"It sounds crazy," he'd told Mickie, later. "But Szeska
was going to try to kill me *in his office*. I felt it. I didn't even
realize it until the banging at the door started. He looked
away for a second, and it was like a mask dropped off his
face."

To Mickie, though, very little that Voort says sounds

crazy. To Mickie, Voort is usually right. Mickie's lips had gone white, and a flinty look had come into his pupils. Mickie, the ex-marine, had probably looked like that during firefights in the North/South Korea neutral zone, a decade earlier, skirmishes that had never even been made public, but that Mickie had revealed to Voort.

Voort had continued, "After my cousins showed up, he relaxed, even smiled. He said he changed his mind and I could go. He reminded me of a TV show I saw once about cobras. How they weave in front of the victim before they bite."

Now, in the present, Aziz shakes his head. "I smell smoke," he tells the two detectives ruefully. "But I need the fire. Anything else I can do? I want to help."

"I see that," Mickie retorts, turning to leave.

Five minutes later, striding toward One Police Plaza, Mickie snorts. "Ambitious asshole. Fucking chickenshit climber."

But Voort shakes his head. "He's right. We don't have evidence. And politicians are the only people who aren't supposed to be ambitious, did you ever think of that?"

"What are you talking about?"

"Cops, clerks, everyone else is *supposed* to be ambitious. If some auto exec says he wants to become president of GM, everyone thinks it's great. But a politician admits he wants something bigger and the whole world's down on the guy."

"Don't get theoretical. If Aziz wants to go after someone, he comes up with a way."

"No Mickie, *we* come up with the way, and we haven't found it yet here."

"Fuck Aziz and fuck you, too. Everyone I love works in that building, and even Syl comes to visit. Half the time I'd like to help Szeska have an accident myself. And the other half I think, let *him* finish Greene. That's what he's doing, right? Knocking off people on Meechum's list? That's what you think, isn't it? So let him, and *then* go after him."

A truck bomb, Voort imagines, blowing up down here, would slaughter hundreds even if it never reached its target. Frank Greene could drive under the municipal building arch, and leap out and run. The blast would kill cops, tourists, journalists, churchgoers.

He halts before St. Andrew's. His chest is pounding.

He says, slowly, "Let Szeska be? He killed Meechum if he's who we think he is. That's the trade-off with somebody like that. Meechum for Frank. But that's okay with you, huh?"

Mickie stops, too. It's a cool autumn day, brisk and bright, and pedestrians wear coats against the chill. Voort sees tourists craning their necks, gazing up at the federal building. Construction workers, on a break, drink coffee. Mothers wheel babies across the plaza. A priest exits the church carrying an empty mesh shopping bag. Two cabbies on the street curse at each other, over smoking engines, waving their fists.

Mickie says, more softly, "Yeah, that's the trade-off. You're right, but sometimes it's hard to control yourself."

And Voort, staring up at One Police Plaza, suddenly is transported in his mind to Meechum's den, years ago, as the two boys stare at the aftermath of the Beirut bombing that took his brother's life. Voort sees the side of the marine headquarters fallen away, the smoke, and swinging girders, and he hears ambulances and fire engines, and sees soldiers carrying stretchers.

Then he imagines that it is police headquarters toppling apart. Bricks fall like rain in his mind. Furniture burns in craters. Screams rise from smoking rubble.

"I'm going into church for a minute," Voort says. "Want to come?"

"Me? Never."

"I'll be up in ten minutes. Start the meeting."

Inside St. Andrews, Voort puts a hundred in the poor box, lights candles, kneels in a rear pew and crosses himself. The cozy church seems far from the hectic pace outside. The nave glows from gold leaf, and the huge-eyed saints regard him peacefully, their irises frozen in reverence or celestial contemplation. The airiness and quiet, as always, lift his spirits, concentrate his thoughts.

I can't make a mistake now.

"God," he says in his head, moving his lips silently, "thank you for my family, and my friend Mickie, who saved my life today. Thank you for the ability to feel conflict, and for perspective. Thank you for strength to control the wrong kind of emotion. Help me protect my family, and friends, and even," he starts to say, "Camilla."

But instead he says, ". . . all the people going in and out of that building. And give me strength to lay off Jill."

He hasn't thought of her all day until now. That lean fragrant body. That soft auburn hair. The memory of her green eyes hits him, even here, like a blast of sensuality.

Voort clears his mind, "Dad, help me remember the things you taught me."

Voort gets to his feet, alone in the church but slightly less frustrated, joined to some greater force that won't solve his problems, he knows, but makes him feel more able to do so himself.

Ten minutes later, he's on the twelfth floor of One Police Plaza, in the Situation Room, the war room, addressing a dozen detectives that Addonizio has assigned to the Szeska/Greene investigation.

"Half of you will watch the brownstone. Follow anyone leaving it. Let 'em know you're there. Screw up whatever they're doing. Push 'em."

The room is long, windowless, and bright with white light from fluorescent tubes. Men and women detectives sit at a pine conference table, or lean against scuffed walls, sipping coffee, looking tense. They come from different precincts, but they all have friends at One Police Plaza.

Voort borrows a slogan from an army commercial, and changes it a little. "Be the best assholes you can be."

They laugh.

On an easel to the right side of the table, in Magic Marker, Mickie has written:

1. Who owns the building? Pays bills? Real estate deeds.
2. Names on Meechum's list. Neighbors. Relatives.
3. Szeska's background. Army? Find gov't agency.
4. ID all people in brownstone. SS numbers. Licenses. Check them all!
5. Charley Mann.

"The rest of you," Voort continues, swinging his attention to a second easel, "will look for Frank Greene."

They regard the sketch, drawn by a Massachusetts State Police artist, from the stable owner's description. They see a white man of early middle age, with a thatch of thick black curly hair jutting above his narrow face. Greene has a small nose and longish ears. His lips, slightly parted, are of average thickness. It's the face of a man you would pass without noticing, on the street.

Mickie's written in black Magic Marker:

1. Blue Ford van. Mass. plates 442AL.
2. Fertilizer buyers in NY? Check farmers markets.
3. Greene's background. SS #, schools, bills, friends, old neighborhood.

An older detective, from the Fifth Precinct, a veteran with one year until retirement, says, "If we find him, do we warn him, or arrest him?"

"We warn him and we take him in for a talk. We warn him and we get into his house, and find that van."

One of the female detectives against the far wall, a small, sharp-eyed brunette from Missing Persons, suggests, "Why not all of us look for Frank Greene, and leave Szeska for after?"

All eyes swing to Voort, and for the second time the option is on the table. Concentrate on the immediate danger to the police and public. Treat Szeska as a potential ally here instead of an enemy, at least for a while.

It will be Voort's decision, Voort to blame later if he wastes manpower on Szeska, and Frank Greene does turn out to have a bomb out there, and has time to set it off.

Voort just looks at her.

"It was just, like, a joke," the woman says, blushing. "Forget I brought it up."

Minutes later, meeting over, the detectives push from the room, worried, hurrying. Mickie will head the Frank Greene end of the investigation. Voort will concentrate on Szeska, and whatever activities are being directed out of Fifty-third Street.

They experience a rush of hope when Hazel calls from the computer room, but this time her information is not helpful.

"Frank Greene is untraceable so far. He doesn't live at the address on his license. His social security number is not on file for a job. No credit card usage. You have to work hard to be this invisible. Maybe the guy knows someone's looking for him, and he's buried himself. He might as well already be dead."

Voort doesn't want to sleep, but he needs it. His muscles ache. His eyes are heavy. He's barely slept for two days, and he's been on the run or on the phone into the late evening, with the mayor's office, the army, the FBI; or he's been monitoring progress, or rather the lack of it, in the cities where police are carrying on investigations into the deaths of the other people on Meechum's list.

"Go home," Mickie says. "Or wherever it is you're sleeping these days."

Hazel's made some progress on the Szeska end, having discovered that the law firm listed on the deed for the brownstone, a Park Avenue firm named Crain & Marshall, "also represents the Department of Defense in civil cases, mostly property matters, pending in local courts."

Mickie says, "You look like you're going to fall over. And don't you have a lady to protect? Or whatever you do with the terrorist at night?"

There's a barely eaten wheat pizza, with extra cheese, black olives, and red peppers, on his desk, and two drained bottles of Evian mineral water. Mickie's jacket is off, his suspenders are red, and his electrical massage machine buzzes annoyingly as he rubs his neck with it.

"Jill stopped treating them," Voort says. "The terrorists."

"Is that what she said? Then it must be true."

"Mickie, don't you ever cut anyone some slack?"

"Yeah, once I did it. A week later, the guy cut someone's throat."

Voort can almost physically feel the ticking of the second hands on his watch, jerking from point to point like a timer on a bomb.

"Before I leave, let's go over what they found so far one more time," Voort says, "in case we missed something."

"Fine." A yawn. "We know he went to high school in Bayside," Mickie says. "We know, according to the only surviving elderly neighbor, who *maybe* remembers him, that he was shy and drew pictures of horses."

"We know *maybe* he had a sister."

"No teachers at the high school remember him."

"Parents dead."

"No taxes filed for six years."

"No credit cards. No friends. No bank account, at least under his name and social security number."

Mickie sighs and shuts off the massage machine. "Now I remember where I heard about this guy. He's the invisible man. You going to eat any more pizza?"

"I'll give the rest to the homeless in the park."

"At least we accomplished one thing this afternoon. We pissed off Szeska," Mickie says, referring to the detectives who trailed his employees to lunch, and their apartments. And to the fire inspectors who showed up at the brownstone, combing the building looking for frayed wires, while a police cruiser parked outside, and the officers sat, watching, until someone came out to politely inquire if "something was wrong."

"He can dish it out, but he can't take it," Mickie grins, referring to the fact that Szeska must have complained about interference to someone in Washington, because Addonizio called a while ago to say the mayor had received inquiries about police "harassment" of a "sensitive intelligence operation" in the city.

"What about the *mayor's* inquiries?" Voort had replied.

"He's working on it," Addonizio had said. "And the senator's on the horn with the White House."

But in the end, any small victories of the day, any petty annoyances inflicted upon Szeska, had paled beside the unanswered questions.

Voort had received a call from Jill at five, which he had not returned, and another at seven, when he dispatched a uniformed patrolman to watch her, on the late shift, instead of going himself.

Now Mickie says, "Wake up. You were nodding off. I'll sleep on the couch."

Voort puts on his coat, and picks up the cold pizza. Grease has stained the cardboard from inside.

I'm just going over there to protect her. We're not going to have sex tonight. I'm too tired anyway.

Yeah, right.

Outside, it's gotten cold with the first hint of winter, and the air is clear, and bright, the stars out, but the plaza is fairly deserted. A few lonely people are out, strolling nowhere, using up time, waiting for the night to end, and their more distracting daily disappointments to begin. Traffic on the Brooklyn Bridge is light, mostly exiting Manhattan. The shops are gated. Most city offices are shut, their lights off, under the mayor's new power-saving policies.

But the lights blaze in city hall. The mayor is working the phones, Voort hopes.

Even if he gets no response, we go into that brownstone first thing tomorrow.

Dim, in the vapor lights, he can see figures of the homeless lying on benches in the plaza, shielded from arrest by the latest round of liberal judge court orders. They have newspapers for blankets, shopping carts for closets, court-ordered drugs for dinner, and the man Voort approaches gives off a faint stench of urine, eyeing the oncoming cop with suspicion that turns to surprise when Voort holds out the pizza box.

"Hungry?"

The man reaches for the box eagerly, and tears it open. With his ripped black leather coat, once the pride of whoever donated it to Coats for the Homeless, his ragged beard and wild hair, the man could be a poster for life's disappointments.

He frowns, looking up at Voort over the top of the open box.

"Are these mushrooms? I hate mushrooms," he says.

"Then give it to someone else," Voort says, exhausted, and heads for the subway, trudging across the shadow thrown down by One Police Plaza, into the darkness beneath the arch of the municipal building, and down the wide stairway toward the rumbling subway below. He hears running footsteps behind him.

He whirls, but the tiredness has slowed his normally faster reflexes.

The homeless man stands there, gasping from exertion, holding the pizza box.

"I was an asshole. People oughtta concentrate on the good side. Thanks," the guy says. "Really."

"No problem." But Voort's spirits lift.

Downstairs, he finds himself alone on the platform. Track work, a badly lettered sign on a girder advises him, has made number six train service even less reliable than usual. He's too tired to go back upstairs and hail a cab. He falls onto a bench. The subway sways into the station, and proceeds uptown, groaning and complaining, carrying Voort to his married lover, moving slower than a broken clock, or a mending heart.

The doorman at her building recognizes him, and waves him up.

"That uniformed cop left an hour ago," he says.

He wasn't supposed to do that, Voort thinks, alarmed.

"He said it was a family emergency," says the doorman, regarding himself as the key source of news in this place.

The elevator is empty, and on the penthouse level Voort rings her bell and is relieved to hear light shuffling footsteps on the wood floor, approaching on the other side of the door. He imagines her smell before he even hears the lock, a faint vanilla odor that makes his groin itch despite his tiredness.

But something is different when the door opens. He sees, behind her, that the curtains have been pulled to the side, something she is not supposed to do. The black, lit city glimmers out there, and the sliding window is open to the terrace, so a light punishing breeze knifes in. The room is cold, and Jill's brow is darkened by a haggard frown, which only adds one more variation to her beauty. She's dressed in a belted robe of purple flannel and matching Chinese slippers. The wide mannish lapels flare to show pink pajamas with leaping sheep on them, and a bit of creamy freckled cleavage.

She's carrying a portable phone at her side. Clearly, she's just been talking to someone, and Voort interrupted her. Her hair is perfect. From the neck up, she could be at her office, the symphony, or sitting in first class on a flight to visit her husband in Rome.

"I didn't think you were coming," she says, and he realizes that bothered her.

"Sorry about not calling," he says, closing the curtains. "Things came up with Szeska." Which is, of course, a dodge because it is only a partial truth.

"What things?"

He tells her, but the mood is strained. The curtains, she says? I opened them because I was "sick of things," meaning police guards, and constraints, and precautions, although that, too, seems only a partial reason. She conveys more of a sense of almost juvenile rebellion, like a teenager who gets bad news and then drives too fast on the freeway, tempting fate.

Only a day ago these two were in bed together, panting and kissing and straining in the dark.

Now the unspoken question—What happens now?—gives an awkwardness to the talk, or silence, or the way they sit or move around. The apartment seems tiny. The couch which converts to a bed seems dangerous. The city outside seems attentive rather than anonymous. A gray dove coos out on the balcony, and she jerks at the sound.

"You look tired," she says.

"Yeah." How eloquent, he thinks.

"You should sleep."

"That sounds good."

"Or do you want to eat first? I ordered in Chinese but the officer who was here didn't eat anything. I can heat it up. Broccoli. Dumplings."

"Thanks. But I had pizza at the office."

"I can't stand this. I lied," Jill says. "This morning. I lied."

At least, with these words, the gap is gone, although

what remains is a tangible uncertainty. Voort's exhaustion turns to curiosity. Jill is sitting on the half-made foldout couch. She has, since he met her, emanated vibrant strength and certainty. Now she shows the less sure side, but plunges into what she wants to say nevertheless.

"I met my husband when I was twenty, in college. He was terrific, Conrad. Handsome. Smart. He played squash, and he sailed. He was attentive, generous, too good to be true."

"And?"

"And," she shrugs, "for the first two years things were perfect. I'd miss him when he was abroad, but believe me, he'd make up for it when he was home. And then one day, when he *was* home, the phone rang. It was some woman, another doctor, in Geneva. They'd spent the last week together at a ski resort. She wasn't supposed to phone him. But I guess she was hoping to mess us up."

"That's too bad."

"I went crazy. I screamed at him. I suppose I expected that he would act the way . . . well . . . like on television," she says, chagrined. "He'd deny it, or cry and admit it. He'd be afraid I'd leave him. He . . . I don't know . . . he'd *crawl*."

"But he didn't."

"He just sat there, looking pained, and heard me out, respectfully, and then he asked me a question. He said, 'If that woman had never phoned, do you think you would have detected any difference in me? In my love for you? My behavior?' Well, to hell with behavior. I was in a rage. I broke things. I said, 'What difference does that make?' and he said, '*All* the difference. I'm not American. We do things in other ways where I come from. Everything I've ever done with you is the truth, and if I sleep with someone when I'm away, and I'm careful medically, and you never hear about it, what difference does it make?' "

Voort realizes that the memory is making her tremble. He thinks, go to her. Give her human contact.

He does not move.

She says, "I threw him out. And a week went by. And I missed him, so much, when I wasn't ranting, that is, that after a couple more weeks I found myself thinking about it. He'd said that the affairs made him treat me *better*. He'd said variety, every once in a while, kept him from feeling confined. He'd asked if I had a complaint, one single complaint about him otherwise, and the truth was, when I made myself think about it, I didn't."

"So you called him back."

"He was smarter than that, and more caring in his own way. He showed up after a while. He let me cool off. But he never apologized. Never said he wouldn't do it again. He concentrated on the good, not the disappointment. His silence told me he would do it again. And that was the unspoken deal. I talked about it once to him, a year later, and all he said was, quite directly, unapologetically, 'When we're away from each other, we, not he, what *we* did was our own business.' He said our time together was sacred. He said the rest of the time, we were bound in a different way. Conrad, I don't know if you've ever loved someone and they betrayed you."

"I have." He sees Camilla in his head.

"Then you know that part of you wants to forgive them."

"Not always."

"Well, I did. After a while I made an accommodation with the pain. I took him back. Our life together picked up, was good, great, and then he went away again. And after that . . ."

"Yes?"

"He came home and it was great again, but for me, the truth is, if I want to admit it, it was not great in the same way. Corrosion eats away at things. I stopped asking little questions. Y'know, like what did you do last night? Who did you go to the restaurant with? I blocked a whole part of his life out. I threw myself into work when he was away."

"It sounds painful."

"Under the surface, but not on top. So this morning I lied to both of us, you *and* me," she says. "I told myself I believed what he said. I told myself, when he's away, whatever happens is not important. He comes from a different culture. It's an equal arrangement. But I didn't like when you didn't come back today."

Voort finally goes to her, puts his arm around her. She stiffens but then relaxes. She lays her head on his shoulder. But her hands remain in her lap.

"I'm not like him," she says. "If I do . . . something like that, it doesn't mean nothing."

"I wouldn't call you a liar," he says.

"You didn't come here to see me tonight. You came because it's your job."

He nods. "That's right. But I don't know if I wouldn't have come otherwise," he says, "after a while."

"This is so stupid. I'm embarrassed. I'm married, not you, and I'm asking *your* intentions."

"At the moment," he says, "they're to sleep."

And that is when the explosion goes off outside.

It's far away, the rumble, somewhere else in the city. It's a deep reverberating sound that rolls through the windows, makes the glass ballerina on the coffee table vibrate, and lifts Voort to his feet with urgency.

He rushes onto the terrace, to the railing.

He sees no fire, no smoke, and he hears no sirens down there.

He's sweating, turning back for the phone, to call Mickie, when he hears her say, "Look!"

Another explosion.

Arcing up, to the west, in a thin green line, and bursting into a shower of glitter over the spires of the high buildings, he sees it now.

"Fireworks."

Christ.

Boom!

Lots of fireworks on the river.

It's some store's October promotional. Some yacht owner's evening entertainment. Some rich New Jersey kid back from North Carolina, doing illegal things in the backyard of his Fort Lee duplex.

The phone is ringing now here, and it turns out to be Mickie.

"Con Man, I jumped off the damn couch."

As if the fireworks released all the other urban noises, the city comes alive with sound; with sirens, and honking, and a distant, whooping car alarm.

Voort, shaken, closes the sliding window, and the curtains, and he drops onto the foldout couch.

They fall asleep together, dressed, their arms around each other.

Until the phone screams at four A.M.

"It's Hugh Addonizio. This is getting to be a habit," she jokes, handing him the receiver. He's been having a dream, but he cannot remember what it is, only that it was uncomfortable, that, in it, he was afraid.

"Voort, the mayor did it!" says the chief of detectives, who has clearly, once again, not been sleeping. But who at least didn't show up personally this time.

"Voort, the damn president's pissed off. Everyone's running around the capital like chickens with their heads cut off, worried about being blamed for bombs. You're taking the first shuttle to Washington," he says. "So start dressing. You'll take a cab to the White House . . ."

"The *White House?*"

"You're not going *into* the White House, but you have to use the Pennsylvania Avenue entrance to the Executive Office Building. Someone will meet you at the gate. Sign whatever they give you, promising to shut up, except for telling us, of course. But you'll get the story. That's the promise. You'll get all the damn answers from some general named Rourke."

EIGHTEEN

Voort hasn't been in Washington since he was twelve, on a class field trip. Back then, he, Meechum, and twenty other seventh graders spent two days touring monuments and museums, and nights in shared hotel rooms, playing spin the bottle, kiss the girls.

"Things have gone downhill since then," the elderly cabdriver gripes, in a deep southern accent, on the way downtown from Ronald Reagan Airport. "The president's a disappointment. Congress ain't no better. Hell, when I was young you could drive into the Senate parking lot without hitting a damn bomb barrier, or walk into the Library of Congress without having five cops pat down the bulge in your shirt.

"Here we are, mister. The White House. Built by giants. Inhabited by mites."

Voort tips the man, strides around the concrete bomb barriers blocking early-morning traffic from Pennsylvania Avenue, and heads for the West Gate. It's a cool, blue-skied day, and the barriers look more like big flowerpots, decorations, but their purpose is undeniable. Tourists can still stroll, RollerBlade, or carry protest signs in front of the White House. They can no longer drive.

At least there was no news of any bombing in New York on the all-news radio in the cab.

Approaching the spiked iron gate, Voort recalls his teacher saying, nineteen years ago, "Andrew Jackson opened the White House to anyone wanting to get in, for his inauguration. Those were the days before Lincoln got shot."

Voort presses an intercom button on the gate, within view of a glassed-in security hut on the grounds. The capital police inside scrutinize him while they ask his name. Guests in front of him are being buzzed into a waiting area inside the gate, but when Voort answers, the guard signals someone behind him, and a small, raven-haired woman in a green army uniform steps out of the booth.

"I'm Lieutenant Roberta White, sir," she says, shaking hands with professional warmth that does not reach her almond eyes. "I'm with General Rourke at NTAA. He apologizes for a change of plans. He was in his office on an emergency until five this morning. He wondered if you'd mind coming to the house."

"Emergency?" Voort says.

"All taken care of. The car's on the corner. This way, please."

"What's NTAA?" Voort asks, noting, with a last glance back, that the visitors being allowed onto the grounds are leaving their names on a sign-in sheet, leaving proof of their presence.

"Sorry about the initials, sir. NTAA means National Threat Assessment Agency." The smile she flashes is slightly more real this time. "You get so used to acronyms around here you stop talking normally. Even when we order food in, at night, we'll say, 'I'll have the HOP.'"

Voort guesses, "Hamburger, onions, and pickles?"

"You learn fast, sir."

A black Chrysler sedan idles on the corner, and Voort sees a puff of gray exhaust rise at their approach. But he's frowning. "I never heard of the National Threat Assessment Agency."

"Most people haven't. I can answer any basic questions, information you can get on the Web, but specific details will have to come from the general. NTAA was set up to assess and react to threats facing the country," she says, as if having memorized a mission statement. "We name 'em and we tame 'em, sir. At least that's the slang. We coordinate intelligence reports from other agencies, and our experts design strategies to deal with threats."

Voort thinks about it. "Threats inside the country?"

"Overseas mostly. War plans. Nuclear terrorism. Big stuff. But we can operate here."

Voort ducks to get into the car. "I always thought the FBI or CIA did that. Why you?"

"I asked that in the beginning, sir. The mandates of those agencies are more limited than ours. The FBI concentrates on domestic problems. CIA stays overseas. And we haven't even gotten to ATF, that's Alcohol, Tobacco, and Firearms, Secret Service, DOD." She blushes. "That's the Department of Defense. We coordinate the bunch."

Then she tries a joke. "It's the government. A little duplication never hurts."

The car, accelerating, makes a U-turn on Connecticut Avenue and proceeds toward the Potomac, retracing the route the cabdriver took.

Voort, remembering the names on Meechum's list, asks, "So, for instance, if NTAA was worried about armed militias in Montana, would that constitute a threat?"

The sexy lieutenant says, "It would depend what they

were planning. Some people think the next war will be here, sir. Our experts would analyze them, I suppose. But we're out of my area."

"How about someone selling military secrets to Iraq?"

"The general will know."

They take the Fourteenth Street Bridge into Virginia, weave through rapidly moving southbound traffic on U.S. 395, and pass bumper-to-bumper stalled commuter traffic, heading north into the city. Suburbs merge into each other. The countryside alternates between new subdivisions and pine forest, with concrete sound barriers lining the road in places, giving it a claustrophobic feel.

"Ever work with someone named Meechum Keefe at NTAA?"

"I'm not familiar with that name, sir."

"How about Colonel John Szeska?"

The lieutenant nods. "I read his articles in war college, but never met him."

"Articles?"

"On personal freedoms versus security issues. Nuclear terrorism in the twenty-first century. That kind of thing."

Twenty noninformative minutes later they leave the Interstate at Quantico. Strip malls give way to subdivisions. Town houses scale their way up to Colonials. They reach a wealthier area of large homes, built in classic styles, but the styles are mixed together, the hodgepodge of architecture out of place, tastelessly showy. A Victorian mansion sits beside a California stucco ranch. A brick Cape Cod lies adjacent to a Shakespearean Tudor. The Chrysler slows at the white gravel driveway of a one-story brick ranch, with Doric pillars holding up the small portico, and twin wings arcing back, onto pine-studded grounds. Hedgerows flank the curving walkway. A red Jeep Cherokee sits in the driveway. Lace curtains obscure whatever lies behind the French windows. There is nothing memorable about the house.

"The general hoped he could get a couple hours sleep before you arrived, sir."

"What was the emergency that kept him up?" Voort says, wondering if it was Szeska.

"General Rourke can fill you in on that"—meaning, "if he feels like it."

The man who opens the door, at the lieutenant's knock, looks like he got enough sleep. He's healthy, ruddy, sixty-ish, with yellow-white hair cut short on the sides, but curling in back over the collar of his knit black crewneck sweater and white shirt. His head is large and squarish, and he has the blocky body of an ex-athlete. His face is shiny, as if he has just shaven. His eyes are unreadable blue, the same dark color as his crisp new jeans. Oddly, he wears sandals.

"Lieutenant, wait in the car."

"Yes, sir."

The lieutenant spins without another word, and walks toward the Chrysler. Voort is alone with the general.

"Good flight?" Rourke asks, perfunctorily.

"Fine."

"They feed you?"

"A bagel."

"I'm grilling steak and eggs in back. I like a real breakfast. Want some?"

"I never turn down a steak, especially well done. I understand there was an emergency last night."

A grunt. The general turns and says, back to Voort, "There's an emergency every night. People have no idea what goes on while they sleep."

Voort has found over the years that it is usually a good

idea to accept a source's invitations of food or drink, even if he's not thirsty or hungry. Dining with someone tends to relax things, and from the coolly polite reception here, this meeting will not be relaxed.

Rourke leads him through a living room that is as unremarkable as the outside of the house. The couch and sitting chairs are forest green, like the shag carpet. The furniture is stained pine, the coffee table glass. Decorations seem to have been selected for memory value, making the room a travelogue.

The wall art is Asian, mostly framed colored-pencil sketches of huts, and fishermen on rivers. Longboats drift under palm trees. Peasants wade in rice paddies. On built-in glass shelves, Voort sees miniature mahogany chests from South America, and pottery which he guesses is Middle Eastern. The wooden masks are African. In the bookshelves he sees the same titles he saw in Szeska's office. Sun-tzu. Napoleon. General Gordon in Sudan.

"Shit. Another bombing," Rourke says as they enter the kitchen. He's stopped, and he's staring at a small TV on the counter, by an open carton of eggs. The picture is on, the sound is off.

Voort's heart turns over.

On screen, he sees, beneath footage of rescue workers, the word *Sarajevo*.

"Come out back. I started the grill already. Detective, I hate what we're about to do. I have a feeling this is going to be one of the worst meetings of my life."

"Why?"

Rourke steps into the grassy backyard, which contains, to Voort's surprise, a glassed-in one-lane lap pool, good for year-round use.

"Because, like Judas, I have a feeling I'm going to fuck a friend."

It's shady back here, with redwood lawn furniture and a smoking Weber grill. The steaks are probably on the covered plate, probably, but a second plate covers it. There's an electric coffeepot plugged into the side of the house. Voort's eyes go to a manila folder on the picnic table, beside a bottle of A-1 sauce, and sliced tomatoes on tinfoil.

"Sign the papers in there," Rourke says crisply as he uncovers the steaks. "They say whatever you learn today you'll keep secret. You can tell your superiors, but not CNN. Otherwise you'll end up in Leavenworth, and that's a military prison, son. Not what you're used to. You don't get Thursday night movies like in the resorts where you send felons up in your hometown."

The steaks sizzle on the grill. Blood drips on fire, and flames leap up, seeking more combustible fat to burn.

Voort signs the documents. Rourke's crisp attitude reminds him of the officers who used to visit Meechum's house when he was a boy. "Let's get to business then," the general says. "All delays are dangerous in war." Rourke looks at Voort, as if testing his knowledge, and adds, "Dryden said that."

The man snaps his wrists, breaking eggs in a bowl.

"I remembered a quote, too, on the flight down."

"What's that?"

"I learned it in college. From Cicero. 'The law is silent during war.'"

Rourke grunts, and places a greased pan on the Weber. He pours the yellow eggs onto it.

"I see." But he seems surprised that Voort knew any quotes. The eggs sizzle. Voort smells charred meat. Rourke says, "They said answer your questions. What do you want to know?"

But of course, the problem is choosing the right questions. The general is under duress, reluctant to talk, and Voort can guess how this meeting came about. He envisions the angry phone call Rourke must have received last night. Everyone fears a late-night call, and last night was Rourke's turn. Had it been an angry general? Had the White House ordered him to betray his friend?

Voort decides to tread lightly at first to avoid making the man more defensive. He must start with something basic.

"Tell me about the National Threat Assessment Agency," he says, staying away from Szeska.

Rourke turns the steaks over. The charred lines on the meat resemble stripes on a convict's shirt. "Do you read history? You must if you know Cicero."

"A little."

"If you read history you know that a big reason World War One started is because the major powers never got enough information to avoid things getting out of hand. Today our problem is that intelligence people are overwhelmed with too much: reports, maps, studies. We coordinate it, narrow it down to key issues, and make plans to cope with threats. Didn't the lieutenant tell you that?"

"Can you give an example, inside the country?"

"Not one we're working on. But I can give one we *might* have worked on if we'd existed at the time. Remember Aldrich Ames, the CIA agent who worked at headquarters and sold secrets to Russia? The agency knew he was spending money like crazy. They knew he had a new house, new car . . . yet they never caught him until it was too late. Why? They're not stupid, despite what the television says.

"The truth was, they probably had about two thousand *other* employees overdrawn at their banks, too, at the same time. The information on Ames was buried in a shitpile of other data. But had the CIA's files been reviewed by another agency, us for instance, we might have picked out Ames earlier. The information was there. Sometimes an outsider can spot things an insider can't."

"And your job is to spot the threats?"

"My job is to pick the right people for the right jobs. I'm retiring in a few weeks anyway, thank God."

Rourke picks the steaks off the grill, puts one on each plate, and adds slices of bloodred tomatoes. He slides the eggs off the pan with a spatula and lays them atop the smoking meat. He places a plate in front of Voort, and one across the picnic table from him. He sits down.

"My wife says I'm a meatatarian," he says. "I hate vegetables."

"Let's get to Colonel Szeska. Did you hire him?"

Rourke carves steak. "I did."

"Is that what he does in New York, reviews files from other agencies?"

Rourke's fork stops halfway to his mouth. "That particular project was supposed to be closed."

"What project?" says Voort, a throbbing starting up in his chest.

"And for all I know," Rourke continues, "it *is* closed. He hasn't done anything wrong to my knowledge. But I've been ordered to tell you about the project, in case Szeska . . ."

"Kept it going instead of shutting it down," Voort suggests.

Rourke looks devastated. Voort takes a forkful of egg. He chews but does not taste. He maintains the illusion of dining. The general, staring at his food, says:

"There was a lieutenant named Meechum Keefe."

Voort feels a stab of loss, but does not reveal the friendship.

"Keefe met Szeska at West Point."

Voort forces himself to keep slicing steak. It seems to make things easier for Rourke.

"No, that's not the way to start. I better start a different way. I'll start with Szeska before they met," the general says, causing Voort to remember something else that his father used to tell him, long ago: "Personalities are like chemicals, pal. Some mix well. Some cause explosions. Look at the mix when you're on a case."

And now Rourke is tracing the path that led Meechum to Szeska. Rourke is talking about Szeska the young hero in Vietnam. Szeska the wounded warrior in Iraq. Szeska's trajectory through the troublespots, through the years, until he was stationed in Ecuador.

"John got back from the jungle. He'd gone on a raid against the ELA, one of those 'liberation armies' that we helped stop before they did damage. He was happy. He was going to see his wife. I had to tell him the ELA had blown up a bus and that she'd been on it."

As the details go on; the funeral, the grief, Szeska's ranting at the cemetery, Voort pictures the man he met on Fifty-third Street, only in the vision the man is younger, torn by the sort of loss Voort has seen so many times on his job. In the vision, Szeska is racked by the same kind of fury that had gripped Meechum's family, when Al died. Voort's on familiar ground now. His whole case—the list, the deaths, the links with Washington, all of which had seemed large and mysterious—is now shrinking to proportions he understands.

Rourke is saying, "I pulled him out of Ecuador. He was a wreck. Finished in the field. He came back to an easier job, lecturing at Quantico and West Point. Years went by, and he was okay again. That's when he met Meechum Keefe."

At the name, Voort feels his own grief coming. He can't help it. Meechum, Rourke is saying, at West Point, was "obsessed" with his dead brother. He threw himself into antiterrorism studies, classes, theories. Meechum, in Szeska's classes, absorbed the colonel's fear of the kind of threats the country would face in years to come. The two men hit it off. They shared loss.

"Meechum was a computer jock and a maverick. An individualist," Rourke says more admiringly, now that they are discussing skills instead of limitations. "When he got an idea into his head he would never let go. He used to say, 'Can we do things my way?' "

"He was a friend of mine."

"I know. One day Meechum came to Szeska, *after* he'd graduated. He'd been thinking, he said. He believed it was possible to come up with a better way, *his* way, for a computer to help identify threats. He said he'd designed a software program more sophisticated than corporate profiling. He believed his way could identify perpetrators *before* they committed illegal acts."

"You mean the computer would tell you who might set a bomb off before they did it?"

"That was the claim. Terrorist. Spy. Bomb maker. Revolutionary. Look," Rourke says, waving a fly off his steak, "the kid was adamant. He said, give me files on suspects, and I'll run the program. It was voodoo to me, voodoo to Szeska. But Meechum camped out in my office. I'm a liaison. Army to NTAA. I wear two hats. He kept saying,

'What harm would it do to give me a chance? Just one test.' "

"So you did," Voort says, heart sinking.

"Why not," Rourke says. "He had high-level clearance. He was a proven resource, a recognized computer genius. And the army had been playing around with the notion of improving software that supplemented human investigative capabilities. So we tried Meechum's experiment. We gave him the files relating to potential threats against one of our bases in Germany."

Voort asks which base.

"Never mind that. Meechum got all the information we had. The interviews, the threatening letters, the reports, the analysis. He wouldn't go to Germany. He'd only use his software. It cost us nothing beside his salary. We dumped all the stuff on his lap and said, laughing, okay, kid, go off for a month with your magic, and come back and show us your way."

Voort listens, captivated. Suddenly an animal scream interrupts Rourke, and both men spin toward the pine trees. Two ravens, swooping and pecking, fight each other in the air.

"Meechum walked out of the office," Rourke continues, "and frankly I forgot about him. A month goes by, and he's back. He's ranked the threats."

Excitement mounting, Voort pictures the Executive Office Building in which he had been supposed to meet Rourke this morning. He sees Meechum, in uniform, signing into the White House ledger. Meechum striding confidently, having done things his way, across the White House grounds.

"In my office," Rourke says, "he explains his system.

Moron Computer Class 101 for me. He says the computer assigns numbers to personality traits. For instance, and I'm making up numbers here, a suspect gets a ten if he was an only child. Six if he had siblings. Ten if his father beat him, if he had no friends, if he liked blue Popsicles maybe, all kinds of things, that Meechum put in. I'm simplifying it here but you get what I mean."

"Go on."

"And our base in Germany, believe me, had no shortage of potential threats." Rourke lifts his index finger, as if counting. "We had Libyans living near the base, legal immigrants, running a store."

Another finger. "We had Green Party environmentalist freaks, y'know the kind who demonstrate against the damn American polluters who kill the trees."

Third finger. "Ex–Bader Meinhoff, released from prison. Meechum's software had looked at all of them, assigned them numbers, tallied the numbers, color-coded the results."

Knowing Meechum, it is completely logical to Voort that his old friend would have attempted this. That he would have the confidence in his abilities. That he would have been sure that his way would be best.

He can picture Meechum in Rourke's office, waving files, insisting he has answers.

"Did he have answers?" Voort says.

Rourke's throat is dry, and he reaches for the cooled-off coffee. His Adam's apple works as he drinks. He says, "Meechum said the program had kicked out one big threat, and then he showed me. Ready for this? *It was the town baker.*"

"The baker?"

"I couldn't believe it! I could imagine the laughter in

the meeting, when he announced his big find. I said, Are you sure this is right? What about the Libyans? And Meechum went red. 'No, I'm right! The Libyans are shop-keepers. The Bader-Meinhoff people went to jail already.' Meechum insisted it was the baker, a one-legged guy with no prison record, no record of violence, a good marriage, a daughter. He'd written a single nasty letter to the com-mander of the base, complaining about soldiers who didn't pay their bills. There was an interview, an intelligence offi-cer dropping into the bakery, pretending to be a customer. Nothing I found alarming. But Meechum was adamant."

"So you shut him down."

"Shut him down? Two weeks later the baker went nuts and shot twelve soldiers."

Voort, astounded, says, "You mean it *worked*? How could a computer do that?"

"How do I know? Maybe it was a fluke! But corporations pay millions a year for profiles of executives, and the CIA has sworn by profiling for years, not that they have any-thing that sophisticated. But there has to be something to it. Meechum said it was a new science, that it was getting better.

"Meechum was good or lucky," Rourke says, remember-ing, "and as soon as the army found out what happened, he got called in again, only this time the audience was big-ger. It wasn't just the army anymore. The NTAA is always seeking ways to supplement threat assessment. This time Meechum was asked if he could design a pilot program . . ."

"His way."

"Yeah. His damn way . . ."

Voort finishes the thought, ". . . to examine files from lots of agencies."

Rourke finishes his coffee and grimaces. "FBI. CIA. Bureau of Alcohol, Tobacco, and Firearms. What the hell, NTAA figured. It worked once. Let's try again."

"And now Meechum had access to everyone's files," Voort reasons, and thinks *That's why the names on his list would have all been of interest to different agencies. That's why there was no common thread.*

"Right," Rourke says, mopping his brow. "Top secret. International intelligence is hard enough. Domestic is a minefield. Americans go crazy if they think the government's checking up on them. We sheep-dipped participants' files, changed their records so it would look like they'd left the army, in case the thing blew up in our faces, if they screwed up.

"But meanwhile, every agency's suspicions, suspects, worries would be fed into one central program, Meechum's threat assessment program. And Szeska wanted to run the operation. He said he'd brought Meechum to me. He said he'd calmed down since Ecuador. He said it was important work and he was tired of teaching. I like Szeska. Meechum didn't want administrative responsibilities. He wanted to concentrate on software. So we set Szeska up in a brownstone and gave him his pick of staff."

"This is insane," Voort says.

"Why? It was an experiment," says Rourke, standing up. "That's what we do. That's how the country stays ahead of everyone else. Some experiments work. The hydrogen bomb worked. Some experiments fail. Mind control. Hallucinogenic drugs. The fucking space program started out as an experiment. All experiments seem far-fetched when you start them. Star Wars or Meechum. This was his big shot."

"You keep saying 'was.' Does that mean it didn't work?"

Rourke calms a little, and shakes his head. "Not the way it was supposed to. It was too good to be true, a computer program that could do all that. But we didn't know it yet. At first there was huge excitement. The computer jocks, of course, had faith in the thing. Science is God around here. Szeska got the best of the best. The CIA's always been big on computer profiling, so their experts were in. SAC, the Strategic Air Command, had the best computer people. The army has psychological warfare people. The FBI has behavior modification experts."

"And all of them worked out of the brownstone in New York?"

"Yes. That building is used for intelligence anyway. Its staff monitors U.N. diplomats . . . well, they're not really diplomats. And we monitor security on military contractors in the Northeast. Szeska's people got the top floor. We left them alone for months. Then there was a big meeting at Quantico, at the war college, to show results. Meechum had processed a couple months' worth of files from participating agencies. He had more predictions."

"And?"

"And he gave us five or six names. 'Purples,' he called them. Unusually urgent threats."

Voort's head begins throbbing. "Let me guess. Jill Towne. Frank Greene."

"No."

Voort, baffled, says, "Then who?"

"Actually, these names are not part of your investigation, and you won't learn them from me. They're classified. But they were all people who were later arrested, and prosecuted successfully, all but one, that is."

"I don't understand. You said the program didn't work, but now it seems it did."

Rourke shakes his head. "It worked in Germany because Meechum had the right kind of information about the baker, when he started. But it turned out that in order to get more information on the new people, Szeska's group had broken every domestic surveillance law. Wiretapping. Breaking and entering. Entrapment. To supplement the information they had. And not just against the guilty ones. On hundreds of innocent people. They'd done the things secret police do in Communist countries. They'd been overzealous in getting information so Meechum's program could work.

"And more. It turns out Szeska, for his field staff, had chosen people with grudges. People who had lost friends or family to terrorists. They were all like Meechum, walking wounded. They were out for blood."

Voort is cast back, listening, to his meeting, just yesterday, at One Police Plaza. He remembers his own detectives, out for blood themselves, suggesting that he leave Szeska alone, for a little while, so Szeska could eliminate the potential terrorist Frank Greene.

"I understand," Voort says.

"At the meeting, at Quantico, the participating agencies were horrified when they understood how Szeska had run the thing. The software became a sidepoint. Every agency there had been burned on domestic surveillance over the last few years. The FBI remembered the Hoover files. The CIA remembered the break-ins and wiretapping. The Secret Service pulled out. SAC pulled out. Everyone's looking at everyone else, thinking, even if I wanted to use this information, there's no way, with all these other guys knowing it, I would even try. I'd land up in jail.

"And that was that. Meechum's way hadn't worked. Oh, the software was useful, it can kick out names, and it's been installed in many threat assessment programs, but without the extra effort, the illegal stuff . . . it's a great tool, but not a miracle."

But now Voort is confused. "I don't understand. If the program was stopped, like you say, how come four of the people Meechum identified were arrested?"

"Independently, agencies went after them, after letting the thing cool off for a couple of months. Thanks to Meechum, they knew who to zero in on, and the project never came out in trial, because they started from scratch on each one. But they knew where to look. They knew who to look at. I said the program was a tool, and face it, how could they ignore potential dangers once they knew about them? It's easy to do an investigation when you know you'll find proof before you start."

"You also said one of the people Meechum identified was not arrested."

And now Rourke sighs, blows out air. He looks stricken. "That's the toughie, the damn toughie. That's the worst part."

He pulls from the back pocket of his jeans a photograph, and hands it to Voort. It shows a bearded man Voort has never seen before, a chubby white man in a peaked tractor hat, sitting behind a table lined with rifles. The man wears a denim shirt and jeans. He's turned toward the right to talk to someone else, but the other person is not in the photo.

"That was taken at a gun show in Texas," Rourke says. "You're looking at Rollo Francis Mott the third. You never heard of him, I know."

Voort says nothing. Rourke hands him another photo.

"Here's the man he was talking to, who was cut out of the first shot."

Voort recognizes this second man, and starts to feel warm.

"That's Timothy McVeigh."

The man convicted of bombing the federal building in Oklahoma City.

Rourke's lips are pressed together, in regret or anger, and they have gone white. "According to Meechum's software, Rollo was a purple. Rollo was into explosives. Rollo, the program predicted, would involve himself in the bombing of some federal building, possibly somewhere in the Southwest."

"Wait a minute. Meechum predicted this *before* Oklahoma City?"

"A month before. The program didn't kick out McVeigh, he never came to Meechum's attention, but . . . and remember the paper you signed today . . . this is secret, Mr. Voort . . . the FBI believes that Rollo is the other man guilty in the Oklahoma City bombing. But they haven't proved it. They have nothing on Rollo. When that thing went off in Oklahoma, Szeska went crazy. He called up, ranting. He said if we had listened to Meechum, we could have stopped it. He said even if Rollo wasn't involved, by going after him, we could have found out about McVeigh."

"Is that true?"

Rourke lays his hands flat on the table, helplessly. "*Could* we have? Yes, we could have. They're friends. Rollo's visited him in prison. It's conceivable. If the program had been instituted, instead of being shut down, Rollo would have been under intense scrutiny, and *if* he was involved, we would have found out about the bomb and stopped it, I think."

The impact of the revelation lifts Voort to his feet. His stomach has gone sour. His head hurts. He knows exactly what Meechum's reaction would have been that day, turning on the television, watching again as victims were pulled from rubble, anonymous victims, doomed because of where they chose to go that day. Like his brother. Men, women, and children, killed.

"Szeska went ballistic," Rourke says.

"And started up the project again."

"I have no idea. You're the one who called us. Your damn mayor's been waking up every influential senator in the city," Rourke says. "After we closed the project, Szeska begged me to stay active. He said, 'Let me run the New York office.' He said he didn't want to go back to teaching. He said he could make a difference, and I knew he was right.

"So I pulled strings, and he stayed in New York for the army, in a different capacity. He was supposed to run the place, the *legal* part of it, keeping tabs on the defense contractors. But last night I got that phone call. If what you suspect is true, yes, he used the office to restart Meechum's project."

"If it's a computer program, it'll be in his computers."

"No. We were up all night getting into his system, top to bottom. There's nothing there. The names you gave us, the people who died by 'accident,' we couldn't find them. But Szeska would keep the files somewhere else if he's activated the project. He could have even lied to his own staff, and said Washington ordered it. But the appropriate people are in the field somewhere. Remember, we're still talking *if*. There's no proof."

Rourke's voice is trembling.

"He killed them," Voort says, certain now in his heart.

"Well, he couldn't arrest them. We'd taken that option away."

"Meechum wouldn't cooperate with this," Voort says. "No matter what Szeska said, he wouldn't go along with killing people. Finding them, yes. But not assassinating them."

"Perhaps Meechum didn't know what Szeska was doing. Look, Szeska is a friend of mine. Do you know how I feel, even suggesting this? But if a bomb goes off in New York today, and you could have stopped it . . . I don't want that on my head."

"Meechum suspected," Voort whispers. And this time it feels right.

"Maybe he was going to tell," Rourke says.

Voort, nodding, remembers Meechum's words at the White Horse. *I don't want to get anyone in trouble. I want to be sure first.*

"I have been directed to tell you," Rourke says, in control of his voice again, "that you have all our cooperation. Our records are open to you. You can see minutes of meetings. You must keep them secret, but if they help stop a bombing, you can have anything you want. If Szeska *does* have a file on Greene, the original report would have been generated at another agency. Every appropriate agency is going through their files, searching for references to him. If we find something, you'll get it."

"But you don't think it will be thorough."

"If Szeska's guilty, the original reports will be supplemented by extra fieldwork. His files will be much more detailed, and completely illegal. Szeska read Sun-tzu, and Sun-tzu said, 'In accord with the enemy's disposition, we impose measures on the masses that produce victory, but the masses are unable to fathom them.' "

"Where is Szeska now?" Voort asks, knowing the thing is starting to conclude, to climax.

And Rourke looks miserable, "You don't know? It doesn't help his case. I thought your people told you. Szeska's disappeared."

NINETEEN

Filled with despair, John Szeska sits in his dark apartment, alone, eight hours before Voort arrives in Virginia. The blasting heat is stuck on "high." Naked, he nurses an iced whiskey and gazes through blowing curtains at the lights of Manhattan across the East River, bright orbs that might be extinguished if Frank Greene has his way.

I am failing you, Lupe.

Sweat collects on his powerful shoulders and runs down his back, despite the breeze blowing in. He is thinking that Voort tracked him down today. Police almost arrested him. If the detective's relatives had burst in five minutes later, they would have found Voort on the floor.

Destroy the evidence before they come for you.

Instead, Szeska pours another drink, eyeing Voort's detectives in an unmarked Ford below, under an oak and in a cone of vapor light. Their presence is intentional harassment, a promise of more scrutiny. Voort will turn up the pressure. In that last fraction of a second today, before his relatives arrived, as Szeska was moving in for the kill, the knowledge of what was about to happen had come into Voort's eyes.

Burn the disks now.

Safe, Szeska tells himself, is such an odd word. But it is as simple as reaching out and snapping the pieces of plastic on his thigh. Or turning on the oven, slipping the three black computer disks inside, watching them melt, bubble, pool. There is no other evidence of their existence.

But safe has never been the point.

At least he's gotten the photographer and researcher away. He warned them this afternoon. By morning they'll be overseas, on "official business." They will have activated whatever escape plans they have made—plans Szeska intentionally does not know. They will stay away forever unless a coded message from him, left in a voice-drop, orders them to return.

Now it's just me and Frank Greene and the cop and the disks.

And things with the cop have become personal.

Szeska feels the great clock of inevitability ticking. He feels all the threads twisting toward culmination. He feels Frank Greene out there, completing final preparations. He senses Voort making phone calls, ordering files opened, asking for search warrants, coming after Szeska with all the implacable rage of a dog attacking the man who killed its master.

The phone rings.

Szeska doesn't even glance at it. It has to be a wrong number at this hour. His own people would no longer call him here. His eyes remain on the disks, which feel heavy as iron, not plastic.

"Frank Greene" reads the label on the top one, a superb achievement in intelligence gathering. It includes the man's professional history, sex and sleeping habits, acquaintances' names, photos, digital voice samples, and copies of letters he sent to the president, FBI, and Bureau of Alcohol, Tobacco, and Firearms, ranting about the New York police—letters which brought him to the project's attention.

Szeska's answering machine clicks on but whoever is calling hangs up.

The other disks contain information on more threats Meechum uncovered. A farmer in North Dakota is constructing a crude homemade nuclear device, in his barn, using plans broadcast on the Internet. The dean of a South Carolina college is, in the misguided belief that he is promoting international cooperation, bringing Sudanese trained terrorists, "students" he calls them in scholarship applications, into his school. A GS-14 in the Commerce Department, whose parents live in Shanghai, is enabling weapons parts to be shipped to Beijing legally by simply stamping them NONMILITARY. APPROVED.

They would be dead already if it weren't for Voort.

The damn phone rings again!

Szeska picks it up to stop the noise, and hears a teenage voice, a black street kid, from the angry accent, say, "Yo! Is this Robert Szeska?"

And with the utterance of the code name, Szeska roars out of his half trance. "Robert" can only mean that Voort has managed to go over Szeska's head to Washington. And someone high up in Washington has reached Rourke.

"My name is *John* Szeska," he corrects, sleepily, as if he has been woken up. "There's no Robert here."

"Don't give me that shit, Robert. I recognize your voice."

"It's late and . . ."

"The Jets lost and you owe me thirty. I'll collect at the store."

The kid hangs up whatever pay phone he has been using. Szeska is already moving.

"Jets" means "trouble."

"Thirty" means "You have thirty minutes to get out of
the house."

"Store" is the goal now, the oasis of safety to which he
has been advised to flee.

And Szeska is swinging into the escape drill he'd lain
out when he moved here, and reviews monthly so it remains fresh. He has always known an enemy might come
for him. He had not accepted until now that the enemy
would be his own side.

*What was that quote from Chinese Gordon? It's your own
side that fucks you in the end.*

He needs only minutes to change into dark clothes, and
retrieve a prepacked overnight bag from a hidden compartment inside his bedroom closet. It contains a silenced
Glock automatic, a car key, $18,000 in cash, a false pass-
port, driver's license, social security card, and credit cards.
There are a half-dozen diamonds, $80,000 in traveler's
checks, two wigs, a makeup kit, an elastic elbow brace, and
open air tickets—to Montevideo, and to Quito.

He puts the disks in the bag.

Szeska has hidden two additional sets of escape needs in
Manhattan. But since the warning came at home, he uses
the nearest cache.

Six minutes up. From the window, he sees, in the quiet
street, Voort's police minders, silhouetted two stories below.
He sees the glow of a cigarette burning in the passenger
seat. He sees exhaust rising. The cops, told to be conspicu-
ous, are running the heat.

That the Minders have not moved in an hour, that they

are not covering the doors, tells him that they do not know the attack is coming, which means the assault will be federal, not local; FBI or DOD. Justice. ATF.

Rourke's men.

But the lapse, not including the police, has given Szeska extra minutes. He must now take advantage of the "repair work" he's been doing around the house—modifications which have added to the property value while facilitating escape.

His apartment door opens on a hallway he carpeted with footstep-muffling pile, so no one downstairs can hear him leaving. The stairway takes him to the basement, where he switches off an alarm system he installed. The lock on a boiler-side window, oiled by him, is easy to open. Ice cold air hits him as he wriggles out, onto a two-foot-wide dirt strip on the side of the house, behind a wall of evergreen hedges he planted. He crawls to the end of the property, where the neighbor's slat fence begins, tall, formidable, blocking any view from the street.

Szeska helped install it.

"John's so helpful," the neighbor told his wife's cousin that day.

"He loves working with his hands," she'd replied.

Thirteen minutes gone. It feels like winter out here, and smells of incoming snow. His breath frosts and his fingers sting. At twenty-four minutes he's on the newly routed Q-19 bus, which drops him two blocks from a long-term parking lot near La Guardia. The LeSabre he keeps there starts instantly. The heating system works especially well.

By three-thirty, evisioning federal agents tearing up his furniture, cushions, closets, and appliances, Szeska is crossing the Goethals Bridge, toward New Jersey, in light, middle-of-the-night traffic. Local airports are out of the question. So is Amtrak or a bus.

That damn Voort has no idea what he's wrecking.

He turns south on I-95, catching a last glimpse of the black towers of the city across the river. But any feeling of relief changes to horror as he sees, in his mind, an orange cloud erupting over there. He hears bomb victims screaming over wailing ambulance sirens.

People will die because of Voort.

He turns on the radio to drown out the destruction. But he can't stop thinking, What is Frank Greene doing now? Loading fuel barrels in his van? Checking street maps of the city?

Szeska switches to the center lane, staying three miles above the speed limit, like a normal driver instead of a drug or cigarette runner trying not to be noticed by police.

Lupe, what else can I do but run?

The news on the radio is bad, adding to the feeling of things going out of control. Strikers have closed auto plants in Detroit and Tennessee. The biggest HMO in California is shutting down, and over a million people will lose health care. Storms in the Midwest have left thousands across a five-state area without homes, and emptied the already strained coffers of the federal natural disaster relief program.

As things get worse, more Frank Greenes will come out.

Szeska pays the toll at the Delaware border, passing out of the outer ring of the primary danger zone, gliding through a cold Delaware River fog toward the looming twin towers of the Memorial Bridge.

In his mind he relives the morning the project was shut down. He sees himself walking proudly into the meeting at Quantico, carrying a list of threats that Meechum had identified. It would be a triumph, he thought. But it had turned into a disaster. Instead of welcoming him, the bureaucrats had been horrified. They'd started distancing themselves from the project as soon as they understood Szeska's methods. The condemnations had grown strident as each representative tried to outdo the other, as if each feared being remembered for ever considering sanctioning what Szeska had done.

He had been dizzy with rage. He had been sent from the room like a naughty child. He had sat, disbelieving, in a hallway, on a wooden chair, hearing the muffled sounds of Washington infighting from the other side of the door, a soldier more at home abroad, away from these suited men and women, who had never battled in the field in their lives.

After a while Rourke had come out. "How about some lunch, Big Guy?"

And so the program had died in the back booth of a Spaghetti House, amid the smell of garlic and premade salad dressing, and the gurgle of cheap house wine.

A waitress was yelling "I ordered a number *two*" as Rourke said, chewing Italian bread, "I don't agree with them. But shut it down."

"But it worked."

"Destroy the files and hard drives. The machines will be junked to stop anyone from figuring out how to retrieve information. The agencies are pulling out their people. They'll be gone by the time you get home. You did a bang-up job, John. Better than I thought possible. They're wrong, but they're the bosses."

It was no use arguing. Of all the waffling, self-destructive decisions inflicted on the military over the years—the early withdrawal from Iraq, the sale of arms to enemies, the inability to commit to Bosnia early on—this had been, in Szeska's mind, the worst.

He had flown home, where the only staff remaining had been the people he brought in; Charley, Laura, Meechum, and Pete, all as upset as he, as dazed and infuriated. A July day, he remembers, hot and rainy with the kind of cloying humidity only an urban center can produce. The dirty moisture had seemed to ooze from brick buildings. It soiled skin and fueled tempers.

Apoplectic with rage, John Szeska had, at dusk, been sitting in his office, lights off, shades up, a putrid rain rattling the half-open windows.

All he could think was, *Now no one will shoot the dogs.*

Outside, the traffic noises; horns and brakes and hip-hop music, had swelled into a nonstop cacophony of disappointment and urgent complaint.

Szeska had barely heard the door open, yet was only half surprised to see his visitors: Charley, loyal Charley, who believed anything Szeska wanted him to; and Laura the photographer, who'd lost a husband on the *Achille Lauro*, and Pete the researcher, whose wife and six-month-old son had died in the Pan Am flight over Lockerbie, when terrorists blew it up.

Charley had muttered, "I can't believe it."

Laura had said, "They act more scared of *us*."

On and on. A funeral before deaths happened. Until finally, after hours of resentment, Charley had fixed him with those West Virginia hound dog eyes, and uttered the words that had occurred to all of them.

"Are we *really* going to stop?"

That was the moment he realized they were still willing

to follow him, and it made him love them and want to protect them more. But he also saw that their commitment was
no surprise. They had killed in Saigon, so what was so
wrong with doing it for the right reason in Sacramento?
Beirut had been acceptable, so why not Boston? Tehran was
as good as Tallahassee. Quito was no different from Queens.

The four of them had lived so long overseas that their
country existed for them more as a concept than as physical
boundaries. Their grudges were their boundaries. The project was over, but the grudges remained.

"We're really going to stop," he'd told them firmly,
keeping self-control that brought bile to his throat. "We do
what they say."

And then, a month later, Szeska had been in his office,
shaving, when a secretary ran in.

"A bomb blew up the federal building in Oklahoma
City!"

He'd thought, *This isn't happening.*

He'd been filled with a dreadful premonition that the
project might have prevented it. He'd stayed in front of the
TV for hours, and on the Internet, calling up reports, talking to Washington, waiting for the other shoe to drop.

And when Timothy McVeigh had been arrested, an
American who'd murdered his own people, Charley, Laura,
and Pete had come to the apartment, and asked to restart
the project again.

No one ever said, "We'll kill these people ourselves."
But they knew what Charley meant.

"No," Szeska repeated. The TV had been on, showing
one more special about terrorism in America, showing victims hurt because, as far as Szeska was concerned, America
had stopped protecting its citizens.

"Washington will see the value in what we did now," he predicted. "And restart the project."

It didn't happen.

What *did* happen was that Charley returned, days later, with the photo of Tim McVeigh with Rollo Francis Mott, the man who had been identified as dangerous, by Meechum.

"Before we destroyed the files, we made copies," Charley said.

Laura had walked in, and so had Pete. His three fates, Szeska realized, were more willing to do what Lupe wanted than he was. And he saw more. *If I say no, they'll do it without me. And they won't do it well.*

So Szeska, whose mind worked faster than a computer sometimes, had merely voiced the first logistics problem of the new arrangement.

"What about Meechum?" he'd said.

And now, as he drives, as the FBI searches for him, the mist outside seems to thicken and become unnatural, obscuring not only sight but proportion, direction. The road shrinks to a miniscule gray strip of rolling tarmac. The radio voice seems to come from all directions. Red carbuncle lights loom suddenly ahead, and in the mist blue police lights are flashing.

They found me!

But there has merely been a fender-bender accident in the fog.

At six, with wan natural light seeping into the day, he passes a two-truck collision that blocked the interstate. At six-thirty he is stuck in early morning traffic, in the Baltimore Harbor Tunnel.

"This just in from New York City," the radio says as Szeska feels a wave of fear:

Greene set the bomb off.

". . . the 737 overshot a runway at Kennedy Airport. No passengers were hurt. . . ."

He shuts the radio.

By seven the fog has burned off, revealing bumper-to-bumper traffic clogging southbound lanes to the capital.

At eight-twenty he leaves the LeSabre in a strip mall near Reston, Virginia. He walks with the overnight bag, a mile, into a suburban subdivision.

"You drive slower than my Aunt Martha," Rourke tells him irritably when he answers the door.

Voort, he thinks, would be shocked if he knew about the phone call, but Rourke is the closest thing to friend or family in Szeska's life. That the general, his old mentor, has gone out of his way to warn Szeska, even as he sent men to Szeska's home . . . that he has risked his own career to get Szeska's side before seizing him, is a remarkable act of loyalty considering that Szeska has been lying to him all along. Rourke had no idea he kept the project going.

"Traffic was stalled," Szeska says.

"Did you keep the project going after we shut it down? Tell the truth."

The truth is, I could have ignored your warning and gone straight to a safe airport. I could have disappeared by now. But then Greene would have had time to set his bomb off. My best choice was my riskiest: obey your summons, lie about the project, find out how much you know, and decide if I can still help.

Szeska the actor stares at the general, mouth agape. He's been preparing for this moment.

He repeats, "Kept it going?"

He breaks out laughing. "Is that why I got the phone call? I thought it was serious! You should have let me sleep."

But Rourke just says, "If you didn't keep it going, why did you clear out of New York so fast?"

"You called me, not the other way around! I figured someone must have learned we started that project in the first place. You have coffee? I've been driving for hours."

They are watching each other. Each man has taken an enormous risk for the other. Friendship can only go so far, and Rourke has enormous resources at his disposal. If he decides Szeska is lying, he can have the arrest done here. For all Szeska knows, he has men in the basement.

But at the moment, a student of human nature, Rourke simply says, "I wanted to talk to you before the detective showed up, but he'll be here in a few minutes, because you're so late."

"What detective?"

Rourke smiles, acknowledging that Szeska has avoided the trap. "You'll recognize him. Get up in the attic. Use the headphones up there. The backyard is wired. You'll hear everything."

"Wired?"

Szeska's puzzlement, the confusion of a fellow professional, is a praise Rourke enjoys.

"Part of the job, Big Guy. In D.C., if you can't bug the enemy, at least eavesdrop on your own side. NTAA holds cocktail parties here. You wouldn't believe the things congressmen and lobbyists talk about after that third margarita, when they think I'm in the house. If they want to cut our budget, they'd better remember the old quote from Calhoun: 'Protection and patriotism are reciprocal.' "

" 'And knowledge is power.' Whatever you've heard about me is not true."

Rourke smiles coolly. "Then we'll celebrate. But you're

a hell of an actor, my friend. Better than me. So after that detective leaves, you'll tell me every detail of what I'm not supposed to be worried about. Then we'll break open a six pack. After the chewing out I got from the Secretary of Defense last night, I could use a laugh."

And now Voort, in Rourke's yard, is wrapping up the story about Meechum and Frank Greene. He's told the general about the sketches, the list, the "accidents," the expected bombing.

Szeska, enraged, thinking, *Those stupid cops have made a bad mistake. They've misread their evidence.*

"Will you be going back to New York today?" Rourke asks over the miniature receiver in Szeska's ear. "Or would you rather work out of Washington, with us?"

There's a folding cot and oval throw rug and a writing table in the room; a stuffed chair by the window and a reading lamp, which is off. It's an overheated cell in here, perfect for a monk.

Voort is saying, "If you're linked with my computer guys, like you say, I'll go home."

Szeska, thinking, *You goddamn amateur. Can't you see the truth when it's in front of your face? You're giving Frank Greene a clear run.*

"Believe me, the second we get a report, *you'll* get the report. Your people are welcome to help," Rourke says.

Twenty feet below the attic window, from where Szeska watches, morning sun gives Voort's blond head a corona, makes him a saint in a leather jacket.

"Contrary to popular belief, we don't keep dossiers on every citizen," Rourke laughs.

"Yeah, just half of them, and the other half work for you."

The men are walking back around the house, toward the car. Rourke's fading voice says, "Until I talk to John, I have trouble believing he did any of this."

Voort, barely audible from a distance, says, "When we catch him, ask."

And then, minutes later, from inside the house, "John! Come down!"

We live our life telling lies, Rourke had said in Vietnam. The lies help people, but the people don't want to know we exist. They want us to do things, but they need us to deny them. They don't want responsibility, just results.

Now the lies have led him here, and Szeska lowers the folding ladder to the downstairs hallway. Rourke stands there like a homeowner awaiting the Orkin man's termite report, hands on hips, demanding face upturned. But something else is there now, too. It's the smallest softening in the eyes. It's fear inside the look of inquiry. It's so subtle that someone who doesn't know Rourke well would miss it, but it gives Szeska leverage. Szeska realizes that the general has become an outsider, too. Like so many others over the years, he wants the story to turn out a certain way. He wants to protect Szeska.

And that desire is Szeska's best chance to get out of here.

The biggest break can be the smallest change in things. Rourke's been in Washington too long. You have to soften when all you do is talk.

"Reception was perfect," Szeska says.

The ladder springs back on its hinge, withdrawing into the attic. Rourke just asks, "Well?"

"I never heard of those names."

"None of them? Not Frank Greene?"

"If you'd like my people to help look for him, we'd be glad to."

Rourke moves so close they are inches apart. He says, trying for toughness, but Szeska has seen the vulnerable core, "I can testify for you. I can explain the circumstances."

"If you thought I had the file, why not wait until whoever raided my house last night found it?"

"Because they wouldn't find anything unless you let them. And because I owed you an opportunity to talk before the Visigoths descended. Have a seat in the living room. I'll get coffee."

Meaning, "Reconsider what you've said."

But Szeska doesn't need to reconsider. Rourke returns with two steaming mugs of coffee that say ARMY on the side and reek of hazelnut. Szeska's drink will have three spoonfuls of sugar in it. It will have the smallest bit of fresh cream. Rourke knows Szeska without needing a dossier.

"What happened to Meechum?" Rourke says, sitting down.

"He and Charley were . . . *that way.* You saw the report. They went to a hotel. They died in a fire. Charley smoked and must have fallen asleep."

"Charley was *gay?* Charley wasn't gay."

Szeska sips coffee, completely unrattled. All he has to do now is leave this house and he will be free. It is time to mix a partial truth with a partial lie. First the lie.

"Charley was experimenting with things these last few months."

Then the truth.

"He was dying of cancer."

Rourke puts his mug down.

Szeska nods. "Check his medical records. He had weeks to live. Drugs could kill the pain, but it would come back. So he tried things. New things. He went to Atlantic City to gamble. He tried cocaine. It was none of my business. Meechum was one of the things."

There had been a time, a long time ago, Szeska knows, when he never could have been able to fool Rourke.

"And as for Charley's family, I arranged full college tuition for the kids. Double pension for his wife. Anything I could do, I did. Between you and me, I wondered if he started the damn fire on purpose. Meechum was the real queen, not Charley. Maybe Charley was mortified. Maybe he was in pain. I don't want to know. A suicide means less benefits."

They are wrapping up their lives together, against one more ticking clock.

Rourke says, "I can't decide if you're telling me the truth, or just what I want to hear. I'll be blunt. If you have the file, leave it with me. I'll get it to them. Walk away. Go where you want. Go to the places you have tickets to in that bag. They'll never know you were here."

No, they'll trace you as an accessory, Szeska thinks. *I can't do that to you.*

Szeska says, "I told you. I don't have any file."

Rourke holds up his hands. "And I wanted to say that if you *did* keep that project going, I don't blame you. And you're *right* to run."

Rourke rises, and over his shoulder Szeska sees one of the colored-pencil sketches of a Vietnamese river. He recognizes the forested bend. It is close to the village where his squad was ambushed, long ago. Close to the trail that led him, eventually, to Rourke.

Rourke says, "For thirty years you've given your life for your country. You've been shot. You lost your wife. You have done enough for ungrateful people. It's not your fault if Washington ignored your warnings."

"Is this another strategy to make me give you a file I don't have?"

Szeska has never, in all the years, seen this kind of emotion in Rourke, whether it is real or an act.

"I wanted to tell you, face-to-face, that you kept your promise to her, which you told me about in the cemetery. And that ten years from now, when this country knows better about the threats it faces, people like you will be heroes. I wanted you to know you never failed me. Your country owes you, not the other way around."

Rourke calms. "But I'm relieved to find out you don't have the file. For a few minutes there, Voort was convincing."

"*You're* relieved? Think how *I* feel. I'll just head back to New York and straighten everything out."

Rourke has not touched his coffee. "Just remember. If, thirty minutes after you leave, I find a disk in my mailbox, that someone else left, it will be easy to make it look like we found it in New York."

"General, you just don't give up."

And with that, the talk is over. They shake hands as if they will see each other soon, which they won't. Szeska picks up the bag, feeling Rourke's eyes on it. But Rourke does not stop him. Szeska is unsure whether it is loyalty or deception, but he's going to get out of here.

Outside, he walks the mile to the LeSabre.

Rourke was right. I owe them nothing.

In October, the leaves are just starting to turn colors this far south. In New York they died weeks ago. It occurs to him that all he sees, these suburbs, so familiar to the people here, are alien to him. He's spent most of his life in places where leaves don't turn colors. And in many places where no leaves exist at all.

Voort ruined everything. And now he's even messing up the search for Frank Greene.

In the car he changes appearance. The curly-haired wig goes on, and the brown-tinted contact lenses. He slips on the elbow brace and wills himself to ignore the pain. A shot of cortisone, administered to the left side of his face, swells the cheeks and adds a sense of weight to the overall appearance. Sunglasses are not recommended for fugitives.

Police seeking fugitives look twice at sunglasses.

He drives west, on U.S. 66, killing time, eventually turning onto the Dulles Airport access road, and the long-term parking lot at the capital's international airport.

I'll leave the car long-term, all right. It'll stay until they tow it away.

Equatoriana Airlines flight 44 is scheduled to leave at eleven-thirty tonight. The MD-11 will carry its passengers six hours south, across the eastern seaboard, and the Gulf of Mexico, and down the west side of South America to Guayaquil, Ecuador's city on the equator, and then, tomorrow at six A.M., he will land in *her* city in the Andes, *her* resting place and his future.

Szeska, or rather, as his new passport says, Mr. Vincent Payne, shows his ticket and tells the clerk he has brought only carry-on luggage. Vincent Payne walks through the bomb detector, minus the gun, which he left in the car. He enjoys the fruit juices, hard drinks, and pastries in the new first-class lounge. There is nothing in the *New York Times* about Frank Greene, or a bomb alert. The *Daily News* has nothing. The five o'clock news has nothing.

After a while, the lounge fills with early arriving passengers. The stars are coming up outside the big glass windows, their lights bright but smaller than the ones on incoming planes.

At ten, when an announcement comes over the intercom that the flight will leave on time this evening, Vincent Payne is frowning at a small item on page eight of tonight's *New York Post*.

He says, under his breath, "Who was I kidding, anyway?"

He picks up his bag, spins on his heel, and leaves the lounge.

He finds the LeSabre where he left it, and a half hour later is back on Route 95, heading north. This time traffic is light, as if fate approves his decision. By one a.m. he's reached the Holland Tunnel. Twenty minutes later he parks on Fifth and Sixty-first Street, in a space which will be legal until eight.

Szeska removes his disguises. His appearance must be normal for what he plans to do next.

Jill Towne's night doorman is a polite, blocky Hispanic with a thin mustache, who reaches instantly for the house phone when Szeska explains that he is here on "urgent police business."

"Please call Detective Conrad Voort in Miss Towne's penthouse. Tell him Colonel Szeska left this envelope for him."

Szeska leaves as the man punches numbers in the house phone. He briskly returns to the LeSabre, and ten minutes later pulls up to a pay phone at Second Avenue and Thirty-seventh Street.

Jill Towne answers on the first ring. Szeska asks to speak to the detective.

"Where are you?" Voort says.

"I want you to be clear on something," Szeska says. "I

collected all the information on that disk myself. No one helped. No one knew. I took the photos. I planted the bugs. I'm completely responsible. Catch the guy before he blows people up."

"Tell me about Meechum."

"He died in the fire. You're wasting time."

"And the accidents?"

"What accidents?"

"Meet me. I'll come alone."

Szeska laughs dryly. A police car is cruising past, and its occupants do not even glance in his direction. "Have you ever been to Leavenworth Prison, Voort? What I just admitted to could put me there for years."

"And Jill?" Voort asks, barely suppressing his rage.

Szeska figured he'll ask if she's safe. He's going to have to give a little on that. He says, "Didn't she decide to lay off the controversial work? Then everyone's happy."

"How do you know what she decided?"

"You told me. And you would have absolutely *nothing* on Greene if it weren't for me. Now listen," Szeska says. "You have things wrong. *He's not going to attack One Police Plaza, or the precinct.*"

A pause. "But the drawings show . . ."

Szeska cuts the detective off, wanting to wrap this up, to get away from this phone. He puts force into his voice. He uses his authoritative "colonel's" voice. *"Think.* He took everything he needed from Massachusetts. He needed the van, the dynamite, the fertilizer. *Don't you think he'd need drawings he made of his target?"*

Voort's breathing slows, deepens.

"Doesn't it make sense," Szeska continues, "that he'd

leave behind drawings he *didn't* need, and take ones he *did*? Of a *third* location?"

And the damn cop argues!

"Maybe he has *other* drawings of One Police Plaza," Voort says, out of his league. A city cop, a sex crimes cop, a local guy with no idea of the big picture, needing help from a man he wants to arrest, not even realizing that they should be allies.

Voort says, "Do you have any idea how many guys have gone down because of things that didn't make sense? They leave pens from their hotel at a crime scene. They leave phone bills, credit cards, fingerprints. *Sense?*"

"You're angry at me so you're not thinking. Do you really want to risk the lives of all your friends because you don't want me to be right? If you don't want to believe me, believe Meechum's profiling. Use the disk.

"Voort, imagine you're Frank Greene. You're smart. You hate police. You want to kill as many as possible—top guys, too—*in an accessible place*. You know you can never get your van past the bomb barriers. You're not suicidal. You want to get away. So *think*, Voort. The papers say you're a hotshot thinker. *Think* of a place where police don't usually go, where there are no defensive preparations, a place that's been in newspapers, and where half the city knows, at a particular time and place, quite soon, Frank Greene can find hundreds of unsuspecting police."

Szeska can almost hear the air go out of the detective.

"Oh, God," Voort says, seeing where Szeska is leading, not necessarily accepting it, but understanding the tragic possibilities.

"God won't stop it. Only you can."

"You're asking me to ignore the only evidence we have."

"The disk is evidence and life's one big guess sometimes. Hitler chose badly at Normandy and lost the war. Good-bye, Voort. You wanted this problem. All those cops, your friends and relatives depend on you. I could have stopped Greene but you came after me. So *you* take responsibility. I'm out of here. I'm far away. You can't hear me anymore. Let your friend help you."

But the cop still comes at him. "You're going far away?" the voice says with driving hatred. "Well, I don't care how far. You killed those people and you didn't do it alone. I'll have your pictures in post offices. I'll get a special on your project on TV."

Of course, Szeska knows, reeling, Voort signed the nondisclosure agreement in Washington, but it is clear the cop will find a way around it, will not, if Szeska is free, remain bound by a piece of paper. Voort will "leak" information in a way that makes it seem it did not come from him.

"I'll take all of you down," Voort says.

Szeska feels the explosive relentlessness in the man, instead of gratefulness. Voort will have Szeska's face and description—and computer-generated variations—broadcast all over the country. He can do it. Any TV network would leap to tell the tale.

Szeska hisses, "Do you know what it's like when you have the opportunity to stop someone like Greene, stop something this bad, and you fail? You never forget. You *never forgive yourself*. You hear people screaming in your sleep till you die. And by the way," he says, forcing himself to the immediate problem, Frank Greene, "in case we're missing signals, try page eight, column two, in today's *Post*, for the location."

"You're just guessing," Voort says as Szeska hangs up. It's incredible. After all the risks Szeska has taken, is the cop actually going to ignore the results because of a personal vendetta? Szeska risked his life putting the file into Voort's hands, and now his rage is so great it robs him of sight for an instant.

Szeska leans against the booth for balance.

Invisible city. Invisible Szeska.

He addresses the detective as if the disconnected receiver can still transmit voices.

"Use what I gave you. I'll come for you afterward. Tragic accidents happen when emotions run high."

TWENTY

V oort sits motionless on the edge of Jill's foldout couch, regarding the black computer disk in his hand. The room is still. Propped against her pillow, Jill rubs his shoulders with both hands. A small table lamp is lit beside Voort, and the disk's metallic piece throws artificial light onto the nearest wall and fashions it into a stiletto-shaped prism.

He's dressed in the clothes he wore when he went down to the lobby to retrieve Szeska's disk: unbelted trousers, a T-shirt, shoes, no socks.

"Aren't you going to read it?" she says.

The disk seems heavier than it ought to be, but Voort tells himself that's probably in his imagination. He also imagines heat emanating from the surface, as if the thing has absorbed not only facts about people but their passions and fears, and the blood pumping through their hearts.

He hears the words of his father, uttered years ago, when he was nine.

You will be tempted one day, when you are a policeman, to break the law yourself, in order to put a criminal away. You'll tell yourself it's for the greater good. You'll tell yourself that it's the only way and that you'll save lives. But if you do it once, the second time will be easier. Then, someday, will come the third.

Voort gazes back into the eyes of the woman that disks like this one put on an assassination list. If he doesn't use the information now, more people might die.

"Jill, do you have a computer here?"

He feels dirty. She retrieves a small Toshiba laptop from a closet, lays it on the kitchen counter, and flicks the appropriate switch. There is time to change his mind. But Voort's fingers seem to move by themselves, inserting the disk into the slot off the keyboard.

"I want to see, too," she says, coming closer. Her face is shiny with greed, and Voort wonders if he looks the same way.

"No. Sit down." Voort feels like a hypocrite, "protecting" Frank Greene's privacy.

"Conrad, this concerns me, too."

"Tell you what. If you're in the file, you can look."

She doesn't argue this time, and at least he's grateful for that.

The disk turns out to contain a single dossier, titled, GREENE, FRANK. Voort watches pictures of the man swim up, and the subheads: "Schedule." "History." "Habits." "Projections."

His father's voice is saying, in his head, "The toughest choices are between good and good, buddy."

"Well?" Jill asks, from the couch, dying to see the file, too.

Voort calls up "Projections" and starts reading.

He does not tell her any of it.

After a while, he whispers to himself, "Oh, God."

TWENTY-ONE

A nd now it is the day.

The date on Frank Greene's sketches.

The clock strikes six A.M. in the police briefing room. The sun is not yet up, but over a hundred cops, FBI agents, and bomb squad experts—an incoming defensive shift, lean forward, riveted by Voort.

"Frank Allan Greene," Voort says at a podium, "was born in Bayside, to middle-class parents. He joined no clubs in high school. He had no brothers or sisters. His father was a salesclerk at Macy's. His mother was a nurse."

Voort is thinking, Szeska was so damn sure nothing would happen today.

Twin screens flanking Voort show photos, documents, and letters obtained by Szeska, provided on the disk.

"Greene graduated from high school without trouble. He drifted from job to job."

Greene, invisible to the department until now, is being given a body, face, voice, history. Szeska, through Voort, is providing the audience background in case they ever have to talk to the man. You never know which approach can calm someone down.

"Greene ran the copy room in a law firm, was a gofer for a TV production company, was a security guard on Ninetieth Street. Seven in the evening till two in the morning. Minimum wage. No benefits. Rain or shine. He patrolled the block."

On-screen, Greene, in a blue uniform, hugs a golden retriever, beside a parked car, on Ninetieth Street. He presses his cheek to the animal's head. Whoever holds the leash is out of the shot.

Mickie growls, from the first row, "The Führer loved animals."

The photo is excellent quality. Greene looks about thirty, pale, with a face pockmarked from teenage acne, according to medical records Szeska stole. Curly black hair recedes at the crown. His sideburns are long, his nose thin, ears round, and in this shot, unlike the police sketch from Massachusetts, he wears wire-rimmed glasses the shape and diameter of robins' eggs.

The mayor, learning at five A.M. how Voort had obtained this information, had said, "Use everything you have. I don't care how you found it. Stop him now. Worry about the ACLU later. Jack Lopez of the antiterrorism squad will run things."

"Frank Greene was good at security. People still remember him on that block. He was polite. He carried shopping bags. He shooed druggies off the street. He phoned the four-one if he saw anything suspicious."

The humiliating part is coming, though. Voort had been mortified, reading it in Szeska's file.

"Then his application was rejected at the police academy."

A collective groan rises from the audience.

"He wanted to be a cop."

How many times over the years has a sniper, a bomber, a phone-threat suspect turned out to be a disgruntled employee.

I never thought to check academy applications. I only checked arrest records, brutality complaints.

But Voort keeps going, feeling sick, hiding it, telling his audience about Greene's failed psychological test, the rejection that eventually turned the man into a rabid hater of the department that had turned him down.

Since midnight, even before Szeska showed up at Jill Towne's apartment, Jack Lopez has been assigning patrols throughout the City Hall area, and to the precinct in Greene's sketches. Plainclothesmen walk the plaza and surrounding blocks, waiting for the opening of hundreds of stores and restaurants, and the arrival of Saturday commuters, shoppers, and tourists. As far as Greene is concerned, a Saturday is as good as a weekday for carrying out a bombing. The commissioner is famous for working weekends, and requiring other department high-ups to do the same.

Like the oncoming shift, antiterrorism squad cops outside carry descriptions of Greene's van, photos of the man and computer-generated variations—Greene with different glasses, no glasses, sunglasses, different hair.

FBI surveillance teams man lower-level office windows. Snipers occupy rooftops. Helicopters patrol entrance and exit ramps of the FDR Drive and the Brooklyn Bridge.

Voort says, "He may have changed the color of the van, but it has other markings. The right rear bumper is twisted from an accident, as you can see in this shot. There's a sticker on the left front window for Greenpeace, and another, for the World Wildlife Fund, on the back window, lower right side."

Szeska had told him, *If you screw up, you never forgive yourself.*

Voort tells the colonel, in his mind, *Ignoring preparations here would be a screwup. Nothing in that file proved he wouldn't show up. In fact, after seeing your damn evidence, I'd say there's a good chance he will.*

"Even if the paint job is new, he may not fix the bumper. Hell, he plans to blow up the van. So be alert for the right model, wrong color. Check the bumper. Look for the stickers."

Szeska had said, *I could have stopped Greene but you came after me.*

Voort answers, in his mind, Meechum would be alive if it weren't for you.

He tells the room, "You are about to hear a tape of Frank Greene calling a talk show in Massachusetts. Remember his voice."

The low, enraged voice says, "John Locke said, 'He who would take away my liberty would take away everything else. It is lawful for me to kill him.' And I'm talking about the brutal New York police."

Voort says, "You hear the *r*? It's like an *uh*. The next call is to a gun salesman."

What I'd like to know, Meechum, is, Did you give Szeska the names of other people besides the ones you told me about? Are they in danger, too?

Greene saying, "You're going to New York in October? Stay away from One Police Plaza! I hear there's going to be a big ruckus there!"

The audience stirs, each person thinking, *I am inside One Police Plaza now.*

"Slide please. This is his handwriting. It's a letter he sent the president. See the long loop on the *p*? Maybe you think you've found him, but he looks different. Get a glance at a shopping list, letter, anything he wrote."

Mickie passes around a bottle of Old Spice aftershave, so they will recognize Greene's scent of choice.

"Any questions?"

Hands go up.

A detective asks, "How long will we maintain this level of preparation if he doesn't show?"

"We'll let you know."

An FBI agent asks, "With all the information on him, how come he wasn't arrested before this?"

"The information's recent."

A bomb squad expert says, "Isn't it against the law to write those kinds of things to the president?"

"Greene didn't threaten him directly."

And then they are breaking up, and Mickie comes up to him with yesterday's *Post*, folded to page eight, to the article on Hugh Addonizio's upcoming retirement party.

HUNDREDS OF COPS EXPECTED IN QUEENS!

"Szeska's sure this is the target, huh?"

"Every damn precinct in the city is a potential target, and there's extra security at all of them. Szeska's not God, Mickie. He's got a computer guessing for him. But we should have checked the academy applications."

"Nobody could have thought of it. Szeska only knew about it because he broke every fucking law to get his information. I just wish you would have passed around his picture, too."

"We've got our hands full looking for Greene. I'll worry about Szeska."

"Well, in the war plans department, you're as good as him, as far as I'm concerned."

"I'm going to have to be better."

Because he's out there. I feel it.

They head outside to check defensive preparations against mistakes.

Frank Greene doesn't show up by noon.

Or by three, when weekend shoppers stroll the streets.

Or by nine, when the few area bars and jazz clubs are filled to capacity. But aside from vehicular street traffic, at night, the City Hall area is relatively quiet.

At eleven, Voort begins counting down the last hour to midnight, stamping his feet to keep warm. In fifty minutes, the date on Frank Greene's sketches will expire. *And Szeska will have turned out to be right.* The night is silent except for his radio. Detectives and ATS cops call in, touch base. Everyone is on edge.

Upstairs, in the Submarine Room—the communications center—wait the commissioner, Jack Lopez, Addonizio, bomb and terrorist squad chiefs, and FBI officials.

All those egos crammed between four walls.

Those guys are ready to kill each other. They're not used to feeling vulnerable where they work.

It is frigid for October. Razor-edged clouds glide above the city, below an ice-white moon. Lights in empty offices glow with a fierce brightness accentuated by cold. From the direction of the East River, he hears the *chuk-chuk* of a police helicopter, over the FDR Drive.

Mickie's gone for coffee. Jill's at home.

Voort walks the plaza. The day has been filled with false alarms, with blue vans spotted a hundred times near City Hall. On each occasion, as squad cars closed in, the adrenaline has surged in the surveillance teams. Each time the alert has turned out to be nothing dangerous. The edge has dropped by one more degree in their awareness. The fatigue has grown one more miniscule bit.

If he comes, I might as well be on the plaza. I'm closer to the action and can reach any point fast.

Voort patrols like the Blue Guy he used to be, alert for any alteration in sight or sound. He descends the wide concrete stairs to the rear of the building, passes bomb barriers out back, embedded in the sidewalk, and more barriers protecting the loading docks on the north side.

He checks the guard booth by the ramp to the underground parking lot, manned by Blue Guys who operate a steel traffic bar shielding the entrance. An attacker would need a large truck to ram through, or more speed than it is possible to build up after making the sharp turn onto the ramp.

Nothing's moving.

But back on the plaza, he experiences an odd itching between his shoulder blades, a throb of expectation.

Is someone there?

He turns and peers into the alternating bands of light and dark. The feeling does not disappear.

Then a voice from the other direction distracts him. "Looks like Meechum got his way."

Mickie, a dark, approaching silhouette, holds two Styrofoam cups in his gloved hands. His shoulders seem unusually wide beneath his camel-haired, calf-length Yugoslavian coat. His gloves are Italian leather. His ears are bright red. Steel-tipped shoes tap on concrete.

"You can dress well for a stakeout as well as down," he always says. "There's no law you have to look like shit."

At least they napped this afternoon, in the office. Voort

takes the coffee as Mickie says, "And if his way works, he'll save a lot of people."

"He had a good track record in the old days."

Voort lifts the plastic cover as Mickie adds, morosely, "But there are a hundred other targets Frankie can choose."

Frankie, Voort thinks. Mickie's given Greene the nickname of a crooner, or thug. A monicker that makes him common, a nuisance, a lowlife. Not a threat.

Frankie Avalon. Frankie Greene.

Eleven-seventeen.

Again comes the uncomfortable feeling, at Voort's back. No one there.

Mickie is saying, "Anyway, Szeska's probably in Costa Rica now, calling himself Joe Smith."

"He's still in the city."

"There's nothing for him here."

Voort shakes his head. "You should have heard him on the phone, Mickie. 'You never let yourself forget,' he said. 'You have nightmares your whole life.' He's on a mission. I don't think he can stop."

"Con Man, even his own guys are after him."

"Remember the Israeli last year?"

"The diplomat we shipped home? What does he have to do with Szeska?"

"Itzik Heifitz," Voort says, imagining the man— handsome, smart, wealthy, arrogant. A U.N. attaché who had a Ph.D. from Columbia, an apartment on Fifth Avenue, a wife who'd been runner-up for Miss Universe, and a lineage linking him to one of the most famous generals in Israel. A man who had been positively identified by three midtown waitresses for harassing them, both at work and at home, over the phone.

"Remember him?" Mickie repeats, blowing on his

coffee. "We warn him, and *the same night* he rings the bell of one of the waitresses, rapes her, and strolls home like he thinks she won't tell."

"He told me a story when we were waiting to put him on the airplane. He said it was from the Mideast. About a scorpion and a frog."

"What a psycho. Watching the World Cup on TV when we show up."

"A scorpion wants to cross a river, but he can't swim, so he asks a frog to carry him across. The frog says, 'Are you crazy? If I put you on my back, you'll sting me and I'll die.' The scorpion says, 'That's stupid. If I do that we both die.'

"So the frog says yes.

"And when they're in the middle of the river, the scorpion stings him. They're going under. The scorpion says, 'I can't help it. It's my nature.' "

And now Voort sees over Mickie's shoulder that another figure is approaching, a plainclotheswoman, from the lean, swaying look. But when she gets close he feels his breathing stop.

"Jill?"

The throb of danger worsens in his head.

Is that who was on the other side of the plaza?

She certainly would have been hard to make out, seeing that she's dressed in black: soft leather, hip-length black jacket, black Calvin Klein jeans, black gloves, black boots, and from the fringe of soft cashmere visible between the jacket's lapels, a black sweater with a foldover collar. Her hair looks less auburn in the gleam of vapor light. Mickie's presence makes her unsure whether to kiss Voort or not.

He has not spoken to anyone outside a small knowl-
edgeable circle about the bomb threat. He had never considered it any direct danger to her.

"I'm free again!" she practically sings. "I can go anywhere
I want. Surprised to see me?"

Mickie says, "It's your nature."

"I was getting sick of my apartment, and usually I love
that place!"

Keeping concern from his voice, Voort asks, "But why
are you *here?*"

"To celebrate! It's Saturday night! I phoned, to buy
you a drink, but they said you were working, so I took a
chance and walked down." Her grin widens, as if she's
caught them goofing off. "Working, huh? So this is how
cops work."

Mickie says, "See you later, Con Man." He nods politely
at Jill. His powerful figure strolls off toward the municipal
building. His departure is a warning to Voort to wrap things
up fast.

"He certainly hides his feelings about things," she says.

"Yeah, he's an unreadable mask."

Her natural radiance is enhanced by exuberance. He
can feel her excitement over her regained ability to just
stroll around. "I've been *everywhere!*" she says. "The Village. SoHo. I've been in prison and I'm out. So? How about
the drink?"

"After I get off, if you're still up."

"I can stay awake as long as you, mister," she says with
the confidence of a woman who knows she will always be
sought after by men. "And Irish coffee would be perfect."

She shivers happily. "Love that whipped cream."

Eleven twenty-eight.

Voort spins, alerted by the rev of an engine in the direction of City Hall. But it's just a Blue Guy on one of the three-wheeled patrol carts zipping along the outer perimeter of the barriers.

When his eyes return to her, she's frowning.

"Something wrong?"

"Nope."

She has no idea that the disk he received last night has anything to do with his being here now. Taking her arm, he turns her gently away from ground zero, One Police Plaza. They stroll toward Federal Triangle. The route to safety is shortest this way.

He tells her, "I'll be off about twelve-thirty. Pick a place to meet."

Fifty yards ahead, across the plaza and beyond the trash can–sized barriers, late-night traffic has been moving swiftly on Centre Street. But now a pair of headlights turns off the road, in his direction. The lights bump up, meaning the vehicle has climbed the sidewalk.

Only police vehicles are allowed to do that.

"How about Veronica's on Greenwich Street?" Jill says. "The owner's a friend. I can catch up on her love life while I wait for you."

"Fine." He's trying to make out the shape of the vehicle. It's no three-wheeled cart this time.

The headlights spread a blinding fan shape across the plaza, toward headquarters. The bomb barriers form stumpy shadows in the light.

Jill says, "Veronica's has great vegetable dumplings."

It's a van.

She adds, "They have wonderful Irish coffee."

"That'll be the place then," he says quickly as the

driver's door opens. "Jill, do me a favor and walk in the other direction. Now. I'll meet you at Veronica's."

"Something *is* the matter, isn't it?"

The radio should have warned me if a van was coming.

"Go," he snaps. And this time his tone produces a flare of resistance in her face. People do not tell me what to do, she seems to say. But there's no time to discuss it. He says, harshly, "Now!"

He thinks she's going to argue but she turns away, clicks off, boot noise receding as Voort heads toward the van, all his attention focused. He pulls out his radio.

"I have a van at the plaza, off Centre Street. Up on the sidewalk."

Static.

Is the radio busted?

Blinded by the twin orbs, he tries again. In the Submarine Room, he'd be able to monitor *all* communication. But down here he's limited to one frequency at a time, to talking to his team, or people upstairs. Field people call headquarters and headquarters coordinates. Jack Lopez said they were like an army, preventing an attack.

He sees me coming.

To hell with the radio. Pull out the gun.

He hears the van's door slam shut and the van jerks back into the street.

Voort starts to run.

And now he hears the screech of rubber. He is still twenty yards off when the wheels catch and the van accelerates, righting itself, speeding north.

He reaches Centre Street in time to see it turn left, up Reade. The paint was dark, but the van was too far off to make out the color or license plate. Voort's radio is answering finally. He gives rapid information—van heading west, after trying to get onto the plaza.

But Greene knows he can't drive onto the plaza. So how could it have been him?

Detectives and agents are running toward him now, from all directions, converging.

And Jill's voice, says, behind him, "Who was in that van?"

Voort feels blood draining from his face. He is horrified that she followed him. He cannot believe she ignored his order.

Seeing her standing in the spot where she would have died if the van had blown up, where she still *could* die if it returns, he feels a furious combustion erupt. All the threads of frustration merge. Meechum's death. Szeska's taunts and disappearance.

By sleeping with her, I put her in danger.

"I told you to leave!"

The city has degenerated into anarchy, so why not him, too? At that instant, Voort believes he will never stop Frank Greene. Even the officers around him, a formidable enough array upstairs, seem puny and ineffective here, yakking into their radios, as helpless as a gaggle of tourists trying to pick their way through unfamiliar terrain with maps.

Voort rages, "Do you have some death wish? Bin Hussein. The open curtains. Now you couldn't even walk away. *I told you to go!*"

The blood drains from her face, and her frosting breath comes in agitated bursts. But outrage turns to wonder as she realizes *all* the people here are police.

"I ... I thought you were just hanging out with Mickie."

And with those embarrassed words Voort remembers something he'd heard in that terrorism lecture last year: *A terrorist turns you against your loved ones. He wants to make your simplest act frightening. He wants you to become so afraid you turn your life upside down.*

He tells himself, calm down, as Jill says, in a much softer voice, "You were afraid I'd get hurt."

Still, he has to get rid of her. But this time he does it right. He leads her a few feet off, out of earshot of the others. He must convince her to leave by using sincerity, not facts; attitude, not information.

"I'll meet you at twelve-thirty. At Veronica's."

"You're really not going to tell me, are you?"

"It doesn't directly relate to you. The deal is, you go now, and I won't bust in when you're operating on a patient, asking how you work."

"I don't do operations," she sniffs. "I do antibiotics. But I'll think of some other thing you have to do."

This notion of a debt to be paid seems to please her a flirtatious bit.

She kisses him on the cheek, her lips dry with cold, and her body is trembling, despite her bravado. "You have strong hands," she says, rubbing her shoulder where he grabbed it.

She walks off. Voort, monitoring the lone figure this time instead of taking the departure for granted, feels something like love flicker inside. A beautiful woman leaving a lover can seem formidable or heart wrenching or inaccessibly gorgeous and far away. She can make a small farewell feel like a big one. But Jill looks vulnerable, never mind the tough-guy black clothes; a solitary female being swallowed into the narrow canyons surrounding the municipal building. Flesh amid the predators. Blood amid the stones.

He sees her walk beneath a lone figure in the window of an office building, looking down at her, silhouetted in light.

Is that one of our detectives in that window?

He calls for a squad car to patrol Duane Street, where she's walking. Veronica's lies straight toward the Hudson, ten minutes away by foot.

Checking, he learns that the figure in the office window is FBI.

The van turns out, ten minutes later, to contain a slightly drunk tourist from Maine, who had pulled up on the sidewalk to get a good view of the lit, beautiful municipal building.

"Back home we park on grass. I figured it would be no big deal if I went on the plaza. But then a guy started running toward me with a gun," he tells the Blue Guys who stop him.

At eleven-fifty, Voort's up in the Submarine as a flurry of messages erupt on the radios. Another van has been spotted near Houston Street, heading south.

But after two hundred sightings since surveillance began, no alarm marks alerts anymore, just mild interest as people in the room follow reports, listen as cops pull over the van at Prince and Broadway, and as a second blue-and-white, idling fifty feet from the stop, broadcasts a description of the stop.

"The officers are at the windows. They're shaking their heads. It's not the guy."

At eleven fifty-five a helicopter reports a van heading south on FDR Drive, from the Houston Street entrance toward City Hall. Another van is coming north on FDR, toward them.

Both vans head over the bridge, toward Brooklyn.

By now the Submarine is littered with half-empty Coke bottles on the conference table, pizza boxes wedged in the wastebaskets, Chinese food containers by the computers, candy bar wrappers by the microphones. The Submarine smells of perfume and cologne and sweaty clothing.

"Once there was a cop named Murphy," Addonizio says, from a steel folding chair he's occupied for the last hour. "If Murphy was ordered to look for a red Volkswagen, all he saw was red Volkswagens that day. If they told him green Studebaker, purple Metropolitan, two-tone Chevy with a green-headed monster inside, that's all that went by. Do you know what Murphy is famous for? They named Murphy's Law after him."

Eleven fifty-nine.

"He's definitely not coming tonight," predicts a detective named Purdy, a perky brunette from Staten Island who's been brushing her long silky hair all night.

"Maybe he moved to Honolulu," Mickie says. "I'm ready to go myself."

"Well, it's midnight, boys and girls. It looks like Colonel Szeska was right about . . ."

But the radio bursts to life, as an FBI agent's voice says, in a soft Alabama accent, "I have a blue Ford van with a red-and-white . . . that's a Massachusetts plate . . . entering Manhattan from the Battery Tunnel."

Voort pictures the agent, who had impressed him with her questions at yesterday's briefing; a tall, doe-eyed brunette, a Yale graduate who carried a squash racket and attaché case to the meeting. She's stationed in a sixth-floor construction law firm office on Greenwich Street, with an excellent view of the West Side Highway.

She says, calm as a Phantom fighter pilot watching an enemy MiG approach, "I see a twisted rear bumper. I see stickers on the bumper but can't make them out. He's gunning it! He's turning east, on Park. . . ."

Detective Purdy puts her brush down. "Toward us."

Jack Lopez takes two steps toward the radio operator, frowning.

Voort and Mickie run for the door.

There's no point staying here, not when it's midnight, and the only way Frank Greene's sketch will be meaningful is if this is the right van.

Behind them, they hear the radio saying, "He ran a light! He's speeding up."

They take the stairs two at a time, radios crackling, jackets left behind. The van could reach the plaza before they do, if it keeps running lights.

The chorus of voices grows at Voort's belt. The van, on Park Street, is not stopping for a pursuing squad car.

Mickie gasps, "So Szeska said he's not coming till tomorrow, huh?"

Voort pictures the emergency teams around them reaching into "repair" trucks for guns, aiming rifles from rooftops, holding fire in case the driver turns out to be an unlucky speeder, or drunk, someone in the wrong place at the wrong time, breaking the wrong laws.

In the Submarine, radios will be chattering like machine guns. "The driver's a lone white male!"

Voort pulls his gun out. Wind blasts into his face.

He hears sirens.

Mickie, having trouble keeping up, wheezes, "Do

you think there's something odd about running *toward* a bomb?"

Ahead, cops and agents have formed a skirmish line under the municipal building arch. Voort joins them where they crouch behind squad cars, girding for attack.

"Here he comes!"

And the van is actually *in the air* when he sees it, having hit a bump. It crashes back to the road. Then, in what at first appears an optical illusion, the whole front end seems to tip forward, rear up, and Voort is thinking, a block away, *It's starting to blow up,* but instead of a fireball, he sees smoke at the wheels, and the van crabbing sideways.

There's no blast. The driver's spotted the array of armor. He's hit his brakes. Trying to turn, to maneuver, he's sent his van into a paroxysm of conflicting motions—sideways as the brakes hold, forward from momentum, upward from stopping power.

Give up, Voort tells him, in his head. *Get out. Put your hands up. You've seen us. Give up.*

Sirens everywhere.

The van, stopped, belches black exhaust smoke. It seems alive, under the streetlamps. It is heaving, catching its breath, deciding what to do.

Voort and Mickie can't help but follow the first rush of bomb squad men charging forward, in their kevlar vests and helmets.

He knows he should not get close but he can't help it. Besides, the van door is opening.

And a man, getting out, is yelling in a high-pitched voice, a wail of horror audible over more sirens, "Don't shoot me! Don't shoot!"

By the time Voort reaches the van, a Blue Guy's got

the driver facedown, on the street, cuffing him. The bomb squad guys are in the van. Voort hears someone in there shouting, "No bomb! *No bomb!* There's paintings in here!"

Voort sees the driver's face now. The cop who cuffed him has spun him on his back.

A kid. Not Greene. A twenty-year-old in a stocking cap and paint-smeared cloth jacket. Shit.

The cop, crazy with fear, is shouting at the driver, *"What were you doing?"*

An FBI agent, a young guy in a dark coat, is bent over, throwing up in the middle of the street.

The driver turns out to be a painter, he says, whose wife called him at his Brooklyn studio an hour ago to say she was moving out of their apartment. He was desperate to reach her before she left, frenzied to convince her they belong together.

"Doesn't marriage mean anything?" the painter weeps, as they take him away. "She's married and sleeping with some other guy."

Weak-kneed, Voort glances in the van. Sure enough, paintings lean against the side. He sees a blue sky and a lake in the top one, through plastic sheeting. A man and woman paddle a canoe, on a sunny day, on the glassy lake.

He slides down the outside of the van. He does not feel the cold of the asphalt, or of the metal, against his back.

Mickie sits down heavily beside him. "I'm sick of this shit," he says. "I'm going home. Where are you meeting Miss Bin Hussein?"

"There's an opening in the Ku Klux Klan, Mickie."

"I'm not racist, and the KKK are killers. But if one of them was in trouble, want to bet she'd fix him up?"

*　　*　　*

In the mayor's office, fifteen minutes later, Addonizio and the commissioner are screaming at each other, going at it at the top of their lungs, wingtip to wingtip, nose to nose; their rage fueled by the long wait and all the false alarms.

Addonizio yelling, "I'm canceling the party tomorrow!"

The commissioner shouting back, "I'm not bowing to terrorism!" which, frankly, to Voort, sounds stupid under the circumstances.

The mayor, who called the meeting as soon as he got the news about the van, sits behind his oversized desk, and lets them fight. If Teddy Roosevelt advised presidents to walk softly and carry a big stick, successful New York mayors walk like elephants and wield big mouths. But today, Hizzoner quietly weighs consequences, risks, choices.

All seem bad.

"*You* won't bow to terrorism?" Addonizio snaps. "*I* won't be responsible for a thousand cops getting killed."

The room is larger then the White House's Oval Office, its size in line with the walk-like-an-elephant theory. In the land of the show-off, the biggest room rules. The windows are open. Hizzoner is famous for loving bracing breezes, Frederic Remington sculptures, and Georgia O'Keeffe paintings, from her New York period. Her canvases of black rising towers in the 1920s, when she lived in the city—looming edifices celebrating the jazz age—hang over the mantel, and along walls.

The commissioner's voice, low and vibrant, is well-suited for argument. He is the only man in the room with his overcoat on. For a Bostonian, he's cold-sensitive. The mayor brought him into the department last year to give it "new blood."

"Should I shut down every precinct, too, until we catch Greene?" he snaps.

"Hell no! I think you should put up big signs, saying, 'No Security at All.' "

That's when Voort says, "I have an idea."

As he outlines his scenario, his "war plan," he sees his partner nodding, approving. Jack Lopez, too. Addonizio does not interrupt, which means, in his case, he's considering it. Hizzoner gazes dispiritedly out the window toward One Police Plaza. The commissioner grows silent, and sits down. The mayor's PR expert runs his hands through his hair, a widely mimicked affectation marking tougher press conferences. The FBI liaison puts an unlit pipe in his mouth.

"Well?" the mayor asks his commissioner, when Voort is finished. "Can you live with that?"

The commissioner gives a single nod, as if he's won the argument. "It doesn't bow to terrorism."

Addonizio says, "I want *all* the cops to live with it, not just him," meaning the commissioner. "Good idea, Conrad."

The FBI man's unlit pipe wafts a tobacco smell through the room.

"Actually, I was going to propose something along the same lines," he says. "If we don't get him tomorrow, it's circle the wagons around every police building in town."

"Then do it," Hizzoner says, "but get some sleep first. I'll get the clearances tonight. I want you fresh in the morning."

"Hell of a thing to look forward to," Addonizio sighs to Voort as they walk down the steps of City Hall, into the cold crisp night, minutes later. "That a van with half a ton of dynamite inside will show up at my party."

Mickie tries a joke which falls flat. "Well, Hugh. I guess he wants to send you off with a bang."

Voort's too wired to go home and just fall asleep. He passed the exhausted state hours ago. He tries Jill on her cell phone and she's still at the restaurant.

Veronica's, Tribeca's new Czech bistro, is bright with energy when Voort pushes through the revolving door. Czech rock music is blasting. Blowup photos line the walls showing Prague on the day the Soviets withdrew. Wildly cheering Czechs stick bouquets of flowers in Russian tank cannons. Czechs drink wine, and sing, celebrating freedom. Czechs kiss and dance in Prague's main square.

He does not see Jill.

Blond waitresses in black minis and tight white sleeveless pullovers circulate with drinks. A photo of Czech hero Alexander Dubček hangs centrally above the bar, beside that of the hot new Prague model, Veronica, who owns the place, and occupies a far stool beside the current food critic for *New York* magazine. Tribeca was a warehouse district a decade ago. Now it is the urban planner's dream—new condos with roof decks, new restaurants, new gourmet supermarkets, new day-care centers.

Frowning, Voort thinks, *Where the hell is Jill?*

The bistro is filled with boisterous Wall Street types celebrating financial gains despite the national turndown, with longtime neighborhood residents, with the inevitable trendies who follow restaurant reviews, and with Czechs who miss the food back home.

Voort feels, just for an instant, the same odd sensation he experienced before, between his shoulder blades. The briefest itch. He turns around.

Nobody looks back from the wall of people.

"You're safe," Jill says as he comes up to her bar stool, filled with relief. "I was worried. Not that I have any idea what you're safe *from*."

Beside her, a good-looking guy in a suit eyes Voort with recognition. He was obviously trying to pick her up. The guy, actor-handsome, black hair slicked down and parted in the middle, Armani suit, Armani shoes, Armani tie, says, "You were on TV!" He seems happier to talk with a celebrity than frustrated at striking out with Jill. "You're that rich cop who solved that serial case last year!"

He even slides left, onto another stool so Voort can take his seat. It's the New York Guy Code of fair play, late Saturday night style. Her kiss is happy, sexy, forgiving, and long. It makes him feel good. It gets his heart going. His groin stirs.

"Why do I think you need a drink?" she says.

"Because you read my mind."

Her hands, soft on his neck, dispel his frustration. As he pulls back from the kiss, he remembers reading a magazine article saying you can tell whether people in a city are happy or not by whether they show affection in public.

The magazine had given examples. Paris, yes. Moscow, no.

"Catch the bad guy?" she asks lightly as Voort tells the bartender. "Vodka. Straight."

"We missed him tonight."

"You still get the girl."

"Then maybe I'll miss him every night."

"Then maybe you'll always get the girl."

The vodka spreads through him, relaxes him, seeps through his veins and makes him more light-headed. They hold hands and chat about the decor and order little vegetable dumplings, and for a moment, at least, he can forget Greene and Szeska. They sit so close their thighs touch, and as always, he feels the rush of heat when she's near.

She eats whipped cream off her Irish coffee with a spoon, licks a remnant off the corner of her lip, says with more delicacy, "You never told me how you feel about our conversation the other night."

Meaning the admission that she's married.

Voort flashes to the driver of the van being led away. The married painter whose wife is cheating on him.

"I haven't thought about it. I haven't had time."

"He called today," she says, meaning, Voort knows, her husband, as one more round of reality intrudes on romance.

"He said I sounded different," she says.

"That's usually the case."

"I thought you said you didn't do this kind of thing."

"I meet a lot of people who do."

"Is that disapproval? Well, you're here. He said he'll be delayed coming home," she says, watching him closely. "He said fighting's broken out in Africa, in Rwanda, and his of-fice wants him to supervise relief. I think he senses some-thing is wrong here. He said he misses me. He asked if I would come with him."

"What did you answer?"

"That I had too much work here."

"Do you?"

"No."

Voort finishes his drink and waves off the bartender's offer of another. "I'm not going to tell you whether to go or not."

"And I seem to be asking you to do that, aren't I? I am and I have no right to." Now she looks flustered. "I'm the one who's married, and I'm like a girl with a crush. I don't understand it. This is supposed to be easy, that's what he always told me. But it isn't. I feel so . . ." She frowns, casting about for a suitable word to describe her confusion, self-disgust, and inability to know herself. She settles on "innocent."

"Everyone's innocent when it comes to something," Voort says. He adds, "And probably guilty, too."

"Let's go to bed," she says. "We don't have to decide anything. We don't even have to talk."

Voort removes his hand from hers. She is so beautiful, and her distress is real. It's hard to be logical, or moral, or to remember principles, when he can smell her. The music seems louder, and outside the plate-glass window, which seems far away, a red revolving rooflight on a squad car rushes past, as its occupants speed toward a crime.

There's a flash of movement in the mirror behind him, as if someone had been coming toward him, and suddenly turned away.

"I think I'll visit Matt tonight," he says. "I haven't spent time with him and you'll be fine now, alone. Besides . . ."

He stops himself. He was going to say that he needs to be up in a few hours, for work.

He changes it to a joke. "Besides, if I go home, instead of your place, no one will know where to reach me, and I'll finally get some sleep. How about dinner Monday?"

If you're not overseas.

"I thought we were going to Addonizio's party tomorrow night."

Voort lies. "I'm not going to that party."

And tells a truth. "I'll be working."

"Well, I think with all this work, they don't pay you civil servants enough. Sweetheart," she adds affectionately, as if they're free, unattached lovers, "you look beat. Let's get you to sleep."

Outside, signaling for a cab, Voort finds himself eyeing the bar door, behind him.

This is the paranoid way Meechum was acting the night they killed him.

On the way uptown, in the taxi, he checks periodically, for Szeska, for a cab or car following him. He is very aware each time they pass a van.

"Monday night," she repeats, like a promise, when she gets out of the cab. She stretches, a gorgeous sight. "Are you sure you don't want to stay?"

"I do. I'll be rested Monday."

Jill kisses him on the mouth. "You may be rested going into Monday, but you won't be rested by the end."

After she disappears into the building, the driver turns and shakes his head. He's a young man wearing a tropical shirt in the overheated cab. He says, enviously, "All my life I've waited for an invitation from a woman who looks like that. You get it and you don't go up. What a waste."

Voort gives him the address of his town house. "On the

way downtown," he says, "go down lots of side streets. Make lots of turns."

Thirteenth Street is quiet when the taxi pulls up, although a green van is pulling away from the front of his house. He eyes the retreating plates, frowning. He's pretty sure that Szeska didn't follow Meechum to the University Place bar the night that he killed him. Which means that Szeska would have been waiting for Meechum when Meechum returned to his hotel.

His heart is pounding when he puts the key in the lock.

But when he gets inside, it's quiet. From the number of jackets hung on pegs in the front hall, he can tell that eight or nine relatives are upstairs. He tiptoes into a couple of guest bedrooms, to see which Voorts are there, and wakes the man in the third room, a cousin named Paul Voort, a detective in the narcotics division; a twenty-six-year-old who's one of the Tugboat Voorts; a kid who's been decorated for valor twice already, who is single, and has a girlfriend up in Croton. He's also one of the Voorts who showed up at Szeska's office two days ago.

Voort explains that for the next few days at least, he'd like some of the family to keep an eye on the blocks around the town house.

Paul frowns. "You think he'll come after you here?"

"He starts fires. He causes accidents. Either someone stays outside, or all of you leave. I don't feel comfortable having relatives here otherwise."

"No prob," Paul says, swinging his legs out of bed, yawning, reaching for his folded trousers.

"I'm off tomorrow. I'll make a couple calls now. I can

get Peter here in an hour, and Tiny. We were supposed to paint Marla's store tomorrow but hell, we can do it next week."

"Arrest Szeska if you see him," Voort says. "There's a federal warrant now."

"For Meechum?"

"For illegal wiretapping."

"Like the IRS man who got Capone said, it's a start."

On the third landing Voort hears the sound of late-night TV from Matt's room. The sick man's sitting up in bed, lights off, watching New York One, the all local news channel.

"I thought of something new I want to do," Matt says, grinning.

"What?"

"Go to a bash tomorrow with a thousand detectives, booze, babes, and music. Know of anything coming up like that? I'm not due for another treatment till Thursday."

"Sure, I'll take you." He'll make up an excuse tomorrow.

"You will?"

"We'll tell everyone you work undercover at Sloan-Kettering."

"Did you say undercover, or under the covers? Look! They're showing a taped interview with your boss!"

Falling into the seat by the bed, Voort sees a reporter on-screen, in a studio living room, chatting with Hugh Addonizio. Since Addonizio was at One Police Plaza all day, the tape has to be at least two days old.

Matt says, "He's been talking about his old cases. Gotti. Gallo. But it's not as good as the stories you guys tell."

"That's because we lie."

On-screen, Addonizio looks relaxed, and radiates strength, not like the worried man Voort remembers at One Police Plaza. The reporter eats up the stories.

Addonizio is saying, "It'll only be a little party."

"Little? The last time a New York chief of detectives retired two thousand people showed up. I understand some big celebrities may be dropping in. People you've helped over the years."

The reporter names a popular movie star, and the former mayor, who now hosts a talk show on Channel Five.

"I'm not comfortable talking about them. I have no idea if they're coming, and they value their privacy."

The taped part ends and the camera pans back to show the reporter, live. "Tomorrow night the city's finest will say good-bye to one of *their* finest, one of the most beloved chiefs in the city's history. We'll miss you, Hugh Addonizio. Stay tuned for . . ."

Matt switches off the set.

"You look like shit," he says.

"It's the light."

"I hope whatever you've been doing, it's been fun. You want the bed? I'll take the chair and tell the stories. Ever hear the one about two patients?"

"Want to go kayaking this week?"

Matt brightens. "You bet, and I won't get seasick either. That's what happened last time. Seasickness. Not chemicals. And speaking of sickness, how come you're not with the doctor?"

"I thought I'd give her a night off, and visit you."

"She's a keeper. Are you really serious about taking me to Addonizio's party?"

There's the sound of a small explosion outside, probably a car backfiring. Voort listens a bit. He decides to wait outside, on the street, to not go to sleep until the relatives get here.

In a way, I hope Szeska is out there right now.

"If I go, you go," he replies.

TWENTY-TWO

The Southern Cross fades. The rising sun brightens the dome of the sky before the edges. The glow seeps earthward, turns clouds pink, illuminates the massive black cone of hardened lava a quarter mile ahead, jutting from the Pacific. Dolphins breach the glassy surface. Dawn is as cool as the day will be hot.

Lupe, coming out on deck of the cabin cruiser, wears khaki shorts and a matching shirt. Sunglasses hang from her neck on a black cord. A peaked cap protects her against the equatorial sun. She is tan and carries a rifle.

"Darling, it is time to shoot the dog."

Szeska nestles into his pillow. His hands squeeze the sheets.

"Do you know the worst part of this job?" she asks as they climb into the launch at the stern of the boat, as he swings the bow toward the island. "I like dogs, but they can't help being destructive. They don't trust us, don't let us take them off an island. Once things go beyond cooperation a bullet is the only way."

They had spotted the animal yesterday, when they anchored in the harbor. The Irish setter, once someone's pet, now wild, had barked frantically, racing back and forth along the black sand beach. It wanted to be friends. But it fled when they landed.

So they returned to the boat, made love, sat on the top deck as dusk fell, eyeing the constellations. Hercules and Sirius the dog star and the Southern Cross. Shapes not visible back home.

In sleep, Szeska flinches as if he has heard two quick shots.

He looks down. The dying dog has Meechum's face. The legs thrash as if the creature is trying to run, but its nerves are severed. It can't move.

Meechum says, "I hid copies of my files."

"You're lying."

"Voort will find you. Your picture will be in every newspaper."

Szeska shakes the animal. Meechum cries out in pain.

"Where did you put the files," Szeska demands.

But Meechum just smiles. "Now the dog will shoot *you.*"

Szeska wakes up, drenched.

An alarm is ringing. For a moment he is disoriented, the heat changing from equatorial to motel baseboard, the smell changing from eucalyptus to bottled Pine Sol, the cloud shapes now mere watermarks on a ceiling.

I'm in the Polynesian Motel.

General Grant said that luck comes to those who prepare for it, and Szeska has been preparing since two nights ago. After hanging up with Voort, he raided his caches in Manhattan for more weapons, communications equipment, money and disguises, headed to Queens, and found a motor lodge within view of Frank Greene's target.

Serving casual lovers, catering hall guests, and probably a prostitute or two.

The bed is adequate, the motel clean. Color prints on the walls show the pyramids and the Eiffel Tower. Come to Queens and see the world. Szeska pads barefoot on cheap orange shag to the window and looks out. It's peaceful, but by tonight it could be a battlefield.

If the police don't show up, at least I can try to stop him.

His third-story view encompasses the intersection of newly named Moynihan Boulevard and Eighty-ninth Street, a commercial strip fronting a residential neighborhood. The six-lane boulevard is spotted with grassy traffic islands with park benches and trees. A Shell station sits directly across from him, bordering the hedge-lined parking lot of The Parthenon catering hall, where Addonizio's retirement party is scheduled to begin in twelve hours.

Unless Voort got it canceled.

The catering hall is two stories high, Mediteranean style, of stucco, painted flamingo pink, and fronted by Doric pillars. Key West meets Delphi. At night, the fountain in the horseshoe-shaped driveway is lit in blues, greens, and reds. Plaster of paris statues of Apollo and Diana flank the lot entrance. A balcony runs the length of the second floor, its wrought-iron railing draped with "grape arbor vines."

A truck bomb detonating within fifty feet of the entrance would blow the floor-to-ceiling glass up there across the ballroom, like shrapnel from a Claymore mine. It would drive shredding pieces of concrete into human bodies, and bring the tiled roof down on whoever was still alive after that.

Why don't I see police surveillance down there?

Using binoculars, Szeska scans the rest of the block. He sees a greeting card shop, deli, candy store, twenty-four-hour A&P. A couple of doctor's offices.

Is it possible that Voort let his hatred of me cloud his judgment? That he's not using the file? I saw a couple of unmarked Chevies in the lot yesterday, but that would be normal for detectives arranging the party.

The block to the left of Szeska's nest, also across from the catering hall, contains a small city park.

At eight-thirty, his disquiet growing, he's pulled a chair to the window, unwrapped the first of a half-dozen sandwiches he picked up yesterday, opened a thermos of water, and divided the scene below into sections. Section by section, he scans the street.

It's raining lightly out there, misty but cold, with a slight electrical burning smell, ozone, and a handful of Sunday commuters—Manhattan handymen, shop clerks, white-collar workaholics, or TV people—hold umbrellas and hunch forward against the wind, their raincoat bottoms blowing. They run toward covered bus stops or subway stations. It's so normal-looking that it takes a few minutes before Szeska realizes he has just spotted the same "commuter" for the second time. The man had walked into the subway minutes ago. He must have exited while Szeska was concentrating on a different section. Now he's coming out of the candy store, and walking to the subway *again*.

Szeska keeps his binoculars on the subway entrance. After several minutes the man exits the subway and heads down the block in the other direction, maintaining his steady commuter's stride.

Szeska relaxes. Cops.

And now Szeska spots a woman in a brown raincoat for the second time. She also had gone into the subway entrance. Now she's back also.

FBI, too?

Could be.

But, assuming that the party is off, he frowns, seeing a purple truck with "Mancini's Catering" on the side, turn into The Parthenon's parking lot, and lurch over the traffic bump as it backs toward a covered loading dock on the north side of the building.

Could they be holding the party anyway?

The truck departs fifteen minutes later, except when it hits the bump it doesn't wobble as much, which means it is now *heavier* than when it arrived, not lighter.

It is carrying valuable equipment *out* of the hall.

Szeska smiles. "Very good, Voort," he says out loud, understanding the plan.

The rain picks up.

Szeska unlocks an aluminum box the size of an attaché case that he brought from Manhattan, and begins assembling the sniper's rifle inside, like the one he had brought to Massachusetts, to try to kill Frank Greene. If Greene shows today and the police fail to see him coming, Szeska will provide backup. He has kept up his shooting skills over the years with regular practice, and knows he could get off at least two silenced shots from his window *and* have time to flee before anyone realizes the derivation point of the shots.

Also, if there's opportunity out there, confusion, and stray firing, I may get lucky.

I may get Voort.

In Manhattan, which receives eastbound weather before Queens, the rain is light but a cold front has blasted into the city, after the storm wreaked havoc with electrical systems in New Jersey. Voort stands in the center of the gigantic police impoundment lot on pier 42, which once served the great cruise liners, and now juts crumblingly into the gray, frigid Hudson. Usually he comes to the river to kayak. Today he scans cars. They are all makes and models, seized from owners who transported illegal drugs with them, or simply never paid tickets.

The cars are slated for auction.

"I want an old one," he tells the Blue Guy beside him, the lot guard. "That works."

The shivering Blue Guy, heavy around the middle even in his poncho, obviously resents being taken from his warm office. "How come *you* get a car? My Toyota's busted at home. Are they giving cops cars? How can I get one?"

"I don't care about the body. But it has to run."

"How the hell do I know which ones run? They get towed in. They get towed out."

Voort settles on an '89 Accord hatchback with 150,000 miles on the odometer. The right passenger door is dented from an accident. The interior smells thickly of cigarettes, and butt burns spot the upholstery. But the engine starts right up, and the radio works, so he can listen to all-news CBS on the way to Queens.

The Blue Guy leans into the open window. "You could take any car and you're passing up the sports models? I got a red Porsche on the south lot, new as a baby."

Fifty feet off, through the thickening rain, Voort sees Mickie pulling out of a space in a battered green Hyundai. Jack Lopez, chief of today's operation, having chosen a '94 Camaro, two spots down, is having trouble starting it.

Voort tells the Blue Guy, "People'll be coming for cars all day. Anyone who's got the requisition form, give them what they want."

He signs the paper and the Blue Guy persists. "Come on. Whaddaya gonna do with them?"

"Bring 'em back tomorrow," Voort answers.

But he's thinking, *Unless they get blown up tonight.*

By ten A.M., the commuters are gone from Moynihan Avenue. Hardier housewives, braving rain, hurry in and out of the A&P. Two-dozen teenagers carrying books—probably college entrance exam course preparation material—rush into the subway. The dog walkers are out, and an "emergency Con Ed crew" is starting to cordon off part of the sidewalk across from the Parthenon. Good, Szeska thinks. That will eliminate pedestrians over there tonight.

The commuter-cop, Szeska sees, is now part of the crew, wearing a hard hat and uniform.

A couple of city "park attendants" have pulled up to the park in an olive-drab Recreation Department truck. They idle, either really goofing off, or looking like they're doing nothing while they scan the street for Frank Greene.

Szeska has no idea whether real city park attendants work on Sunday or not.

Come on, Frank, visit the block one more time to scout it. Get caught now.

Suddenly Szeska freezes. Someone is banging at his door.

From out in the hall, a woman yells, "Can I clean your room, señor?"

Is she really a maid?

Szeska picks up the Glock .38 off a table by the window. "No thank you!"

He hears tinny music, probably from a transistor radio on the cleaning cart, fading as the cart squeaks off.

Or is it a trick to relax me, and they will break down the door?

But no one tries to get in, and he turns back to the window. Now that he's satisfied with the street surveillance, it's time for the next task, figuring out if it is safe for him to go out.

Do the cops have my description as well as Greene's? Does Voort have them looking for me?

Szeska's fairly certain he fooled Voort when he said he was leaving New York, but he can't be sure.

To check, he focuses on the Con Ed crew and follows their gazes when they give passersby extra attention.

But the crew seems to watch men who are shorter than Szeska; men with black hair, thinner features, narrower frames. Like Frank Greene.

Szeska turns his attention to pedestrians, picking out one who *is* built like him. The man has big shoulders, short hair, a wide forehead, and a round face.

But when the man walks past the Con Ed crew they pay him no attention. The man passes the Recreation Department truck and the men inside don't seem to care.

I can go out.

But of course, there is only one dangerous way to make sure, and now is the time to do it, before the street below is packed with cops. If the FBI or Rourke's people are looking for him, and carrying computer-generated disguise sketches, sooner or later today there's a good chance they'll start knocking on doors. It might be too late to flee then.

He locks the now-cleaned rifle away first. It's been over ten years since Szeska went up against trained enemies, but his instincts are sharp, his anger focused. He's even excited, feeling his blood rushing.

He rejects the businessman disguise: the dark suit and

curly wig. In this part of Queens, on Sunday, the white-collar workaholics going to Manhattan are more casually dressed, in expensive jeans, topsiders, brand-new sweat-shirts. He rejects the cop uniform, which may be useful later.

The handyman clothing, however, is just right.

On goes the painful elbow brace and soiled light brown uniform with stitching on the shirt that says "Vinnie." On goes the matching zip-up jacket and brown wig with a widow's peak, which he wore when he checked into the motel. Rubber-soled shoes complete the image, supplemented by a rubber rain poncho in the same drab hue. The Glock is in his waistband.

As Szeska walks into the hallway, the maid, two doors down, looks over eagerly.

"Clean your room *now*, señor?"

"Leave it alone, please."

He hangs the DO NOT DISTURB sign on the knob and strolls into the storm. He'd rather not have to leave the motel, but has to admit that he enjoys the way his senses expand, the way his heart speeds up, as he exits the protection of the motel, as he reaches the field.

At the steady pace of a bored Sunday workman, Szeska walks directly past a "mom" cop, who does not seem to notice him; does not even, reflected in the rain-smeared dry-cleaner window, turn to look after he passes.

Szeska the shopper picks out Granny Smith apples in the A&P, where another mom cop is "shopping," feeling plums and tomatoes right beside him. He buys a surge protector in the Rite-Aid drugstore, an item he actually needs if a power disruption occurs. Back in the room he's got a miniature state-of-the-art Zenith QH-76 radio scanner, fifty times better than anything you can get in even a high-end spy store, designed specifically for NTAA to break through jamming into digital private radio frequencies, the kind sophisticated terrorists use, and the antiterrorist guys at the FBI. The researcher brought the equipment into the project in the beginning, when Washington was funding it, giving them anything they needed.

Szeska reported it lost when the project was canceled.

They'd never given it back.

Now, with his purchase, he reaches the line at the checkout counter just ahead of a black cop in a civilian windbreaker, feeling the man's eyes on his back.

The clerk nods approvingly as he bags the surge protector. He's a kid with spiky hair and a small earring in his right ear.

"Smart move, man, buying this, with this weirdo storm coming," he says. "Did you hear it blew out half the power in Pennsylvania?"

"The greenhouse effect is making the weather crazy," Szeska says, and turns to the cop behind him, giving him, daringly, a full look at his face and a shot at his voice. Szeska says, "It's people like us, you and me and our wasteful energy policies, that cause this kind of storm, don't you think?"

The cop rolls his eyes. "It's El Niño," he replies.

Safe!

But when Szeska gets back to the motel, he doesn't like the nervous way the clerk rushes from the office to intercept him. The Glock, under the poncho, will be hard to reach.

"Mr. Payne?"

She's young and pretty and she glances back toward the office, where he can't see anyone, but someone is there.

"I'm Sheila, from the front desk?"

"I'm in a hurry."

"One of the other guests?" she says, unable to utter a phrase without making it sound like a question. "He's asking if you would mind switching rooms with him? He says he stayed in your room on his wedding night? He says it has sentimental value?"

Rain blows beneath the overhang where they stand.

Sheila says, "I told him I'd ask?"

Szeska's senses are roaring. Is it a trick to get into the room? Does a cop want the room for surveillance?

He says, like a man who dislikes being disturbed over small matters. "I want that room."

"How long will you be staying with us?" she asks, preferring, from her expression, that he check out soon, hopefully only because she has been offered a big tip if he does.

Szeska heads up the stairs. The rain is getting hard.

He snaps, "Until my wife lets me back in my house."

At one P.M., while antiterrorist squad cops prepare a franks-and-beans lunch in the catering hall kitchen, Voort, in the main ballroom, tonight's command post, briefs a half-dozen FBI agents who have just arrived inside the "catering truck." It's been agreed by cooperating law enforcement agencies that for political and PR reasons police will officially take the lead role today, but Jack Lopez of the AT squad has coordinated every aspect with the FBI.

"Since early this morning," says Voort, who has no problem letting the more experienced Lopez run the operation, "e-mail messages have advised all precincts that the party is canceled due to busted water pipes. So detectives won't show up tonight."

One agent, the Alabama woman who spotted the van at the Battery Tunnel yesterday, asks, "What if reporters see the messages? And the news gets out?"

"Canceled parties and broken catering hall pipes don't make news."

Downstairs, he hears the sounds of AT people hauling The Parthenon's better china, financial records, artwork, and office furniture to the catering truck. It's being moved out until tomorrow.

"We'll have the whole place to ourselves," Voort tells the agents, indicating blueprints tacked to a corkboard, beside detailed sketches of the block outside and nearby streets. "Downstairs is a bar, atrium, coatroom, a dining hall for smaller parties. Upstairs is the main ballroom. Kitchen and office in the basement. Staff dressing room, too."

The sound system comes on, blasting Latin music so loud that a couple of the agents wince from the noise. The Parthenon's usual Panamanian setup crew plays loud music while working, the cooperative owner had told police, so the police are doing the same.

As the windows are open, anyone in the parking lot will think things are normal inside.

"Thanks to you people at the FBI, we've got cardboard cutouts, from your shooting range, to be positioned behind windows tonight. It'll look like lots of people are in here. The city buses will be diverted off Moynihan Boulevard. The subways will bypass the stop, and use the express line, due to, eh, flooding from the rain. ATS people dressed like gas crews will close any stores still open at six, with a story about a gas leak. They'll shut down the Shell station but leave the lights on. The rain and cordoned-off block across the street should keep pedestrians to a minimum. We'll have a stream of couples, 'guests,' you people, going into the catering hall, coming out back, recycling themselves around the block. We'll have FBI and cops inside parked cars on the street. The big problem will be civilians in cars, so we want to keep them moving. If Greene is spotted, the instant he enters the box area, traffic will be stopped behind him."

"What about the cars in front of him?" asks the Alabama agent. "Won't they be caught in the box if things hit the fan?"

"Half the cars will be filled with plainclothes police. We're trying to keep civilian exposure to a minimum," Voort sighs, "but it's like any stakeout," meaning that it is impossible, any time police try to trap a criminal, to eliminate every risk.

"In the end, we create a cordon around a two-block area. When Greene drives in we seal off the box. Those of you outside, if you see the van, report it but pretend to ignore it. Stay where you are unless you get orders. We want to give civilians time to get out. Let the flow of traffic slow Greene naturally. The lights will be timed. When you get the okay, approach from both sides. If he makes any sudden move he could be going for the button. *Any quick moves* and you shoot."

"What if we're inside the hall when he comes?" the woman asks.

"Wait for instructions. And no one goes out without a raid jacket. We don't want anyone shot by accident."

After the briefing Voort takes his paper plate of franks and beans and a can of orange soda to a folding chair in a corner, with a view of the rainwashed street.

There's so much electricity in the air that he gets a shock when he touches the chair.

Mickie joins him, looking funny in his white starched "catering staff" uniform. His hair is perfect. He's removed his jewelry—his watch and Detective Benevolent Association ring.

"The more I think about it, the more I wish you would have handed out Szeska's picture, too," he says.

"I told you. One man at a time."

"But if he's here, like you think, he may be . . ."

"I don't want our people distracted," Voort interrupts. "You know how hard it is to find even one guy. I don't want to confuse them with two."

The food is tasteless but he forces it down to keep up energy. After two cans of soda, his throat stays dry.

You will have nightmares forever if you make a mistake, Szeska had said.

Mickie asks, finishing his hot dog, "What are all those books you had delivered to the office?"

"What *he* reads. What Rourke kept quoting from. I opened the Churchill to a part called 'two-front wars.'"

"Like when a country fights two enemies at the same time?"

"The Germans fought England in the west and Russia in the east, in World War Two."

"That's what you're dealing with, Con Man. Two enemies."

Voort takes his last bite of hot dog. The music grows louder. Tambourines jingle behind trumpets. The notes swell with Latin glee.

He says, morosely, "Yeah, Szeska and Greene. My two-front war."

*   *   *

At three, at his window, Szeska sees the high school kids returning from their college exam preparation course. But visibility is getting harder, rain thicker. At four, the moms are out, dim forms in the storm, finishing last-minute Sunday shopping. At five, as Con Ed starts closing the block off, the blue-collar dads are back, and the day-tourists to Manhattan's museums or theaters start climbing from the subway.

"The damn rain's turning icy," a voice on the police scanner behind him says, thick with worsening static. "People are slipping all over the place."

Outside, traffic stops, and honking reaches him. The slick road has caused a fender bender on Moynihan Boulevard.

At seven, more impounded cars start filling the parking lot, as "guests" arrive. Lights blaze in the catering hall, but with the rain getting worse, it is getting almost impossible to see that far. Szeska makes out people behind the sheer curtains, except, when they don't move, he realizes they are not people at all.

Outside, a sporadic stream of couples walk through the rain into The Parthenon. Several minutes later they reappear on the block. It's a clever little plan.

Rock-and-roll music reaches his ears, from the catering hall. It mixes with messages—thick with static—coming over the radio. The cops and FBI are using four channels: one for observer teams, one for sniper teams, one for the bomb squad and ATS assault crew, who have been given the job of attacking the van. The last channel is for medical personnel.

Party time!

Szeska, trained to lie still and observe for hours, is able to monitor the radio and allow a small part of his mind to go back to the day things fell apart between him and Meechum. A bright and sunny day when Meechum had walked into the office, a frown on his face.

"Colonel? Can I ask a question? Which agency gets our information in Washington?"

In Szeska's memory, his alarms go off. He sits back, laces his fingers, picks a sucking candy out of the jar and unwraps it.

"You know that's classified. Why ask after two years?"

"Because I never see anything in the news about arrests of these people. And I'm talking about the very first batch. There's been plenty of time to bring them in."

"Candy?"

"No thanks."

"Washington doesn't exactly advertise what they do. This stuff is secret."

Szeska remembers urging Meechum in his mind, *Walk away. I don't want to have to hurt you.* He remembers Meechum shaking his head doggedly, saying, "But whenever anyone gets arrested for the kinds of things we've been investigating, it makes big news."

"Maybe it made local news."

"No, I've been going over reports, and there's been nothing on any of those people in their papers."

A cop voice on the scanner pulls Szeska's attention away from the memory. "South corner? How's visibility?"

Voort's voice answers, "Terrible, it's . . ." Static drowns out the rest.

South corner is downstairs.

Szeska looks down. A figure, Voort, stands there under an umbrella.

He's right here.

Szeska uses the scope of his rifle to get a better view of Voort. The cop seems inches away in the crosshairs. Szeska pushes off the urge to fire. He casts back and sees himself waving Meechum into the stuffed chair in his office. Acting wry, as if Meechum has amusingly missed some obvious point. Telling his old student, "Meechum, *think*. You leave them in place. You learn who they contact. This is pretty basic. I'm surprised at you. And what are you doing checking up on old subjects anyway? You have enough to do with the new ones."

Outside, Voort strolls off.

Szeska switches channels on the scanner and hears a sniper saying, "Anybody got extra gloves? My hands are freezing."

"You're kidding. You didn't bring gloves?" someone else says.

The wet cold fragrance of rain fills Szeska's nostrils. When he returns to the window, the fringe of curtain swishes toward his knee, from static electricity. His memory returns to his office. He sees Meechum leaving, the others arriving. He hears the argument that had erupted then.

Pete saying, "He's only checking the first batch now, but what if he reaches the people we've done something about?"

Laura saying, "We shouldn't have told him Washington restarted the project. We should have let him in on things from the first. Colonel, let's offer him the chance."

Outside, Szeska hears a crash, an accident on Moynihan Boulevard. A delivery truck's slid into the back of a pickup out there. Men start screaming. A horn blasts, and there's another crash. This time a bus—on the Atlantic City casino run—has hit the truck. Traffic is backing up.

In his head, Charley tells Pete and Laura, "It was lie to him or never start the thing. He'd never go along."

A knock at the door startles Szeska into the present. The maid's voice calls, "Can I turn down the bed?"

"No! And don't come back!"

Muttering out there, something about "not letting me do my job."

And Charley, in his memory, is saying, "I tapped his phone like you wanted, Colonel. I'm following him when he goes out."

But now a cop cries, on the scanner, clear for once, "It's him! It's him! It's Frank Greene! North side!"

Szeska turns from the window. Meechum is forgotten. His senses are roaring. He is utterly in the present.

His mind, as usual in times of combat, functions on an instinctive level, reducing thought processes to fractions of seconds. He rejects the rifle because visibility makes it useless. His original plan is worthless. He can accomplish nothing from this room. He will take the Glock, a cop's kind of gun. If he fires it later, if an "accident" occurs, and investigators recover bullets, odds are they'll conclude that they came from a cop's private weapon. No one will be surprised when the cop does not come forward.

He is his finest, most able self at this moment. He realizes that his rising tide of excitement has nothing to do with Voort, Meechum, or even Lupe. The chemistry inside him was there long before they existed in his life. Szeska turns to leave as the scanner pinpoints the location of the first of tonight's targets. He feels brilliantly, totally alive, at home with action and with long odds.

Grabbing his waterproof jacket, Szeska understands at some subconscious level, more as a stab of satisfaction than an actual thought, the final element that has kept him in place here and that, in the end, determined his inability to give up the project.

I love this.

The truth, he sees as he experiences the animal immediacy that for him only comes in combat, is that for a person with the right attitude, *his* attitude, war is the only thing in life that never disappoints, never disappears or diminishes.

Is it so bad to love your job?

Use the weather to your advantage.

A good field operative improvises.

Make your own luck tonight.

TWENTY-THREE

Voort might as well be blind.

You make plans, careful plans, he tells himself, but they don't seem so careful later in a violent electrical storm. You don't plan for a traffic accident. For the sudden appearance of dozens of civilians in an Atlantic City bus. For rain so thick your spotters can barely see.

Over his earpiece he hears details. "The van's white now, with New York plates. But the bumper's twisted. It's got the Greenpeace sticker. Greene's wearing a red parka and . . ."

Static drowns out the next words, even though the anti-terrorism squad's digital radios are supposed to be the best.

Voort shouts into his set, "What else is he wearing?"

Static.

Thunder seems to rip the sky apart, and send shock waves across the city. Hail smacks against the Shell station, where Voort has paused in his rounds of the police perimeter. He is alone. His job this evening, ordered by Jack Lopez, was to be "Rover."

"Sounds like the name of a dog," Voort had said.

"Yeah, you're a bloodhound," the fierce and diminutive

captain had said. "You're not trained like us, but your instincts are great. We wouldn't be here if it weren't for you.
So be my outsider. Go where you want. Stay on the tactical
channel and tell me if you see anything that looks wrong."

But what's wrong is nature itself. The storm has made a
mockery of all their logic, of even the carefully detailed
sketches he'd used in his briefing, in which shops were la-
beled, sidewalks and parked cars delineated, Greene's easily
spotted van a large, isolated X.

The static turns into English again.

". . . slowing at the light. Collins and Goldberg are approaching from the east side. . . ."

They're not supposed to do that until civilians are cleared out.

The quick explosion of gunfire erupts in the earpiece,
more distant-sounding than the real shooting coming from
two blocks north.

Damn!

Voort groans as the earpiece blares, "Officers down!"

The attack has begun on the far end of the cordon.
He yanks down the Velcro flaps of his Gore-Tex waterproof field parka, exposing the gigantic yellow NYPD letters
against a field of blue to anyone closer than ten feet away.

He hurries north, a sick feeling in his belly. In the first
seconds he passes cops and FBI agents who have slipped out
of parked cars they occupied along the street. Now they
crouch behind them, ordered to stay in place.

Voort has sat in on enough briefings to understand that
plans are, in the end, only calculations, only hopes. Now he
must concentrate on the job. He tries to shut out the image
of detectives on the ground, bleeding, in the rain.

The radio said nothing about Frank Greene being shot.

More firing erupts from the north end of the box.

And now the ground shudders violently and Voort braces, thinking, *The van is blowing up.* But the sound is thunder, fading into a woman's high-pitched keening coming from out on the median strip. A truck horn starts blasting; its operator hurt or, incredibly, indulging in the New York driver's universal acknowledgment of disappointment: Traffic delays. Football scores. Gunfire.

The voice in the earpiece says, "He's out of the van. . . . People are all over the place! We can't see him anymore!"

Static.

Voort tries another channel, hears Lopez issuing instructions which the field staff should know anyway. "Don't fire unless you're positive of the target, and you have a good shot. Plainclothes people, get your field jackets . . . (static)"

Maybe if I'm closer, the radio will function.

He pounds toward the catering hall, runs past the line of plaster-of-paris Greek gods bordering The Parthenon parking lot. Bacchus drinking wine. Zeus holding a plaster-of-paris lightning bolt. Hera on her plaster-of-paris throne.

The air smells of ozone, of chemicals. Lightning cracks and suddenly Voort is flying, arms flailing.

The sidewalk is coated with ice.

He crashes against a parked car, hip striking chassis, elbow smashing hood, ass glancing off steel, and he's sliding across the hard concrete.

Pain rips through his right ankle when he stands up.

Ahead, more screams accompany the rapid report of small-arms fire, and the duller, faster thud from an automatic rifle.

Is that one of our snipers? Or him?

Out on Moynihan Boulevard, people are screaming, and Voort sees forms through the storm, civilians who have left their cars, fleeing in all directions. Any one of them could be Frank Greene. Ahead is a nightmarish, half-obscured panorama of confusion: running figures, stopped cars, swinging traffic lights, blowing trees. Panicked civilians are fleeing through police lines, several at a time. For all Voort knows, the bomber could have escaped by now.

If that's the case, we're shooting at each other.

Head down, staying along the periphery, Voort limps along the sidewalk toward whatever madness is going on up there. He passes ATS officers crouched behind parked cars, every few feet.

The plan, the logical plan had been surround the van. Evacuate civilians. Isolate Greene.

Some plan.

A bullhorn ahead, from the direction of the fighting, the low, confident, measured voice of the ATS negotiator, is announcing, "*Stay in your cars. Lock the doors. Stay in . . .*"

Voort tries to ignore the shooting pains lashing his ankle. The whole city reeks of ozone, as if, were a match to be lit, the atmosphere would explode.

"Two more cops down," a lieutenant, hooded against the rain, tells Voort, when he stops, wincing, behind an Isuzu truck.

"Where's Greene?"

"Who the fuck knows. Who knows if he's even the one who shot them. I can't see a goddamn thing out there and the fucking storm is screwing up every other word on my radio."

The rain, touching any hard surface—street, car, radio—almost instantly congeals to ice. The bullhorn switches messages, urges people who have left their cars to "get down."

And now, looming, a man charges out of the rain directly at Voort, *wearing a red jacket.*

Voort fumbles in his holster, for his .38.

But the man turns out to be a teenage boy fleeing past in panic.

I could have shot him, Voort thinks, shaken. If the gun had been in my hand, would I have fired?

Then he realizes the shooting has stopped.

In the pause, the monumental assault of nature continues. The barrage of hail strikes cars and stop signs. The dull reverberating thuds of thunder get worse. The radio has fallen silent as if the storm has sucked power from it.

Did we get him? Then why don't they say so? Has he escaped? Is he hiding in a car or truck or on the median strip? There must be two dozen unlocked cars out there.

The lieutenant shouts, "I feel like I'm back in fucking Kosovo!"

On the medic channel, Voort hears EMS people conferring over a patient, a woman who staggered out of the rain, and collapsed between parked cars. She is hemorrhaging blood.

On the bomb squad channel, the assault crew announces they've surrounded the van.

"We're going in."

When the Oklahoma City bomb exploded, shrapnel was hurled hundreds of feet. Windows fell off buildings. Brick and mortar were torn from each other. The front of the federal building was wrenched off its mooring by the blast, and a vacuum was created that sucked the roof to the ground.

Voort braces again. Behind him, lights in the catering hall flicker out. Szeska's voice comes into Voort's mind: *You wanted this problem.*

Suddenly, a series of shots erupts from Voort's right side, from the direction of the motel, the opposite end of the box from where the fighting has been taking place so far. Voort switches channels on his earpiece control, and hears a detective shouting, "Friendly fire! Hold your fire! That's FBI you're shooting at!"

On the bomb squad channel, he hears, "*All clear!* We defused it!"

Voort reels from success. He can't believe it! *We stopped it!* He needs to see personally that at least part of his plan, *his* idea, refined by others but originated by him, worked. Gun out, at a crouch, he runs toward the van, threads the mass of blocked, abandoned, or still occupied cars.

Greene could be anywhere.

The van materializes through the rain, its doors open, exhaust rising as it idles between an abandoned landscaping truck and a cab. Two cops in raid jackets are exiting the back. The first catches sight of Voort and pumps his fist jubilantly into the air. At least something is going right out here.

His jubilant act lifts Voort's spirits. The worst disaster in the department's history has just been averted.

But the celebration ends a fraction of a second later when Voort stumbles over a body, sprawled on its back. The dead man's eyes are open, his white shirt stained a mass of watery red. From the shoulder holster it's clear the man was a cop, *except his raid jacket and earpiece are gone,* and Voort, on his own radio now, is shouting, trying to get through to Jack Lopez, yelling that Greene's not wearing a red parka anymore.

"He took clothes off a cop! He's got a raid jacket and a radio! He's *dressed like a cop!*"

Voort's unsure if he's getting through.

On Moynihan Boulevard, all around him, assault crew

cops are going car to car, checking vehicles for Greene, and evacuating civilians. Ahead, bomb squad guys are trying to maneuver Greene's van out of the fight zone, inching it around traffic, toward The Parthenon.

A fantastic burst of lightning brightens the median strip and the civilians who have taken cover on the ground. Lopez is ordering, urgently, through the earpiece, "Everyone out of the box, now! He's got a raid jacket! Everyone out with IDs up!"

Voort backs out of the box to the sidewalk with a wall of retreating cops. He can't stand leaving civilians on the median strip. He can hear them crying for help out there, from the cars, the grass, the Atlantic City bus.

Everything is falling apart.

The negotiator, back on the bullhorn, is announcing, "Frank Greene, this is the police. Please understand that we have a warrant for your arrest. . . ."

FBI agents at the Polynesia Motel call in saying that one of their crew seems to be missing. She may be wounded or captured, on the median strip.

The helpless rage seems to spread among the rain-battered cops. There's a palpable ballooning of desperation. The city seems engulfed by anarchy. Greene could have escaped or he could be anywhere in the damn box, or in one of the cars, holding hostages. Voort, at the entrance to The Parthenon's lot, watches a man and woman, a hysterical couple, begging a lieutenant to send help back to their teenage daughter. She failed to follow them to safety when they fled from their car.

But the lieutenant can do nothing. The lieutenant tells them no.

The loudspeaker calls, "Mr. Greene, I would like you to

walk slowly toward the catering hall, without your weapon, and with your hands raised."

The storm seethes, explodes, rocks the city.

Why isn't Lopez doing anything?

Sirens now. The local precinct, having received frantic phone calls about shots, will have dispatched squad cars. And as police radios are monitored in newsrooms around the city, reporters will be on the way, too.

Voort runs at a limp for The Parthenon command station. Upstairs, he finds Lopez and the lead FBI agent, a Virginian named Mike Cullen, locked in an argument beside the field communications controls.

"We should go in now," Lopez, the ex–Delta Force captain is urging. "There are injured civilians out there. We use the night vision PVS equipment. We belly crawl in and evacuate everybody!"

But Cullen pats the air with both palms, in a calm-down gesture. "I hate waiting, too," soothes the rangy ex-lawyer in an FBI field jacket. "But give your negotiator a chance to do what he's good at. If Greene's still here, he can't get out. He lost his chance. But if shooting starts we could lose more civilians. Hell, they followed *your* instructions and hid in their cars."

"He could take hostages. I say we go car to car," Lopez insists.

Voort is remembering that Meechum's profile of Greene said that if he was cornered, and there was any chance of escape, even a small one, he'd fight.

The FBI man shakes his head. "Jack, listen to me. You Delta guys always want to rush things, but if *one person gets hurt*, anyone, their families, a bystander that gets hit, can bring a civil suit against everyone from you and me to the Director in Washington."

"*That's* what you're worried about? A lawsuit?" Lopez says, aghast.

Meechum's profile had said, *Greene believes he will be killed if we arrest him, so in my estimation he would die first.*

The agent says, "I'm worried about a hundred things that could go wrong, and a lawsuit is just one. Let's try the negotiator, okay?"

Voort, dripping rain, breaks into the conversation. "How do you know those wounded people weren't shot by us, by accident?"

Mike Cullen regards Voort as if he were a bum who just wandered into his cocktail party. "Who's this guy?" he asks Lopez, having missed Voort's briefing before.

Voort says, "How do you know the injured people weren't hit by *your* guys, and *your* delay will bring on the suit?"

Lopez is grinning.

Cullen pauses. "I have to call Washington."

"While you do," Lopez says, "we're going in."

And to Voort, "If you ever want to leave that pansy sex-crimes division, come work for me."

"I want to go with your guys now."

Lopez has already turned to his tabletop map, and is running his finger along the south perimeter, as if envisioning his moving skirmish line. He says, without looking up, "Sounds personal."

"It is."

"Keep your head down when you go in. I like a guy with a grudge."

Voort dons a black body suit, black boots, a black helmet, and a PVS-4 monocular on one eye, for night vision. It will pick up any heat radiated in front of him, and show it in red and green. He wears a kevlar vest and headphones, enabling him to receive messages quietly in one ear, and to whisper to the command center over the microphone. He carries, at his waist, two flash-bang grenades for diversions only. Unlike the ATS cops getting ready for a wet, cold belly crawl, he's taking his .38 Browning. He is not trained to use the lightweight semiautomatics with which they have been equipped.

Out on the median strip, in the dark, a woman is screaming.

"Somebody help me!"

She must have been unconscious before. Awake now, she is in agony.

"Pleassssse!"

The sound grinds into him, cuts at him, but there is nothing he can do to help except keep his position in the line. He must keep his position in the line. The assault team, like an invading army, is arrayed across Eighty-seventh Street, the south border of the cordon. Spaced every five feet, cops face the long way across, a direction assuring that if they have to start shooting, it will be along the median strip, making it less likely that bystanders will be hurt.

Over his earpiece, Lopez's voice says, clear at least, "Keep within sight of the person on both sides. If you find wounded, EMS people will be right behind you. If you find unhurt civilians, send 'em back. People in front go through every car, every truck. People behind take their position. *I never want a break in the line that he can get through.*"

Voort flips the safety off his .38.

The voice says, "And for Christ sake, no shooting

unless you're sure who you're firing at. If shooting starts on the other side of the box, hit the ground or take cover. And aim low."

They start crawling, attacking.

The pavement is slick, and freezing. It's like belly crawling on an ice skating rink. Voort imagines that local squad cars have arrived by now. Local Blue Guys will be holding a crowd back, blocks away, out of ricochet range.

The woman on the median strip screams, "Oh, God!"

He has, of course, with Mickie, practiced assaults during training exercises. In sessions taking up whole days, they've rushed into abandoned houses, the point man responsible for the enemy in front, the backups covering corners and doors.

They've practiced in brownstones, elevators, offices, airports. In a citywide "antiterrorism" week with the FBI last year, they spent nights in the World Trade Center, Museum of Natural History, Shea Stadium, Stock Exchange. They rappelled down buildings. They "monitored terrorists" with binoculars, from roofs.

But in none of the sessions did Voort experience the kind of operation he is involved in here, wriggling through puddles and ice-slick grass over a median strip, sliding over dogshit, twigs, pebbles, a soda can.

This is probably the kind of exercise Meechum practiced at West Point.

Rain flies into his mouth and ears and it batters his helmet and slicks his hair down against his skin. His clothes are soaked. His gun seems to be altering, molecule by molecule, into a sculpture of ice. His gums hurt from cold, and his ankle is throbbing. His feet are wet.

And now the line pauses at the first abandoned vehicle,

a white Chevy, its driver's door open. A cop crawls into it. "Nobody here!" Next is a Toyota Corolla, and the bus from Atlantic City. Greene could be inside either. But it turns out only three old ladies are hiding in the bus.

Voort removes his hand from the gun, wiggles his fingers to increase circulation.

As they move, to hide their noise, the negotiator is on his bullhorn again, at the opposite end of the box, urging Greene to walk out, and hopefully at least distracting him.

There's a sharp pain in Voort's left hand, and he realizes he's cut it on broken glass. He hears himself breathing, a wet, cold, sucking sound.

A voice in his earpiece says, calmly, "I have a man and a woman, unharmed, in a Dodge van. I'm sending them back. A man and a woman."

On the far end of the line, too distant for Voort to see, crawling cops reach the screaming woman.

"We need a stretcher here!"

It feels like I've been out here for hours. How far have we gone? Is that shooting I hear? No, it was a car backfiring. Is the cop on my left still there? He was there a second ago. Where did he go?

Over his earphone, his link to the world outside the five square feet around him, he hears that a whole family—a dad, mom, and two sisters—have been found in a car. Safe.

Where the hell is the cop who was on my left?

Ah, he's back, except it's a different guy now. The first guy must have stayed in the last car.

But now, as they move again, Voort sees a flicker of dark green materializing on the ground ahead, in his monocular. Squinting, his attention is drawn away from the officer on his left, to the civilian on the ground, an adult from the size, in a green parka; someone who, judging from the fact that he is rising without effort, spotting his rescuers, must have dropped down, obeyed the loudspeaker, and now he sees he's safe. He's up on one knee, pointing toward Voort, his rescuer.

"I have a contact," Voort says into his radio.

The man's features, discernible in the flash of lightning, are recognizable from Szeska's surveillance photos. The hair is plastered down. The skin has a rubbery washed-out hue. The glasses are small egg-shaped wire rims. Water pours down the lenses. Frank Greene is pointing at Voort.

He got rid of the police jacket!

Greene must have retreated back to the median strip, as confused as everyone else, must have avoided hiding in a dry car, afraid of being trapped.

There's something in his hand!

Voort shouts, his .38 coming up, "Put it down!"

Greene. As solitary and inexplicable at the end of his life as he has been all along.

Yellow lights burst from his extended hand.

Voort fires back as something hot zips past his face. Greene seems to freeze, to paralyze. But the hand moves up again and Voort empties the .38 as firing erupts from down the line. Greene jerks from multiple impacts. He sinks down on his knees with exaggerated slowness. In the next flash of lightning, his shoulders cave forward, and then he drops.

Voort is the first to reach him. Greene lies on his side, pellets of hail slashing into his open mouth. Blood pours from his nose. Voort pulls Greene's gun away, and leans down to hear him. The man gulps for air, blinking wildly. He's lost his glasses.

Looking up at Voort, his eyes are wide and terrified. Greene is trying to say something.

"I wanted to be a policeman," he whispers.

His mouth loses animation, forms a jagged, still O.

Voort sinks to the ground. He does not feel the rain. He is aware that people, cops or agents, are around him, asking if he's hit, hurt, needs a doctor.

He can't talk.

He can't hear anything.

Then he hears sirens, soft and muffled at first, as if far away. Sound comes back into the world. Lopez and Mickie are kneeling in front of him, and a helicopter has appeared above them, bathing them in yellow light. It came from nowhere. It's probably the FBI Nightstalker copter, arrived too late from Washington.

Mickie is saying, "Con Man, are you okay?"

He manages to stand with Mickie's help. The cops around him—elite professionals—have jobs to do, cleaning up, gathering evidence, finding Greene's gun, but emotion is in every face regarding Voort. It's gratefulness. Relief. He has saved their friends and relatives who might have died tonight. Every officer here, even had they not attended Addonizio's party, would have lost an uncle, brother, partner, neighbor. Almost every detective would have probably been in the catering hall, dancing, drinking, dying in the blast.

God, thank you.

Declining help, Voort limps on his own out of the rain. He feels like it has always been raining, like there has never been any entity called the sun. The catering hall is dry, and there's hot coffee, hot showers inside, and fresh clothes in the basement, spare sets used by setup crews. More officers are waiting when he comes out.

Cops saying, "Way to go!" "Good job." "You did it."

Voort, shivering, accepts more coffee. But it has no effect. The cold is embedded in the atoms of his bones.

"Voort?"

It's Lopez, asking if he wants to do paperwork tonight or tomorrow. If he wants to go back to One Police Plaza.

"Tomorrow."

Lopez saying fine, but get out of here now in that case, before the reporters get here, and the big brass, and the place becomes a circus. Maybe Lopez is being considerate. Maybe he wants the credit.

Voort repeats, "The place becomes a circus."

Lopez says be sure to be at One Police Plaza first thing in the morning. "Now get going or you'll be here all night. And I meant what I said. You ever want to get away from the bed beat, come in with me."

Voort and Mickie slip out of a side entrance. It's a half hour since the shooting, and although only cops are outside, the mayor is on his way, and the commissioner, Addonizio, and probably about a thousand reporters, too.

The rain has stopped finally, like a joke, a punch line. The night is cold, and through clear icy air they see forensics crews combing through the median strip and street for bullets, pieces of clothing, looking for blood, bone, anything dropped by Greene or the victims. Traffic will remain blocked on Moynihan Boulevard. The abandoned cars will, for a while, remain in place.

"Scotch or Irish?" Mickie asks.

"Irish," Voort says. "A whole bottle of Jameson's."

"Patrick's Pub," Mickie says, nodding, clapping his hand on Voort's back, "a fine old Irish emporium, would be glad to take my money, and it is only a few short blocks from here."

"I want to walk."

"Your ankle looks like shit."

"He fired first, Mickie. I was lucky."

A fact that was observed by John Szeska, who prefers walking also, and follows now, half a block behind.

TWENTY-FOUR

"Pubs," Mickie says theatrically, waving his index finger like a drunk professor making a distinction, "are the great climactic leveler. Take a night so cold even an Eskimo won't go out. Visit your pub and won't *that* be your warmest memory. Two more here!"

Patrick's is lit and full and the thick wooden walls are the color of peat; the rows of lit bottles beneath the long, polished mirror seem to emit warmth. A real log fire crackles in the tavern.

Mickie says, "I forgot what I was saying."

The place smells of pine smoke and sawdust. At midnight, they've occupied the same stools, heard the same Celtic tunes on the jukebox, had the same jowly bartender fill the same glasses from the same amber bottle, for two hours.

"You're a philosopher, Mickie. Of cold."

"What are you a philosopher of?"

Voort rubs his throbbing forehead. "Disappointment."

The talk is loud, and wind rushes in whenever customers enter. Above the far corner of the bar, the vodka section, above the clear backlit bottles of Stoli and Goose

Point and Finlandia and Icelandic, a TV is showing, yet again, the scene at the intersection of Moynihan Boulevard and Eighty-seventh Street.

The newscaster is almost drowned out in the noisy pub.

"Unconfirmed reports indicate police found three thousand pounds of explosives in the van."

"Meechum," Voort explains exhaustedly, sadly, fondly, and half slumped at the bar, "was an absolutist. Everything, to him, was white or black. He would have stayed loyal to Szeska unless I proved absolutely what was going on."

"An absolutist, huh? Are you talking about Meechum? Or you?"

"*That* is an interesting query. Perhaps we're talking about cops, us, incapable of seeing moral distinctions. A bunch of ten-year-old minds in thirty-year-old bodies. We can see the shit in front of our faces. But in our heads the world's as pure as the Saturday matinee."

"To cops," Mickie says, raising his drink.

"To Meechum."

The glasses clink, the throats tilt back. Mickie says, "Meechum. Go on."

Behind them the front door opens, and a Blue Guy comes in, a patrolman in uniform, big and gray. Foot patrols have been reinstituted in this neighborhood. The raincoated cop walks past them toward the men's room, or the phone, without looking up.

"Meechum," Voort says, extending his empty glass to the cooperative bartender, "gave everything he had to whatever he loved, but would cut himself off if it stopped being perfect. His brother was perfect, but that's easy when you're dead. The army was perfect. The project was perfect. Szeska was perfect. When they weren't perfect, he couldn't deal."

"Stop me if I'm wrong, Con Man, but are we working this around to your married girlfriend?"

Voort draws himself up. "You want to reduce the great philosophical question of the ages to my sex life?"

"You're talking about disappointment. But you hit the nail on the head when it comes to love life. Love, my best pal, is the ability to feel the old ticker pounding even after the lady disappoints you. That's what the great man said."

"What man?"

"Me."

Voort peers at his partner. "When did you turn into Ann Landers?"

"Hey, what do I know? I've been married forever. And we're both babbling from chemical overload."

"Don't tell me this headache is caused by alcohol!"

Mickie throws money on the bar. "Con Man, are you okay to drive?"

"If I drive," Voort announces, "and get a ticket, the police will impound my already impounded car. I shall take the subway."

Mickie winks. "Not me. I'm at home with imperfection, especially my own. Not to mention that the nearest Long Island Railroad stop is . . . where is it, anyway? But, Mother," he says, leaning down toward Voort, "I promise I'll drive slow."

Voort jerks his hand in the direction where the Blue Guy has disappeared.

"What a night to walk a beat."

When they get outside, the drizzle has started again. The pavement is slick. The stores are grated, the block quiet. The apartments over the shops are dark, their occupants asleep.

They walk several steps back toward the catering hall.

"Voort, the subway's the other way."

Voort spins and heads toward the F train, which is two blocks off, he thinks.

Weaving slightly, but feeling sharper than he had in the bar, he takes in cold air, which seems fresh and friendly again.

"I don't have any problem with disappointment," he mumbles irritably. "And it wasn't about Jill at all."

John Szeska moves out from the shadows of a Mobil station, across the street from Patrick's Pub. Mickie, walking faster than Voort, is disappearing around a corner. Szeska crosses the street, closing on the weaving figure.

He wears soiled jeans, a grimy zip-up jacket, a stocking cap whose dark color matches the grease smears on his face. His hands are dirty. His rubber-soled work boots are dirty. He looks like a thousand subway line repairmen, emergency services electrical repairmen, late-night garage mechanics, or water pipe or sewer workers who get off their jobs at all hours in New York.

Ahead, the detective slumps against a thin, bare maple, as alone in the city as he. He heaves, but nothing comes out.

I never got a chance at him earlier this evening.

Voort starts walking again.

Szeska increases speed.

Use a knife. Take his wallet. He was drunk. He was mugged. That's what the police report will say. My face will stay off TV.

Ninety feet and closing.

Seventy.

A car glides up the street, a Golf, foreign-made, so it is not a plainclothesman's. It slows opposite Voort, it's driver

interested in a parking space. It maneuvers while the passenger looks out toward Szeska.

Szeska turns his head, slows, and Voort pulls away.

Szeska speeds up after passing the Golf, and, at forty
feet, the cop lucks out again, as a cone of light shoots onto
the sidewalk from the opening door of a street-level apartment. A man steps into the cold wearing a bathrobe and
slippers. He shouts back into the apartment, "Go to your
mother then. I don't care what you do!"

A woman inside screams back in another language,
Eastern European, thick, low, enraged.

Cursing under his breath, avoiding more potential witnesses, Szeska crosses to the far side of the street, and after
passing, crosses back.

And now he sees the glowing green globes ahead which
announce the entrance of a New York subway station. The
architecture hasn't changed since 1920. Gas-lamp style, the
globes perch above wrought-iron poles.

Voort reaches the subway, leans against the poles, heaving again.

Unbelievable! *Another* car cruises down the street and
by the time it passes, Voort has stumbled down the stairs.

But Szeska realizes happily as he reaches the entrance,
and reads the sign, that this particular stairway does not
lead directly to a tollbooth, which would be occupied, but
to a tunnel that connects to a subway platform—one of
those underground passageways that designers, in their
blissful, civic-minded ignorance, created to protect citizens
from unpleasant elements on the surface, or enable them to
pass safely beneath busier streets. One of those tunnels that,
in reality, harbor the homeless, rats, an occasional mugger,
and provide a superb setting for an attack.

Szeska, knife out, hurries down the stairs.

It worked out perfect, so perfect, as perfect as a . . .

Trap?

Voort's standing there as Szeska rounds the corner at the bottom of the stairs. His gun is out. He's not been drinking. There's no smell of alcohol. His eyes are sober. Szeska screams, inside, *tricked!*

"Do you really think," Voort says, "I'd let myself get that drunk with *you* around?"

Szeska, more as an impulse than an actual thought, knows, *He reacted slowly when Greene shot at him. I can kill him if I move fast.*

The impulse reaching his hand and . . .

Another voice, from the stairs, behind Szeska, the hated partner's voice, says, "And do you think his friends would leave him alone?"

TWENTY-FIVE

*T*wo weeks later, on another Sunday, Voort rises at six in the morning, alone in his bedroom, on a cold November day. He showers, dresses, and eats a light breakfast. A half-dozen Voorts are still sleeping in guest rooms in the house.

Matt has taken a turn for the better in the last two weeks.

Taking a soft leather attaché case he packed last night, Voort goes down to the garage for the Jaguar.

It's a bright day outside, bone-hurtingly cold, and Voort encounters little traffic on his way to Jill's apartment. She's waiting in the lobby, with a suitcase, when he arrives.

"What time's the flight?" he says.

"Eight-thirty. Yours?"

"Plenty of time after I drop you off."

She places her hand on his knee, in the car, as they reach the FDR Drive. The sun is dazzling on the East River. Harlem is quiet at this hour. The housing projects lining the road look much more peaceful than Voort knows they are inside.

He takes the Triboro Bridge to Queens, and Kennedy Airport.

"You're not angry I'm going," Jill says.

"I'm glad."

"Are we going to be friends?"

"We are already."

It will be, she says, slightly flustered, at least two months before she returns to New York, during which she'll work with the husband, which is the way Voort thinks of the man, in Rwanda. "Leishmaniasis. Malaria. Bilharzia. Guinea worm," she says, fixing her hair in the passenger-side cosmetic mirror, giving her hands something to do. "And thanks for the donation."

"It'll buy lots of medicine at African prices."

"It will buy more than a lot."

Over the last couple of weeks they've seen each other a handful of times, and slept together, and each time the sex was good, Voort thinks, but the core of whatever had drawn him to her had receded farther into the distance. Conversations had grown more strained, lovemaking more detached. The husband had called two or three more times from Geneva.

"I don't know what will happen when I see him," she says. "There's been a lot of damage over the years."

"If you knew, there'd be no point going."

Her touch, on his thigh, is light enough to almost not be there. There's no sex in it, just connection and affection, whether or not that will include, in the future, actual contact or not.

Voort parks in the short-term lot, and carries her suitcase into the Swissair terminal. The airline has donated seats for relief workers going to Geneva, the jump-off point for Red Cross flights to Africa.

He waits while she sends the luggage off, then walks her

to the portal separating passengers from well-wishers. Their kiss is long and memorable.

"Stay away from the wrong people," he says.

"Who? Abu? If he shows up, I'll treat him," she says. "I'm ashamed that I acted so afraid before."

Forty minutes later, Voort parks the Jag in the day-rate lot at the other Queens airport, La Guardia. The Delta shuttle to Washington leaves every hour. On a Sunday morning it is fairly empty, although by noon it will be filled with the Washington workaholics—congressmen, aides, reporters who visited New York for the weekend, all rushing back to their legislation, investigations, or Sunday-night bone-up reading of newspapers for the week's battles ahead.

Voort sips coffee during the uneventful flight, opens the leather attaché case and scans underlined passages in the book inside.

He ignores the newspaper which a stewardess has lain on the seat beside him. "Life of a Bomber," reads the headline, promising an in-depth story of Frank Greene's past.

The jet touches down, and Voort picks up his Toyota rental at the Hertz counter. Washington is sunny and cool although warmer than New York.

He knows the route by memory.

At eleven-fifty, he turns the Toyota into General Rourke's graveled driveway near Quantico, Virginia, where he sees the same red Cherokee as before.

"Who is it?" says a woman's voice over the intercom when he rings the bell.

"Conrad Voort. I'm hoping to talk with General Rourke. Is he in?"

Several moments later the door opens, and Rourke

stands there, in a tennis shirt and white warm-up pants and sneakers. The blue eyes are curious. The hair is in place.

"You really must like my breakfasts, Mr. Voort."

"Some things," Voort answers, standing on the front step, "you can't get out of your mind."

Rourke inclines his head slightly.

Voort holds up the attaché case. "Like books. Sun-tzu. Chinese Gordon. The ones you told me about, that you gave Szeska to read."

Rourke holds the door open wider, and calls, to the woman, in back, "Honey, I've got a meeting I forgot about. I'll meet you at the court. Tell Louie we'll kick his ass, double or nothing."

The voice calls back irritably, "Nick, the court's reserved at one."

Rourke winks at Voort. "It pisses her off if I have to work on Sundays. Do you play tennis?"

"I like kayaking."

"Never tried it. Half the places I've been stationed, you don't want to go anywhere near the water. Get dumped in a kayak, you come out with typhoid. Let's go out back."

"I ate already."

"Me, too. We're going for a swim."

Without waiting for a reply, Rourke leads the way. The pool house is hot and humid, and light pours in from the skylight and is refracted in the chlorinated lap pool. Voort starts to sweat from the heat.

Rourke unties his sneakers and takes off his shirt.

"I said talk, not swim," Voort says.

"If you want to bullshit," Rourke says, sliding off the warm-up pants, "stay out of the pool. If you want to really talk, then I want to see every inch of that body."

Voort hesitates and Rourke adds, "Son, you have no idea how tiny those receivers can be. But in the water, even if you've got one in the crack of your ass, it won't work."

Voort strips to his underwear. Rourke shakes his head. "Uh-uh. To the skin." Voort does it and steps down into the shallow end of the pool. The light is pale blue, and he hears water lapping over the gurgle of electrical pool machinery. Light is refracted between the surface and the glass ceiling.

Rourke, his clothes off, looks fit, with solid belly muscles and biceps. The thick black chest hair is turning gray.

Rourke swims a vigorous lap and returns; delaying, readying, calming, and controlling. Then he nods toward the deeper water.

"Chest high, Mr. Voort."

They walk to the middle of the pool, where Rourke says, "Okay then. What about books?"

"Two things keep bothering me," Voort says, his voice echoing.

"One!"

"The sheep-dipping," Voort says. "You said when the project started, you falsified records. You wanted to avoid embarrassment if your people broke laws. You said with records falsified, the press would have a harder time confirming things."

Rourke considers. "That's more or less right."

"So why," Voort asks, watching for a response that he suspects Rourke is too practiced to give, "when the project was canceled, didn't you change the records back?"

"Oversight," Rourke says without hesitation, but Voort is unsure if the man is speaking the truth or is simply a practiced liar.

Rourke says, "We were supposed to change the records

back but nobody did. Szeska and Meechum were still getting paid, so there was no rush. It was a paper change. Sergeant Smith thought Sergeant Jones was doing it. You know how things are."

Rourke holds up two fingers. "And the second thing?"

"The books," Voort says, "in your shelves, and also in his office. I've been reading them."

Rourke's brow goes up.

Voort says, "I've been especially interested in the British general, Chinese Gordon. That biography of him."

Rourke nods. "I can see why you like it. He was a fascinating man. Too bad about the way he died, though. With his head on a pike, and reinforcements arriving too late."

"General Gordon," Voort says, "was sent to Sudan by the British Foreign Office, to evacuate Khartoum when the Muslim army was coming. He had plenty of time to do the job."

"Yes, yes, you remember correctly."

"But he refused to evacuate when he got there. He decided to fight. And because he stayed, and disobeyed orders, the British had to send reinforcements. They'd planned to get out of Africa. They ended up staying. His disobedience reversed their whole foreign policy."

"You get an A in history, Detective, but this happened a century ago. What's the possible relevance to Colonel Szeska?"

"Well, the author of that book, Strachey, kept speculating on why the Foreign Office chose a man with a record of disobedience for such a mission. The book suggested that the Foreign Office *wanted* him to disobey orders. I mean, I'm not a scholar. I won't get the details exactly right. I didn't get a chance to study the book . . ."

"You're doing fine," Rourke says dryly.

"The book said that the Foreign Office did not agree with the idea of getting out of Africa. So they picked Gordon and hoped he'd disobey."

"You think I did that with Szeska? That kind of thinking is a little devious for me." Rourke smiles. "I'm a straightforward guy."

Voort feels the warm water lapping at his chest. "Like you said, it's just us here now. No microphones. Just speculation from an ignorant sex-crimes cop who knows nothing about national policy." Voort taps his forehead, as if to say he is not smart. He says, "And the dumb sex-crimes cop thinks you supported that project. You told him to shut it down, but you made it easy for him not to. You never changed the records. You let him keep the job, in New York, far from Washington, where the project might be discovered. You made sure he picked his own staff. No oversight. You knew his background better than anyone. You told me so. You said, *My job is, I pick the right people for the right jobs.*"

"I picked the wrong one this time."

"Because he kept the project going? Or because he got caught?"

"I'm retiring in two weeks," Rourke remarks. "I'll be out of the army. Little golf. Little tennis. Visit the kids in Minnesota."

The humidity seems cloying now. The water is lukewarm, lapping against Voort's body.

He says, "Maybe someone should have run a threat assessment on you."

"I will say one thing," the general says, more slowly, choosing words carefully, as if, safe here, retiring soon, he wants to let Voort glimpse his point of view.

"John Szeska was a hero to me, just like the men in

those books. He knew what was right and he did it. Things are breaking down in this country. The dangers are inside the country now. Soon people will understand how vulnerable they are to the dangers that project identified. Meechum was ahead of things. So was John.

"And when people *see* that, *realize* that, all the things those two did will become legal. The Italians went the extra mile against the Red Squads. The Germans did it against Bader Meinhoff. They stayed democracies. And we will do it here when people get disappointed enough, when the money runs out and this country starts disintegrating."

Voort says, "I've read those kinds of words before."

"Who said them?"

"Adolf Hitler."

Disgusted, Rourke says, "Give me a break. You're a bleeding heart, my friend. You understand nothing. John Szeska saved a few hundred people, cops, including you maybe, from a bombing, and he's in Leavenworth now."

Voort climbs from the pool. "I came to tell you that if he's ever let out of that cell, *ever*, I'll tell what I know. I don't care if I signed a paper or not."

Rourke says nothing.

"So if someone's got some idea of releasing him a couple of years from now, of making up some bullshit excuse . . . no evidence . . . or whatever technicality you come up with . . . remember what I said. Not to mention, I've written it all down. You keep saying when the shit hits the fan, but things have gotten bad before in this country, and we've come through the bad times without murdering each other."

Rourke eyes Voort, and then the light dies in his eyes.

"I've got to get ready for that tennis game now."

Voort climbs from the pool and dries himself. The general ignores him. Voort has ceased to exist.

Voort makes his way through the house and drives back to the airport. The day has grown colder. The sun seems to have shrunk, withered, and to be burning itself out. The sky has dried to washed-out winter blue. The husk of the moon hangs above the Washington Monument, even at two in the afternoon. The city's mastery of illusion extends all the way to the sky.

When he lands at La Guardia at least New York looks the same. It has the reassuring permanence at times of a natural wonder, a mountain, a canyon. He steers the car toward the towers in the distance. But when he reaches the FDR Drive, he passes his exit and heads downtown. He parks the Jaguar, police visor sign down, behind One Police Plaza.

He's remembering Meechum. Meechum as a kid. Meechum graduating from West Point, throwing his hat in the air. Meechum in the White Horse Tavern, saying, "Things didn't turn out the way you planned."

On Sundays, this part of the city is generally deserted, devoid of the workers who comprise the bulk of its population during the week. Voort mounts the stairs to the main plaza, passes the entrance to headquarters, and lets himself into St. Andrews Church fifty yards later. Morning Mass ended hours ago.

Kneeling in a back pew, he murmurs, "Thank you for life, for friendship, for Mickie and Meechum. Thank you for helping us stop Frank Greene. Thank you for the ability to make distinctions, and experience emotions, including disappointment. But, God, if you can give me the ability to grow from disappointment, that would be great."

To his father, he says, rising, "Dad, the tips helped a lot. But I had to use the disk."

Rising, he puts three one-hundred-dollar bills in the poor box, leaves and walks west on Chambers, the arterial boulevard linking the mayor in City Hall with his top policemen. Realizing his destination, he is filled with surprise. He passes Veronica's, the cafe where he met Jill for drinks two weeks ago. He comes in sight of the Hudson River, turns north on Greenwich, and stops in front of a redbrick condo with a green awning in front; a former warehouse, which like half a dozen other renovation projects on the street, have led the revitalization of the neighborhood.

Entering the foyer, Voort encounters polished brick, and clay-colored tile, and he sees British prints of jockeys on thoroughbreds hanging on the spankingly clean wall beyond the locked, inner hallway door, also of glass.

Last time he was here, blood drenched the foyer. He can smell it in his mind, and hear sirens coming.

Last time he was here he watched someone die.

Voort regards the bells, and corresponding names identifying occupants. His gloved finger presses a buzzer for an apartment on the fifth floor.

No answer at first.

Then Camilla's voice, the now-bright and cheery voice of his old girlfriend, who aborted their baby, says, "Who is it?"

After some moments, when Voort doesn't answer, Camilla says, "Is someone there?"

ABOUT THE AUTHOR

ETHAN BLACK is a pseudonym for a bestselling New York journalist who has written twelve novels and books of non-fiction, including the thrillers *The Broken Hearts Club* and *Irresistible*.